WATCH DOG

WATCH DOG

GUARD DOG SERIES - BOOK 2

KATT ANDREWS

CRIMSON QUILL
PUBLISHING
LLC

WATCH DOG

Guard Dog Series - Book 2

Copyright © Katt Andrews 2025

All rights reserved.

First published in 2025

This is a work of fiction. All names, characters, places, organizations, and events in this publication are products of the author's imagination or are used fictitiously. Any resemblance to actual persons, living or dead, or real businesses, establishments, organizations, locales, or events is entirely coincidental.

ISBN (Paperback) 979-8-9991952-3-4

Also by Katt Andrews

The Guard Dog Series
Guard Dog

CONTENT WARNING

Watch Dog is a mature, high-heat, dark cartel romance with characters who are sometimes irredeemable and have extreme proclivities towards violence. It contains situations that some readers might find offensive, distressing, or triggering. Reader discretion is advised as this book contains:

- Sexually explicit content, including detailed sex scenes
- Physical abuse, emotional abuse, and psychological manipulation
- Kidnapping/abduction
- Stalking
- References to childhood trauma and domestic abuse
- Blood, gore, violence, torture, and graphic injury
- Use of firearms, knives, explosives, and other weapons
- Death including remembered death of a sibling, death of parents
- Remembered childhood trauma
- Remembered car accident involving drunk driving

- Criminal activity including murder, assault, hacking, surveillance, and theft
- Invasion of privacy via hidden cameras, microphones, and other means
- Cartel-related violence and organized crime
- References to drug dealing, human trafficking, and forced prostitution
- Power imbalance in romantic dynamic (bodyguard/client)
- Themes of trauma, PTSD, and survivor's guilt
- Mentions of alcohol abuse/addiction
- Alcohol consumption

1

———

A REDDIT THREAD

Source: Reddit
Subreddit: r/TheDarkDuke
[Created Three Weeks After Publication of *The Dark Duke*]
Thread posted 3 hours ago | 367 upvotes | 6 downvotes
Posted by u/rachelreadsthings

Thread Title: Okay but WHY is *The Dark Duke* actually good?

u/rachelreadsthings
Started this book as a joke. What even is this genre?
Bridgerton meets Arrival meets Legally Blonde?
Tentacle porn with a moral compass?
And why do I need more of this in my life?

u/thatgirlwiththetabs
RIGHT??? Alien Regency Romance??? I thought it was going to
be all kink and slime and brocade waistcoats and suddenly I'm
crying about language barriers and interspecies loneliness???

u/petrichorloop

"Nobody will silence your voice again" is actually going on my gravestone. And maybe a thigh tattoo.

u/charliedowntown
Not to be that guy but... the prose is legitimately good. Like I was not expecting that. Actual literary structure in my alien romance. Wild. But also - more suction cup sex please

u/rachelreadsthings
The pacing, the world-building, the way the Duke respects her boundaries before he touches her. 10/10, no notes.

u/dramionealways
Book club didn't take me seriously when I picked this and now we're all in discussing tentacle fucking. While wearing tiaras.

u/dukesdisciple
Okay but where is Mercede Sanchez from? No bio, no photos, no interviews... just vibes, porn and suspiciously good grammar

2

MARIA

THE LIBRARY IS MINE NOW, officially my "office." But it still smells like cigar smoke, old books, and wood polish. Like my father might walk in at any second and ask what the hell I think I'm doing in here.

I adjust the angle of my laptop, trying to frame the shot just right. Bookshelves behind me. Advance review copy of my next book, *The Stellar Sovereign*, at the edge of the screen. Cup of coffee in hand. Nothing too staged. I sit back and check the lighting. Natural from the east window, soft and golden. My skin looks dewy instead of sleep-deprived. I hope.

I smooth my hair. Touch up my lip gloss again. I want to look like a *real* author. Someone who belongs in this world, even if I feel like I'm faking it most days and it could all just disappear.

I haven't been sleeping. Too many late nights rereading *Stellar* scenes, revising the same ones over and over, writing bonus content I never send, refreshing my sales dashboard like it holds the answers to questions I don't know how to ask. What if I only had one good book in me? What if *The Dark Duke* was a fluke?

I want to do well. I want to prove I'm not just a rich girl who bought her way in with a flashy debut and the connections of her famous writer friend. Why is this second book so much harder than the first?

I want my father and my brothers to be proud of me. I want Natalie, my publisher, to be proud of me. And I especially want my mentor and my new friend, Ami Zadegan, to be proud of me.

That word—*friend*—it still feels strange, like I don't quite know how to wear it. I didn't grow up with friends, not really. I went to boarding school in Vermont from first through eighth grade—a lonely Hispanic girl from San Antonio surrounded by cold weather, ugly uniforms, and icy stares. Then high school back in Texas, where the girls at my Catholic school already had their cliques, and I was a nobody with a crime lord father, a team of bodyguards, and a chip on her shoulder.

I had Fidel, of course. We went to the same high school, Saint Ursula's Prep in San Antonio. But he was three years older than me. A senior when I was a freshman. He had friends, played all the sports, looked like something out of an 80s movie. Jake from *Sixteen Candles*. Girls whispered when he passed them in the hallways. Giggled when he smiled. He didn't just fit in. He ruled the place without even trying.

And me? I was the awkward transfer student with a cartel last name and no idea how to belong. He acknowledged me in the halls. Sometimes walked me to class. Made sure no one messed with me. But that was it.

He was untouchable. And I was invisible.

But now, I have two real friends. Natalie and Ami. My publisher and my mentor. And while that makes me happy, it also terrifies me. What if I mess it up? What if they realize I don't know how to be someone's friend? What if they decide I'm not worth it, not as talented as they are, and they leave me behind?

This all started because of Ami. She coached me through my first novel. Believed in it when I wasn't even sure what I was doing. Forwarded it to her publisher, and the next thing I knew, I was on a call with Natalie Morris, owner of Crimson Quill Press, and she was actually interested in my book.

Now, Ami's off doing a whirlwind press tour—New York, Chicago, LA—promoting *Beneath a Persian Sky,* her novel about her Iranian-American family and her difficult childhood. It hit the *New York Times* bestseller list in its first week, and the critics are obsessed. It's the biggest release Crimson Quill has ever pulled off.

I know Ami's working nonstop, but she still sends texts when she can. Little check-ins. Reminders that she's in my corner, that she believes in me. I still can't believe I'm friends with this amazing author.

Sometimes I wonder if Ami regrets it—getting involved with me, a "cartel princess," and my family, the leaders of the pre-eminent criminal organization in Texas.

But then I see her with Marco, head of my father's security team, the Guard Dogs, and definitely part of my family. I see the way he looks at her. The way she looks at him. And I remember —she knew exactly what she was getting into with all of us. She wanted it.

And she hasn't said anything to me about regretting becoming a part of this weird and dangerous world. My family's world.

Maybe if I can succeed as an author, I can prove to Ami that she didn't make a mistake believing in me. Maybe if I can hold onto this shot at friendship, at belonging, I won't have to keep being alone.

And maybe if I can succeed, I can show my family that I don't need to be kept "safe" and hidden. That I matter in my own right.

I click the video call link on my laptop.

Chime

Natalie Morris appears instantly—all Nordic poise and polish in a long-sleeved navy blouse, her ice-blue eyes sharp behind tortoiseshell glasses she removes with one manicured hand. Her long honey-blonde hair is pulled back in her signature, no-nonsense style. She's only a few years older than me but she radiates calm authority—the kind of woman who could turn a literary mess into a marketing plan before her second cup of coffee.

I've never been to her Houston office, but Ami told me it's in a strip center in the Heights, wedged between a vape shop and a dry cleaner. Ami said that Natalie plows all of her profits back into the business. So it's not exactly glamorous. But what I can see on screen still feels like a mission statement: paperbacks stacked everywhere, a string of Christmas lights curling around a leaning bookshelf, fan art taped above a whiteboard full of deadlines and promo ideas. Scrappy. Determined. Completely hers.

Ami told me Natalie built Crimson Quill from scratch, starting with nothing but a dream, a logo, and a whole lot of hustle. And now? It's on the verge of becoming a major voice in romance publishing—bold, steamy, diverse. Everything about it reflects Natalie's vision. I admire her. Fierce. Brilliant. Untouchable. But under the polish, she's warm. And fiercely loyal. She's always there when I need her.

And I do need her. Because some days, like today, I feel like an imposter. Like me thinking that I'm a real author is a joke.

She sips from a black mug printed with the company's red quill logo and levels her gaze at me through the camera. She looks like she's already read three manuscripts this morning and is ready to pass judgment on all of them.

"Mercede," she says with a smile. I appreciate that Natalie is always careful to use my pen name in these meetings. "You're glowing. As always."

"I don't feel glowing. But I got some sleep, so... "

"Excellent. You're going to need all the energy you can fake once Callie joins us."

I hear a second chime. A clatter. "Shit. Sorry!"

Callie Park launches into view—half in frame, ponytail lopsided, iced coffee in one hand, phone in the other. Callie is Crimson Quill's Marketing and Social Media Manager. And she is truly weaponized enthusiasm.

"I'm here! Okay, so I have six things to discuss—"

Natalie sighs. "Down from ten things? Good work, Callie."

"Should I be taking notes?" I ask.

Callie gasps. "No, absolutely not. You just need to sit there and look amazing while I tell you the internet is losing its actual mind."

I blink. "What? What does that mean?"

"First of all, *The Dark Duke* is spiking on BookTok. Like, climbing-faster-than-I-can-track levels. The sucking-his-tentacle-into-her-mouth scene? It has a fan edit. It's everywhere. Seventeen thousand shares and counting. I just watched an Insta reel of a kid acting out the scene where the Duke bends the knee for Lady Penelope in his promposal. Promposal, Mercede!"

Promposal? I sit there, frozen, while my brain goes static. People are reading it. They're quoting it. They're talking about it like it matters. They think *The Dark Duke* is a real book worth spending their time and money on.

And all I can think is—what if I can't give them more? What if I disappoint everyone who believed in me?

"Also!" Callie continues without pausing for breath. "There's a whole subreddit, called the Dark Duke of course, and I cannot believe no one told me about it before this morning. Oh, and you have a fan cult, Mercede. Like a real one."

Natalie looks up from her notes, and tilts her head. "A fan cult?"

Callie grins. "They call themselves the Duke's Disciples. I think it started as a joke. Like, 'I'd kill for him' kind of stuff. But now they have custom emojis and merch and there's a whole Dark Duke Discord and a Substack. The Discord posts tentacle thirst traps on Thursdays. They're graphic but sweet."

Natalie raises a brow. "And are we okay with 'fan cult'?"

Callie's eyes bug out. "Honestly? This is the dream! They're well-organized and terrifyingly literate. They might take over a small government. Or form one."

"Also," she continues, completely serious, "someone got the Duke's tentacles tattooed on their thigh last week with the words 'Bend the Knee.'" She pauses. "It's all on YouTube."

I try to laugh. I really do. But something clutches in my throat. I started writing weird stories in a spiral notebook in middle school, sitting alone in the library, with no expectation that anyone would ever read my words—let alone brand them onto their skin. I don't know how to be part of a "fan cult." I certainly don't know how to lead one.

Natalie folds her hands together. "And all of this good news is why we wanted to talk with you, Mercede."

I freeze. "So this isn't just a... 'check in and keep writing' call?"

Callie shakes her head. "Girl, no. You're a brand now. We have to act fast."

Natalie smiles. "Don't worry. You're not *just* a brand. You're our best shot at making tentacle love mainstream." She winks. "And also, you're my favorite author right now. Please don't tell Ami I said that."

I laugh. Then take a deep breath. "Okay, tell me what you need from me."

Natalie nods, slipping right back into business mode. "We're redesigning your website. MercedeSanchez.com needs to reflect where you are. Right now it's just a book blurb and a stock author photo. We want a clean, modern launch site by next week."

"Next week? Launch for what?"

"Your career," Natalie says smoothly. "Callie's lining up podcast interviews, BookTube features, newsletter swaps. The usual. We also want a welcome blog post from you. Something fun and personal. Maybe a bonus scene? Maybe an author Q&A?"

I stare blankly. "Do people actually read author blogs?"

Callie's phone buzzes in her hand. She looks down at it but keeps right on talking. "Not when they suck. But when they're spicy? Emotional? Real? Absolutely."

"I don't know if I'm any of those things."

"You wrote *The Dark Duke*," Natalie says. "Trust me, you are."

I nod, but inside my stomach twists. They see Mercede Sanchez. My pen name. The name I made up so my father wouldn't find out what I'd been doing. So the Sandoval name wouldn't hover over every review, every deal, every interview request.

But he did find out. And, while Raul is proud of me, he still doesn't like it and probably never will. He tolerates it. Because I keep it separate. Because I'm careful to stay hidden as Mercede Sanchez. Because my father wants to keep me safe. And because Fidel Cedillo, my father's security specialist and resident hacker, makes sure whatever I do as Mercede, it stays far, far away from the Sandovals.

Before I can respond, I see movement behind me through the corner of my screen. Speak of the devil and he doth appear. Fidel, suddenly lurking behind me in the library.

"Seriously?" I mutter as Fidel steps fully into view. I don't turn but I can see him through my laptop screen.

He's all in black—long sleeved dress shirt, cuffed to his elbows, dark trousers, dress shoes that don't make a sound on the thick rugs in the library. Handgun holstered in the small of his back. Of course. We're at home on a Tuesday morning. Why wouldn't he be packing a gun?

He's holding a tablet, his mouth tight as he scans the room. "You didn't clear this call," he says, low enough that I think only I can hear.

I turn toward him, whispering over my shoulder. "I'm meeting with Natalie. About my book."

"External connection. Unverified access point. You notify me next time."

His voice is flat. Not angry. Just... annoyed.

"Noted," I mutter.

He moves to the east window and taps something into his tablet. Then glances at my screen, realizing he can be seen. His eyes land on Natalie.

"Miss Morris," he addresses her politely. They met at my first bookstore signing for *The Dark Duke*.

She nods. "Mr. Cedillo."

Callie leans closer towards her camera, eyebrows up. "Wait —who *is* that, Mercede? Your brother? Your assistant? Is that your boyfriend?" Callie does not have social boundaries.

"He's security," I say.

Fidel doesn't look back. Doesn't speak. Just walks out.

Through her camera, Callie can see the doorway where he exited and watches it for a beat. "Your security's real sexy, Mercede." Then she waggles her eyebrows at me. Like I said, no social boundaries.

Natalie clears her throat. "And are there any lingering *concerns* since the incident?"

She means the Calderons' siege of our estate eight months ago. The breach. The blood.

"Everything's stable," I say. "The team has been... thorough."

Natalie arches a brow. She's one of the very few outsiders who knows what happened. Who knows exactly who I am and who my family is. "Good," she says. "Because you're about to become very, very visible."

Visible. It's everything I was taught never to be. But maybe it's also the only way I'll ever matter on my own.

Callie jumps back in, bouncing in her seat. "Oh! One last thing—tiny idea—what if we tried to set up a mini book tour for you? Something we can put together fast. Just indie bookstores here in South Texas? To expand your reach and give you some face time with the fandom, and..." her voice goes sing-song, "get you ready for MAVFessssst!"

"MAVFest?" I blink. "That's not even remotely realistic."

The Music, Arts & Vision Festival—MAVFest—is Austin's premier event for film, music, tech, and digital innovation. A buzzy showcase for the next big thing in the creative world. Exactly the kind of place where a mysterious tentacled-alien romance could break out. To be a part of that, *The Dark Duke* would have to be a full-blown viral juggernaut.

Natalie grins. "I said the same thing about publishing a romance about a slick-skinned, suction-cupped alien duke, and yet, here we are."

Callie shrugs, like it's no big deal. "We already submitted your name. Natalie's making calls. I might have... mentioned you in a few group chats. It's not a guarantee, but they're watching. They know who you are now."

They believe in me. Natalie. Callie. My fans. Ami. Marco and the rest of the Dogs. Even my father. And that's the scariest part. Because I'm not sure how to be this person they see. Mercede Sanchez. I'm not sure I'm her.

I think I know how to write. I definitely know how to hide. But this? Being out in the public with it all? Meeting people face-to-face? Letting them see me and know who I am. Letting them read my work. Judge it. This is new.

My phone buzzes.

Fidel: Use the secure system next time.

I swipe the message away before they can see the way my hands are starting to shake.

Because I know Fidel's listening to all of this. And I know what he's really saying to me. *Think about what happened, Maria. Think about when the Calderóns were inside this house. Think about what could happen again if you're not careful.*

Our home was nearly destroyed. My father was shot and almost killed. I shot and killed two men. We were fighting for our lives.

Since then, I've trained nearly every day with the Guard Dogs. Self-defense workouts with Marco and Chuck in the gym. Shooting drills with Rafe on the range. Elias gave me a knife small enough to strap to my thigh. Taught me how to draw it fast. Where to stab to make it count.

And Fidel keeps me on my toes security-wise. Monitoring my computer, my phone, my every digital move. He says real security is about what you *don't* ignore. I hear his voice in my head more than I'd like to admit. Especially when I'm second-guessing myself.

But the threat we faced is over. The Calderóns are gone. Everything's fine. My father says we're fine. We're fine.

And if everything stays fine, then maybe I can pull this off. Make a bestseller list, land a deal, go to MAVFest on my own merit. Maybe I can finally prove that I'm more than what I came from. I'm not just a Sandoval. I'm me.

I focus back on my laptop screen and the rest of the call flies by—bonus scene discussion, a fantasy casting post idea for the website, and Callie's promise to draft a reader poll asking what color the Duke's undulating torso really is. Callie believes "lustrous obsidian" will be the winner.

The call ends with a cheery "Byeeee!" from Callie and a smile and a click from Natalie's side.

The video call ends.

I sit back in the chair. Two hours have passed and the library is now warm as the sun streams through the windows.

I check my phone again. Nothing more from Fidel

I glance at the shelves—my father's books, my books, the laptop still open to a blank "About the Author" page.

The Duke's Disciples. Fan cult. Website. Signing tour. MAVFest.

Visibility.

My father isn't going to like that. I wonder what Fidel will think. Pretty sure he won't like it either.

3

———

FIDEL

MARIA DIDN'T CLEAR the call.

A flagged external connection, unsecured, initiated from the library. It's a blind spot I fixed two weeks ago. I know she likes working in the library because the lighting, the big windows, the rows of old books make her feel more like a "real" author. I know it matters to her.

But she needs to be cautious. She needs to clear all calls with me. She probably doesn't want me listening. Or reporting back to her father.

Too bad. She has to be careful. I have to keep her safe. It's my job.

After checking in on her, reminding her, texting her, I tap into her video feed. Just a quick check. Routine. Standard protocol.

Natalie Morris is on the call. Good. Expected. She's professional. Smart. I trust her. She knows who Maria is. Knows the Sandovals.

The other one—Callie—is the wild card. Loud, fast, unpredictable. The kind of person who leaves digital breadcrumbs everywhere she goes. Sloppy. I've already archived her IP logs just in case.

Then I see Maria.

Hair down. Loose waves falling over one shoulder, light catching the ends. Wearing one of those soft blouses that looks casual but probably isn't—silky, pale, precise.

Her posture's straight. Her expression composed. But her eyes...

There's something in them that makes me lean in. A flicker of something she doesn't show anyone else.

She looks good. She always does.

Not that it matters.

They're talking about *The Dark Duke*. Correction: they're talking about *her*.

About *Mercede Sanchez*. About a "promposal." Whatever the fuck that is. A tattoo. A fan cult. *The Duke's Disciples.*

Callie says the name like it's amazing. An achievement. Something to be proud of.

I start running searches before the call even ends.

The Dark Duke subreddit: active. Growing fast. Cross-referenced with Tumblr, TikTok, a handful of private Discord links. High engagement. Erotic fan art. Conspiracy threads. One post speculates Mercede is secretly an heiress.

I don't like that.

Not because they're close—yet—but because *they're looking*. And all it takes is one person finding a photo, an old classmate, a sideways mention, and suddenly Maria's not anonymous anymore.

I keep one ear on the call. They're talking about her website. The new version. Suggested blog posts. Possible book tour. MAVFest.

MAVFest?

I pause the surveillance feed. Let the silence stretch in the space where her voice was.

MAVFest would be a nightmare. If she gets in, if Raul actually lets her go, I'll have to make sure Marco doubles security. Triples it. I'll need to run background checks on every studio exec, bookstore owner, panel moderator, Uber driver, and hotel maid in Austin.

Maria won't want extra protection. She won't think she needs it. Because she thinks she's safe now. Because Raul told her it's over.

It's not.

I swivel in my chair and pull up the Calderón file again. Eight months old. Officially cold. I've chased every lead, scrubbed every data set. And still nothing concrete tying Maria to the Calderóns. Nothing that explains why *she* became their target.

But I did find a connection between the Calderóns and Los Cuervos. Los Cuervos. The Crows. A ghost cartel. Brutal. Ruthless. Known for vanishing people, posting execution videos. Not known for negotiation or backing down.

Everything I've pulled from the black-market intel, cartel dumps, and backdoor networks confirms it—Los Cuervos was backing the Calderóns in their failed play against the Sandovals.

But if the goal was to destabilize the family and take over, why go after Maria? Why not Raul Jr.? Or Carlos? Both are the heirs apparent. Why not Raul himself? Maria makes no sense.

And that's what I keep circling back to. Because it doesn't add up. The goal was never chaos for chaos's sake. They didn't want a war. They wanted to send a message. And taking Maria was how they wanted to do it.

I'm sure of it now. The attack at La Cascada, the night Maria met Ami Zadegan—that was a kidnapping attempt. And the follow-up at the nightclub, Luz? Same plan. Ami was drugged, but Maria was the real target.

And the man behind it? Tommy Dawson. A fake identity with a flawless resume, spotless references, nothing out of place. Whoever built his cover knew exactly how deep I'd dig in my background check. And made sure I'd find nothing.

Tommy played the long game. Quiet. Professional. He became manager at Luz, earned our trust. Never once slipped.

Until he did.

The tattoo on the back of his hand—small, easy to miss. But I didn't miss it. Found it in the video footage. A black crow. The mark of a Los Cuervos foot soldier.

He waited for the right night. He was the manager of Luz and Elias would've told him we'd be there that night. He created the right distraction. The fight that broke out near the dance floor. And then, he made his move.

I can feel it in my gut—the plan was to drug and kidnap Maria. I know it. Even if I don't yet have enough proof to take to Raul.

And Tommy wasn't the end of it. Los Cuervos came for her again. They used the Calderóns one last time when they launched the assault on the Sandoval compound.

That attempt nearly succeeded. And it told me everything I need to know. Los Cuervos doesn't give up. They don't stop coming. They test the perimeter. They study responses. They adapt.

They'll try again.

And now Maria wants to step into the spotlight. Like they're not still out there. Like they're forgotten her. They haven't.

I tap open a private browser and access her website's backend.

Mercedesanchez.com was registered with a shell domain service. Sloppy. Whoever set it up, probably Callie, didn't scrub their metadata. I trace the admin trail. Clean, but not clean enough.

There's a buried redirect ping in the site traffic logs. It doesn't go anywhere dangerous—yet. Could be a bot. Could be someone probing the admin panel. Could be nothing. I set a digital tripwire. If they come back, I'll know.

She won't see it. She doesn't need to. She's already been targeted. Lived through a violent attack.

That's enough.

I glance at the corner of my screen. Her video call's ended. The feed is blank. But I can still see her sitting there through her laptop camera. The way her smile slipped the second the call ended. The tension that hasn't left her shoulders. That look she gets when she's pretending to be fine.

She thinks I don't notice. She thinks no one ever has.

But I do. I always have.

She thinks none of this is real. The praise. The sales. The hype. She thinks she just got lucky.

But she didn't. She's good. Better than good. She just doesn't believe it yet.

She never has. Not back in high school, not now. She walked those halls like she was bracing for a fight—quiet, defensive, always alone.

I used to worry about her. Not that I ever said anything. I figured the last thing she wanted was to be seen talking to the guy who grew up in her family's kitchen. Whose brother worked security for her father. I wasn't exactly anonymous at school, but I knew my place. And I figured she wanted to keep her distance from it.

But every day, I tracked her. She'd walk those halls like she didn't care. Like she was fine. But I saw the way she kept her eyes down. The way her mouth tightened when other girls passed. She wasn't fine.

She didn't see me. Not really. But I saw her. Every damn day. And I see her now.

I pull up the files on *The Dark Duke*. Even though it's been published, I still have the manuscript archived in three versions. She rewrote Chapter 17 a few times. I like the final version. The first two were too careful. The Duke didn't beg properly.

She got it right in the end. She always does.

The Stellar Sovereign is a little rougher. I've read it. Twice.

Her voice is sharper in the second book. Bolder. Angrier. She kills someone in the prologue and doesn't apologize for it.

I think she's preparing herself. Or maybe trying to write something she can't say out loud.

I get it.

Some things you can't fix. You just reshape them. Turn them into fiction and hope nobody recognizes the truth you're saying underneath.

The cursor blinks at the top of my code window. The IP reroutes again. Different proxy. Someone's poking around the subreddit now. Commenting under an alias. I cross-check their username with my flagged database.

Nothing yet.

But I'm watching.

4

LEAD UP TO MAVFEST

Email from Natalie Morris to Mercede Sanchez, cc: Callie Park

From: nat@crimsonquillpress.com
To: msan@email.com
CC: callie@crimsonquillpress.com
Subject: The Dark Duke: Strategy & Next Steps

Maria:

This is your official notice: you are no longer just a debut author. You're a rising voice in romance—and one a lot of people are suddenly very interested in.

Sales for *The Dark Duke* have exceeded projections across every format. The hardcover is in its third printing. The audiobook hit #1. Foreign rights auctions are moving fast, and your name just showed up in *Variety* under the headline: "Spicy Storm: Hollywood Targets Dark Fantasy Breakout Authors" (Callie - please send her the link).

We're getting real offers now. From producers, streamers, studios. Half of them don't even understand what "alien Regency romance" is—but they know they want in.

Which brings me to the point of this message: MAVFest. It's three months away—perfect timing with promo for *The Stellar Sovereign* ramping up. The festival is a convergence point for film, television, publishing, and media. And you're going.

You'll have Platinum access through Crimson Quill. If we play this right, we walk out with a serious option deal, potential development package, and real industry momentum.

But this has to be strategic.

We'll need planning, coordination, and a willingness to stay visible.

I'll take care of scheduling and high-level negotiations. Callie will handle promotional support, interviews, socials, and fan engagement.

You just keep writing, and be ready to show up as the voice everyone wants to hear.

Let's talk tonight. Yes, it's about Lily Renshaw. Yes, it involves a tiara.

—Natalie
Natalie Morris

CEO, Crimson Quill Press

————

Reply Email from Callie Park to Mercede Sanchez, cc: Natalie Morris

From: callie@crimsonquillpress.com
To: msan@email.com
CC: nat@crimsonquillpress.com
Subject: The Dark Duke: Strategy & Next Steps

Mercede!!!

Okay, deep breath: I am FREAKING OUT (in a good, productive, totally-on-brand way).

Natalie already gave you the serious version, but here's mine: Your fandom is EXPLODING!!!!

The subreddit is up. The fan art is coming in hourly. Someone built a Pinterest board called "DukeCore" and I'm not at all concerned about how often it gets updated. It's often.

You're a brand now. I mean that in the most loving way. You're not just Mercede Sanchez. You're Lady Penelope's emotional support system, and the entire internet is rooting for our tentacled duke.

Here's what I'm working on (remotely, with 3 screens and 2 iced coffees):

- Relaunching MercedeSanchez.com with a sleek new design, updated bio, and teaser graphics for The Stellar Sovereign
- Lining up podcast interviews, BookTube features, and BookTok influencers (don't panic—we'll curate the list)
- Scheduling a fandom AMA thread (Reddit is READY)
- Coordinating a bonus scene drop around Chapter 17 (yes, that scene)
- Drafting poll options for Duke casting. We're calling it "Who Should Undulate With His Grace?"

You are not allowed to ghost me, disappear, or go off-grid. I will track you down. With tentacle porn gifs - they now exist!! ;)

MAVFest is going to be HUGE, and while I won't be there physically (per Nat and I'm sad but OK I get it because $$$), I am spiritually present in every panel, every signing, and every lipstick shade you wear. Do not let Natalie talk you out of a DukeCore cape and tiara moment.

This is happening. You're happening.

Let's make it iconic.

—Callie
P.S. - *Variety* article attached - you're Hollywood!
Callie Park
Marketing & Publicity Manager
Crimson Quill Press

———

Text Message Thread - Maria Sanchez and Fidel Cedillo

Maria: hey. URGENT. can you check this file for malware or whatever.

Natalie says it's fine but she opens email like she's defusing a bomb

Fidel: send it

Maria: [File attachment: Lily_Renshaw_Dark-Duke_Audition.mov]

Fidel: what is this

Maria: her audition tape

lily renshaw

yes THAT lily

apparently she wants to play lady penelope

Fidel: this better not be porn

Maria: ??well??

Fidel: what the actual fuck maria

don't send me shit like that

Maria: 😂😂😂😂

Fidel: she's wearing a tiara

and moaning

in a fake british accent

while getting railed by tentacles

Maria: omg tell me how amazing it is 😵 💀 🔥

Fidel: there were multiple takes

MULTIPLE

Maria: she really wants the role

she said she's "emotionally attached to penelope's arc"

also the tentacle prosthetics were her own

also pretty sure looking at this stuff is your job

Fidel: i'm deleting this from my phone

and hopefully my memory

Maria: too late

it lives in your soul now

like the duke 🐙🩶

Fidel: warn me next time

i feel sick

Maria: nope

also you're my MAVFest security detail

you're stuck with me

and lady penelope

and... the suction cups 🐙🫧

———

Text Message Thread - Marco Cedillo and Fidel Cedillo

Marco: you're heading to austin with maria next month

Fidel: copy. security detail?

Marco: you're running point

Fidel: just me?

Marco: carlos crew will assist

elias is also going

he'll handle Sandoval business and assist

but primary protection's on you

Fidel: understood

Marco: raul signed off

so did i

don't fuck it up

Fidel: i won't

Marco: don't

she's got press, fans, cameras

eyes everywhere

keep her locked down and out of trouble

Fidel: copy

starting event map and site analysis

Marco: she'll stay with Carlos. Less exposure
for now

Natalie's building the schedule

coordinate with her and elias

don't let maria run the show

you run the show

Fidel: copy

Marco: and try not to kill anyone

even if they deserve it

Fidel: no promises

———

Email from Natalie Morris to Maria Sanchez, Fidel Cedillo and Elias Vasquez, cc: Callie Park

From: nat@crimsonquillpress.com
To: msan@email.com
fid@sandovalgroup.org
eli@sandovalgroup.org
CC: callie@crimsonquillpress.com

Subject: MAVFest Day 1 Breakdown + Full 9-Day Schedule (PDF Attached)

Hi all,

MAVFest kicks off tomorrow, and I want the four of us aligned from the outset. Day 1 will lean promotional—fan-facing events, media visibility, and soft-entry press. I'll be handling high-level logistics, press interactions, and industry handoffs as needed.

Callie has prepared the working schedule (attached), including RSVP confirmations, location maps, and key contacts. Some of the times may flex based on crowd size or delays. We'll stay adaptive.

Day 1 – Saturday:

- 10:00 AM – VIP Welcome Brunch @ Violet Crown Rooftop Garden
- 12:30 PM – Book Signing @ Stardust Books
- 3:00 PM – Panel: "From Fandom to Film" @ Arthouse Theater, Room C (optional; we're just attending so may skip if signing runs over)
- 6:00 PM – Private Cocktail Reception @ Hotel Hermosa Rooftop

All four of us are credentialed with Platinum Badges. These grant full access to MAVFest venues, green rooms, VIP lounges, and private receptions. I'm texting out the digital badge files immediately after this email. Please save them somewhere you won't lose them. Please.

Mercede: Your only job is to show up, stay centered, and be the brilliant, grounded star everyone wants to see.

I'll coordinate all initial meetings with streamers, studios, and reps. Based on momentum, the strongest offers will come in quickly. Likely within the first 72 hours. Once we've filtered for legitimacy, I'll assist on contract and negotiation strategy.

Let's keep things sharp, professional, and legendary.

—Natalie
Natalie Morris
CEO, Crimson Quill Press
Attachment: MAVFest_Schedule_9Days_FINAL.pdf

5

———

FIDEL

THE FIRST PROBLEM is the number of tentacles.

The second is where they're placing the tentacles.

The third—and I didn't see this one coming—is that I'm somehow the primary bodyguard for the queen of a fandom that genuinely wants to be suction-cup fucked.

And judging by the feral energy inside this bookstore, a lot of people have spent serious time thinking about that.

The line for Maria's book signing coils through Stardust Books, a deceptively cozy indie shop jammed between a CBD dispensary and a vegan taco stand. MAVFest has turned downtown Austin into a circus, and somehow, this event ended up center ring.

The fans? Unhinged.

Cosplayers in midnight-blue frock coats and black sclera lenses pack the aisles. Some have gone full Duke, tentacles sprouting from shoulders, wrists, and, in at least one case I noticed near the travel section, a disturbingly low-slung belt.

One aisle over, someone throws up the Duke's salute—three fingers raised, waggling like little tentacles. The signal ripples outward as more fans respond, a silent cult call echoing through a crowd that's clearly not here just to buy books.

I spot a woman in elbow-length gloves and a tiara, clutching a stack of paper to her chest. Fanfic, judging by the prominent cover page:

Blood on the Ballroom Floor: A Regency Space Romance - NSFW, Tentacles, Dom/Sub, Breeding Kink, Suction Cup Kink, Edging

I look away before I read anything else. I've seen a lot of weird shit in my life. But everything in this bookstore tops it.

I've already done the research—forums, edits, cosplay accounts, Discord servers. I know this fandom better than I want to. Because one of these people might decide Maria belongs to them. Might want to touch her. Get close. Make a scene. And I need to see that coming before it happens.

Yeah, Maria thought using a pen name kept her safe. That being "Mercede Sanchez" created distance.

I definitely disagree.

I adjust my earpiece. It's military-grade—encrypted, discreet, and lets us communicate in crowded rooms like this. "Elias. Eyes on exits?"

"Got 'em. Also got eyes on a woman wearing a full tentacle harness. Where do you even buy that?"

"She's not a threat."

"Not to Maria. But I'll be seeing that thing in my nightmares."

I keep scanning. Phones flash. The buzz of whispers rises every time someone realizes I'm with her. I hear someone murmur, "she's got a bodyguard." I'm not just security. I'm *her* security.

Across the room, I can see Maria at her signing table, poised and perfect, autographing a battered copy of *The Dark Duke* while a woman in Lady Penelope cosplay sobs through her thanks.

Maria's hair is loose, black as ink, hanging in thick curls down her back. Her dress is deep blue, dusted with rhinestones that catch the light like stars. Her own version of Duke cosplay. She's smiling, with flushed cheeks, and that sharp gaze that never misses a thing. Even now, with a line of strangers crying and rambling in front of her, she looks beautiful.

And she's locked in. Focused. There's nothing fake about it. Maria doesn't think tentacle harnesses and velvet capes are weird. She loves it. The fans, the chaos, the raw emotion. She was built for this.

I shouldn't be watching her like this. So intently.

But I do.

I see the way her tongue dips out when she signs a book. The tilt of her head when she listens to a fan. I see the intelligence in her eyes. The strategy. Maria isn't just signing books. She's claiming ground. Stepping out of the shadow of her last name and into something that's hers alone.

This is the future she's been fighting for.

And it's drawing attention.

I clock the bookstore clerk watching her from behind the register. Some guy in line keeps stealing glances at her chest. Everyone's staring. None of them should be looking at her like that. But only I know what they'd be risking if they tried anything.

Raul gave me one directive before this trip: Keep her safe.

I intend to.

Even if it means standing in a sea of velvet capes, ball gowns, and suction-cup gloves.

Even if it means ignoring the way she smells when we're close—citrus and warmth and something spiced. Even if it means pretending I don't notice everything about her.

"Security update, *jefe*," Elias says in my ear. "No threats. Just a lot of questionable eyeliner and one guy wearing Duke ears over AirPods."

"Copy."

Through the comm, I hear Elias again, this time talking to a fan.

"Can you point me to the Duke's Disciples line?" a male voice asks him.

Elias, dry as ever, replies, "Go to the coffee bar and ask the barista for a double-tongued lap dance. That's the code."

I sigh. Elias thinks this is hilarious.

I shift my weight, scanning the room again. No weapons. No odd signals. No signs of anything about to go sideways.

But something still feels... off.

And then I see him.

Back corner, near the sci-fi section. Hat low. Arms crossed. The edge of a black tattoo peeks out from the sleeve of his gray t-shirt. The talons of a bird. A crow? He's too stiff. His gaze sweeps the room like he's tracking patterns. Cataloging targets.

I move. Fast.

"Elias," I mutter into the comm. "Possible problem."

The guy turns just as I reach him. I grab his shoulder, shove him against the bookshelf, and yank up his sleeve.

Tattoo. Sharp black wings spread across his bicep.

My breath locks.

But it's not a crow. It's an eagle.

The adrenaline turns sour.

"Jesus—what the hell?" the guy barks, pulling his arm back. "What the fuck is wrong with you?"

He's mid-thirties, gym-built, normal. Not cartel. Not armed. Just a guy with an eagle tattoo.

He jerks his chin toward the line. "I'm here with my sister. She wanted her book signed. You gonna tackle her next?"

I follow his gaze. She's in line, wearing a tiara. Can't be older than sixteen.

People are watching now. I release his arm. Step back.

"Just... stay out of trouble," I mutter.

He scoffs and walks off, shaking his head.

"You good over there, watch dog?" Elias teases.

"Wasn't a threat," I admit.

"So you're just throwing innocent guys into bookshelves now?"

I don't answer. I make my way back to the signing table, to where Maria sits with Natalie.

Maria doesn't look up at me, just hisses at me in a low voice, "Fidel Mateo Cedillo! You cannot assault my fans!"

I hate it when she uses my full name. That means she's really pissed. "He looked suspicious," I say quietly.

"Everyone here looks suspicious," she spits out. "They're cosplaying as tentacled aliens. You just scared the crap out of one of my fans!"

"I'll try to restrain myself."

She shoots me a glare but turns back to the next fan with a smile on her face.

And that's when the door to the book store opens. A woman steps inside—platinum blonde waves, white trench coat, massive sunglasses, five-inch heels. A man trails behind her, his phone aloft and a greasy grin on his face.

Lily Renshaw.

The whispers quickly spread through the crowd. Her name ripples across the room like a shockwave.

Phones rise. Flashes pop. Someone drops a book and gasps.

Maria exhales slowly. I tense.

Because of course Lily Fucking Renshaw is here.

She wants *The Dark Duke.* Wants to be Lady Penelope. And

she wants it badly enough to send Maria an unhinged audition tape—ball gown, suction cup sex, fake British accent and all.

She wasn't supposed to be here. Her appearance is not on our schedule. No one cleared her. No one invited her.

But she's here now. And she's making a scene.

Lily dramatically lowers her shades, smiles at the crowd, and actually flashes them the Duke's salute. Three fingers up, waggling like she just declared herself the High Priestess of Tentacle Fuckery.

The room erupts in cheers. Shit.

Maria sees it all. Her smile freezes.

Natalie, seated beside her, mutters under her breath, "She's got some fucking nerve." She is *not* pleased.

Lily and her greasy escort make their way to the signing table. The guy steps forward, hand out to Maria, all smarm and self-importance. "Wes Solano. Solano Studios. You've probably heard of my work. *Blood & Asphalt? Neon Cowboys?*"

"No, Mr. Solano," Maria says flatly, not taking his hand. "I haven't."

He drops his hand. Doesn't miss a beat. "Lily and I would love to discuss adapting *The Dark Duke*. Big-screen potential. Streaming rights. A franchise."

Maria's jaw tightens. Natalie doesn't let it slide. "Here? Now? During *Mercede's* book signing?"

This is Maria's moment. And Natalie's not about to let anyone hijack it.

Wes Solano is unfazed. He shrugs, still grinning. "Thought it was a good photo op. Big crowd, lots of buzz. But maybe you and your team could join us for drinks tonight?"

Lily dramatically places a hand on her chest. "Please, Mercede. It would be such an honor."

Elias, still in my ear: "Fifty bucks says Maria stabs her in the eye with a pen in the next five minutes."

I don't take the bet.
Because I kind of hope she does.

6

MAVFEST DAY 1

**Text Message Thread - Natalie Morris and Maria Sandoval
Timestamp 5:47 p.m.**

Natalie: pls tell me u saw lily throw up the duke's salute 😵

Maria: they cheered

like full-on standing ovation

i think i blacked out

Natalie: girl they ate it up

penelope cosplay + duke worship = kink profile checked

Maria: who the fuck is wes solano?

he looked like he was there to sell timeshares

In 2007

Natalie: at a phoenix holiday inn

but welcome to MAVFest

they all pitch

none of them r real

        Maria: so we're really doing drinks w them later?

Natalie: we smile

we nod

we sip something overpriced since Wes paying

we ghost them by tuesday

        Maria: wes called the dark duke a "buzzy high-concept property"

        buzz seems to be a major part of his vocabulary

Natalie: i need a drink

armadillo bar after signing

we'll do our fake polite industry thing before the rooftop party

        Maria: fine

        but if lily flashes that salute again i'm throwing a book at her

Natalie: not the dark duke

Something hardcover and irrelevant 😈

7

MARIA

After the book signing, Lily suggested we grab drinks at the Gilded Armadillo. Of course she did. It's exactly the kind of place she thinks deals get made. Dim lighting, overpriced cocktails, and just enough curated charm to make her feel important.

And Fidel is on edge. As usual.

He's been that way since we were kids. Always watching, always assessing, always convinced something is about to go wrong. Back then, it wasn't cartel threats or security breaches keeping him up at night. It was me. He scowled when my music blasted too loud, telling me I'd go deaf before I hit thirteen. He grumbled when I stayed up too late watching TV, muttering something about eye damage. He hovered by the pool like I was one wild splash away from drowning and nearly had a stroke every time I swung a tennis racket, worried I would knock myself unconscious.

Fidel has spent our entire lives bracing for disaster. Some things never change.

Sitting beside me, he shifts slightly, his gaze sweeping the bar with the quiet intensity of a predator watching for a threat. Not that the Gilded Armadillo, a swanky bar in the Hotel

Hermosa, is particularly dangerous. Unless you count the influencers making out with their smoked jalapeño margaritas at the bar.

It's a high-end Austin hotspot, and during MAVFest, it caters to industry people—actors, directors, anyone who wants to be seen. The bar is packed on MAVFest's opening night, crawling with producers, agents, and actors pretending they aren't just here to network. Elias, with his charm and more than a little cash, has secured us a corner with a cowhide leather couch, a few velvet chairs, and a low table.

MAVFest hosts screenings, panels, concerts, rooftop parties, AI demos, influencer mixers. You name it, it's here. It's an eleven-day sprint through networking hell disguised as a nonstop party. Events are spread out all over Austin—historic theaters, luxury hotels, rooftops overlooking the city, private estates, and outdoor stages designed to look exclusive while still being heavily Instagrammable.

I lean in to Natalie, seated to my left on the couch, pitching my voice low so only she hears. "Remind me again why you're not in LA with Ami?" I murmur.

She doesn't look at me, just whispers, "Because you are my tentacle queen, and this is MAVFest." Then, drier, "Also, Ami's doing a book signing in Cleveland. So I sent Callie. I don't do Cleveland."

Natalie is convinced that if we play our cards right and make it through all eleven days, we'll come out the other end of MAVFest with an amazing deal for turning *The Dark Duke* into a movie or streaming series under my control.

We've already had several people reach out with interest in *The Dark Duke*: producers, directors, actors, a few studios. Lily Renshaw is just the most persistent.

So here we all sit, in the Gilded Armadillo, having a "casual business meeting," the four of us with Lily and her sidekick, Wes Solano.

"And when I read *The Dark Duke*, I just knew… it had to be a film," Lily says, both hands gripping her wineglass to her chest like it's a crystal chalice and she's imparting a great cinematic prophecy. "The tension, the longing, the intergalactic stakes. It's begging to be on the big screen."

Natalie offers a polite nod, the kind of carefully neutral response that reveals absolutely nothing. The more time I spend with her, the more I realize—she knows when to play charming, and when to go ice cold. At this moment, as she gazes at Lily, I know she's in full ice queen mode.

She's here for me but she's also here to make sure Crimson Quill gets a good deal on the subsidiary rights for *The Dark Duke*. If the book becomes a hit series, it drives sales, prestige, and leverage for the imprint. Everyone wins—*if* we get the contract we want.

Elias, seated in a chair on the other side of Natalie, is even harder to read, his fingers resting lightly against his tumbler of tequila as he lets Lily talk. Where Natalie is glacier and steel, Elias Vasquez is silk and switchblades. He's tall, lean, elegantly built, and always impeccably dressed. His dark hair brushes his collar, a little too long for most boardrooms, and his clean-shaven face is striking. Not movie-star pretty, but sharp in a way that makes people look twice. He gives off the quiet confidence of a man who's survived things most of the people at this table can't imagine. And came out the other side polished, lethal, and utterly unbothered.

I know Elias is here for my security. But he's also the Sandoval negotiator—the one who closes deals, moves money, and makes sure every contract ultimately benefits the family. He doesn't care about books or industry chatter. He cares about power, influence, and how much leverage a successful adaptation of my work can buy for his boss, my father. Which means, in this case, his interests might not line up with mine.

As I take in everyone, I'm trying very hard not to scream into one of the oversized velvet throw pillows lining this couch. While I appreciate Fidel's protectiveness, Natalie's insights, Elias's business acumen, Lily's enthusiasm, and whatever it is Wes brings to the table, I'm not sure any of this is actually about me.

Sometimes I wonder if anyone at this table actually sees *me*. Not the cartel daughter. Not the author with "potential." Not the girl who grew up so sheltered she had to learn how the real world works from romance novels and social media.

Just me.

I know where I come from. I know what my last name means. But this—the books, the attention, the deals—it's the first thing I've ever done that's mine. No brothers calling the shots. No favors traded. No shadow of Raul Sandoval hanging over the contract.

If I can pull this off, if I can turn *The Dark Duke* into something real, it won't just be a win for me. It'll be a declaration. That I'm not here because of my name. That no one bought my success. That I built this for myself. And I can stand on my own.

Meanwhile, Lily keeps selling herself.

"I just know I'm meant to play Lady Penelope," she continues, sounding like she's delivering an acceptance speech. "I'm sure you all saw my portrayal of the next-door neighbor in *Six Doors Down*." She pauses just long enough to take a sip of her wine. Elias looks over at me and shrugs. "And, of course, we really need to get ahead of this before someone else scoops up the rights."

Fidel exhales sharply through his nose. I don't even have to look at him to know exactly what he's thinking: *self-absorbed bitch.*

Natalie, ever the professional, sets her own glass down gently before responding. "Mercede owns her film rights," she says smoothly. "So there's no need to rush into anything."

I appreciate that Natalie uses my pen name. Lily doesn't need to know about my family.

Lily's smile flickers—just for a second—before she recovers with award-worthy finesse. "Oh, of course," she purrs. "I just want what's best for the project."

Natalie makes a small sound of acknowledgment. A subtle warning that she's seen this play before.

Elias, still watching Lily with measured patience, finally speaks. "Do you have a director attached?"

Lily's expression brightens. "I have options."

Elias tilts his glass slightly, studying the liquid like it holds the patience he needs to get through this conversation. "So no."

I almost choke on my Prosecco. Maybe Elias knows more about the film industry than I give him credit for.

Lily barely falters, flipping her hair over one shoulder. "It means I'm having conversations. Right, Wes?"

Her gaze flicks to Wes Solano, who has been mostly content to let Lily take the lead, focusing less on the conversation and more on draining the expensive scotch he ordered.

"I mean, obviously, Solano Studios has great connections," Wes says smoothly. "We've got a real *in* with the film scene here in Austin. With the vision Lily and I have, this is the perfect city for a project like this. There's so much happening right now. Austin is the new Hollywood, you know."

Natalie raises a brow, unimpressed. "Is that so?"

"Absolutely," Wes says, flashing me a toothy grin I immediately don't trust. "Mercede, this is the kind of project that could change the industry. A high-concept, female-driven sci-fi romance? It's fresh. It's bold. It's exactly what the studios are looking for right now."

Lily nods, unfazed by our obvious skepticism. "All of the streamers are looking for prestige content. That's why we need to move fast. I want to position this for a MAVFest premiere next year. *The Dark Duke* is exactly the kind of buzzy, high-concept crossover hit they'll eat up."

I press my lips together. The idea that anyone can just snap their fingers and make a MAVFest premiere happen is laughable. But Lily says it with such breathless certainty that I half expect her to pull out a festival badge for next year and wave it at us.

Lily leans toward me, lowering her voice conspiratorially. "The attention is building, Mercede. You're the next big thing. But you have to strike while the iron is hot."

Wes nods. "Exactly. Give us the go-ahead, and we can bring in some major players. Directors, investors, actors."

As much as I want to roll my eyes, I know why we're still here. Lily has seven million followers across multiple social media platforms, a growing acting resume, and an algorithm-friendly face. She's everywhere right now.

Fidel clocked it days ago. He didn't say much, just sent me the numbers.

And I know what that means. If Lily wants to play Lady Penelope, people will listen. If she starts pushing her version of the character to her followers—the costumes, the tone, the story —before I've had a chance to shape what *The Dark Duke* even is on screen? Then I'll lose control. It'll be her version of the story, not mine.

Fidel shifts on the couch, letting out a small, unimpressed sound that might be a laugh.

Lily, either oblivious or deliberately ignoring the tension, turns to Fidel with a slow smile. "You must be so protective of Mercede," she purrs.

And for the first time tonight, Lily Renshaw has stopped

talking about herself. Now, she's looking at Fidel like she wants to take a bite out of him.

Her gaze drags over him, slow and assessing, taking in the sharp angles of his face, the shadow of stubble along his jaw, the way his charcoal gray suit stretches across broad shoulders. Even sitting, his presence hums with quiet, restrained threat.

And I hate that I know exactly what she sees.

Because the suit does things to him. It's not just the way it fits, the expert tailoring emphasizing his powerful frame, long, muscled legs, solid chest, thick arms. It's the way he wears it. Other men wear suits to impress. To posture.

But Fidel wears his comfortably, easily. Like it's perfectly fitted to him. Because it is. It has to be to let him hide a gun. Probably more than one.

Even now, under Lily's scrutiny, he doesn't fidget, doesn't shift, doesn't react. Just lifts his glass with those strong, capable hands, takes a slow sip of water, and swallows.

Something low in my stomach clenches. I tell myself it's nerves. Tension. Frustration.

But I usually don't feel tension *that* low.

Lily is still watching him, her smile sharpening, her body shifting ever so slightly—testing. Waiting for him to react, to see her.

And Fidel, in classic Fidel fashion, does nothing.

There's a flash of relief when I see that. Something that I don't want to feel. I hate that I do.

Fidel, to his credit, simply stares at Lily, unreadable, before saying, "Protecting Mercede is my job."

Lily's smile stretches a fraction wider, and I have the sinking suspicion that she's just decided to make Fidel her new favorite game.

As if on cue, the check arrives. Elias, without a word, reaches for it. Wes makes no move to stop him.

Of course. Wes and Lily invite *us* for drinks at one of the most exclusive bars in Austin... and the Sandovals foot the bill.

Typical.

Lily pouts, sighing dramatically. "Oh, *come on*, Mercede" she says. "We could wrap this up *now*. You know we'd make magic together."

I tighten my grip on my glass of Prosecco.

I've worked so hard to keep my writing separate from the Sandovals, to prove, if only to myself, that I can build something on my own. But as Lily leans back, flashing that too-bright smile like *The Dark Duke* is already hers, and as her gaze keeps drifting, lingering, circling back to Fidel, I have the sinking feeling that I'm about to lose control of everything.

8

FIDEL

The Platinum Soirée is a fucking nightmare. MAVFest's first-night Platinum badge mixer is the kind of over-the-top bullshit that makes rich people feel important. It's a who's-who of industry elites—directors, producers, tech moguls, streaming execs, and a sprinkle of A-list actors thrown in for show while everyone pretends they're not here to cut deals.

The whole thing sprawls across the rooftop of the Hotel Hermosa which has been transformed into some kind of luxury jungle, with manicured palms, glass fire pits, and an infinity-edge pool that spills toward the skyline, backed by the Texas Capitol glowing against the night sky.

Low lighting glints off every surface—gold-rimmed glasses filled with branded cocktails and flakes of edible gold, crystal-clear ice cubes, foil-stamped napkins bearing the MAVFest logo. A live DJ pulses ambient beats from a glass booth near the pool while some influencer types pose with drinks they're probably being paid to hold.

Even I recognize a few of the faces here. That guy from the revenge Western who won an Oscar last year. Or maybe the year before. The redhead from that assassin show that swept some awards. If I'm recognizing the actors, it's only a matter of time before this turns into a media circus.

Which means this is a security disaster waiting to happen.

Too many people. Too many angles. Too many Platinum badge holders who think they're important enough to get close to Maria.

Maria stands close at my side, a glass of Prosecco in hand, eyes bright with excitement as she scans the rooftop.

"Fidel," she whispers, leaning in like she's telling me a secret, her breath warm in my ear. "This is so much better than I thought it'd be." She's more relaxed now that we've gotten away from Lily and Wes Solano.

I grunt, scanning the crowd over the rim of my glass of water. Daniel Castillo is somewhere nearby, helping cover the perimeter. He already checked in with a quick update through the comm confirming Carlos's security team is in place. Guards on the exits. Drivers outside.

Carlos didn't come himself. He has no patience for this kind of shit.

Carlos Sandoval—Raul's second son and Maria's older brother—runs the Austin operation. Tech, politics, culture. All the high-gloss sectors the family needs to keep in check. And when Carlos doesn't want to deal with something directly, he sends Daniel.

Daniel solves problems so efficiently it's like they were never there. Enforcer. Strategist. Quietly lethal. While I'm in town, he and I are coordinating the security rotation.

If there's a problem tonight, Daniel's my back-up.

The problem we are all currently handling is keeping Maria safe.

And right now, she isn't making that easy.

She tips her glass back, finishing the rest of her Prosecco. Her cheeks are flushed—from the heat, the Prosecco, or just the thrill of the night. Hard to tell. There's a shimmer in her eyes that says she's riding the edge of tipsy. Not drunk. Just fearless enough to forget how close we're standing.

"I think I need another one and then I'm going to mingle," she announces.

I catch her wrist before she can slip away. Warm, delicate. Too easy to break.

"You don't need another one and you stick by me," I tell her.

Maria pouts, pressing closer to me, a teasing lilt in her voice. "You're no fun, Fidel."

No. I'm not fun. I'm just here on a rooftop full of self-important pricks trying to make sure she gets through this festival alive.

Across the terrace, Natalie and Elias are deep in conversation with a group of gray-haired men in golf shirts. Probably studio execs, all circling the same thing: distribution rights, adaptations deals, and who gets to control the future of *The Dark Duke*.

Natalie, despite her tailored dress and polished charm, has the cutthroat instincts of a war general. Elias? He's worse. Patient, methodical, and terrifyingly good at making people think his deal is the only deal worth taking.

Maria knows what that conversation is. She knows exactly what it means. But she's choosing not to join them. At least, not yet.

Right now, she seems focused on the fun. The buzz. The feeling of being here as an author, not a product.

But the longer she stays out of those talks, the more likely it is that someone else decides to speak for her. To take control of her future.

I clench my jaw. Maria's future isn't my problem. Not tonight.

Tonight, I just need to make sure she isn't an easy target on this fucking rooftop.

I lift my glass, bringing it to my lips. "Starting tomorrow, I want direct access to every meeting, every appearance, every invite." I take a drink. "No more *'drinks with Lily'* surprises. No last minute changes."

Maria groans. "Fidel—"

"No arguments." I set my glass down and level her with a look. "I'll coordinate your schedule with Daniel and the security detail. Who's driving you, which guards are assigned, how they're rotating shifts."

Maria blinks, momentarily thrown by the sharp shift in my tone.

"You're serious."

I arch a brow.

She sighs dramatically, turning back to the crowd and shifting so that her back is lightly pressed against my chest, her body aligning against mine in a way I am definitely not going to acknowledge.

She fits against me like it's normal. Like it doesn't mean anything. Like she hasn't been driving me insane for years.

"Fine," she mutters, tilting her head back to look up at me. "Whatever you want, *Fidel*."

I exhale through my nose, pressing down the heat curling low in my gut.

It isn't all I want. Not even close.

I want her mouth, her laugh, her skin against mine. I want to be the one she leans on—because she wants to, not because she's assigned to me.

But she can never know that. If I cross that line, I won't come back.

Maria smiles, oblivious to the way I'm unraveling with every goddamn breath she takes. She acts like pressing against me, whispering in my ear, tilting her head back to smile doesn't mean a goddamn thing. Maybe it doesn't to her. Maybe I'm the only one falling apart.

She lifts her empty glass between us. "Now, be a good body-guard and get me another drink."

I get it. Why she wants to be here. Why she needs it.

She's never had a single part of her life that wasn't under someone else's control. Raul, Carlos, Marco, even Elias. Even me. We all orbit around her like we know what's best. And maybe we do.

But the thing about Maria? She doesn't want anyone's permission. Not anymore. She wants to make her own choices, go her own way, win or lose, succeed or crash and burn.

And I want that for her.

Because I know what it's like to be born into a world that already has your whole life mapped out. Every move scripted, every choice made for you by someone else. A name like Sandoval comes with power, but it also comes with chains.

And Maria's trying to break hers.

I take the glass from her hand and lead her to the bar. Just to be difficult, I don't get her another Prosecco.

I get her a water.

And I make her drink every drop.

9

FIDEL

THE COVERED terrace at Hotel Zavala overlooks a golf course carved into the hills of far west Austin—wide open, rolling green fairways. And useless from a security standpoint. The terrace is too open. Too accessible. No barriers worth a damn.

Beyond the manicured greens, the landscape becomes wild. A late-afternoon haze hangs over limestone ridges patched with brush, twisted live oaks and scruffy mesquite. That Hill Country blend of elegance and dust. Pretty to look at. A nightmare to monitor.

Nothing on this job is easy to protect.

I'm waiting for the "Team Dark Duke" meeting Maria has called for. She wants all of us on the same page about the future of her book. Specifically, the importance of negotiating a film deal here at MAVFest.

But I have bigger problems. This morning has already been a headache.

It started with the weekly status check, a meeting Raul insisted upon to keep himself fully informed of every business dealing that impacts the Sandovals and their interests, legal or otherwise. He expects complete transparency, from the empire's financial expansions to the day-to-day movements of his family. The moment he accepted that these meetings could be securely conducted as encrypted video calls, he tolerated no excuse for missing them.

Elias and I met up with Carlos at his place, an upscale, modern mansion in West Lake Hills, just across Lady Bird Lake from downtown Austin. Carlos sat at the head of the conference table in his home office, espresso in hand. I sat to one side of him, Elias to the other. Each of us connected to the video call on our laptops.

On my screen, I saw Raul and Marco joining from San Antonio; Raul, as always, composed and unreadable, Marco already impatient, his fingers tapping against the desk.

RJ—Raul Jr.—called in from Houston with his in-house legal advisor, Isabella Morales, seated beside him, each on their own laptops. He was wrapping up a report on two new oil and gas-adjacent companies with whom he was on the verge of signing contracts. One specialized in deep-sea exploration for offshore drilling sites; the other provided equipment for rigs. The ultimate goal was acquisition of these companies.

"Impressive," Raul intoned. "These will be excellent for expanding our oil and gas reach. And for financial movements."

Financial movements. A polite way of saying smuggling and money laundering.

Then Raul shifted to Carlos. "Austin?"

Carlos delivered his usual report. Business at the clubs, music venues, and underground casinos was running smoothly. Political ties remained solid, and lobbying efforts—wining and dining the right elected officials, law enforcement personnel, and government insiders—were proceeding without issue. No disruptions, no surprises.

Then, he dropped the bombshell.

"I've had an idea that I think might work for us in a number of ways."

Marco stopped tapping his fingers. Raul gave a slight nod. Continue.

"Solano Studios is a small production company here in Austin," Carlos said. "Owned by Wes Solano. Big talker, but no real financial resources or backing. He's been trying to lock down Maria's film rights for *The Dark Duke*. With Lily Renshaw attached, maybe he thinks he can pull in funding. She's got a massive social media presence, so he might be right."

Carlos leaned back, already calculating the angles.

"If Maria ends up working with them, that gives us an opportunity to move in and take over. A production company would be a strong investment, drawing in outside investors and allowing us to move cash through the system."

Money laundering.

Elias hummed in interest. "Hollywood is nothing but expensive illusions. The amount of unchecked cash flow in that industry is insane. A company like Solano Studios? We take it over, we control how it moves."

Carlos's gaze flicked to the screen. "And *we* control what happens to *The Dark Duke*."

Ah. There it was.

I felt a muscle in my jaw tighten.

"So that's what this is really about," I said. I couldn't help myself.

"Not entirely," Carlos replied smoothly. "But let's be honest— if we're going to expand into film production, and I think we should, we might as well start with something that benefits us. And keeping Maria's project in-house ensures no one screws her over."

It was a smart pitch. Solano Studios was vulnerable. Taking

over would give the Sandovals a foothold in a new industry, expanding financial operations and influence.

But it also meant one more part of Maria's life falling under the Sandoval umbrella.

"Maria wants control over her career," I said, voice even.

Carlos exhaled, shaking his head. "You think I don't know that? I also know she doesn't know shit about how the film industry works. Frankly, I'm not sure Natalie does either. They think they do, but publishing and film are different worlds."

"So we just take the choice away from her?"

"We give her the best option available," Carlos corrected. "And we make sure no one fucks her over. You think that's a bad thing?"

I didn't answer.

Raul, silent until this point, finally spoke. "Carlos, I see the appeal. But this is a new industry for us. I want numbers. I want risk assessment. And I want every potential liability accounted for."

That was as close to approval as Carlos was going to get.

"Understood," Carlos said. "I'll put together a full proposal. But let's be honest—Maria needs protection in this, whether she likes it or not."

Maria needs protection. That was something we could all agree on.

But why was I the only one still watching the shadows?

It wasn't Hollywood that worried me. It was Los Cuervos. And they weren't gone.

I sat forward, shifting the conversation. "We need to stay focused on the real threat," I said. "Los Cuervos hasn't made a move since the Calderón attack, but that doesn't mean they're gone."

Raul studied me. "Fidel, that was eight months ago. If they

were planning retaliation, we would have seen signs of it by now."

"Or they're waiting for the right moment," I mutter.

"Paranoia isn't strategy," Carlos pointed out.

"Neither is underestimating the enemy," I shot back.

Raul focused on me, his gaze steady. "Los Cuervos miscalculated by using the Calderóns. They learned the hard way that we are not an empire they can muscle into. For now, I consider them neutralized."

I didn't. But I clenched my fists under the table and kept my mouth shut.

"Obviously," Raul continued, "if I am presented with new information, I will consider it."

New information. Fine. I'd find that information.

In the meantime, I had another priority—locking down Maria's security.

I glanced at Carlos. "I'm vetting Maria's full schedule for MAVFest. Again. Every single event she's attending. I need to coordinate her movements with Daniel so we're all in sync. No gaps in coverage, no miscommunications."

Carlos frowned. "She'll have security. She'll be fine."

"She won't be," I said flatly. "Not if someone starts tracking her. And I need to make sure she's invisible digitally. Frank is good, but I need access. We keep her off the radar. No one follows her movements unless we want them to."

Frank Lin was not an enforcer. He was a hacker, an analyst, a ghost in the system. We'd gone to college together and I'd helped him get a job with the Sandovals. He ran Carlos's tech operations, gathering data and making sure no one could see the Sandoval footprint where it wasn't supposed to be.

Carlos sighed, rubbing his temple. "Jesus. Fine. I'll have Daniel reach out. You guys can talk. Again. And you can use

Frank. Make sure he does his job. You're in charge of Maria's security. They'll answer to you."

"Good."

Raul's voice cut through. "Fidel, Maria's security is your responsibility. Continue doing what needs to be done. And, if you're this certain that Los Cuervos is still a threat, bring me proof."

Now, I glance out across the terrace. The heat's still hanging in the air and the meeting with Maria is about to begin.

But since the call with Raul ended, my priorities have shifted. Finding that proof is now at the top of the list. Right after keeping Maria safe.

Keeping Maria safe comes before everything.

10

MARIA

NATALIE and I step onto the Hotel Zavala terrace. Late afternoon heat clings to the stone, but a breeze off the golf course cuts through it, carrying the scent of cut grass. I slip into a chair across from Elias and Fidel.

The Zavala is the kind of hotel where real power moves behind closed doors. Not just a five-star luxury spot. This is where the A-listers, studio heads, and deep-pocketed investors set up shop during MAVFest, away from the noise and crowds of downtown. Million-dollar deals are made here, over dirty martinis and cigars. It's the kind of place where a single suite costs more per night than some people make in a year.

Everything about it radiates exclusivity. The sleek, glass-paneled balconies that overlook the pristine golf course. The private concierge staff who cater to their guests' every whim. The blacked-out SUVs lining the valet entrance, each one carrying someone with a name people recognize.

Natalie's room is here so she's close to the power players. Mine isn't.

Because Raul had put his foot down.

Instead of letting me stay here, where the "action" is—where connections are made, where the people who matter would see me—he planted me at Carlos's estate, safely insulated from the entertainment industry's power circle.

Typical.

Zara Caldwell, Natalie's recommended attorney, will arrive soon. But first, I need everyone on the same page.

Both Fidel and Elias stand as we sit.

"We won't be bothered here," Elias says. "I had the hotel clear the terrace."

"And I have several of Carlos's security detail stationed at the door to keep out intruders," Fidel adds.

Fidel. Always vigilant. Always a stick in the mud.

Natalie shoots me a glance before turning to them. "The attorney we're meeting with is Zara Caldwell. Entertainment and publishing law. I've worked with her in the past. She's excellent."

Elias nods. "Carlos's team vetted her. She is who you say she is. It's worth taking the meeting."

Natalie's nails tap against the table, slow and deliberate. "Thank you for your approval, Elias."

Elias leans back, stretching one arm over a chair. "No problem," he says with a smirk.

For a second, neither of them moves, the air between them stretching tight. Fidel and I exchange a glance and he gives me a small shrug. *Yeah, what the hell?*

Elias gives Natalie a lazy, unreadable smile, just as Zara arrives, right on time.

Zara Caldwell is polished. Early thirties. Smooth brown skin and dark cornrows braided straight back into a low, coiled bun —no frizz, no flyaways, just clean, perfect lines. Her navy pantsuit is tailored within an inch of its life, structured and sharp despite the heat. Gold hoop earrings glint under the soft lighting, and her manicure—short, glossy, and blood-red—

matches the flash of her lipstick. She walks toward us with fluid precision, the kind of presence that says she bills by the quarter-hour and doesn't waste a second of it.

But I still feel a bit skeptical. Is she here for me or for the Sandovals?

She puts her hand out to me. "Zara Caldwell," she says. "Entertainment attorney specializing in publishing and film rights. Langston, Blake and Saavedra. You must be Mercede Sanchez."

I take her hand and we shake. "It's so nice to meet you, Ms. Caldwell. Please call me Mercede."

"Only if you'll call me Zara," she replies with a quick smile.

She takes a seat as introductions are made all around and then I just ask her, "So you're the lawyer Natalie trusts?"

Zara gives me a small, knowing smirk. "Yes. And more importantly, I'm the lawyer who's going to keep you from getting screwed over."

Natalie shoots me a quick wink.

Zara sets down her leather folio and leans forward slightly. "Before we begin, just know that I am here at your request to provide legal advice. This meeting is with you and your team, and we are in a private setting. Further, I understand that, at this time, I am dealing with Mercede Sanchez, author of *The Dark Duke*, and we are discussing the possibility of you hiring me to represent you regarding that work. Everything we discuss, and by we I mean all of us sitting here, is confidential and protected under attorney-client privilege—whether or not you hire me."

She meets my gaze directly. "Even if Mercede Sanchez is a pen name."

Okay. She knows exactly who I am.

There's no judgment in her tone. No hesitation. Just a simple acknowledgment of fact.

"So we can all speak freely. Is that agreeable to everyone?"

We all nod.

Elias, having dealt with countless attorneys, both in business and other matters, seems satisfied. That alone puts me slightly more at ease.

All eyes turn to me. This is my deal, and for once, I'm the one taking charge.

"All right, Zara. Tell me what you can do for me."

Zara gives me a wide grin and begins her spiel. "If you decide to sell the media rights to *The Dark Duke*, my job is to protect you and make sure you get exactly what you want. That means negotiating option agreements, securing creative control, structuring payments, ensuring profit participation, protecting international rights, and fighting against 'Hollywood accounting' scams. I can do any of those things for you. I can do all of them if you wish."

Elias and Natalie, as expected, both perk up.

"I've worked with several major authors," Zara continues. "I helped secure rights for *Blood & Blade*, which is currently filming in Spain, and *The Rise of House Ashford*, which is now in production for *Season 2* on UltraVision."

I know both of those books. And I had watched *Season 1* of *House Ashford*. Twice.

"Natalie is already one of my favorite clients," Zara adds, giving her a brief smile. "I have represented several of her authors. I assume she's told you—my job is to fight for you. If you want full creative control, I can negotiate that. If you want a better percentage of profits, I can get it. But that only works if you have a team that knows how to fight for you. A team that would include me. Does that sound like what you're looking for?"

For a second, I just stare at her. No one has ever asked me what I want. Not like this. Like I just have to say the word and someone will fight for me. That's not how it's worked before. But maybe... it could.

Zara picks up on my doubt instantly.

"No one can force you into a deal, Mercede. Not me. Not a studio. Not anyone."

That should reassure me. But it doesn't.

I think back to when I was twelve, home from boarding school for the holidays. I went to my father's office, knocked on his door. Marco opened it. He was already working security by then. My father was on a call but waved me in.

I sat in the large leather chair in front of his desk, clutching the folder in my hands, trying to steady my nerves.

When he hung up, he looked at me and smiled. "Yes, *mija*. What is it?"

I asked him if I could go to a summer writing camp in New York. I had the flyer printed, the application filled out. I'd even written a short story as a sample.

He barely glanced at any of it. Just kept smiling and said, "Writers don't survive in this world, *mija*. They get eaten. You can spend the summer here, like always."

And then he took his next call.

Marco walked me out without a word. I didn't cry until the door shut behind me.

That was the day I began to realize that if I wanted a life of my own, I'd have to fight for it. I'd have to take it. No one was ever going to hand it to me. Not my father, not my brothers, not even the version of myself who once believed asking nicely was enough.

My family had never *forced* anything on me. They just took my life over, removing every option until all choice was gone.

But maybe this time can be different. If I speak up and claim this... maybe I can decide what happens next.

Elias leans forward. "If she signs an option contract, how long before production starts?"

"Best case scenario? Six months to a year," Zara says. "Worst case? Indefinitely, if the studio shelves it. But I'll make sure we don't allow that to happen."

I exhale sharply, dragging a hand through my hair. Too many unknowns. Too many things potentially outside my control.

"You don't have to decide today," Natalie reminds me.

"No, you don't," Zara agrees. "Take your time. But if you do move forward, I can get you the best deal, structured exactly the way you want it."

She's damn confident. I like that.

Zara finally takes her leave, leaving several business cards and shaking hands all around.

The four of us stay on the terrace as the sun dips lower.

"Well?" I ask, looking around the table.

Natalie answers first. "I've seen adaptation deals fall apart before. Even if *we* love *The Dark Duke*, we need to be sure we get a deal that has real financing and guaranteed distribution. Something beyond Lily Renshaw and whatever deal she's trying to cook up."

"And you think we can get that kind of deal?" I ask, wanting a real answer.

Natalie gazes up at the sky for a moment, contemplating. She then looks back at me, locking eyes. "I do. Especially with Zara's help. And the fact is that Lily's too tenacious not to get this project noticed. I'm sure she's also talking to other producers, not just Wes Solano. Maybe even major studios. The question is whether you want to steer this adaptation yourself... or let Lily and someone else decide how the deal goes. How your story ends up on screen."

Elias adjusts his cufflinks. "Zara knows her business. If Lily lands a big studio deal, they'll have an army of lawyers. And they'll come in with their own terms. You could be forced to give up control. If you want to move forward, on your terms, I believe you need Zara on your side."

He turns to Fidel. "Thoughts?"

Fidel is looking down at his hands, folded neatly on the table. Finally, he looks up.

"I think Zara Caldwell is exactly who you need," he says carefully. "If you don't move quickly, a studio might scoop Lily up, and you'll lose your chance to shape the adaptation the way you envision."

He glances at me.

I smile. "Thanks, Fidel. I agree."

I set down my glass. "Okay. Let's hire Zara Caldwell and move forward."

Elias and Natalie stand, still talking contracts as they head inside. Fidel stays. Doesn't tell me what to do. Doesn't hover. Just... stays. Like he's anchored here for me.

He turns to me. "I'll walk you to the car."

Instead of getting up, I lean back. "Can we sit and watch the sunset? Just for a minute?"

Fidel looks at me for a moment, as if checking to see if I'm all right. Then, "Sure. But just for a minute. You need to get back to Carlos's."

We sit in silence, watching the sky burn orange over the golf course.

For once, Fidel doesn't tell me to be careful. He doesn't remind me about security.

He just lets me be.

11

———

FIDEL

Carlos would lose his shit if he saw this setup.

This house, in Tarrytown, is one of his many high-end properties in Austin. It's usually spotless, minimalist, a catalog of sleek surfaces and curated neutrality. Now it looks like the war room of someone preparing for a digital siege.

The dining table is covered with open laptops, hard drives, satellite printouts, and stacks of reports organized by type and threat level. A whiteboard I dragged in from the garage glows under the overhead light, crosshatched with connections—names, dates, locations, everything I've gathered on Los Cuervos and anyone they've touched.

The air smells like fresh coffee and hot plastic, thanks to the printer I've been working to death since 7 a.m.

I know it looks like chaos. But it's not. Not to me. This is my kind of order.

I'm running three laptops: one for intel gathering, one for surveillance feeds, and one for encryption. Next to them: burners, encrypted cell phones, and secured lines, all within easy reach. Flash drives and portable power banks sit in neat rows beside the printer. Nothing out of place.

Carlos would still walk in, take one look, and shake his head.

I know that because I spent years watching him work.

Carlos runs Austin like a silent algorithm—efficient, deliberate, unshakeable. Where Raul rules through force and Marco through fear, Carlos plays long game chess. Every deal, every relationship, every donation to a crooked senator is just one more move on a board only he can fully see.

And I've been lucky because he let me look at that board. Let me study it up close.

I know I wasn't supposed to make it this far. Not into this world, not into the rooms where real decisions get made. Not into Raul Sandoval's inner circle.

Guys like me don't get mentored by guys like Carlos Sandoval. We don't get trusted. We get used. Or ignored. Or locked out entirely.

Or at least that's what my father, Hector Cedillo, believed. He was convinced that the cards were stacked against him, against our family. For him, that was the natural order of things. And he saw any attempt to rise above that, to change our circumstances, as weakness. As a personal insult to the great Hector Cedillo. So he tried to beat it out of us—any dream, any defiance, any hope that things could be different.

When he was around, he hit first and explained later, if he explained at all. My mother did what she could, but she was too busy surviving to protect me the way she wanted. Marco tried. Took more hits for all of us than I can count. But when you grow up with a man like Hector, the damage is inevitable.

Some days, I could feel it inside me, a rage I didn't know what to do with. A tight, electric fury that felt like it came from nowhere. Except I knew exactly where it came from. My father.

Back then, it scared me. Still does.

Because no matter how much trust I earn, how many systems I lock down, how much loyalty I prove—part of me still thinks it's only a matter of time before my luck runs out and the blood wins. Before I become him.

Raul knew about Hector. He didn't say much. But he knew. When he brought my mother on as household staff, I was three years old. When he let us move into the quarters near the kitchen, I was four. He took care of us, tried to help us. He paid for my education—uniforms, books, tuition, all of it. He told me, "You're the smart one." And I never forgot.

That's where I met Maria. That's where it all started.

We were kids in the same house but in two different worlds. And somehow, we kept finding each other. Her with scraped knees and a mouth full of fire. Me trying to stay invisible.

Then Elena died. Sudden. Stupid. Senseless. A year later, my mom passed away—quiet, almost like she'd followed her. Marco was overseas, with the Marines. And my father was long gone.

So it was just me. Twelve years old, no family. A boy living alone in the staff quarters of a house that wasn't mine. Raul let me stay, kept me clothed and fed, as I waited for Marco to come home from the Marines.

And Maria was there for me, during the summers and holidays. She was the only thing that still felt... good. Easy. Someone who wanted to be with me. Someone I wanted to protect.

And maybe I've been doing it ever since.

When I finally left for college in Austin, Raul sent me to work for Carlos and, over time, he became more than a mentor. He was my blueprint. Raul always made sure I had the best education. Marco made sure I knew how to see the angles, to fight smart. But Carlos? Carlos taught me how to see the game board and always think at least five steps ahead.

I spent more nights in his guest room than in my own shitty off-campus apartment—setting up security systems, reviewing his club surveillance, running background checks on competitors, and locking down financial records with airtight encryption.

And he didn't treat me like a tech guy. He liked me so he brought me into his strategy meetings. Let me sit at the table. Asked what I thought. And actually listened when I told him.

Carlos didn't just train me to protect his assets. He showed me how to build an empire.

Now, I'm camped out in one of his immaculate houses, watching my own board and setting up my own battlefield.

Yeah. He'd lose his shit if he saw what I've done to this place.

It's only been twenty-four hours since Raul's video call.

Since I told myself: Keep looking. Keep digging. Find the proof.

So far, all I've found is confirmation of what I already knew. Los Cuervos hasn't disappeared. They've just gone quiet.

And that's when they're most dangerous.

I tap the keyboard of my primary laptop, pulling up the newest data packet.

Los Cuervos has come to power quickly over the last few years. They operate out of Monterrey, with roots that stretch across northern Mexico—smuggling, weapons, extortion, human trafficking. Where the Sandovals run their empire like a corporate machine, Los Cuervos has built theirs on brutality and fear.

They don't negotiate.

They don't build coalitions.

They don't make offers.

They take.

And if they want Texas, and I'm certain they do, the Sandoval operation is a turnkey solution.

The smuggling corridors are already built. The money laundering networks, the casinos, the real estate holdings. They won't need to construct anything new.

They'll just take Raul's empire and make it their own. Unless we stop them.

But something still feels off. Something doesn't make sense. This isn't just about expansion.

It's about Maria.

The attempted kidnapping in San Antonio.

Ami Zadegan, drugged at a Sandoval club.

The breach of the compound.

Too many attempts. Too much coordination.

And every time, it traces back to Maria. Why? I've followed the digital footprints, scraped every source I trust. But the motive still doesn't track. It's not just cartel business. It's personal. I just don't know why.

I reach for my coffee, grimacing at the cold bitterness. Doesn't matter. I'm not here for comfort. I'm here for answers.

There's a piece missing. Some motive I haven't uncovered.

And I won't stop until I do.

I rub a hand down my face and refocus on the screen. Daniel's already working Maria's MAVFest schedule, syncing with Natalie, securing each location. Frank's triple-checking the tech setups at the venues and hotels. If any venue has a data blind spot, we'll close it. If any room has a camera, I'll know who's watching.

I'm running every angle. This is the only way I know how to breathe.

Then—

A knock at the door.

I go still. I'm not expecting anyone. Elias is out with Natalie and Zara. Carlos doesn't do pop-ins. And I didn't hear any alerts from the outer perimeter. Which means whoever is at the door, doesn't belong.

Quietly, I slide my chair back and reach for my Glock. Safety off. Muzzle down.

Another knock. Lighter this time. Not urgent. Not aggressive.

I move silently to the door, every nerve on high alert. Whoever this is, they've got the wrong fucking house.

I exhale, calm and steady, and unlock the door.

Then I open it.

12

MARIA

FIDEL ANSWERS the door like he's preparing to kill someone.

The moment it swings open, I'm greeted with a gun aimed in my direction, a sharp glare, and Fidel's entire body coiled tight, like he's ready for an ambush. Only in Texas can a man open the door pointing a Glock in your face and still technically be within his rights.

I sigh. "Okay, first. What the hell?"

His gaze flicks behind me, scanning the driveway where Carlos's driver and a bodyguard linger by the car. I can feel the calculations running through Fidel's head. *Threat level: minimal. Annoyance level: extreme.*

He exhales and lowers the gun, stepping back. "You shouldn't be here."

I breeze past him into the house. "Yeah, yeah. Nice to see you, too."

He shuts the door behind me with a sigh that screams I do not have the patience for this.

"So," I say, turning to him with my best innocent smile. "What's for lunch?"

Fidel's expression barely shifts, but I catch the subtle flicker of disbelief. "Lunch?"

"Yes, lunch. I was bored."

He pinches the bridge of his nose. "So you came to bother me?"

"Bother? No. Enhance your day? Absolutely." I grin, plopping down on the couch. "Besides, you're in one of Carlos's houses. That means it's basically a Sandoval property, which means I can basically show up whenever I want."

Fidel folds his arms. "That is not how this works."

I wave a dismissive hand. "It is now."

I expect more grumbling. Maybe another dramatic sigh. What I didn't expect was to actually look at him.

Fidel is always put together. Always. Tailored suits, crisp dress shirts, expensive watches. Even when we were kids, he was the neat one, clean and serious, while I ran around the compound like a feral Disney princess.

But now?

Gray sweatpants. Fitted black t-shirt.

The shirt clings to his broad shoulders, stretching across his chest like it was sewn onto him. His arms—strong, lean, defined —are on full display. The kind of arms that don't belong to your childhood best friend.

His hair is tousled, like he's run his fingers through it, and the scent of clean soap and something warm and dark lingers in the air between us.

And the gray sweatpants.

I'm not a fool. I know what they say about gray sweatpants. They leave nothing to the imagination. They give you visual proof of just what you're working with. I've just never had cause to... verify the theory. But now I have to look away, because if I keep staring, I might find out exactly what's under those gray sweatpants.

When did being around Fidel turn me into this?

He's supposed to be the guy who growls at me about security and drinks black coffee like it's his primary personality trait. Not someone who makes me forget how words work.

I catch myself staring, and Fidel catches me catching myself staring. For a split second, something flickers across his face. A flash of amusement. Almost a smirk.

Great. Now he knows I was looking.

I recover immediately. "Wow. Didn't know you even owned casual clothes."

Very cool, Maria.

He looks down at himself, then back at me, expression flat. "Didn't know you were going door to door, harassing people in their own homes."

I grin. "I told you. I was bored. Thought I'd check in on my favorite overprotective watch dog."

Fidel lets out a slow exhale, shaking his head. "So you're bored, and you want to play Dora the Explorer?"

I gasp, delighted. "You remember my favorite TV show? That was so long ago! We were little kids!"

"I remember you forcing me to go on imaginary adventures across the entire compound. Acting like a monkey named Boots. And that if I didn't play along, you'd tell Raul I was being mean to you."

I beam. "It worked every time."

Of course it did. Fidel has been playing along with my ridiculous games for as long as I could remember.

He, his mother, and his sister, Elena, moved into the compound when I was barely a year old. His mother cooked for us, but she also helped raise me when my own mother was busy running the household or meeting with the wives of my father's business associates. And when my mother died, she was there for me. And Fidel? Fidel was always there, always mine.

Three years older, scrappy and serious. Trying to act like the man of the house before he even hit double digits. He was just a kid, but already he thought it was his job to protect everyone.

And he did.

He followed me through every wild fantasy. Every tantrum. Every stupid obsession. I made him read the entire *Harry Potter* series to me one summer. Made him address me as "Princess Maria." One time, I wrote a seventeen-page revenge plan against a girl from my boarding school that included cutting off all of her hair while she slept. I made him help me "edit" it. He never told me no. Never laughed. He just... showed up.

Because for a long time, he was my only friend.

There were no other kids on the compound. And by the time I realized why, realized that my father was a "crime lord," I'd already been sent to boarding school in Vermont. Because my father wanted me smart and safe and far away from what it meant to be a Sandoval.

And yet, every time I came home, Fidel was there.

And now?

Now, he's standing in front of me in gray sweatpants. Dangerous. Ridiculously hot. And I'm starting to think this is a problem.

Because I'm thinking about things I've tried very hard not to think about Fidel.

It's not that I've never dated. I have. Sort of. Mostly guys who didn't understand why I had a driver and a bodyguard when I was in high school. Guys who looked at me and called me "exotic" like it was some kind of compliment. Guys who quickly disappeared when they finally realized who my father was.

It never worked out. They never stayed very long.

No one has. Except Fidel.

Now he's standing here in front of me, six foot four and 195 pounds, all muscle and patience, acting like I'm some kind of nuisance.

I put a hand on my hip. "Well, don't worry, *Boots*. I'm not here to make you reenact my childhood fantasies."

His expression doesn't change. "I wasn't worried."

He lets out a sigh, then gestures toward the inside of the house. "You want a tour of *your house*?"

I shrug. "Might as well. What else am I supposed to do while Elias is off playing lawyer with Natalie and Zara?"

Fidel grumbles something about Elias being smart for leaving, then leads me from the entry through the rest of the house —kitchen, living room, bedrooms. All sleek and modern and eerily empty.

Then we reach the dining room.

And I stop cold.

This room isn't a mess. It's a battlefield. A war map.

Laptops. Cables. A huge whiteboard. Sticky notes. Satellite maps. Charts. Printouts. Screens flickering with information I don't understand. One monitor is running a live chat in Spanish. Another shows a map with shipping routes and cartel names marked in red.

It's chaos.

But it's not messy. Every wire, every note, every thread has a place.

I turn to Fidel. "Are you solving murders in your free time, or...?"

He ignores me, stepping around the table. "This is why you shouldn't be here."

I pick up a page and skim it. "Los Cuervos?"

Fidel's jaw tightens. "They were behind the Calderóns. They're not done. People keep acting like they are, but they're not."

"My father says they've been quiet," I say softly.

He nods once. "Cartels don't just disappear, Maria. They regroup. They wait. They look for the right opening."

I glance around the room again, absorbing the weight of what he's working on.

And for the first time, I see him not as my childhood bodyguard. Not as my loyal protector. But as something else. Something colder. Sharper. More dangerous.

Fidel isn't just playing defense. He's planning an offensive strike—mentally, strategically, obsessively.

I look at him again. Really look. He's unhappy. He doesn't like what everything in this room is telling him.

He's truly worried. About me.

And it feels like something inside me shifts.

It's probably nothing. Stress. Sleep deprivation. The gray fucking sweatpants.

I turn away quickly and grab a new page. Change the subject. "By the way. Lily wants me to go on a fake date."

Fidel stiffens. "A what?"

"A fake date. Tonight. For PR. She's setting me up with some actor she thinks should play the Dark Duke. She says it'll be good for fan engagement."

Fidel crosses his arms, slow and deliberate. "That's not on your schedule."

"I know, but now it is."

He glares at me. "Well... good luck with that."

That's it? No argument? No classic Fidel shutdown?

"I think you should be there," I say, still looking at the memo I've picked up, trying to sound offhand.

"I've got work to do." He gestures to the table. "Elias and Daniel's guys can cover it."

I shrug, feigning indifference. "Cool, cool. Maybe I'll ask my dad if he thinks you should be there." I glance up at him. "I mean, since you're in charge of my security and everything."

His brow furrows. He takes in a deep breath and then frowns. He knows I've won.

"Fine," he mutters. "I'll be there for your *fake date*."

"Great." I flash him a smile. "I'll let you know the details after I talk to Lily. And," I look down at the gray sweatpants one last time, "try to wear something nice."

He turns back to his screens, muttering under his breath.

And suddenly, I'm annoyed that I had to convince him to go. Which is ridiculous.

And also—why can't I stop thinking about what's underneath those damn sweatpants?

13

———————

MAVFEST DAY 3

Text Message Thread - Lily Renshaw and Mercede Sanchez

Lily: THIS is the event for our "date"

did you get this email - you have to go girl

Hunter is super cute and perfect for duke 

SAY YES!!!

                Mercede: sounds fun so YES!!!

———————

Email to All MAVest Gold and Platinum Badge Holders

From: mkting@lonestarzhardseltzer.com
To: MAVFest gold, MAVFest platinum
CC: publicity@MAVFest.com

Subject: LET'S ROLL!!! Strike a pose, Sip a seltzer: Lone Starz x MAVFest pop-up Collab

HEY MAVFEST! Are You Ready to roll?
🎳 Lone Starz Bowling Bash @ Lucky Strike Lanes 🎳
📍 Downtown Austin – Open to Gold and Platinum Badge Holders
💥 Sponsored by Lone Starz Hard Seltzer 💥

Join us at Lucky Strike Lanes for the most flavor-packed, clout-friendly night of MAVFest!

🥂 **Lone Starz Hard Seltzer Bowling Bash** 🥂
WHEN: Tonight, 8 PM 'til they kick us out
WHERE: Lucky Strike Lanes (4th & Lavaca)

Proudly presenting our newest, juiciest, dangerously sippable flavor:
PINK PRICKLY PEAR 

🎳 **Tonight's Line-Up Includes:**

- Ice-cold tastings of **Pink Prickly Pear Hard Seltzer**, served in collectible MAVFest cans
- Wild visuals & custom lighting across the lanes
- Limited-edition bowling shirts, balls & merch (first 50 guests only)
- Sets by **DJ Suzy Sparkle** (yes, she'll be there!) spinning cosmic country-core all night long

Confirmed influencer appearances from:

- *The Smoosh Bros* (TikTok legends, chaos agents)

- *NeonEvie* (IG alt-cowgirl + beauty collab queen)
- *CryptoYeehaw* (YouTube finance-meets-ranch-wear personality)
- *Lily Renshaw* (actress, creator, verified Duke Disciple)

Come for the vibes. Stay for the viral content.

Whether you're striking out or racking up wins, Lone Starz Hard Seltzer has the fuel to keep the party rolling.

Lone Starz Hard Seltzer: *Real flavor. Unreal fun.*
#PinkPricklyParty #LoneStarzGoesHard #LoneStarzBowlz
#MAVFestMoments

14

FIDEL

The fake date is at a bowling alley.

A MAVFest influencer event. Open to Gold and Platinum badge holders, sponsored by Lone Starz Hard Seltzer, featuring their new Pink Prickly Pear flavor plastered across every neon-lit screen in the venue.

I've spent over a decade protecting Maria Sandoval from cartel threats, kidnappings, and high-stakes negotiations. But I'm rapidly realizing I've never protected her from anything quite as insufferable as this.

Lucky Strike Lanes has been transformed into a hipster nightmare—low lighting, black leather seating, a DJ blasting indie remixes, and every wannabe TikTok-famous asshole clutching a pink Lone Starz can like it's currency.

Once again, it's a security disaster.

Daniel sent two men to help cover Maria tonight, Luis and Jorge. They're new and taking it seriously. But it's not enough. Not with this crowd. Not with the sheer number of cameras, proximity, digital livestreams. Anyone could slip in, blend in, make a move, disappear.

I'm going to have to rework the entire security plan. Again.

Coordinate with Daniel. Get Frank on digital lockdown. Make sure Maria isn't being tracked in real time.

Because right now? She's way too visible.

Lily Renshaw, on the other hand, is visible and thriving.

She's running this event like it's the Met Gala and not a brand-sponsored bowling night.

Her new "digital strategist," Sloane Cross, has her camera trained and ready as Lily hits pose after pose like she's starring in her own hard seltzer commercial.

"Okay, now one with the can and the bowling ball," Lily directs, grabbing a pink ball that matches her pink stilettos and the pink Lone Starz can she's holding. She flashes a sultry smile. She's got a whole look for this event, curated down to the color of her lipstick.

Sloane doesn't say much. She just angles the camera, adjusts something on her phone, taps rapidly on her tablet, and mutters, "Uploading."

She's not as overly enthusiastic as I would expect. Her actions are almost bored. Mechanical.

"Now one with me and Mercede!" Lily chirps, eyes laser-locked on Maria.

Maria steps in. Calm. Effortless.

Black crop top. Gold hoop earrings. High-waisted jeans. No flash, no filter. But somehow she looks like the one everyone came to see.

The picture is taken. Maria steps out of frame immediately and walks toward me, shaking Lily off like pink glitter.

Lily is already on to the next victim. "Hunter! Let's do one together. Just for fun. Never know when we'll be cast as romantic leads."

Hunter Novak grins like he's heard that line before. He probably has.

Hunter is Hollywood pretty. Dark-haired, blue-eyed, tall,

smug. The kind of guy who definitely peaked during a Disney Channel summer movie and never quite recovered. His jawline is sharp. His confidence is sharper.

He's the "fake date" that Lily brought along and has been hovering around Maria all night, brushing her arm, cracking jokes, calling her "Mercede" like they're on a first-name basis.

I tighten my arms across my chest as Maria drops into the chair beside me to change into bowling shoes.

"You look like you're having fun," I mutter.

She glances up, arching a brow. "And you look like being here is a personal insult to you. Loosen up."

Hunter appears beside her like a fungus. "So, Mercede, be honest—are you any good?"

Maria tilts her head, all innocence. "At what?"

"Bowling. You're up."

A slow smile spreads across her face.

"Oh, Hunter." She stands, selects her ball, fingers finding the holes with practiced ease. "I don't know. I guess we'll find out."

He has no idea what's coming.

Maria glides to the lane, plants her feet, takes four perfect steps, and releases.

Smooth. Precise. Merciless.

Strike.

Silence.

Then—

Lily shrieks like she's just discovered a new make-up sponsor. "OMG! Mercede! Sloane, tell me you got that!"

"Already uploading," Sloane says without looking up.

Lily clutches Maria's arm. "This is amazing. Hashtag the Dark Duke bowls! Wait—no. Hashtag Mercede strikes! Or— hashtag bowling is the new sexy!"

Maria throws me a look. With that same smug, competitive spark she's had since we were kids.

She used to bowl like that at the compound's private alley—focused, perfect, relentless. I used to think it was funny. That she was good at bowling of all things. Now watching her just makes my chest ache.

She raises a brow. *Want to play, Fidel?*

I keep my face neutral. *No.*

Lily perches beside me like she belongs there. "Do you bowl, Fidel?" she asks sweetly. "I mean, you look like you might be good with balls."

I look at her. Blink once. *Is she serious?*

"No."

Lily pouts and turns to Maria. "Does he ever have fun?"

Maria lifts her Lone Starz can and takes a sip. "He used to. But now he's just my cranky bodyguard."

She's right. That's all I am. Her bodyguard.

Hunter, oblivious to it all, rolls. It's a mess. The ball veers. Two pins drop.

Maria doesn't even try to hide her laugh.

"I think you hustled me," he says, turning toward her. Grinning. Like an idiot.

She sips her drink and gives him a little smirk. "I didn't lie, Hunter."

Fucking Hunter Novak.

I turn and start scanning the crowd again.

And then I notice her. Lily's publicity hack. Sloane Cross.

She's no longer filming Lily. She's pulled back, standing at a bar table, posture tight, laser-focused on her screens. One hand on her phone, the other swiping rapidly across a tablet.

But here's the thing—there's no way she's editing. She's not queuing up the perfect reel or cropping Lily's latest pose. Not posting to Lily's live feed. Not filming every moment with Lily like a PR strategist would.

She looks like she's running ops.

I recognize the rhythm—toggle, scan, adjust, backtrack. Never looking up. Never taking her focus off her screens. Eyes locked on the digital information in front of her.

She glances around once, shielding the tablet as she zooms in on something. And I feel it—that itch at the base of my skull.

She's not filming Lily. Not curating a feed. I swear she's tracking something. Or someone.

And Wes Solano?

He's next to her, sitting on a barstool, drowning in his scotch, sweat bleeding through his "trying too hard to be a hipster" shirt. He keeps glancing over at Sloane like she's holding a detonator and he just heard the click.

A bad feeling coils low in my spine.

I head toward the bar area to try and get a better look at what Sloane's doing, keeping to the edges.

I'm almost there when some girl I don't recognize slides up to me. Tan skin, cropped leather jacket, camera crew badge. Not dangerous. Not even flirty, really. Just a quick smile and a "Hey, I love your vibe." She touches my forearm lightly. "You an actor?"

I shake my head. "Security."

She laughs. "Figures. You've got that 'brooding-hitman-in-a-prestige-drama' thing going."

I don't respond. Just nod once and turn back toward the lanes—

—and catch Maria watching. Watching me and this girl. This girl who's still touching me.

Maria takes a long sip of her drink. Then stands and crosses over to us like she's in no particular hurry. Reaches us and puts her hand on my shoulder. She turns to the young woman with something that might be a smile. But isn't.

"I'm sorry, sweetheart," Maria says lightly, "but could you excuse us?"

Sweetheart?

The girl blinks at Maria. "Oh... sure." Then she looks at me and says, "See you around, Security," and gives me a wink as she walks away.

Maria steps closer. "Stop flirting," she mutters. "You're supposed to be my bodyguard. You're not here to pick up girls."

I let a beat pass. "Jealous?"

She rolls her eyes, but the blush on her cheeks deepens. "Of course not. I'm just trying to help you do your job."

I don't say anything. But I know Maria. And I'm pretty sure she just lied to me.

And for a second, I let myself feel it. That flicker of hope.

Then I bury it. Because hope is dangerous. And Maria is not mine.

She bumps me with her elbow. "You're really not going to bowl?"

"I have nothing to prove."

"Scared I'll beat you?"

Before I can answer, Lily flutters in, throwing an arm around Maria's shoulders. "Tell me you're having fun!"

Maria hesitates—just a second—then smiles at Lily. "Yeah. I am."

She's having fun. Laughing. Smiling. With fucking Hunter Novak, her fake date. Who gets to be close to her. Gets to touch her.

I fucking hate it.

15

FIDEL

The house is quiet.

Elias is still asleep. Maria is at Carlos's. And for the first time in days, I've got a moment alone.

I should be using it to get some damn rest.

Instead, I'm at the dining table, laptops open, monitors glowing, fingers moving fast across the keys. One name. One target.

Sloane Cross.

I lean back and roll out the tension in my shoulders. But my head's not cooperating. It keeps drifting back to the bowling alley.

Too many people. Too many eyes. Too many fucking cameras.

I'd told myself I was there for security. Told myself I was watching everyone.

But the truth? I couldn't stop watching Maria.

The way she laughed when she knocked over a single pin. The way she stretched her arms over her head, that little moan only I heard, her shirt pulled up and baring a soft sliver of skin.

That moan—quiet, unthinking, pleased.

I shouldn't be thinking about the way she sounded. I shouldn't know that sound. But I do.

And it plays on a loop in my head at the worst possible moments.

Focus, *cabrón*.

I exhale, shove the thought aside, and pull up the bowling alley footage again—specifically, the footage I tagged of Sloane.

Not Lily and her chaotic energy. Not Hunter and his twitchy flirting. Sloane.

While Lily posed for selfies and engineered viral chaos, Sloane barely looked up. Phone in one hand, tablet in the other. Not coordinating content. Not managing appearances. She was working. Live-monitoring something.

And the second I really focused on her?

She noticed.

Not directly. But I caught the shift. The subtle tilt of her screen. The flick of her eyes. The way she repositioned herself when Wes Solano leaned toward her, like she was used to operating under surveillance—and knew how to hide from it.

Which makes no sense. Because Wes? He's her boss. She ultimately works for him. But he looked scared of her. Like he didn't know whether he was paying her... or being blackmailed by her.

So who the hell is she?

I turn back to my screens. Time to find out.

People lie. Data doesn't.

I start with Solano Studios. A quick trace of connected accounts confirms what I already suspected. Wes is in deep.

Maxed-out credit cards. Private lenders. Overdrawn accounts. His whole operation is a financial house of cards held together by desperation and debt.

And yet... he's suddenly flush enough to hire a high-end "digital strategist" like Sloane?

No. Doesn't make sense. Someone else has to be bankrolling this. Someone tossed him a lifeline. And I'm betting it wasn't out of kindness.

I shift searches, digging into Sloane Cross.

Surface-level stuff looks passable. LinkedIn account—clean, curated, maybe a little too much. A website registered two years ago. A handful of blog posts, mostly fluff. Job history that reads like someone copied and pasted a PR starter kit.

It's the kind of digital footprint that screams fabricated. Which means its time to dig beneath the mask.

Most people leave behind clutter. College projects. Internship announcements no one ever took down. Old bios. Deleted tweets. Metadata.

Sloane has none of that. Her online presence isn't just thin. It's virtually nonexistent. Sanitized.

I run a deeper scrape—archived versions of deleted social profiles, Whois data on her domain registration, and hidden admin contacts.

Then I hit a flag.

Her domain was registered from an IP out of Bratislava. Then rerouted through a ghost node in Chicago. Then masked again through a VPN exit node I know is used by private intel contractors.

That's not how a PR strategist operates. They wouldn't care.

That's how someone who wants to be invisible operates.

I sit back, my mind racing.

And the kicker? The ghost node she used in Chicago—it pinged once before, six months ago. On a device that also accessed Raul Sandoval's internal server.

Not a coincidence. Not a glitch.

That means whoever set up Sloane's site—or Sloane herself —has been inside our firewall before. Someone with skills. Someone who knew exactly what they were doing.

And now she's attached to Wes Solano, hiding behind influencer bullshit like she's just another hype girl?

No fucking way.

This isn't about PR. This is about gaining access. A direct threat.

Something's not right.

16

MARIA

I'D TURNED down MAVFest's offer to put me up at the Hotel Zavala. It was generous, sure, but both my father and Carlos insisted I stay with him. For security reasons. And because family should be together. Carlos had also told me, "No sister of mine is staying in a place where the minibar charges twenty bucks for peanut M&Ms."

While part of me wished I was staying at the Zavala with Natalie and the MAVFest A-listers, I honestly loved being with Carlos. His home is sleek and modern as he prefers—floor-to-ceiling windows, minimalist furniture, everything spotless. Plus, I knew it made him happy to have me here, to be the big brother taking care of his little sister.

Carlos is ten years older than me, a full-grown adult by the time I hit middle school. But somehow, we've always been close —maybe because neither of us ever quite fit the mold our father wanted.

We've spent the day getting ready for the "family dinner" Carlos planned for tonight. Fidel, Elias, and Natalie will be here, of course. But he's also invited Christopher Harding, the man he's been dating for the last few months. Chris is Deputy

Director for the Vital Statistics Section of the Texas Department of State Health Services. At least, I think that's his job title. Carlos had explained it all quickly, somewhat nervously, and asked me to, "Call him Chris. And don't embarrass me. And please don't talk about Papa or the family business. He knows but I try to keep him away from all of that."

I actually enjoy seeing Carlos wound up like this.

Carlos is private. Always has been. In a family where every move is scrutinized, he made sure there was nothing to scrutinize. He never paraded women around like Marco had in the past. Never settled down like RJ. His dating life, if he even had one, had never been anyone's business but his own.

Then, at some point, he hadn't wanted to live that way anymore. He hadn't wanted other people to control his life. I certainly knew what that felt like.

He had come out to all of us, including my father, just two years ago. I'm sure, at the time, he was expecting the absolute worst.

But if there's one thing I know about Raul Sandoval, it's that he loves his family. I think he's seen too much death in his own life—the death of his first wife, then his second wife, even the tragic death of Elena—to reject his son over his decision to live his true life openly.

So I'm excited about our family dinner.

I've spent most of the day in the kitchen with Carlos's cook, Esmeralda, because it reminds me of home, of the long hours I'd spent in the kitchen as a child, watching Fidel's mom, Miss Ana, cook.

I spent half my childhood in that kitchen, sitting on a barstool at the island, chattering nonstop—asking a million questions, sharing every new obsession, soaking up the warmth of her presence. Elena was often there, being the big sister I never had. And Fidel was there too, sitting beside me, listening, asking his own quiet questions. And the two of us were always eating—sneaking bites of whatever she was making, the kitchen filled with the scent of spices, simmering sauces, homemade tortillas, freshly baked bread.

Miss Ana was an incredible cook. And she was the closest thing I had to a mother. Because I barely remembered my own.

At Carlos's request, Esmeralda prepared a Tex-Mex feast for us to enjoy tonight—ceviche, thick chile con queso with roasted peppers, chicken enchiladas verde with homemade mole sauce, cheese enchiladas covered in oaxaca cheese, a massive bowl of guacamole, steamy yellow rice, and a huge pot of borracho beans. She tells me these are all Chris's favorites. She even helps me bake a Mexican chocolate cake spiced with cinnamon and just a bit of cayenne. It was Fidel's childhood favorite and, while mine doesn't look as perfect as the ones his mother made, I think I did a damn good job.

Chris arrives first, gives me a hug, and then heads into the kitchen with a bottle of wine and a cookbook he brought for Esmeralda. Natalie comes in next with another bottle of wine and immediately starts asking Carlos about prices in the neighborhood, the architectural style of his home, and what kind of restrictions the HOA puts on new construction.

Elias and Fidel arrive last. I open the door, letting them in. More wine, and Elias has "beautiful flowers for the beautiful ladies," meaning me, Natalie, and Esmeralda. Natalie accepts her bouquet, rolling her eyes and telling Elias he is a "true gentleman." But I can see the pink that flushes her cheeks as she holds the flowers.

Fidel stands in the doorway. I'm sure he spent the entire day buried in surveillance feeds and cartel research. He's dressed just a bit more casually than usual, in a black dress shirt, sleeves rolled up, forearms distractingly solid, and dark gray trousers.

He looks tired. Tense. Dangerous. And way too good. Since when do forearms make me flustered?

He steps in, and it hits me again—just how big he is. So tall, all sharp lines and quiet force, with the kind of lean, controlled strength that doesn't need to shout to be dangerous. Broad shoulders, long legs, a body made for precision, not show. He's built like a man who could snap you in half. And might, if you pushed him far enough. But most of the time, he keeps that fuse tamped.

I grab his forearm, pulling him forward and shutting the door. I notice that he's not wearing his usual holster but has a pistol tucked into a small-of-back holster.

Of course. Wouldn't want to be underdressed at a family dinner.

I stand up on my tiptoes, holding the bouquet Elias gave me, and whisper in his ear. "No gift for me, Fidel?"

He blinks. "What? Why—" His jaw clenches slightly. "Why would I get you a gift?"

I smirk. "You tell me."

His scowl deepens, but before he can come up with a comeback, I give him a wink and flounce off, savoring the frustration in his face.

We gather around the bar in Carlos's living area where the enormous windows look out over the Austin skyline at sundown. Carlos pours an "amazing tequila" he has purchased for this dinner for Natalie and the men. Chris and Carlos go into a discussion about the aging process and the finish on different tequilas. Apparently barrels are involved. Natalie sips her tequila carefully and asks lots of questions.

I drink Prosecco, watching Fidel over the rim of my flute and wondering just how much tequila it would take to loosen him up.

At dinner, Esmeralda loads up the table before taking off for the night, going home to her three miniature dachshunds, Penny, Charlie, and Daisy. She showed me photos earlier.

We eat family-style, with Carlos and Chris sitting at each end of the table. Elias and Natalie sit across from me and Fidel takes the chair next to mine. For some reason, I feel a small flutter in my stomach as he pulls his chair close.

We dig into Esmeralda's delicious meal, eating as if we're starving. Chris tells story after story of the truly weird and hilarious things he's seen in his job.

"You'd think, of all things, a death certificate would be straightforward. But no. Last month, a funeral home accidentally put the wrong cause of death on a guy's record." He pauses to take a sip of the beer he's drinking with dinner. "Instead of 'barbiturate overdose,' they wrote 'barbecue overdose.' Now, the family's furious, the funeral home is mortified, and I've got a grieving widow screaming at me that we are 'dishonoring his legacy.' Ma'am, I agree. If anything, 'brisket-related complications' would've been more respectful."

We all break out in peals of laughter and I try not to choke on my Prosecco.

It's Carlos who finally brings it up. He has a bite of enchilada on his fork when he gives me an easy, almost amused look. "So, Maria. How was your fake date last night?"

I don't miss the way Fidel stiffens slightly, fork pausing for just a second before he forces himself to keep eating.

Elias, already smirking, leans back. "Yeah, tell us all about it."

Natalie raises an eyebrow. "Fake date?"

Carlos wipes his mouth, completely unaware of the storm he may have just kicked up between me and Fidel.

"Well," I start, "Lily Renshaw thought it'd be good publicity. We went bowling and she set me up with some actor. Fidel played bodyguard."

Fidel puts his fork down on his plate. He takes a sip of the tequila he's brought to the table.

"It was actually so *fun*," I say, dragging out the words just to see if Fidel will react. "Huntley was so charming—"

Fidel mutters, "That's not his name."

I turn toward Fidel and give my best innocent look. "I'm sorry. What?"

"His name. It wasn't Huntley." He's grinding his teeth, spitting out the words like they taste bad. "His name was Hunter."

"Oh?" I reply. "Hunter?"

Carlos snorts. Elias lets out a quiet chuckle. Natalie grins.

Fidel, very pointedly, does not look at me.

"Yes, well, *Hunter* was charming and I had a wonderful time." Fidel picks up his fork again and I can see his fingers whiten as he grips it. "He was so sweet and so handsome. He might make a good Dark Duke." Fidel stabs his fork into an enchilada. "I hope I'll get to see more of him."

Fidel huffs out a breath and jams a huge bite of enchilada into his mouth.

I know I'm getting to him. And I should stop. But I don't. Because it's funny. And I want him to look at me, see me. Me. Only me.

We keep eating and laughing as Chris tells several more unhinged stories, including one about a man who broke down in tears because he was not allowed to register his dog as his son. Finally, dinner's over. Carlos stands and says, "Maria has a special treat for dessert. So let's head back to the bar and I'll make you all a carajillo to go with her cake."

As everyone stands to follow him, I elbow Fidel. "Hey, will you help me with the cake?"

We gather some of the plates, utensils, and half-empty glasses and carry them into the kitchen. Esmeralda left my cake on the island with plates and forks nearby.

"Look what I made!" I sweep my hand over the cake, gesturing like a game show hostess. "Mexican chocolate cake. Just like your mom made."

I swipe my finger through the chocolate frosting on top of the cake and bring it to his mouth. "Taste it. It's just like hers."

Fidel takes my wrist, pulling my frosting-covered finger into his mouth. His eyes meet mine as he sucks the chocolate off my finger. His grip is firm. Hot. Possessive. And it sends a pulse straight through me.

What is happening?

Then, he slowly pulls my finger from his mouth, continuing to suck.

I step closer to him, close enough that I can feel the heat coming off of him, close enough that I could put my hands on him if I wanted. So he could feel the warmth spreading through my body.

I don't move away.

Neither does he.

His eyes are half-lidded as he looks down at me. And he pulls my wrist to his chest, bringing me even closer.

"Maria..." he whispers my name, and I feel his breath on my lips. If he leaned down, just another half inch, he could kiss me.

Is he going to kiss me?

He takes my jaw in his other hand. The look in his eyes nearly knocks the air from my lungs.

Raw. Dark.

Like he wants to grab me, shove me against the counter, and do things to me that have nothing to do with being my bodyguard.

And suddenly, I want him to do those things. I want Fidel so badly my entire body is humming.

We stand like that for a second? A minute? Longer? I can't tell.

And then his eyes snap open, like he's received an electrical shock. He pushes me back with the wrist he's still holding and then drops it. He shakes his head, as if to wake himself up, to come back to his senses.

"The cake, Maria. They're waiting for the cake." He's talking fast, too fast, his eyes darting around the kitchen, on everything but me.

And all I can think is: *The cake? What cake?*

"I'm sorry. That was stupid of me. I don't know what I was thinking." He runs both of his hands through his hair, still talking too fast. "I apologize. Maria, I shouldn't have done that. I am so sorry." He's flustered. Is he angry? Embarrassed? I don't know what's happening.

He finally looks at me, waiting to see how I'll react.

"Oh, sure," I say. "No problem. The cake."

What the actual fuck am I saying? The cake? I sound like an idiot.

Fidel takes a deep breath, picks up a knife, and begins slicing the cake. "Yeah, let's get this cake out there. They're waiting for cake."

He puts a slice on a plate, places a fork next to it, and jams it at me, waiting for me to take it from him.

"Maria. Here. Take this cake out to Carlos." He says it without looking at me.

How many times is he going to say the word cake?

"Okay. Yeah. I'll take the cake to Carlos."

I feel like I'm floating out of the kitchen, carrying a piece of Mexican chocolate cake to my brother.

I walk back into the dining room with a smile that doesn't feel real, a plate of cake that I hope I don't drop, and one thought spinning in my head: *What the actual fuck just happened?*

17

———

FIDEL

I HAVE to get myself under control.

I have to shut this down.

I shove open my bedroom door, letting it slam behind me, but the sound doesn't shake anything loose. Doesn't ease the coil of tension wrapped tight in my chest, my gut, my fucking cock.

Maria.

I exhale sharply, rolling my shoulders, forcing my mind anywhere but back in that kitchen, back to her, back to what I had done.

I shouldn't have touched her.

I shouldn't have let her get that close.

But the moment she lifted her frosting-covered finger to my mouth, the moment she whispered, *Taste it*, something in me had snapped.

I had meant to take a small taste, just to appease her. But the frosting on her finger—rich chocolate, warm cinnamon, and something undeniably her. Before I could stop myself, I had pulled her in, had taken more. Had sucked her finger deeper into my mouth, let my tongue swirl against her skin, let my teeth scrape just slightly before pulling back.

Her eyes had gone wide, her lips slightly parted.

And I had wanted to ruin her.

I clench my jaw, raking both hands through my hair, my pulse pounding.

No. Stop this.

I've had plenty of sex. High school. College. A few hookups since. All quick. Clean. Forgettable.

No one's ever stuck. No one's ever made me feel like this. Not like her.

But Maria isn't some woman I can take to bed and forget about in the morning. She's a Sandoval. Raul's only daughter. The one thing in his world that's truly untouchable. One day, she'll be with someone rich. Powerful. Respected. A man with a name that means something, someone with an empire at his feet, a man Raul approves of, a man who can give her everything.

And me? I'm none of those things. I'm a foot soldier who takes orders, who works in the shadows, whose only value is keeping the right people alive. I'm the man who makes sure those people don't get shot in the street. That's all I'll ever be. That's the natural order of things.

We had grown up together. Been kids playing whatever stupid games she demanded we play. She had been small and loud and stubborn. A little menace. And now she was someone I had been ordered to protect, to watch over, to keep safe from men exactly like me.

Except she had just offered me chocolate on her finger, looking at me like she wanted my mouth there and everywhere.

I curse under my breath, yanking my shirt over my head and tossing it to the floor. I need a cold shower. Need to scrub this night from my mind, drown the heat from my body.

I stride into the bathroom, undress, and shove the shower handle to cold, stepping under the spray before I can think twice. Ice water slamming against my skin. I grit my teeth, bracing my hands against the tile.

Breathe. Control. Forget.

The icy water burns against my skin, a sharp contrast to the heat still coiled inside me. I force myself to stand under it, letting it soak my hair, slide down my back, willing it to wash her off of me.

But it's not working. She's still there.

Maria.

I squeeze my eyes shut, but I can still see her. Smell her.

My hand curls into a fist. *No. Shut it down.*

I exhale, long and slow, but the tension in my body shifts from resistance to something darker. Despite the cold water, I'm getting hard. Starting to throb.

I roll my shoulders, still standing under the freezing spray. The cold isn't enough to kill it. It isn't enough to kill thoughts of her.

I swallow, dragging a hand through my soaked hair, my breath uneven.

And before I can stop myself, before I can think, I reach for the dial. Twist. The icy water turns lukewarm. Then warmer. Then hot. The steam rises around me, curling against my skin, and I let it. Let it happen.

Maria.

In her tight jeans at the fucking bowling alley, smiling up at some idiot actor while I stood there, fists clenched. Sitting beside me tonight at dinner, so close I could feel the warmth radiating from her. Maria in that goddamn kitchen, breath hitching when I sucked the frosting from her finger.

The way she smelled—orange blossoms, cinnamon, warm sugar and heat.

The way she watched me, like she had known exactly what she was doing to me.

I groan, dragging a hand down my face, gripping the back of my neck.

Fucking stop.

But I can't stop. I'm hard. Painfully hard. My cock stiff and aching, so fucking desperate I can feel my pulse in it. The memory of her taste, her scent, the way her body had pressed closer, had made me want—

My hand slides down.

I exhale sharply, fisting my cock, squeezing the base, trying to force it down.

But the second I touch myself, I'm gone.

Maria.

Consumed by fantasies of her standing between my legs, eyes big and dark, pulling her closer, shoving her against the counter, taking what I want.

Maria's mouth, pink and perfect, so close to mine.

Maria's skin, so soft, the way her breath would catch if I pulled her in.

I grit my teeth, working my fist up my cock, slow and rough. My hips jerk forward, chasing the friction.

You shouldn't be thinking about this. You shouldn't be doing this.

But I am.

Because I can still taste her. Can still see the way her lips had parted, the way her chest had risen and fallen so fast as I sucked her finger, like she was waiting for me to kiss her.

Like she had wanted it.

I groan, squeezing tighter, pumping harder.

I imagine her looking up at me with those big brown eyes, sticking her frosting-covered finger past my lips and whispering, *Taste it again, Fidel.*

I imagine grabbing her wrist, sucking her fingers into my mouth, licking her clean.

I imagine her dropping to her knees in front of me, taking

my hard cock in her mouth, licking me, sucking me, taking me all the way down her throat.

Fuck.

The image is too much. The way she had smelled, the way she had looked at me, the fucking heat of her body so close to mine—

I curse, bracing one hand against the wall, stroking faster, rougher, jerking my hips into my hand, chasing the release I shouldn't fucking need.

The knot in my stomach tightens.

I imagine her licking, moaning on my cock, pulling back and begging me—*Fidel, please, fuck me*—

That's it.

I groan deep and low, spilling over my hand, heat flashing down my spine as I come, hips stuttering, my entire body trembling under the water.

For a second, all I can do is stand there, panting, forehead pressed to the tile.

Then, shame creeps in.

I swallow hard, letting the water wash away the mess on my hand.

I'm losing it.

Maria isn't an option. She will never be an option.

I exhale slowly, pushing back from the wall, forcing my body to calm, my pulse to settle. I will lock this down. I have to.

Because Raul trusts me.

Because she deserves better.

Because if I let myself have her, if I let myself touch her the way I want—

I'll never fucking stop.

18

———

MARIA

I STEP out of the SUV into the thick, sun-soaked heat of downtown Austin. The high-rise office buildings gleam in the late morning light, casting long shadows over Congress Avenue.

This is potentially one of the most important days of my life. The day Zara tells me whether she can put a deal together for *The Dark Duke*. The day I might finally find out if I can take charge of my future instead of letting other people do it for me.

And I'm completely exhausted.

My head aches. My feet hurt. And, despite the fact that it's only 8:30 in the morning, the heat is already making me sweat.

I barely slept. My mind wouldn't shut off, replaying the moment in Carlos's kitchen over and over again, like I could somehow make it mean less if I dissected it from every angle.

It didn't work.

Every time I closed my eyes, I saw Fidel's mouth. The heat of his hand on my wrist. The slow, deliberate way he sucked the frosting from my finger, like he was starving, like I was the only thing that could satisfy him.

It shouldn't have meant that much. But it did.

And now I can't stop thinking about what would've

happened if he hadn't stopped. If he'd pulled me in and kissed me. If his mouth had moved lower. If his hands had kept going.

I wanted it. I still want it.

It's embarrassing. I'm twenty-four and still a virgin. And not in some precious, waiting-for-true-love kind of way. Just... it never happened. Not all the way. Not with anyone.

Being Raul Sandoval's daughter means most guys ran scared. The few who didn't? I ran first. There were always security issues, complications, threats, risks. And if they got past all of that? There was me—hesitating, unsure, afraid I wouldn't know what I was doing.

Fidel's not like them. He never has been. He doesn't run. He's been part of my security detail, part of my life, for years. Which means...

He knows.

He sees everything. Every background check, every risk profile. He knows I've never had a serious boyfriend. He knows I've never been with someone for that long. I'm sure he knows that I've never had sex. That I'm more experienced in writing Regency alien sex scenes than actually living anything close to one.

It's humiliating.

But last night, I felt like he saw *me*. Not as the "asset" he's been tasked with protecting. Not as Raul Sandoval's untouchable daughter. Not as Mercede Sanchez, my weird alter ego. And certainly not as the pseudo-little sister he grew up with.

I felt like he saw me. Maria.

And the way he looked at me? My panties were soaked. A hot, wet mess. The most turned on I've ever been in my life... from a man licking frosting off my finger.

It's embarrassing.

My security detail hustles me along, one man lingering by the car, the other at my side as I make my way toward the glass entrance of the office tower. I try to ignore them, even though their presence is impossible to forget.

Inside, the air-conditioning hits like a shock. Polished marble floors. Floor-to-ceiling windows that overlook the street. Elias and Natalie are already waiting by the elevators, looking like they were born for high-stakes negotiations.

Elias glances at his watch. "Cutting it close. And you don't look so great."

I roll my eyes. "Thanks for noticing. And I didn't realize I was on a timer."

Natalie smiles but doesn't comment, pressing the button for the elevator.

Fidel stands slightly apart from them, his broad frame tense, eyes locked on his phone. I expect something. Maybe a snarky comment about how I'm slowing down the security team, or how I should've checked in before leaving Carlos's house. Maybe something to acknowledge what happened last night.

But he barely even looks at me. And that pisses me off more than it should.

Like—what? That moment meant nothing to him? Just some accidental frosting foreplay while he was thinking about surveillance cameras and escape routes?

Meanwhile, I've been spiraling about it for twelve straight hours like a teenage girl with a crush.

I frown. *Really, Fidel? This is how you're going to play it?*

The elevator carries us up twenty floors to the sleek lobby of the offices of Langston, Blake & Saavedra. The view from the bank of windows stretches across the city. The receptionist makes a quick call, and a secretary appears to lead us back.

Zara's office is understated and powerful—framed degrees, black glass desk, a direct view of the Capitol. A tray of coffee and sparkling water is waiting as we enter.

Carlos is already here, lounging in one of the chairs like he owns the place.

My stomach tightens. Of course he's already here. Because, while I love him, why wouldn't he insert himself into yet another decision that's supposed to be mine?

"Now that we're all here," Carlos says smoothly, taking the lead as usual, "let's talk about *The Dark Duke*."

I sit across from Zara, doing my best to keep my expression neutral.

Zara offers a polite smile and a slight nod in Carlos's direction. "It's good to have the full team together. I understand Mr. Sandoval has a vested interest in the project's success."

Carlos gives a modest smile, like he's just been publicly knighted. I resist the urge to roll my eyes. He loves being part of "the team"—as long as he's the one calling the plays.

Zara continues, folding her hands over the stack of files on her desk. "Wonderful. Since we last spoke, I've been looking into Solano Studios since they have made an initial offer." She pauses, glancing around the room. "I won't sugarcoat it—what I found isn't great."

Carlos tilts his head. "How bad?"

Zara flips open the folder in front of her. "Wes Solano is deeply in debt. Deeply. He's over-leveraged, but more importantly, his money isn't coming from traditional investors. He's taken out multiple private loans from off-the-books sources that don't report to banks."

I frown. "So he's desperate."

Zara nods. "More than that. My belief is that he's controlled. At best, he's a front. Someone owns him. And whoever that is? They're not making themselves known."

Silence settles over the room.

Natalie mutters a quiet curse under her breath.

Carlos remains unreadable, fingers lightly tapping the arm of his chair.

I exhale. "So if I sign with Solano, I could be walking into something worse than just a bad deal."

"Exactly."

This isn't good. So far, Solano Studios is the only real offer on the table. Has no one else taken me seriously? Surely, there's something else—

Before I can even finish the thought, Carlos leans forward, bracing his elbows on his knees.

"Which is why I'm making him an offer."

My pulse spikes. "What?"

Carlos shrugs. "If Solano's in real trouble, that's great. I can buy him out, clean up his operation, and keep *The Dark Duke* in-house where we can actually protect it."

I stare at him. "We can *protect* it? How is that the answer?"

Carlos gives me a surprised look, like I'm being difficult. "I'm giving us a way to keep control. This is the best move."

Us. My jaw clenches.

He thinks this is helping. But this isn't about protecting my book. It's about the Sandovals owning it. Keeping me under Sandoval control. Dressing it up like support when really, it's just another form of control.

I'm about to snap at Carlos when Zara leans forward slightly, her voice cool and precise.

"Just to be clear, Mr. Sandoval. I represent Mercede Sanchez. If this becomes a matter of internal control, we'll need to revisit the scope of engagement."

Her tone isn't confrontational. It's clinical. But it lands like a gavel on the table.

For the first time this morning, I feel like someone's actually on my side.

Carlos goes still. Elias shifts in his seat. Even Natalie raises an eyebrow.

And that's when I catch movement from the corner of my eye. Fidel. Still silent. Still focused on his phone.

My frustration twists into irritation. "Okay, and *what* is going on with you?"

He doesn't answer right away. Then, with a slow exhale, he turns the phone toward me.

I take it, scanning the screen.

A social media post. A photo of me, earlier, walking into this building. This morning. The caption reads:

SPOTTED: MERCEDE SANCHEZ MEETING WITH AUSTIN POWER PLAYERS! The Dark Duke author seen downtown—right now! Exclusive deal in the works? #MAVFestMercede #DarkDukeNation #CommerceBankBuilding

I frown. "Okay... and?"

Fidel's voice is low, controlled. "Look at the timestamp. The hashtags."

I check. #CommerceBankBuilding. Weirdly specific. And it was posted twenty minutes ago. I've been in this office for less than thirty. Was this posted by Lily's PR team? How would they even have this information? Or is this something else?

I glance up at Fidel again. Still unreadable. Still distant.

Elias leans over to look. "It's MAVFest. People are tracking everything."

Fidel's fingers flex as he takes back his phone. "It's too accurate." His jaw tightens. "Someone is posting Maria's exact location in real time."

"Mercede's location," Elias replies, like that's somehow different.

I don't love it. I don't love the idea that someone is watching me this closely. But I'm not panicked. That's what the whole team is here for—security. I trust that part of the operation.

What I don't trust right now? Fidel. Or at least, how he's acting. His silence.

I look up at him again, trying to read his expression. Nothing. Not even a flicker.

Was last night really just... nothing? Did I imagine the whole thing?

I fold my arms, pulse rising. Not from fear, but frustration. "Fine. Great. So you'll handle it, right? You're my bodyguard. That's your job."

He blinks, but says nothing.

And I just sit there, fuming, while everyone else talks around me—about deals, about risk, about my life—wondering when exactly the man who looked at me last night like I was the only thing he'd ever wanted had decided that now I wasn't even worth a glance.

19

FIDEL

As with all things MAVFest, the Hotel Hermosa's conference level is a security disaster.

After the meeting with Zara, we went straight to the hotel for "MAVFest Publisher Push," a morning focused on publishers, literary agents, and authors. Crowds pack the hallways, attendees and presenters spilling from one panel to the next, all of them trying to make deals before the weekend parties erase half the conversations. Our Platinum badges are not getting us the special treatment I'd expected.

The elevators are jammed. Someone bumps into my shoulder without apologizing. A woman with a MAVFest lanyard is sobbing into her phone just outside the conference room. I clock three separate people carrying tote bags big enough to conceal a weapon. One guy's wearing an NPR baseball cap and a MAVFest backpack that could easily be packed with explosives.

In other words, security sucks and MAVFest Platinum badges are just overpriced invitations to a fucking migraine. All the access. None of the exclusivity.

And I have no fucking idea where Maria is.

"She's supposed to be here," Elias says beside me, arms crossed as he scans the packed conference room.

Natalie's panel—*The Business of Book-to-Screen: Lessons from Top Adaptations*—has already started. She's on stage with a few other publishing executives, all of them talking adaptation trends. Maria's supposed to be here for this. She has her own panel right after.

Except she isn't.

I check my phone again. Nothing. No text from Maria. Nothing from Daniel, either.

I glance at Elias. He checks his watch. "She texted a few minutes ago," he mutters. "Said she was heading this way."

Then where the hell is she?

I pull up my phone, tapping into her GPS tag. She's inside the hotel—Daniel must've brought her in—but she should be right here.

And then I hear her voice.

"I don't care what your schedule says, Daniel. Mine says Mesquite Room."

I turn just in time to see Maria striding down the hall, Daniel at her side. Both of them are clearly annoyed.

They stop in front of us. Maria crosses her arms, looking at Daniel like he's the problem. "I told you, Natalie's schedule must've had an error when she sent it to me."

Daniel's jaw flexes. "Maria, your schedule's wrong. Ours isn't."

I frown. "What the hell is going on?"

Maria sighs. "Daniel said we were supposed to come here. But my schedule said Mesquite Room. My schedule should be right. Except it isn't." She gestures vaguely. "The Mesquite Room was empty."

My stomach tightens.

I take her phone from her hand before she can argue,

scrolling through her calendar. Sure enough, her schedule lists Mesquite Room for Natalie's panel, while mine—and Daniel's, and Elias's—all say Live Oak Ballroom.

Maria is still talking. "It's not a big deal. My panel is actually in the Mesquite Room. My schedule must've gotten mixed up when Natalie sent it to me."

But that doesn't make sense.

I built our security schedule based on Natalie's itinerary. I confirmed it against the official version multiple times. Natalie walked straight into the ballroom without a hitch.

So why the hell is Maria's version wrong?

The schedule came from Natalie. But Maria's calendar? Could've been modified. Deliberately tampered with.

And there's only one person I suspect. One person who keeps slipping just under my radar.

Sloane Cross.

She was too polished. Too precise. Her setup at the bowling alley was clinical—like she was running ops, not PR. When I started watching her, her posture shifted, shoulders curling in, tablet angled out of view. Subtle, practiced, like she expected someone to try and read over her shoulder. I've seen that move before. I've done that move before.

And now Maria's location gets spoofed on social media and her schedule gets redirected?

This isn't a glitch. If Sloane, or someone working through her, is messing with Maria's calendar, they may have already breached the system I built. The system I thought was bulletproof.

My system. My firewall. My protocols. All of it might be compromised.

My pulse spikes, sharp and sudden. A cold flush crawls down my spine, and for one second, I swear I can feel every unsecured access point in this entire fucking hotel pressing in on me. My hand twitches towards the gun under my jacket. But there's no one to shoot when the breach is digital.

Elias peers over my shoulder. "Weird."

Daniel crosses his arms, letting out a slow breath. "Doesn't seem right."

Maria rolls her eyes. "Oh, for fuck's sake."

I ignore her, tapping through her phone again. Comparing timestamps. No other discrepancies. The rest of her schedule matches mine exactly, down to the minute.

That doesn't comfort me. It makes it worse.

Because if someone wants to lead her somewhere else, somewhere isolated, it could happen. One wrong calendar entry. One room swap. One empty hallway. That's all it would take.

What if I don't catch it? What if I don't stop it in time?

Maria snatches her phone back with a huff. "Now that we've all solved the great mystery of my screwed-up schedule, can I go inside?"

I narrow my eyes but step aside, letting her pass.

She breezes toward the ballroom entry, her posture straight, chin lifted—like this isn't worth a second thought. But I catch the flicker in her eyes as she walks past me. She's not scared. She's pissed.

At me.

"Just do your job, Fidel," she says without looking back. "Keep the *asset* safe."

And then she's gone.

Yeah, she's pissed.

20

MARIA

THE LIGHTS on stage are way too hot. My mic is crooked. And someone definitely wrote "Alien Anal Sex Logistics" in glitter pen on the nameplate in front of me.

God, I love it here.

The audience is packed into the small MAVFest conference room—the Mesquite Room—standing room only. I knew I was supposed to be in this room. At some point.

The calendar glitch is still bothering me, but not enough to ruin this. Not yet. Natalie's schedule matched Fidel's. Mine didn't. And I didn't change it. I know I didn't.

It was minor. Probably nothing. Hopefully. Just a bug, a bad sync, or whatever excuse Fidel is too busy brooding over to share with me.

But maybe it was something. I can't be sure. I just know I'm not going to let it ruin this.

And I'm trying really hard not to be annoyed with him. Not just because he's being cold. But because I let myself think last night meant something. Turns out a guy licking frosting off your finger is not a sign that he's into you. I'm an idiot for thinking it was.

Anyway, it's not like I'm being hunted by a death cult. I write about alien sex. My fans are sweet. Obsessed, yes. But loyal. Passionate. Harmless.

And yet I still hear a small voice in my head, whispering, *What if Fidel's not being paranoid? What if he's right and someone changed your calendar?*

I push that thought down. I have to.

Because right now—right this second—I'm here in this room.

And this room is full of people who showed up because they love what I created.

There are at least a dozen people in capes. Four Penelopes. One full-body Vraxian Duke cosplay that includes six fingers on each hand and suction cups on his sleeves. One person in the front row has brought an actual goblet labeled "Goblet of Desire" in rhinestones and is sipping something green and fizzy. Someone is holding up a sign that just says: SUCTION CUP ME.

And to my left? A whole row of people wearing black leather aprons with plastic udders strapped to their chests. Fans of my fellow panelist, Lexi Jett.

These are my people.

The panel is officially titled *Alien Anatomy: Making It Work*, and I'm seated next to three authors with varying levels of scientific rigor and pure chaos energy. To the far left, near her udder-aproned fans, is Lexi, author of bestsellers *Orc Milk Maids*, *Creamed by the Chieftain*, *Udderly Yours*, and the entire *Breeding Pit of Gorgoth* saga. Next to her is T. G. Langston, whose book *Rogue Planet Mating Rituals* is both a *USAToday* bestseller and currently being read by Katya, one of my dad's cooks. On my right is Harper Chang, who writes an online serialized alien romance, *The Nebula Brood Saga*, and once live-tweeted her explicit critique of 100 alien sex scenes over 10 hours while high on Sudafed and Monster Energy drinks.

And in the middle is me. Sitting with these amazing authors. I am definitely not worthy.

As the crowd settles, someone lets out a deep, low "mooooo" from the back of the room. The moo is quickly picked up by others until it rolls through the audience like a weirdly affectionate battle cry. Lexi throws her arms up like a conquering queen.

"Long live the Herd!" she shouts.

The crowd moos louder.

"I swear to God," Harper mutters into her mic, "one of these days her fans are going to riot and it'll be over an orc breeding kink."

T.G. calmly sips his tea. "The anthropology of it is actually quite sound," he says, completely deadpan.

Our moderator, Mila Kerrigan—editor of *Galactic Gaze,* the quarterly journal of speculative romance and fantasy—leans into her mic and flashes the audience a wicked grin.

"Welcome, tentacle-lovers, milk maids, and xenophiles, to *Alien Anatomy: Making It Work*—where physiology meets erotica." The crowd cheers. Mila lifts her clipboard like she's about to conduct a symphony. "We've got four absolutely feral bestselling authors and an audience that clearly knows its suction cups from its udders."

She nods toward the front row, where, for some reason, a huge plastic spaceship is being passed around like a communion icon.

"All right," she says, flipping to her notes. "Let's get into it. These are the questions fans are asking. I'm going to direct these to all of you and just ask that you respond in turn. We'll let the audience ask questions at the end if we have time. Sound good?"

Everyone in the room nods in agreement, anxious to get into the discussion.

"First up—Mercede Sanchez. Your first book *The Dark Duke* has taken the alien sex-loving readership by storm. And it looks like your follow-up, *The Stellar Sovereign*, will do exactly the same. Tell us—how did you approach the anatomy of the Duke? Did you use biology textbooks? Build a silicone model? Make it up? Phone a friend?"

I try to keep my face neutral. Don't look at Elias. Definitely don't look at Fidel.

"Well, I did... a lot of research on teuthology," I say carefully, smiling as a few people in the crowd giggle. "Learning all about mollusks and focusing, naturally, on octopuses. Their anatomy. Mating habits. And I also consulted some very patient people in my life who happen to know a thing or two about tactical gear, functioning in close spaces, and advanced field logistics."

I sneak a glance toward the back of the room. Elias is grinning like a devil and punches Fidel in the arm. Fidel rolls his eyes up to the ceiling, muttering something under his breath. Not looking at me. Not smiling at me.

Fidel helped me with the Duke's anatomy. He remembers how much time we spent on cephalopod biology. I want him to remember. I want him to look at me and smile. I want him to look at me like he did last night.

"I mean, if you're going to write a six-fingered, dual-hearted, low-gravity warlord with a prehensile mating appendage," I continue, "you need to know how that thing theoretically holsters. It's not just about where it fits—" I pause, grinning as the audience hoots, "—but what it does once it's there."

The crowd erupts. Someone in the front row flashes the Duke's salute.

I can't help it. I throw it right back, three fingers in the air, tentacles waggling.

Instantly, half the room responds with the salute.

Lexi leans into her mic. "I mean, I can't compete with the Duke's suction logistics, but some of us prefer the handling of our anatomy to be *hands* on."

Her fans moo in unison. Loudly. Lexi nods like a general acknowledging her army.

"I did a reverse-engineered physiology map for the Gorgoth species," T.G. says, pushing his glasses up the bridge of his nose. "Including three urinary tracts and a separate intromission canal."

"Boring!" Harper interrupts, waving her hand. "I base all my alien sex anatomy on dreams I've had while on muscle relaxers. They are sexy. They are chaotic. They are canon."

The audience loses it. I grin. This is what a panel should be. Smart, stupid, loud, ridiculous, and weirdly validating.

This is what I want. Not just the books. Not just the deals. But this—readers laughing, nerding out, finding joy in something I made up in a coffee-stained notebook at two in the morning.

Not power. Not protection. Not whatever Carlos or my father think I need.

This.

"So tell us," the moderator says, eyes sparkling. "Will we get more anatomical exploration from each of you going forward?"

I lean toward the mic, smirking. "Well, tonight is the FutureFic event. And to celebrate, I may have posted something this morning. Something... extra. A Dark Duke bonus scene. A little something involving suction cups that's not in the original text."

A few people gasp. Someone in the back shouts, "I need that!"

I grin. "Details are on my website."

I pause for effect.

"Let's just say—if you've wondered what more the suction cups can do... your Duke delivers."

The crowd roars. Someone screams. One of the Penelopes fans herself with an actual fan.

T.G. sighs softly. "And people say science fiction is dead."

"Please," Harper says. "Sci-fi's never been hornier."

I beam at the crowd.

And still—under all of it—I feel a small flicker of unease.

I'm not scared. Not really. I've got an entire security team. And I've got my bodyguard, Fidel, who practically breathes paranoia for a living. If something were wrong, he'd handle it.

But still... I can't get it out of my head. Fidel could be right. He usually is. Someone messed with my schedule. And I don't like not knowing why.

So while the crowd is laughing and cheering and calling out, "All hail the Duke!" I'm scanning the back of the room. Not afraid. Just annoyed. Just tired of being the only one who doesn't get to know what's going on. Like I'm the thing being protected instead of the actual person at the center of all of this.

But I smile anyway. I give them what they came for.

And I throw one last salute to the crowd.

21

———

MAVFEST DAY 5

**"Dark Duke Bonus Scene" Blog Post on
https://mercedesanchez.com**

Galactic Greetings to my Beautiful Disciples 

As part of this evening's FutureFic Night celebration at MAVFest
—and to thank all of you for the overwhelming love you've
shown for our magnificent Duke—this is a never-before-seen
bonus scene that didn't make it into the final edition of the book.
It's also definitely NSFW or for anyone who still thinks Lady
Penelope is a virgin.

You asked about the suction cups.
You've begged for the Pleasure Chamber.
You demanded tentacle penetration.
And honestly? You deserve this.

So here you go! Welcome to the Duke's Pleasure Chamber...

Mercede

Bonus Scene - The Dark Duke, posted on MercedeSanchez.com

FutureFic exclusive – not featured in the published edition of The Dark Duke

Lady Penelope Hargrove braced herself against the cryo-forged obsidian walls of the Duke's ancestral pleasure chamber, her breath shallow, her skin slick with condensation. The gown she'd worn for modesty's sake lay shredded at her feet, reduced to silk tatters and forgotten inhibitions.

Above her, the Duke loomed in his true and utterly inhuman form. Towering. Radiant. His six-fingered appendages traced reverent lines along the planes of her body, mapping her curves with a scholar's devotion and a lover's hunger.

"I must warn you," he rasped, voice thick with restraint. "My kind... do not take gently."

"I do not want gentle, my Duke," Penelope whispered. "I want you."

With a guttural growl, he shifted—his prehensile limbs flexing in the low gravity, the smooth violet skin along his torso pulsing with bioluminescence. One of his lower appendages, thick and slick with his own pheromone-rich secretion, uncurled from beneath his waist wrap. Along the underside, suction cups flared open, twitching as they tasted the air, glistening with heat.

Penelope's eyes widened as the appendage slid up her thigh —slow, deliberate, coaxing. A whimper escaped her throat.

"Your body will know mine," he said. "And it will remember me."

The first suction cup latched onto the delicate skin of her inner thigh with a wet pop, followed by another, higher. The pressure sent sparks dancing through her nerves. By the time the third suction cup found the tender crease of her hip, her knees had buckled.

She didn't fall. His arms caught her, lifted her, held her open for him like she was weightless. And then the lower appendage curled forward, poised, pulsing at its tip.

He didn't rush. He pressed the tip of the tentacle to her slick entrance, letting the suction cup there kiss her clit—soft at first, then tighter, like a mouth forming a seal.

She cried out.

The tentacle slid into her with maddening control, inch by inch, the ridged surface dragging along her walls, suction pulsing in rhythm as he moved—pressing, pulsing, tasting her from the inside.

"Stars," she gasped. "You're... I can feel you *everywhere.*"

The Duke made a low, satisfied sound, his dual hearts beating against her heaving breasts like war drums.

"Let me show you what it means," he murmured, "to be claimed by a Vraxian Duke."

And then he thrust the tentacle in to the hilt.

———

Source: Reddit
Subreddit: r/TheDarkDuke
Thread posted 1 hour ago | 1.3K upvotes | 2 awards
Posted by u/dukeskisses4life

Thread Title: **I just read the bonus scene and I am NOT OKAY**

u/dukeskisses4life
Was anyone else at the panel today? I mean I know we joke about how much we would love more tentacle penetration.

I know we MEME about suction cup mechanics.
But Mercede?? She dropped another suction-cup-fuck scene!
And it was... beautiful?? Filthy?? Sacred?????
I'm shaking. I'm sobbing. I've blacked out and am posting this
through my astral projection.

u/dukenightmares
Sorry but is anyone else rereading the scene and noticing the
Duke says "Your body will *remember me*" which is also what he
says in Chapter 14 RIGHT BEFORE THE DREAM
SEQUENCE??
So this is either a parallel or foreshadowing.

u/mercedehasmyheart
No thoughts. Just suction.

u/dukesdisciple69
me: "I'll just read the bonus scene and go to bed early"
also me: up at 2 am writing 5K of smutty fanfic called *Tentacle
Thrust to the Hilt*

———

**Comment on https://mercedesanchez.com to "Dark Duke
Bonus Scene" Blog Post**

User: WingsofBloodandGlory

You looked beautiful today Maria. You always do.
I hope you enjoy my gift. Perhaps one day you will wear it when
you come to me in our pleasure chamber.

22

MARIA

THE PANEL WRAPS and I stand to leave with thunderous applause still echoing around me. My throat is dry. My feet hurt. And I've never felt more tired. Or more alive.

The Mesquite Room empties fast, the crowd shifting toward the next event like a tidal wave of velvet cloaks, glitter, and adrenaline.

I load into the SUV with Natalie and Daniel as we drive to the venue. FutureFic Night is about to begin. And the line into the event space stretches out the doors.

The crowd is huge. A surging, excitable, glittering madhouse of readers, influencers, cosplayers, and industry insiders.

I knew it would be big. Natalie had warned me that MAVFest FutureFic would be insane—a high-profile, multi-author book signing event with some of the biggest names in sci-fi and fantasy and hundreds of attendees. But I didn't expect this.

The venue itself is massive, a converted convention center that is now part pop-up bookstore, part fan festival, and part intergalactic marketplace. There's an entire section devoted to merch: enamel pins, plushies, signed prints, exclusive character candles, even Dark Duke-themed temporary tattoos.

124

One corner holds the bookstore, glowing with spotlighted displays. *The Stellar Sovereign*, *The Dark Duke*, and a dozen other titles all getting the VIP treatment.

High ceilings. LED panels glowing in deep blues and purples like something out of a sci-fi film. A DJ in the corner spinning remixed scores from famous fantasy movie soundtracks. Giant banners hang from the rafters, showcasing the covers of *The Stellar Sovereign* and at least four other fantasy/sci-fi bestsellers, each with their own devoted army of fans.

As I take my place at my signing table, the buzz is already in full swing.

Elaborate cosplays flood the room, readers dressed as battle-worn space captains, armor-clad fae warriors, shimmering intergalactic royalty, and more than a few Dark Duke fanatics in custom Regency-inspired outfits. Capes swishing, cybernetic helmets flashing. Someone is operating a drone above the crowd like a sentient AI companion.

It is beautiful chaos.

Harper Chang appears at the edge of my table, grinning in a crop top that says KNOT OR NOT.

"The panel was a blast," she says, giving me the Duke's salute. "You've got a sick mind. I love it. I've got to interview you for my podcast. We'll do suction cup mechanics and character trauma. Interested?"

I laugh and salute back. "Text me. I'm in."

Lexi Jett struts by a few minutes later, headed to her own signing table, carrying a milk pail full of bookmarks. She tosses me the Duke's salute, which I return with pride. The fans following her moo at me enthusiastically.

And yet, even as I sign book after book, smiling and thanking each reader, I feel the weight of it pressing down on me. Not the crowd.

Carlos.

Fidel.

The men in my life, always watching. Always waiting.

I keep my expression poised as a couple with both of my books in hand steps up next—a young man and woman in black leather aprons with plastic udders strapped across their chests. The girl beams. "We're hardcore *Orc Milk Maids* fans, but after your panel we read the bonus scene." The guy nods seriously. "Suction cup sex. Life changing. Just... thank you."

I blink, then grin and sign their books with amusement. "Thank you so much!"

Natalie slides in beside me for a quick second, murmuring into my ear, "You've had over twenty-three thousand hits to your website in the last two hours. Two-thirds of them from mobile. Callie is in full-on heart attack mode. The bonus scene is blowing up."

Across the store, I spot Lily Renshaw in her element, live-streaming in a silver tiara, surrounded by influencers and entertainment reporters, holding court like she owns the place.

Wes Solano stands nearby, sweating profusely, looking like he might pass out from stress at any moment.

And next to him—the ever-present Sloane Cross, the calmest PR strategist I've ever seen.

I'm sure Fidel has eyes on her.

I can feel him close by, watching me from a few feet away, arms crossed, face unreadable.

Another event for him to hate. Too public. Too chaotic. Too many unknowns. But he's here now because wherever I go, Fidel follows.

Which would mean more if he hadn't spent the entire day pretending I was invisible. I'm such an idiot.

Trying to recover some small shred of my dignity, I refuse to turn toward him, to look at him, to give him the satisfaction of knowing I'm aware of him.

My phone buzzes in my bag. I take it out, look. A text from Fidel. He hasn't texted me all day. Not once.

For a second, I almost check it. Almost let myself believe he might actually be texting about last night. That maybe I hadn't imagined the heat in his eyes, the way he whispered my name.

But then I shove the thought down and drop my phone back into my bag.

I'm not doing this right now.

Two older women step up to the table. "We love *The Stellar Sovereign*, but *The Dark Duke* changed our lives," one of them says. The other places a small jewelry box on the table and opens it to reveal a pair of glimmering tentacle earrings. "We run a Duke-inspired Etsy shop. Starcrossed Sisters. We wanted you to have these."

My eyes sting. I clear my throat. "I'll treasure them."

I love my fans.

A woman in a tailored blazer then steps forward, her presence different from the others in line. Not a fan. Not a journalist. Someone with intent.

"Mercede." She smiles, extending her hand. "I'm Kara Lasater. I'm with UltraVision."

I glance up, my heartbeat kicking up.

UltraVision. The streaming giant.

I stand and take her hand. Kara's handshake is firm, her smile polished.

"I've been watching your rise," she says, holding up a copy of *The Dark Duke*. "And I have to say, it's exactly the kind of property we're looking for at UltraVision."

From across the venue, I see Lily's attention snap to us like a predator catching the scent of blood.

"Oh?" I say, keeping my voice even.

Kara nods. "We're always looking for high-concept, serialized storytelling with strong world-building. And your work—

especially with the level of online engagement you're generating —has serious adaptation potential."

Lily materializes beside me, dazzling. "Kara! We've been hoping someone from UltraVision would stop by. You're a fan of *The Dark Duke*?"

Kara offers a smooth smile. "Hello, Lily. And yes, I'm a fan of smart investments."

My grip tightens around my pen.

This is it. The validation I've been waiting for.

Because if UltraVision is interested, then Kara may be talking about an episodic series. A real budget. A real vision.

"What's your timeline?" I ask, fighting to keep my voice calm.

"We move fast," Kara says. "We're already in early development on new acquisitions for the next cycle. Which would include whatever we pick up here at MAVFest. If you're open to discussing—"

The presence at my back shifts.

Carlos. The air changes the second he steps closer.

He isn't looming over me, exactly. He doesn't have to. Carlos Sandoval knows how to control a room. His dark eyes flick from me to Kara, assessing her in a second.

"Mercede," he says smoothly, using my pen name, playing the role of the supportive brother. "I wasn't aware we were fielding other offers."

Kara lifts a brow, clearly unruffled. "I wasn't aware you had any offers. At all."

My stomach twists.

Carlos's tone stays dangerously pleasant.

"We're currently exploring multiple opportunities," he says. "Solano Studios has put in an offer for an option agreement."

"Solano Studios? I'm not familiar with them," Kara replies, unshaken.

A muscle ticks in Carlos's jaw.

This is not good.

I turn back to Kara, keeping my voice professional. "I'd love to hear more about UltraVision's approach."

"I'd love to tell you." Kara's eyes stay on Carlos, like she knows exactly the game we're all playing. "Here's my card. Let's set a time to talk."

I accept it, pulse pounding.

Carlos stays silent.

Kara gives me one last nod before disappearing into the crowd.

Lily turns to me, gleeful. "Omg, Mercede! UltraVision!"

Carlos ignores her completely, his focus all on me. "Mercede—"

"No," I cut him off, tucking Kara's card into my bag. "Don't. Not here."

His jaw flexes.

And behind him, Fidel is watching. He hasn't moved, but I saw the way his focus was locked on Carlos this whole time. Like he was waiting. Waiting to see if Carlos would push me too far.

I take in a deep breath and then slowly exhale. I am so done. With all of it. With Carlos, trying to take over. With Fidel, giving me incredibly mixed signals. With every single man in my life, telling me what I should want. Telling me what to do. Telling me that I have no say in my own future.

I smooth down my skirt and sit back down, reaching for the book held in the hands of my next fan.

"Hi," I say to her, as if everything is completely normal. "What's your name?"

But everything is not normal.

Because I am done.

23

FIDEL

I WATCH her from across the signing floor. Back straight, pen moving, smile perfectly placed as she chats with readers in orc horns, ball gowns, and full-on medieval armor.

Maria Sandoval is working the crowd like a goddamn pro.

Even after the pre-panel chaos—being routed to the wrong room, accompanied by Daniel but with no real backup—she's still standing. Still glowing. Still poised.

And I should be focused. I should be scanning exits. Watching for pattern breaks in the crowd. Tracking Wes Solano's flop sweat, Lily Renshaw's press performance, and Sloane Cross's complete disinterest in any of it.

Instead, I can't take my eyes off of *her*. Maria.

Watching how easy she makes it look. How she laughs at someone's joke. How she leans in when she signs a book like it matters. Like *they* matter.

How she shines.

She shouldn't be here. Not like this. Not in a room this loud, this crowded, this exposed. And not under my protection if I can't get my shit together.

Because if I screw this up—if I miss something again, miss

another glitch in her schedule—it won't just be on me. It'll be *her* who pays the price.

She's trusting me. Raul is trusting me. And all I can think about is how goddamn beautiful she looks. How easy it would be to step over that line. How hard it's getting to stay behind it.

Focus goddammit!

Sloane Cross is standing just fifty feet away from her, near the merch table, right beside Wes Solano. She's calm, controlled, polished in her skin-tight black blazer.

But she's not looking at Maria. She's looking at me. For just a second, our eyes lock.

And then—she smirks.

Her look isn't PR-friendly. Not polite. It's cold. Knowing. The kind of looks that says *I know something you don't.* My jaw tightens.

She doesn't know I'm a hacker. She thinks I'm just the bodyguard, the guy who glowers at her from across the room while she manipulates the press and puppets her client.

But that smirk? It tells me she's right. She knows something that I don't.

Not yet.

I shift my weight and bring my phone up in one hand, opening Maria's website like I always do. I monitor it constantly, whether she realizes it or not. Traffic patterns. Bounce rates. Referrer tags. And always the comments.

Same for her socials. Same for Reddit.

Part of the job.

And if someone gets a little too creative with the fan art? Or crosses a line in the replies? I flag it. Scrub it. Make sure they never post again. She hasn't seen the worst of it. She doesn't know I'm blocking the creeps, scrubbing the unhinged stuff before she ever sees it.

Today's bonus scene drop lit the whole thing on fire. Engagement's spiked, site traffic more than doubled, comment thread already hundreds deep.

As usual, the fans are complete lunatics.

"I need Duke tentacles tattooed on my soul."

"Lady Penelope, teach me your ways."

"I too would like to be pressed into the Duke's bioluminescent torso."

"I blacked out from the suction cups."

I recognize half the usernames: *dukeskisses4life, tentaclelover, ladypenhargrove.* The same regulars who treat every chapter like a religious event and every blog post like it's sacred canon.

I scroll past dozens more, half amused, half horrified.

And then I see it. A comment that stands out from the rest. No emoji spam. No thirst-core caps lock. Just quiet. Precise.

From a commenter I don't recognize. WingsofBlood-andGlory.

"You looked beautiful today, Maria. You always do.

I hope you enjoy my gift. Perhaps one day you will wear it in our pleasure chamber."

I freeze. Not "Mercede."

Maria.

Whoever this is, they aren't just a fan. They know her. They know who she is. And they might have been at her panel today. Watching her.

The tone of the comment is calm. No typos. No emojis. Just quiet, confident obsession. Like whoever this is thinks she already belongs to him.

This commenter isn't just some horny troll. This is about possession.

My stomach turns.

My thumb hovers over the screen, ready to text her. Warn her.

But I don't. Not here. Not yet. She won't like it. She'll tell me it's a simple mistake. An autocorrect error. She'll say I'm over-reacting.

So instead, I screenshot the comment and start to run a quick packet check on the IP.

That's when I spot something in my peripheral vision. A delivery runner, a kid, maybe nineteen, cutting through the crowd with a massive bouquet in one arm and a small gift box in his other hand.

The bouquet is filled with blood-red roses, dozens of them. Wrapped in thick black paper and tied with a black silk ribbon. The rose scent is heavy, overwhelming. It's like something for a funeral.

My feet are moving before I even realize it. I intercept him five feet from Maria's table, cutting him off with a palm flat to his chest.

"Delivery," the kid says, blinking up at me. "For the writer." He jerks his chin toward Maria.

"Who are you? Who sent this?"

He shrugs, uneasy now. "I'm just TaskRunner. Picked it up two blocks over. Guy handed it off. Paid cash."

I press a finger to my comm. "Elias. Grab this kid I've got near the merch table. Quiet hold. Get the full relay chain on his delivery."

"Copy that," Elias replies instantly.

I pluck the bouquet and the gift box from the runner's hands and move to Maria's table just as she finishes signing a book for a woman wearing a glittery fishbowl helmet.

Maria's eyes widen when she sees the bouquet.

"Fidel, what the hell?" Her voice is too loud. Her smile falters. For a second, she looks confused. Like she doesn't know whether to be touched or terrified.

I keep the gift box close but set the bouquet down in front of her. "Show me the card," I tell her.

She frowns, digging gently through the flowers. Pulls out a stiff white card, pinched between her fingers.

She reads it. Her mouth twitches like she's about to say something.

I take it before she can. Handwritten. Elegant. Just one word.

Maria

That's all it says.

No sender. No message. Just her real name—on a public delivery, at a public event, in a venue that didn't even publish the location of Maria's table until this morning.

My pulse spikes. "This isn't safe," I murmur. My voice is low, just for her. "We need to go. Now."

Maria flashes a tight smile for the fans still lined up at the table, her voice all sunshine. But her eyes are hard. "You can't just... Fidel, this happens all the time. People send me stuff."

"Not like this."

"I get gifts all the time. Flowers. Cards. My fans are... extra."

"This isn't fan extra. This is *targeted*. This is someone who knows who you are."

She tilts her head. Still smiling. Still furious.

"I'm finishing this signing," she hisses. "You want to hover behind me? Fine. But stop being so paranoid. I'm not bailing because someone didn't know how to spell Mercede."

I don't answer. Just slip the gift box into my jacket.

She sees. Glares. But she doesn't stop me. Doesn't say another word.

Not yet.

Natalie slides up to me a second later, glancing at the bouquet like it might be contaminated with some kind of transmissible disease.

"Jesus. That thing looks like it costs more than the venue." She glances at me, raising a brow. "You okay?"

"No," I answer. "You?"

"Also no." She watches Maria for another beat, then returns to her chair next to Maria, finally putting her phone down, eyes scanning the crowd.

In my comm, Elias murmurs: "Delivery kid's clean. Doesn't know who it's from. Picked it up from another guy on 6th Street who vanished. Paid him cash. No signature. No log. Just a hand-off."

I nod once, jaw tight.

The website comment. The card. The flowers. The gift.

Someone knows her real name. Her current location. And how to time this damn delivery to the second.

And I missed it. All of it. Another fuck-up.

She keeps signing. Keeps smiling. Keeps acting like none of this matters.

But it does. I'm not paranoid. Someone's watching. Someone who may be an unhinged fan. Or worse.

I'm going to find him. Take him apart. Slowly and painfully. Make sure he never gets close to her again.

Even if she never knows it.

24

MARIA

By the time FutureFic wraps, my cheeks hurt from smiling. My hand is still cramping from signing books. My voice is raw from small talk and my skull is buzzing with exhaustion.

But I stay until the last book is signed. Until the last fan gets their moment. Because that's what you do. You show up. You smile. You keep smiling. Even when everything inside you is unraveling.

Natalie was watching me. Watching the way I didn't react to the blood-red bouquet, to the gift box Fidel snatched out of my reach. She didn't say anything else about it, but I saw the look on her face. Like something didn't quite add up.

It doesn't.

The bouquet. The gift. My real name on the card. It's specific. Personal.

But I can't deal with that right now. Because I am just one breath away from setting everything and everyone on fire.

Fidel hovered for the rest of the event. Didn't say another word. Just stood there like a brick wall, watching everything, intercepting every odd movement, noting every flicker of attention directed at me.

He kept the gift box. Didn't let me open it to see what it was.

And of course, he hasn't mentioned the chocolate frosting incident. Not a glance. Not a word. Like he didn't take my hand and lick that frosting off my finger like he was starving for it. Like *I* was the thing he wanted, not the sugar.

Like I imagined the whole thing.

Maybe I did.

Because this morning he went back to silent, stoic Fidel. The Fidel who answers questions with one-word grunts, keeps his face in his phone, and acts like feelings are a security threat.

Maybe I'm crazy for wanting anything more from him.

By the time we get back to Carlos's house, I am vibrating with frustration.

Carlos is already home—waiting, of course. He wants to talk about Kara Lasater and UltraVision. But I tell him I'm too tired and we'll talk later.

Natalie and Elias left FututeFic and headed to her hotel, strategizing over a possible UltraVision deal. Fidel's gone to his safe house, probably already working on a full tactical report about the events of the day to give my father. I'm sure he'll log the bouquet as something like a "Class B Threat, Non-Explosive."

I go to my room. Stand in the middle of the floor for a full minute, staring at my reflection in the mirror.

When did I become this? I don't recognize myself anymore. I look like some polished, palatable girl who smiles and nods and does whatever every damn man in her life tells her to do.

Fuck *that* girl.

I strip off my blouse. My skirt. My stilettos. My armor.

Fuck it. I'm not doing this anymore.

I yank open my suitcases.

I gave Carlos his chance. I gave my father my quiet cooperation. I even gave Fidel the benefit of the doubt.

But all they see is a pawn. A little girl to be protected or packaged or positioned. None of them see *me*.

I jam everything into my suitcases and zip them closed, my heart pounding.

Fidel doesn't get to touch me like that, look at me like that, and then act like it never happened. Like everything is back to normal and I don't matter.

I grab my phone. Pull up the Uber app.

If he won't act, I will.

I'm done playing the obedient little heiress doing their bidding. I'm going to start giving the orders.

And I know exactly where I'm going.

25

FIDEL

MARIA IS MISSING.

I stare at the text I just received from Carlos. *Where's Maria?*

FutureFic ended just two hours ago. Two hours. And now she's gone. I clench my fists, trying to think through the pounding in my skull.

Not kidnapped. Not attacked. Just... gone.

And that is a fucking problem. My fucking problem.

My stomach tightens as I pull up the security feeds from Carlos's estate, fast-forwarding through the last hour of footage.

And there she is.

Maria. Walking out of the house alone. A suitcase in each hand. Calm. Unhurried. Getting into a fucking Uber.

I grit my teeth. No security. No driver. No detail shadowing her like they're supposed to.

Jesus Christ, Daniel. Can you just do your fucking job and watch her?

My pulse spikes sharply as I track her movements.

Where the hell is she going?

I pull up another screen, hacking into the Uber system. Within seconds, I have the car's plate, driver name, route.

Where is she heading?

Another few keystrokes. The live GPS feed loads.

I exhale slowly, pressing the heels of my palms into my eyes.

She's headed here. That's where she's going. She's coming to me.

Not kidnapped. Not in danger. But still making the worst possible decision.

I push back from the table, grab my gun, and head out to the front porch.

Twenty minutes later, I'm still standing there, arms crossed, weapon in hand, waiting.

A silver Prius slows to a stop at the curb.

Maria's silhouette shifts in the back seat, unhurried, calm, as if she hasn't just made my blood pressure spike through the roof. She pats the Uber driver on the shoulder. Like she hasn't just destroyed every security protocol I spent weeks putting into place.

Her legs swing out of the back seat. She adjusts her purse strap like she's stepping out for brunch. The Uber driver gets out, opens his trunk, pulls out Maria's suitcases, and hands them to her. She smiles at him sweetly, telling him, "Thanks, Jean Pierre. Best of luck with your screenplay!"

She turns and walks toward me, but pauses when she spots the gun in my hand. "Still with the gun?"

I don't holster it.

She tilts her head, a smirk on her face. "Didn't anyone ever tell you it's rude to greet guests with a weapon?"

I inhale through my nose, forcing my grip to loosen. "It's late. You shouldn't be here."

She arches a brow. "And yet here I am."

A black SUV screeches to a stop at the curb. Carlos's personal bodyguards. Late. Scrambling. Fucking useless.

Maria barely glances at the SUV before turning back to me. "You gonna let me in, or are we doing this on the lawn?"

I wave Carlos's guys off with a sharp motion. They hesitate, looking at me through the car windows, then wave and peel away.

Maria steps inside without another word, leaving her suitcases behind. Like I'm her valet and need to take care of the luggage.

I don't move at first. I just stand there, still holding my gun, pulse hammering in my skull. *What the hell is she thinking?*

I exhale sharply, holster my gun, pick up the damn suitcases, and kick the door shut.

Maria stops a few feet in, surveying the space like she's scoping out her new territory. Calm. Confident. No hesitation.

I watch her. Wait. Wait for some flicker of doubt. Some sign that she knows it was a mistake to come here. But nothing.

I know she's still mad. Has been all day. I just don't know if it's because of what happened in Carlos's kitchen—or because I didn't take it further. Didn't touch her. Didn't kiss her. I'd been hard for hours after because of it and jerked off like a goddamn teenager. I still couldn't look her in the eye.

Because wanting her is one thing. Believing she could ever want me? That's something else.

She exhales slowly and I can see the tension slipping from her shoulders. Like she's been holding her breath for days and this is the first time she can actually breathe.

My grip on the suitcases tightens. This is not good. Not good at all.

She turns, catches me watching. She lifts a brow. "Elias here too?"

"No, not now," I say, jaw tight. "He's with Natalie. Working for you."

"Good," she shrugs, completely unfazed. "When you have a chance, let him know I'm staying here now."

I exhale, slow, controlled, trying to process the sheer absurdity of this situation. "Excuse me?"

Maria turns, puts her hand on her cocked hip, casually, looking at me like I'm the crazy one.

"After what happened tonight at FutureFic, I'm done," she says simply. No dramatics. Just finality. "With Carlos. With my father. With the Sandovals and their constant, never-ending control."

She straightens, gaze steady. "I'm not doing it anymore."

I study her carefully, her shoulders set, chin lifted, fire in her eyes. She's not bluffing.

Maria isn't just pushing back. She's walking away.

And she walked straight to me.

26

MAVFEST DAY 6

**Note on Maria Sandoval's Phone
Timestamp 1:42 a.m.**

TO DO

FIDEL - WHERE'S MY GIFT?? He has it - get it!
- Daniel – bring king silk sheets
- Daniel – white fluffy towels
- Daniel – blow dryer, makeup mirror (in my bathroom)
- Esmeralda – enchiladas??? 🙏
- Get rid of creepy deer painting in hallway ugh 😬
- Natalie - post bonus chapter to socials?? - did we?

GROCERIES
- 6 bottles Prosecco (more??)
- 12-pack Modelo
- 12-pack Diet Dr Pep
- 12-pack Diet Coke (for F)
- what does E drink???
- Veggies – kale, spinach, carrots, bananas, berries

- Eggs
- Protein powder, collagen powder
- Yogurt
- Oat milk
- Elderberry syrup
- Cookie dough ice cream
- ORGANIC coffee!!
- Tortillas (Esmeralda??)

HOUSEHOLD
- Toilet paper!!!
- Sponges
- Dish soap
- Dishwasher soap, cleaning sprays, soaps (all)
- Hand soap
- Bath soap
- Laundry detergent
- Dryer sheets

CANDLES!!!

?? Pink vibrator/dildo, cute, rechargeable, downtown shop?? ask Lily?

27

MARIA

I'M smart enough to know that leaving Carlos's house in an Uber is freaking my family out. So, once I've kicked Elias out of the master bedroom, I bite the bullet and call Carlos and then my dad.

Carlos picks up on the first ring.

"Where are you?" No greeting, no preamble, just Carlos being Carlos.

I tuck my legs under me on the bed, bracing for the lecture. "I'm safe, if that's what you're about to ask."

A beat of silence. Then a slow, measured exhale. "And where exactly is 'safe'?"

"At one of your many other houses. With Fidel and Elias."

Another pause. Then, dryly, "So... you've downgraded from a security fortress to two exhausted bodyguards and a house that probably doesn't have toilet paper?"

I sigh, rubbing my temple. "Carlos, I know you're trying to help. But I need space. I need—"

"Control?"

I swallow. "Yes."

Carlos doesn't argue right away, which is somehow worse than when he's in full big brother mode.

"Papa won't be happy," he finally says.

"I know. And I don't care."

Another exhale. "You should. But fine. I won't drag you back." A pause. Then, pointedly, "Yet."

I scowl at the unspoken threat. Classic Carlos. Always letting me screw up just enough before stepping in.

"Just tell Fidel I expect daily updates," he adds.

I groan. "I'm not a hostage, Carlos."

"Not yet," he mutters, then hangs up.

I stare at my phone. Not yet? *Fuck you, Carlos.*

My call with Papa is shorter and more to the point. "I'm fine, Papa. I'm with Fidel and Elias. I just don't want Carlos micromanaging me anymore."

I hear Papa's sigh. "Make sure Fidel and Elias are with you at all times. I just want you to be safe *mi preciosa*."

"I'll stay with them Papa. I know how to be safe."

But seeing how Fidel and Elias are living is making me question just how "safe" I can be with them.

The living room is the only room that inspires confidence. It's an arsenal—gun lockers lining the walls, rifles leaned within easy reach, ammo boxes cracked open, tactical knives, meticulously arranged on the coffee table, ready to go.

The rest of the house is not as inspiring. Because Fidel and Elias aren't just living like bachelors. They're living like bachelors living like college students living like Spring Breakers, which means they've designed conditions for maximum convenience and minimum effort.

The kitchen is piled with pizza boxes and questionable takeout containers, the sink full of dirty dishes, the trash can overflowing.

Every bathroom has exactly one-fourth roll of toilet paper

on the holder. No extra rolls in the cabinets. Or under the sinks. Or anywhere in this house that I've looked.

The laundry room is pristine because no one is doing laundry. We've been in Austin for almost a week. Where is their laundry?

Standing in the kitchen the next morning, I look into their refrigerator and find exactly three things: three cans of beer, an empty takeout container, and a bottle of hot sauce.

I shut the door and turn. "Do either of you realize that you live here?"

Elias, lounging on a barstool at the kitchen island, barely looks up from his phone. "Not really."

Fidel, sitting next to Elias and buried in his laptop, doesn't even acknowledge me.

I cross my arms. "So what's the plan? Are we just... ordering takeout until MAVFest ends?"

That gets Fidel's attention. He glances up, expression flat. "Yes."

I let the silence drag for a second. Then, sweetly, "That seems like a possible security breach."

His brows pull together.

I pick up my phone. "We're shutting down the takeout. For safety reasons, obviously."

Elias looks up. He smirks, setting his phone down. "This should be good."

Fidel leans back in his chair, crossing his arms. "Safety reasons?"

I nod. "It's a risk. Predictable movements, unvetted food in open containers. You wouldn't let me accept random drinks at a bar. Why should we be comfortable with an endless stream of questionable people having access to our food and making deliveries from unknown locations?"

He narrows his eyes, the little tic in his jaw telling me he hates that I'm using his own paranoia against him. And I'm right.

Elias, meanwhile, is openly grinning.

I shrug. "So I'm taking care of it." I look down at my phone and finish the order. "Groceries will be here in an hour."

Fidel exhales through his nose. The slow, aggravated kind. "No one asked you to do that."

"No one had to."

I beam. Because I'm in control now. Of this house. Of Elias. Of Fidel. Of everything.

28

———

MARIA

It's almost midnight when I step out of my bedroom and into the hallway, the wood cool under my bare feet. My phone is buzzing with texts—Carlos, Natalie, a half-dozen press inquiries—but I ignore them and cross the hall.

Fidel's door is closed. I raise my hand and knock. Once. Then again, louder.

The door creaks open a second later. Fidel stands there in the open doorway. He's not shirtless, but he's ditched the usual jacket and trousers for a soft white t-shirt and the gray sweatpants. His hair is damp and I can smell soap, like he just stepped out of the shower. But there's a tension in his shoulders like he was about to sit down and brood.

We stare at each other for half a second.

"I want my gift," I say.

His eyes narrow. He exhales through his nose, then steps back and disappears into the room.

I lean slightly, trying to catch a glimpse into his bedroom. It's all cold order. A laptop glowing on the desk, a disassembled handgun on a towel next to it. No photos. No mess. Like a hotel room for a spy. Or a sociopath.

He returns, box in hand.

"You've been holding onto it for hours," I say, arms crossed.

"I needed to make sure it was clean."

"Clean," I echo.

"No listening device. No microtracker. No chemical residue. It's not bugged. Not poisoned. Not explosive."

"Wow," I say, accepting the box. "A gift from a fan that isn't going to explode. What a surprise."

He doesn't smile. I lift the lid.

The earrings inside are... ridiculous.

Thick platinum settings, gleaming like molten silver, each holding an emerald the size of a chickpea—oval-cut, impossibly deep green, and haloed in tiny, perfect diamonds. They dangle from heavy platinum hooks, bold and ostentatious, the kind of jewelry Cleopatra might have worn. Or maybe a drug lord's mistress.

My eyebrows shoot up. "Holy shit."

Fidel says nothing.

"These are... bizarre?"

"Yes," he says quietly. "And they're real."

I trace a finger over the emeralds.

"I won't wear them," I murmur. "They're too much."

"I know," he says. "You don't like emeralds."

I look up sharply. He meets my gaze. Steady. Unblinking.

"You wear diamonds," he says, voice low. "Sometimes sapphires. That's what looks best on your skin. You don't wear green. Not in jewelry. Not in your clothes."

My chest tightens.

He keeps going. "Your earrings are always delicate. Usually gold. But sometimes silver. You hate anything that pulls on your earlobes."

My throat goes dry. "How do you know all that?"

He blinks once. "It's my job to know."

"No," I say softly. "That's not a security detail thing. That's a 'staring at me' thing."

He looks down at the floor and doesn't answer.

I glance back at the earrings, then close the box. "This doesn't feel like it's from a fan. It's too over the top. It's wrong." A chill runs down my spine.

Fidel's voice is quiet. "Whoever sent this doesn't know you."

"Do you? Know me?" I ask, voice just above a whisper.

Another pause. Another beat of tension stretching between us in the narrow hall. His gaze flicks up, to my eyes, and the corner of his mouth quirks up, just a bit. Like he might smile, but doesn't want to. It's a look I feel like I've seen so many times on Fidel's face.

And suddenly, I think back to high school. My freshman year. Fidel's senior year. My very first football game.

I had just started school in San Antonio. After spending all those years in boarding school, my father finally wanted me at home, at the same school as Fidel. Saint Ursula's was a blur of plaid skirts, whispered gossip, and tight social circles I didn't belong to. At that first game, I was so clueless, I wasn't even sitting in the right bleacher section. Just a lonely freshman in braids and cherry lip gloss, sitting by myself with the upper classmen, clutching a stupid pom pom, and thinking if I went to a football game, I might fit in.

Behind me, two senior girls were half drunk and wholly terrifying. I could smell their perfume and the alcohol hidden in their water bottles.

"Jesus," one of them whispered, leaning into her friend, "when did Fidel get so fucking hot?"

They were talking about Fidel. My Fidel. He was down on the field in his uniform, standing on the sidelines, watching the game, and waiting to go in.

"Mmm. He's so fine," the other purred, her words slurring together. "I'd get on my knees for him."

"On my knees and suck his cock until he exploded down my throat." They both laughed loudly, not caring who could hear.

I froze. I was trying not to listen. Trying not to understand what they were saying.

Then Fidel turned toward the stands. His helmet was off, sweat gleaming on his forehead, eyes scanning the crowd.

He locked eyes with me. Gave me that almost smile and raised a hand, giving me a quick wave.

My heart jumped. For one stupid second, I raised my hand to wave back.

"Hi Fidel," one of the girls murmured in a low, syrupy voice, lifting her own hand in a slow, lazy wave. "Will you fuck me after the game?"

They both burst out laughing again.

"He totally looked at us."

"Totally. You know I'd let him choke me with that mouthguard."

Their laughter was loud. Confident. Sharp.

I turned halfway, just enough to see their eyes glued to the field. They didn't see me. I was invisible to them. But I saw them watching him. Like he was a prize. A prize they could have.

I turned back, curling my shoulders around my chest, my face burning. I didn't even fully understand what they were saying. But I understood how it made me feel. Embarrassed. Confused.

Angry. Possessive.

I hated those girls. Hated how they thought they could claim him. Hated the strange heat that crawled up my spine when I realized I didn't want anyone else looking at him like that. Thinking of him like that.

Because he was mine.

That was the first time I saw Fidel differently. Not as the boy who helped me build a Hogwarts diorama or tried to braid my hair while I cried about how much I hated boarding school. Not as the silent protector who walked me back from the tennis courts at home when it was dark.

But as someone girls wanted.

And even worse—someone who might want them back.

That was ten years ago. But I think that might be the moment when everything shifted. And I've been pretending not to notice the shift ever since.

I shake off the memory and meet Fidel's gaze.

"Go to bed, Maria."

I take a step back, but hand him the box. "Fine. You keep it. I don't want it near me."

He takes the box from me and his fingers just barely brush against mine.

I walk to my door, then glance back once more.

Fidel's still watching. Still silent.

And the tension between us is thrumming, alive in the space between our doors.

29

FIDEL

Maria has made herself at home.

Which means my life is officially over.

I expected her to be a slight disruption to the routine Elias and I have created. Instead, she's pulled us into her completely chaotic orbit.

I have no idea what's going on.

In less than forty-eight hours, she has taken over the house. Elias has been exiled from the master bedroom to a guest room down the hall. All of our food and beer has been thrown out. The kitchen has been stocked overnight with a ridiculous amount of groceries, half of which are things I don't recognize or want to eat.

I opened the fridge this morning to find Icelandic yogurt, organic oat milk, something called elderberry syrup, and an entire drawer full of leafy green crap.

There are pink sponges by the sink. Spray bottles of five different cleaning products are on the counter. Two candles in the kitchen, one in each bathroom, and a massive one in the living room. There is now more toilet paper in this house than we can use in a year.

The earrings still sit in their box on my dresser. She hasn't brought them up again. Good. I don't want her touching them.

I rub the back of my neck, staring at the absurdity of it all. Elias texted me last night:

> Elias: If she starts lighting all the candles and making us chant, I'm burning this place down.

It had been a joke, but barely.

Still, none of that compares to the upheaval she has inflicted in my dining room. I stalk toward it, coffee in hand, but stop cold in the doorway.

Maria has taken over.

The dining table, my workspace, is a fucking disaster zone. My laptop, multiple monitors, loose notes, and decrypted files on cartel transactions are shoved to one end. The other end? A hurricane of Maria's shit.

Her laptop is open, a half-drunk coffee sits next to her annotated manuscript, and a mess of notebooks, sticky notes, and highlighters are spread around like she's preparing for war.

And at the center of it all—Maria. Curled up on a chair, wearing my hoodie.

Not hers.

Mine.

How did she get a hold of it? It's too big for her, the sleeves swallowing her hands when she moves, the collar stretched just enough that I catch a glimpse of smooth, golden skin at her collarbone. The hem barely skims the top of her thighs, revealing just enough leg to fuck with my entire morning.

She isn't even trying to look sexy. And that makes it worse.

I force my feet to move, stepping into the room, gripping my coffee like it's the only thing keeping me from losing my goddamn mind.

Maria looks up, wide-eyed, sleepy, soft, still waking up.

"Morning," she says easily.

I exhale through my nose. *Fuck.*

"That's my hoodie." My voice sounds rougher than I intended.

Maria blinks, like she hasn't noticed. Like she isn't on the verge of shattering my last shred of restraint.

She tilts her head. "Yeah?" She tugs at the oversized sleeves, a lazy, indulgent movement, like she's settling deeper into it. "You weren't using it."

"That's not—" I clench my teeth, exhaling sharply again. Not worth the fight.

I drop into my chair, fingers flexing, forcing my focus onto my actual job, onto anything but her.

She focuses on me, staring like *I'm* the one invading *her* space.

She rests her chin on her hand. "You've turned this place into quite the..." She waves vaguely at my monitors, where strings of data crawl across the screens. "...place. What are you working on?"

"Nothing you need to worry about."

She makes a face. "Wow. Okay."

I ignore her. Force myself to focus. Keep scrolling through the offshore accounts I've been tracking, my fingers moving while my brain sifts through the pieces of a puzzle that still refuses to come together.

Something's wrong. Something's missing.

Money keeps flowing into Solano Studios. Steady, strategic transfers from a carousel of offshore accounts, each one owned by a different shell corp. They're all scrubbed clean on paper, but I know what I'm looking at. Layered routing paths. Round-trip laundering. Phantom entities registered in jurisdictions with zero oversight. It's a fucking nesting doll of financial fuckery.

I can't prove it yet, but I'm almost certain all of the money traces back to Los Cuervos. They're bankrolling Wes Solano. And they're doing it dirty.

But even if I had the proof of the connection to Los Cuervos, it still doesn't explain why Maria keeps getting dragged into this. She's not a power player. Not a decision-maker. She's not running product or calling shots. She's not even supposed to be a pawn on the game board.

So why the hell is she being tracked? Why is someone screwing with her schedule? Sending her gifts? Watching her like she's the goddamn key to something?

Unless she is. And nobody told me. Or her.

I rub my jaw, my mind racing, but I keep being drawn back to Maria's presence. It's impossible to ignore. A slow, persistent charge in the air, settling under my skin, making it hard to breathe. And that scent. Orange blossoms. Cinnamon.

Goddamn it. She's always like this—too close, too in my stuff, too confident, too much.

And she's wearing my goddamn hoodie.

"I really need your opinion," she says suddenly, tapping at her chin.

I shoot her a look. "No, you really don't."

Maria smirks, completely unfazed. "Which title's better? *A Marquess from the Stars* or *The Viscount's Alien Bride*?"

I blink. "What?"

"For book three." She glances at her screen. "I have a vibe, but I can't decide on the title. *The Viscount's Alien Bride* is fun, but *A Marquess from the Stars* has a little more gravitas, you know?"

I stare at her. "You want me to weigh in on historical alien romance titles right now?"

She lifts a shoulder. "Why not? You're smart, clever. You read."

I freeze for half a second, long enough for Maria's smile to sharpen.

"You do read, don't you? I mean, you've read *my* books, right?"

She does this all the time. Asking cutting questions, tossing out backhanded compliments like casual, effortless weapons.

Maria is waiting for an answer.

Of course I've read her books. Multiple times. The sex scenes maybe too many times. Maria's alien sex scenes are hot as hell. I've learned that I can get myself off in less than three minutes to the idea of a two-tongued alien lord going down on a scandalized virgin in the middle of a moonlit garden. But I won't let her know that.

"I've glanced through them."

She rolls her eyes. "Right, *glanced* through them."

I sigh, rubbing my temples. "Go with the marquess one. For the title. It sounds less stupid."

Her eyes light up. "You think so?"

I exhale slowly, realizing my mistake too late. She has tricked me into actually engaging.

She grins. "Good. Marquess it is."

I huff out a breath and go back to my screen.

Maria settles in across from me, humming, typing away as if we're just two normal people working side by side.

Not a crime family's hacker tracking cartel money.

Not a billionaire's daughter trying to escape the weight of her last name.

Not a gorgeous, infuriating woman who somehow has made my hoodie the sexiest thing I've ever seen on her.

Stop it! Stop thinking about the damn hoodie!

We're just two normal people.

For one quiet, impossible moment, I let myself sit in it. The domesticity. The ease. The feeling that Maria fits here. With me.

And before I can decide what the fuck that even means, my screen flashes.

Her itinerary is being altered. Right in front of me.

The schedule for the next event, a film industry brunch at the art museum tomorrow morning, is being modified. At first, it's subtle—an adjustment to her pickup time, a minor change to the security detail. But then I run a trace. And the request isn't coming from a MAVFest account or anyone in the Sandoval system.

It's bouncing, masked through layers of commercial proxies. One of them's military-grade.

I dig deeper. And then I'm locked out.

What the fuck?

My fingers freeze over the keyboard. Someone just kicked me off the system. No one should be able to lock me out. Not out of my own damn system. *I built this fucking system!*

Is this Sloane Cross?

Wes Solano can't pay his bar tab, so why is he paying for her? Everything about her feels off—too curated, too smooth. She talks like a PR strategist, but doesn't act like one. No hype, no performative enthusiasm. Just cool calculation, like she's studying the room, waiting to make the most efficient move.

Is she really a hacker? None of these glitches were happening until she came on board.

Maria hums to herself, still typing across from me, completely unaware that the control she thinks she's finally taken, might be slipping away.

None of this makes sense. I should be able to pull the threads and watch it unravel. But it's not unraveling.

It's holding. Tight.

Which means either I'm missing something big—or this is Sloane and she's a hell of a lot better than I thought.

30

MAVFEST DAY 6

Timestamp: 13:06 CT

Direct Message to Frank Lin, IT Specialist for Sandoval Group, LLC, Austin Division

Signal Burn Notice Active
From: [Encrypted contact]
To: KillBit
Timestamp: 13:06 CST
404 BACKDOOR – one night only
MAVF hacker underground meet // exploit drop // 1am
6th-Brazos // top floor // elevator code: 0037
No feeds No feds No tourists
BYORig whisper auctions code-for-cash
Zero-days for sale. Proof-of-pwns.
if ur seeing this someone thinks ur still useful.
forget u got this u never saw it.
signal auto-wipe engaged...
3... 2... 1...

31

———

FIDEL

I haven't slept.

Not because of Maria. Not entirely.

But because someone locked me out of my own fucking system.

Someone walked in, wiped the logs, and walked out clean.

The backend firewall I built. The alert tree I coded. The real-time tripwire system I designed to protect Maria. Someone else was inside it. And when I traced the signal?

They kicked me off.

Hard.

I've rewritten that firewall three times since. Rebuilt the traceroute protocol. Pulled a clean backup from one of my off-grid vaults and reinstalled every custom script.

And after twelve hours of pure hell—I'm back in.

But it's not clean.

Whoever did this left no signature, no access logs, no point of entry. Just a blank space where my code used to live.

That shouldn't be possible. And if it happened once, it can happen again.

I looped Frank in this morning. Sent him the full traceback

report and everything I've got on the shifting MAVFest sched-
ules. Told him I need eyes on any digital infrastructure tied to
Maria's event schedule. And I need it now.

While I dig through her press credentials and travel schedule, he's combing the digital badges, access keys, and event
routing protocols.

We're running out of angles.

A notification pops up on my phone. Frank calling.

I answer with a clipped, "Tell me you found something."

A faint laugh. "Nice to talk to you too, bro. And no. I'm not
seeing shit."

I frown. "Nothing?"

"Nothing. MAVFest's IT isn't amateur hour. They've got solid
protocols. But if someone's fucking with the schedule, it's not
happening through official systems." A pause. "And if that's the
case, I don't know where to look."

I rub my jaw, thinking.

Frank is good. Really good. If he's coming up empty, this isn't
a simple infiltration. It's something deeper.

Then he says, "Listen, I've got an idea. It's a long shot, but
might be worth it."

I lean back. "Go on."

"You ever hear of 404 Backdoor?"

I narrow my eyes. "Sounds like a low-rent Defcon ripoff."

Frank snorts. "Nah. It's exclusive. Austin's underground
hacker circuit. Invite-only, no socials, no livestreams, no
amateurs. If someone's working a side angle at MAVFest, there's
a good chance they'll show up there."

I exhale through my nose. He's not wrong. With so many
industry players in town, hackers would all be looking for free-
lance gigs, black-market buyers, and corporate scouts.

He continues. "Look, if someone's fucking with MAVFest's
scheduling, odds are they aren't working alone. These kinds of

jobs always have a backend. Someone handling logistics, someone running interference, someone selling access. If we poke around 404, we might find someone who knows something."

I pause for a second and he knows I'm not convinced. Frank pushes. "Come on. It'll be fun. Just like the good old days."

The good old days. College. The summer after junior year, when Frank and I ran half the darknet bounties coming out of Austin. If a company wanted a stress test on their security, we cracked it. If someone needed a government server breached, we did it. We weren't thieves. We weren't activists. We were just two ambitious assholes who wanted to prove we were the best. And we got paid like we were.

I glance at my screen. The schedule anomalies aren't giving me shit. Maybe it's time to try something different.

I exhale. "Fine. Send me the details."

Frank laughs. "That's the spirit."

Several hours later, around 2 a.m., we arrive. The tech company's office building off Sixth Street that's been hijacked for this is a hive of activity.

On the ground floor, a MAVFest invite-only DJ party pounds with bass, a tech industry event flooded with startup founders, crypto bros, and overpriced cocktails.

But six floors up, hidden behind an unlisted elevator code, that's where the real event is happening.

404 Backdoor.

No security at the door. No check-in. If you made it here, if you've got the code, you're already vetted.

Inside, rows of custom-built rigs hum in dim lighting, glowing monitors reflecting off black-painted walls. Groups of hackers cluster around demo stations, trading exploits, testing scripts, exchanging workarounds for software yet to hit the market.

And then past them, the real action. A central hub where high-stakes bids happen. Encrypted drives swap hands for cash or crypto keys. Code snippets flicker across overhead displays, each line a vulnerability someone is willing to buy or sell.

All of this will be gone tomorrow.

Frank and I stick to the edges, watching.

"See anyone interesting?" he mutters.

I scan the room. I know a lot of these people. Mostly Austin locals, some West Coast tech guys, a handful of foreign players I don't recognize.

Then—

A figure at the far end of the hub, leaning casually against a workstation.

Sloane Cross.

What. The. Fucking. Fuck.

I nudge Frank. "Far right, in black, standing by the encrypted rigs. I know that girl. Sloane Cross."

Frank looks over and when he spots her, his expression flickers with recognition. "No shit."

"You know her?"

He exhales. "Yeah. We ran a job together a couple years back. She wasn't called Sloane then. I don't know what her real name is. Back then she used the handle Blackmatch. She's pretty good."

I shake my head. "She's doing PR now. For Lily Renshaw. Solano Studios."

Frank snorts. "Yeah, no. She may be selling herself as a brand architect or viral strategist or whatever. But that's bullshit. She's a high-level hacker. She's worked cartel jobs."

He leans in slightly, voice low. "She goes where the money is. No loyalty to anyone but herself. Doesn't even vet her clients half the time—just follows the biggest payout. Honestly? It's a miracle she hasn't ended up in a ditch."

Sloane Cross is a hacker. I fucking knew it.

It's no coincidence that Solano has her on payroll. She's not just doing PR. She's a hacker. No ties. No line she won't cross. That's why I can't find anything on her.

She's good at covering her tracks. But following the money? Stupid. And in our world, stupid eventually gets you dead.

Frank glances at me, amused. "She wouldn't be into you, or any guy, if you know what I mean. But how do you know her?"

Before I can respond—

Sloane looks up.

Her gaze flicks over Frank, then lands on me. A slow, knowing smile spreads across her lips. And then, she starts walking toward us.

Shit.

Frank huffs. "Well, this should be fun."

Sloane stops in front of us, arms crossed, weight shifted onto one hip. "Well, well. Look who showed up."

She glances at Frank. "Didn't peg you for MAVFest, KillBit."

KillBit. His old handle. Only a few people still call him that.

Frank shrugs. "Gotta keep up with the scene. Plus, I like the DJ downstairs."

Her eyes flick to me. "And you brought a bodyguard?"

I stay silent.

"Old college buddy."

Sloane's gaze lingers on me, amused. She thinks I'm just Frank's plus-one. Then—

"Ohhh. Right." Her lips curl. "I know you. You're with *Mercede Sanchez.*"

She draws the name out, saying it too carefully. Like she knows exactly who Maria really is.

I don't move. Don't react.

Sloane watches me for another second, then tilts her head. "Well, maybe I'll see you around, bodyguard. After all, your boss's name is all over MAVFest right now." She smiles. Sharp, knowing.

She turns and leaves, threading her way back through the crowd.

I exhale through my nose.

Frank watches her go, then turns to me. "You gonna tell me what the fuck that was about?"

I clench my jaw. "She's working for Solano Studios. For Wes. And she's attached to Lily Renshaw's PR team."

Frank laughs, humorless. "I promise you. She's not doing PR."

"No shit."

Frank exhales, running a hand through his hair. "You know... when we worked together, she was good, but she was sloppy, always left loose ends." He hesitates. "I might have something from that job. I kept it because—paranoid—you know?"

Yeah, I know.

I look at him. "What do you have?"

"Might be nothing. But I'll send it over tomorrow."

We stick around a little longer, talk to a few guys, look at equipment. And then head out.

Later that morning, a black SUV rolls up to the house. One of Carlos's drivers steps out, comes to the door, hands me a package.

No note. No explanation.

Inside? A USB drive.

I don't plug it in right away. Frank is careful. Paranoid like he said. But this? A USB with no explanation? This is old-school spy shit. And old-school spy shit is usually fucked.

I grab one of my secondary laptops—one air-gapped from everything else—and boot it up. Only then do I plug it in.

There's one file. Only one. A backdoor encryption key. From that job Frank did with her.

Well, fuck me.

Frank was right. Sloane Cross wasn't just sloppy. She left herself exposed. And maybe, this is something I can use against her.

Maybe I now have a way in to Sloane Cross.

32

MARIA

THE MORNING SUN filters through the live oak trees, casting shifting patterns of light over the white-clothed tables, the soft hum of conversation blending with the clink of glasses.

I inhale slowly, forcing my shoulders to relax.

Okay. This is it. This is where things are going to happen.

MAVFest's "Mimosas at the Museum" on the grounds of Laguna Gloria Art Museum is one of the most exclusive events on the festival schedule. Platinum badges only, high-level networking, the kind of place where real deals are made.

It's supposed to be chic yet casual. An open-air brunch, champagne flowing, industry people chatting under the dappled shade of towering live oaks. But nothing about this feels casual to me.

I spent over an hour choosing my outfit—a white silk blouse tucked into a red pencil skirt, the kind that hugs just right but still says I mean business. Red stilettos that are stupid for grass but worth it. Small gold hoops with pavé diamonds. Statement watch. Bold red lipstick, in my signature shade, *Dangerous Rouge*. I look like the kind of woman who signs deals before her second mimosa. Hopefully.

Because I need this event to go well.

As far as I'm concerned, Solano Studios is off the table. And UltraVision still hasn't sent a real offer. Kara Lasater seems interested but we haven't come to terms.

So MAVFest is winding down, and I don't have a deal yet.

And it's not just about one book anymore. The second has to be just as successful.

The Dark Duke was my breakout. And *The Stellar Sovereign* is supposed to prove it wasn't a fluke. That I'm not just a one-hit wonder. But all week, I've been running on adrenaline and half-promises. Meetings, smiles, panels. And nothing locked down.

If I walk away from MAVFest empty-handed, it won't just be a disappointment. It'll mean I can't do it. I can't break free of my family. Can't control my career, my future. My own life.

I smooth my napkin over my lap, glancing at Natalie sitting next to me. She's already working, leaning in toward a streaming exec on her other side, nodding, making her case. She's in her element here.

And Elias is trying to out-charm her. As always.

Across from me, he looks effortlessly at home, sipping a mimosa, half-listening to someone talk about a buzzy new adaptation. But I can see it. The sideways glances Elias and Natalie give each other. The arched eyebrows. The competitive little digs dressed up as compliments.

They've been like this all week. Subtle sniping over who can impress more industry people, who gets noticed first. They might hook up. They might murder each other. Could go either way.

Fidel, on the other hand?

He's not relaxed. Not drinking. Not talking to anyone.

He hasn't stopped scanning the crowd since we arrived. I saw him checking his phone three times before we even sat down. He muttered something to Elias about being "back in the system," that "the firewall's holding." But his posture tells me he doesn't believe it's enough.

He sits stiffly on my other side, arms crossed, eyes flicking between me and the people moving through the space. His jacket is open, but I know his gun is right there, easy to reach.

He looks so good—charcoal suit, white shirt, red tie, jaw clenched like he hopes to crack at least two molars. I see his lips pull tight, just like they did right before he tried to yank me out of FutureFic.

At the next table, Kara Lasater sits with a group of UltraVision studio executives, half-listening to a producer drone on about "prestige storytelling."

She hasn't come over to talk to me.

Instead, when she catches my eye, she lifts her glass in a small, effortless toast before turning back to her conversation.

She hasn't waved me over. It's like she's pretending to see me without actually engaging. A silent boundary.

What does it mean?

I swallow, forcing my expression to stay neutral. Is UltraVision pulling back? Are they passing on *The Dark Duke*?

Before I can dwell on it, a voice cuts through the conversation at my table.

"Mercede, I have to ask..."

I glance up, smiling automatically at the woman across the table from me. An older polished blonde, her name tag says she's someone from a mid-level production company that hasn't approached me.

"How have you not signed a deal yet?"

The words hit me like a gut punch, but I keep my expression easy, polished.

I shrug lightly. "Just making sure I find the right fit."

She tilts her head, a polite but knowing smile. "You don't want to wait too long. Momentum is everything."

I hear it for what it is. A warning. People are starting to notice.

I sip my mimosa, ignoring the way my stomach tightens.

UltraVision, the deal I want, hasn't made a move. And Solano Studios? It's not an option. Not with Wes running things into the ground. And definitely not if Carlos takes control.

I'm running out of time.

I glance toward Fidel, hoping for the grounding presence of his steady, unreadable face.

But his expression isn't unreadable anymore. His jaw is tight, his shoulders set. He's focused on something—or someone.

I follow his gaze. A security guy, standing near the garden entrance. He doesn't blink. Just watches, expression hardening. I don't know what Fidel sees, but I can feel his tension winding tighter.

Nothing about the security guy looks suspicious. He's standing where he should be, scanning the area.

Fidel is still watching him.

Then, slowly, he pulls out his phone. Makes a call.

I turn back to my conversation, keeping my expression normal, but I can feel it—the shift in the air.

He's whispering but I can hear every word he says.

"Daniel, where are the guys you sent? The schedule says Jorge and Luis will be here."

A pause for Daniel to answer. Then—

"What do you mean you don't have anything on your schedule? The schedule says we're at the fucking museum and your people should be here."

Another pause. The skin on the back of my neck prickles.

Fidel disconnects. His hand is on my chair, and he's pulling me up before I even process it.

"Fidel, what—"

"We're leaving."

I glance at Elias. He's already pushing his chair back. Natalie exhales sharply but doesn't argue.

I, however, do. "Wait—"

Fidel ignores me. His grip tightens on my arm. Not enough to hurt, just enough to tell me this isn't up for discussion.

"The schedule was changed. Again." His voice is low, controlled. "We're leaving." I can hear something raw in his voice. Not just frustration. Fear. And something else—rage, maybe, that whoever's been fucking with his system got this close again.

I don't argue. Because I know what it means. Daniel's security people are supposed to be here. They're not. The schedule was changed without our knowledge. That's bad.

But I need to stay.

I need to speak with Kara about a deal for *The Dark Duke*. I need to make other connections, figure out my next move. MAVFest is almost over. This might be my only chance.

And Fidel is *ruining* it.

He's dragging me away from the one thing that could secure my future, and he's not even explaining why. Why this small change in security is so important, why he and Elias aren't enough to protect me. He's just gripping my arm, trying to lead me through the tables like I'm some helpless idiot who can't understand what's happening around me.

And maybe I could take it—if he'd said one word about what happened at Carlos's. The frosting on my finger. The way he looked at me. The way I was so sure he wanted me.

But he hasn't. Not once. Not since I walked into his house. Not since I put on his damn hoodie. Not since I've been sleeping under his roof. He just watches me like I'm a threat and touches me like I'm made of glass.

I'm not glass. I'm not fragile. I'm trying to hold everything together, and he's treating me like I'm a liability.

I wrench my arm away, glaring at him. "Fidel, let me—"

And then movement. A man who is not Jorge, not Luis, takes a step toward us, his mouth opening like he's about to call out.

Fidel sees him too.

The man is close now, hands raised, calm but firm. "Sir, I need you to step back from the lady."

It happens fast.

Fidel shoves him. A hard, controlled strike—flat palm to the chest, sending the guy stumbling back.

Gasps ripple through the nearby tables. Heads turn. Someone's glass tips over, a mimosa spilling over white linen.

"Fidel, *what the fuck*?"

But he isn't listening. His stance is already shifting, bracing, ready.

Shit.

The man recovers, stepping forward again, this time with purpose. And I realize—*he has a badge clipped to his belt.*

Museum security. Not a threat. And Fidel just *shoved* him.

Heat flares through my chest, fury snapping into place. I want to scream. At him, at the schedule, at this whole damn week that's slipping through my fingers.

This is it. This is exactly the kind of thing that will ruin everything for me.

I know what's going to happen. Because Fidel is calm and cool. Until he's not.

The first time he pulled something like this was the summer I turned seven. Miss Ana and Elena tried to organize a birthday party for me by the pool. Streamers, cake, plastic crowns. I think my father asked them to because he knew how unhappy I was with boarding school. They invited a handful of kids from their church and Fidel's school. I didn't know any of them. One boy— older, mean—kept laughing at me, calling me names. Said I was just a maid's daughter pretending to be a princess.

I didn't understand half of it. But Fidel did.

One second he was sitting quietly by the pool, watching. The next, he was on the kid—swinging, wordless, furious. Giving the boy a bloody nose, a busted lip, and a black eye. I'd never seen him like that. So angry. So violent. It was like he couldn't stop.

I remember grabbing his t-shirt. Tugging it, hard. He didn't look at me. Not at first. But I shouted at him, the way his mother did when she wanted him to stop.

"Fidel Mateo Cedillo!"

And he stopped. That fast. Just... stopped.

Now I see that same storm building in his eyes, jaw tight, body bracing. And I know—Fidel is about to ruin everything.

33

FIDEL

I DON'T THINK. I just react.

The second the guy steps forward, I hit him. Flat palm to the chest. A controlled strike. Measured. Precise.

The guy stumbles back, arms flailing like he didn't expect to get hit.

I step forward, closing the distance. "Who the fuck are you?" My voice is sharp, cutting through the murmurs rising around us. The adrenaline surges through me, hot and fast.

The guy holds up his hands, breathing fast. "I'm Eddie. Uh, museum security," he says, voice tight with shock, like I'm the one who's out of place here. "Sir, you need to calm down."

Gasps. A chair falling over. Silverware clinking onto plates.

"Isn't that..." someone whispers behind me. "That's Mercede Sanchez," someone else murmurs.

A glass tips over. The bright splash of mimosa against white linen.

I want to hit him, lash out. I pull my fist back to do it. But then—

"Fidel Mateo Cedillo!"

Maria's voice cuts through everything.

My body stills.

I don't even look at her. But I feel it. The command to calm down. To stop.

She says my name just like my mother used to.

My pulse is hammering, my jaw clenched so tight it aches. This isn't right. Nothing about this is right. The schedule change. The missing security detail. Maria's location compromised. Again.

The guy steps forward. Not as some unknown threat, but with the stiff-backed authority of someone who believes he belongs here.

And that's when I see it. The badge on his belt. Museum security.

Fuck.

Maria steps away from me like I'm the problem. "Jesus, Fidel," she hisses, voice low but sharp enough to flay me open.

The guy exhales hard, adjusting his stance. "Sir, you need to leave."

The words hit like a slap. I force myself to actually *look* at him.

Scuffed black dress shoes. Slightly too tight security uniform. Gold name badge that reads "Edward." Older, thick around the middle. Not trained for real combat. Just a guy used to watching security cameras and standing around in galleries. Museum security.

Not cartel. Not Los Cuervos. Not a threat.

And now, half the people here are staring. Conversations have died. Phones are coming out. I spot a man holding his phone just low enough to record without being obvious. A woman whispers to her friend, eyes wide.

They're not looking at a security incident. They're watching a scene. A scandal. Something to go viral. Something to ruin her. Ruin Maria.

I fucked up.

Elias steps in before I can say anything, smoothly cutting between us. "Apologies, Eddie," he says, flashing a smile that's all charm and no sincerity. "Misunderstanding. We're going."

The guard scowls, brushing off his uniform. "That wasn't a misunderstanding. That was *assault*."

Maria is still staring at me, but the fury in her eyes isn't only about what just happened. It's about the negative attention I've put on her. The deals I may have jeopardized. She's looking at me like I've *ruined* something.

And she's right. I didn't protect her. I embarrassed her. I didn't think. I lost it.

Because it wasn't about the job anymore. It was about her. The idea of something happening to her again, on my watch...

I couldn't breathe through it. I just moved. And now she's looking at me like she doesn't even recognize me.

"Fidel, let's just go." Her voice is controlled, but her hands are clenched at her sides. I know—she's *furious*. The kind of furious where you don't yell because if you start, you won't stop.

She doesn't wait to see if I listen. She just turns and walks away.

Elias doesn't give me a choice. He clamps a hand on my shoulder, steering me away.

"Let's go, *jefe*," he mutters.

I let him push me toward the exit. Not because I want to.

Because for the first time in a long time—

I completely fucked up. I lost control.

And I don't know if I can fix this.

34

MAVFEST DAY 8

Text Message Thread - Carlos Sandoval and Fidel Cedillo

Carlos: What the fucking fuck Fidel?

Fidel: Daniel was supposed to send Jorge and Luis

They weren't there

Guy looked weird

Carlos: Your excuse is the old fat security guard looked WEIRD???

Fidel: Misidentification.

Thought Maria's location compromised

Handled it

Carlos: She's not happy

That means I'm not happy

Keep her safe but DONT FUCK UP!!!

Fidel: Her safety is my priority

Always

Carlos: Good

———

Text Message Thread - Marco Cedillo and Fidel Cedillo

Marco: Heard about the museum

Fidel: Carlos already lit me up

Marco: Good. Raul also unhappy.

Fidel: I made the call. Misread the scene.

Marco: You don't get to misread.

Not on this job.

Not with her.

Fidel: Understood

Marco: You're in charge.

Get your shit together.

Don't let Maria run you. You run her.

She pushes. That's who she is. You don't get to break.

Not with her. Not with this family watching.

Fidel: Copy

Marco: You've still got her trust.

Don't waste it.

———

Text Message Thread - Maria Sandoval and Ami Zadegan

Ami: Omg. Maria. The museum. 😊

Fidel still breathing? Or should I send Marco to kill him?

Maria: Barely breathing. Both of us.

And no - don't need Marco to kill him.

Yet.

Ami: Just remember - it's all about you. You're in charge

Get what you want.

Maria: I miss you

Ami: I miss you too

Finish the festival - get the deal you deserve

Then we celebrate

———

Text Message Thread - Maria Sandoval and Natalie Morris

Maria: I think any chance at a deal just died

Kara and UV people saw the whole thing

Everyone saw

Natalie: LOL 😂

Those people? They live for chaos

You've just become 10x more interesting

Maria: You think its not over?

Natalie: Babe we've got you

Me El and Zara working back channels

Callie is turning it into a "moment" for socials

You WILL have a deal - even if we have to blackmail someone (maybe that blonde bitch - "you don't have a deal yet Mercede??? - fuck off lady)

Maria: kk thanks Nat 

Natalie: you know I love you and live for the duke!!

35

FIDEL

THE HOUSE IS QUIET.

I sit at the dining table, the glow of my laptop screen throwing sharp shadows across the room. My fingers hover over the keyboard, but my mind is stuck, replaying this afternoon at the museum. The way Maria yanked her arm out of my grip. The sharp snap of her voice—"Fidel Mateo Cedillo!"

I exhale slowly, pressing my knuckles into my eyes. I so fucked up.

Not in a way that put her in danger, not in a way that should matter. But in a way that matters to her.

I saw a threat and reacted. That's what I do. But she saw something else—me embarrassing her, making her look unstable in front of people she needs to impress. I shoved Eddie. A goddamn museum security guard. Overreacted like an idiot.

Even Elias didn't try to defend me. When we got home, Maria didn't say a word. Just stomped off, heading straight to her bedroom, leaving us both in the entryway.

Elias let out a slow breath, then slung an arm around my shoulders. "I'm only saying this because you're like a little brother to me," he said, voice dry. "But you fucked up, *cabrón.* Bad."

He dropped his arm, his tone turning serious. "You're the boss right now when it comes to security, Fidel. You give the orders. We follow your lead. But that means you can't lose your shit." His gaze sharpened. "Not again."

He was right. I should have kept my head. I should have assessed, calculated. But when I realized Daniel's men weren't there, when I saw that security guard watching us, when I knew someone had screwed with the schedule *again,* something in me snapped. Too fast. Too hard.

I can't make mistakes like this. I can't let emotion override instinct. I can't.

But with Maria. Shit.

I should apologize to her, beg her to forgive me. And I will. But right now, that won't fix the problem. The problem being someone is fucking with us.

I shove a hand through my hair, exhaling hard. I need to get my shit together. The screen in front of me blurs for a second, the lines of text bleeding into each other. I blink, refocus. *Fix the problem.*

And I start doing what I do. First, I pull up Maria's itinerary. The one that keeps changing when it shouldn't.

I start adding decoys, false events. I create fabricated itinerary entries in the schedule. Lunch at a downtown Austin café tomorrow. Meetings with Zara. Other MAVFest happenings. It will be confusing but I'll tell Maria and Daniel what to ignore. And if someone changes these events? I'll know.

Next, I set up notifications to monitor and track in real time. Any edit, any deletion, any fucking comma moved? I'll know. Every modification made—down to the second—will alert me. This means I'll be getting a lot of pings but I'll be able to check them as they happen. No delay. No lag.

I'll also trace signatures. No one gets in without leaving something behind. I'll track IPs, timestamps, encryption methods. I'll track everything. No matter what it is.

I finish rerouting the last of the live feeds through my hardened dashboard—four encrypted layers deep, with traceback scramblers and dead-man pings set to trigger on tamper. This isn't a patch job. It's a full reset. New protocols. Harder locks. Sharper blades.

I reassert full admin control and reclaim the back-end access. The tripwires I've laid aren't just passive—they'll bite back.

If it's Sloane Cross, she's not just erasing logs anymore. She's testing me. Watching to see if I can keep up.

And I can. I will.

I sit back, watching as the data streams in, clean for now. If it's Sloane, why? What the fuck does she gain by messing with Maria? I still haven't made the connection between Sloane and Los Cuervos. Between Maria and Los Cuervos. But I know it's there.

I close the laptop and rub at the ache between my eyes. This isn't just about the schedule.

Maria's been under my protection for years, and I've always done my job. Always handled it professionally. But lately—fuck, lately—it's like my brain short circuits when it comes to her.

I let my temper go hot today when it should have stayed ice cold. I let my hands move before my brain could catch up. Why? I don't fuck up like that. Not in a public place, not in front of people.

It's not just the job anymore.

I take a deep breath. Because right now, I need to do one more thing. It's the one last thing I hope will make things right.

I need to apologize to Maria.

I push up from the table I've been sitting at for hours. I roll my neck, working out the stiffness. It's late but I can see a soft glow in the living room. I know she's in there, alone.

I move toward it, the flickering light and low noise from the TV breaking the silence.

She's curled up on the couch, blanket pulled over her legs, watching *Harry Potter and the Goblet of Fire*. One of her favorites. A childhood comfort movie.

I stop at the threshold, watching her for a second.

She doesn't turn her head, but I know she hears me. Knows I'm here.

I exhale, dragging a hand over my jaw. Then I step forward.

Time to fix this.

36

MARIA

I know he's there.

Standing just inside the living room, watching. Waiting.

I don't look up. I don't acknowledge him. I let him stand there and suffer.

The Yule Ball scene flickers across the screen—the music swelling, Hermione descending the stairs in that floaty gossamer dress, the entire Great Hall turning to stare. It's as beautiful as I remember. Soft candlelight, glittering frost, everything transformed into a winter fairytale.

I pull the blanket higher, curling deeper into the couch.

Fidel still doesn't move.

Good. Let him feel how pissed I am. Let him think about how he humiliated me in front of Kara Lasater and a dozen other power players who will now remember me as the girl dragged out of the brunch by her violent bodyguard. The girl who couldn't keep her shit together long enough to finish a mimosa.

People saw that. Kara Lasater saw that.

I don't know what she thinks of me now, but it can't be good.

And if I can't close a deal for *The Dark Duke*, then what? My independence is slipping through my fingers, and the one person who's supposed to protect me is making it worse.

A deep breath. Measured. Controlled. I know him. He's trying to figure out how to do this. How to apologize.

Finally—

"Maria."

I don't answer.

Another second passes. Then, in a quieter voice, more careful this time.

"I screwed up today."

That gets my attention.

I glance over, just enough to see him standing stiffly near the couch, hands shoved in his pockets. His jaw is tight. His expression, usually so impossible to read, looks... troubled.

He hesitates, then exhales. "I overreacted. I saw a threat. I didn't think. I just reacted." His voice is low, rough around the edges. "I don't want to make excuses. But my job—the only reason I'm here—is to keep you safe. This whole trip, your security, all of it is on me. Your father put it on me. And when I saw that guy, when I realized Daniel's men weren't there..." His throat moves as he swallows. "Something in me snapped. And I'm sorry for acting that way. For treating you that way. I won't let it happen again."

He hesitates, then adds quietly, "And I should've said something sooner. About the other night in the kitchen. The frosting."

My breath stills.

"You looked at me like you were waiting for something," he says. "And I..." He trails off, jaw working. "I crossed a line."

A beat.

"I work for you. I protect you. That's it." His voice is rough. "Your father wouldn't approve. Your brothers wouldn't approve.

And I know you were just caught up in the moment." He swallows. "It was inappropriate. I apologize."

I study him, still curled under my blanket.

He's not just saying this because he feels guilty. He *means* it.

And that's the problem. Because he still doesn't see the real issue.

I shake my head slightly, turning my attention back to the screen. "You always do this, Fidel."

Another beat of silence. I don't have to look at him to know I have his full attention.

"You act like it's only about protecting me," I murmur. "Like I'm just your job." I take a slow breath. "But you don't react this way with anyone else. Only me."

The words settle between us.

Fidel doesn't move. Doesn't speak. And maybe that's answer enough.

For a long moment, neither of us says anything.

On-screen, the camera sweeps over the Yule Ball. Candles glowing, music drifting, the fairy-tale shimmer of it all.

Finally, I sigh and shift, making space on the couch. "Come sit down."

He hesitates, like he thinks this might be a trap.

Then, after a long pause, he lowers himself next to me.

He's stiff at first, like he's hyper-aware of how close we are. I toss part of the blanket over him.

His entire body tenses.

I smirk. "Relax, Fidel. We're just watching a movie. I won't bite you."

A slow exhale from his nose.

The movie keeps playing, the Yule Ball glowing with soft, golden light.

"When I was a kid," I murmur, "this was my favorite part of the movie."

Fidel shifts beside me. "I remember. Because of the dress."

"And the hair," I admit, smiling slightly. "The way it felt like magic. The winter wonderland of it."

I pause, staring at Hermione's face as she glares at Ron. "But now..." My voice is quieter now. "Now I see something else."

Fidel doesn't say anything. Just waits.

"It's not just about the dress or the hair." I watch Hermione blink fast, trying not to cry as Ron ruins everything. "It's because for the first time, we see her differently. Hermione is *strong, brilliant...* but her friends only notice her when they need her." I glance at the screen. "And then Ron finally sees it. That she's not just the useful sidekick. She's beautiful. She's magic." I take in a small breath, "I always hoped one day someone would see me like that."

Fidel is quiet for a long moment. Then, finally, he nods. "I can see that."

Something warm flickers in my chest. For a second, it's just the movie. Just the glow of the screen, the quiet, the soft flicker of candlelight on Hermione's face.

And then...

A memory.

I'm nine years old.

That long summer after Elena died. Fidel's big sister. My wished-for big sister.

Fidel was twelve. And he wasn't just quiet that summer. He was hollow. Like something had been scooped out of him and there was nothing left but an empty shell.

I remember the silence in the house, thick and heavy, pressing down on both of us. Miss Ana in the kitchen, crying softly into a dish towel. Marco wasn't home yet. He had to return to Afghanistan and was trying to get back. And their father? Hector? Fidel never talked about him but I knew. He wasn't around.

I knew Hector used to hit them. Miss Ana. Marco. Fidel. I never saw it but I knew enough. Knew that Marco took most of the hits. That Miss Ana flinched sometimes when people raised their voices. That Fidel tried to stay quiet and small.

And I knew that losing Elena, after all of that, broke something deep in all of them. Especially in Fidel.

It felt like everything was broken back then. Like nothing was safe anymore.

And the two of us—Fidel and me—we didn't know what to do. How to fix it. How to make any of it hurt less.

So we both stayed quiet. Stayed out of the way. Sat on the couch, under a blanket, and watched one movie. *Harry Potter and the Goblet of Fire.*

We watched it again and again and again.

It wasn't just a movie for us. It was something familiar. Something safe. Something that didn't change, even when everything else had.

I exhale slowly, shaking off the memory. But some part of me still feels it. The way it felt back then.

The way it feels now.

Maybe that's why I lean in without thinking. Not a lot. Just enough. Just the soft weight of my head against his shoulder. Like when we were kids.

Fidel tenses.

I half expect him to pull away. But he doesn't.

He stays still.

And after a long moment, I feel it. The slow, hesitant shift of his hand. Just the barest touch against my thigh. Not possessive. Not protective. Just there.

Like maybe, just maybe...

He *wants* to stay right here, too.

37

FIDEL

I SHOULD GET up and leave.

Maria is warm against me, curled under the blanket, her cheek resting lightly against my shoulder. Just like when we were kids. On screen, the Yule Ball glows with soft candlelight, but I don't see it. I don't see anything except her. The way my hoodie is too big on her, the way the cuffs swallow her wrists, the way the scent of her shampoo surrounds me.

I should move.

I don't.

I tell myself it's because I still need to fix things, that I'm still making sure she's okay after earlier. But that's a lie. It's not about the museum. It's not about the fucking schedule. It's her.

She shifts slightly, the barest movement, but I feel all of it. The press of her body, the warmth bleeding through the fabric, how she doesn't even hesitate before leaning into me like this is normal. Like we haven't spent years keeping a careful distance.

Like she isn't the one thing I can't have.

My hand is resting between where our thighs are pressed together, and I feel a buzzing in my fingers where they touch her. I should move.

Maria doesn't even look away from the screen as she murmurs, "You're always so tense, Fidel."

My chest tightens. I've heard that from her before.

It was Maria's prom night.

She was eighteen. I was twenty-one, home from college for the weekend, crashing in the guard house with Marco. Raul had made it clear—as with all of her dates—he wanted background checks, digital sweep, a full social media scrape. He wanted her prom date vetted like a potential business partner.

I knew everything about the kid before he even showed up at the door. Clean record, honor society, Catholic youth leadership program, GPA north of 4.0. A choir boy. Due for a refill on his acne medication. Raul approved.

I didn't care who this kid was. I was just doing my job.

She came home early.

The prom ended at midnight, and she was back by 12:05. Barefoot, holding her heels in one hand, eyes still sparkling from whatever magic the night had offered her.

I was in the kitchen, laptop open, pretending to work.

She floated in like a spell had been cast on her. Like she was still dancing.

Hair curled and pinned up, glitter dusted across her collarbones, lips a soft pink. Her dress was a pale rose color, layered and floating, off the shoulder, cinched at the waist. Just like the one that Hermione wore in the Yule Ball scene.

She twirled, just once, the skirt flaring around her like liquid light.

"Fidel," she said, grinning, "don't I look pretty?"

I couldn't speak.

Because she did. She looked... beautiful. Not a little girl anymore. A young woman. Gorgeous. Glowing. Alive. And for the first time, I saw her not as a mission or a responsibility. But as a woman.

A woman I wanted.

She stood beside me at the counter, talking about the prom decorations, the playlist, the stupid dancing, nibbling on a cookie like nothing about her had changed. Her perfume was soft and sweet, citrusy. I remember not looking directly at her because if I did, I wouldn't stop.

I remember thinking, *she has no idea what she does to people. What she's doing to me.*

She smiled, licked sugar off her fingertip, and kissed my cheek before skipping off to bed.

I didn't sleep that night. Something had changed in Maria. And worse—something had changed in me. I wanted her. In a way I wasn't supposed to.

And I knew that, no matter how long I protected her, or how much I wanted her, I'd never be good enough for her.

Now, sitting here with her against me again, older, bolder, and so fucking close... I feel it all over again. The want. The guilt. The hunger. And I'm just as wrecked as I was back then.

"Fidel? Hello?" Her voice brings me back to the present. I exhale slowly through my nose, refusing to react.

Only now? I'm not sure I can resist anymore.

She turns slightly, tilting her head up, just enough for her breath to brush my jaw. My pulse slams in response, but I keep still, rigid, locked down.

Maria waits. Watching me. Teasing me. Testing me.

Then, soft as silk—"Always so serious, Fidel. We're just watching a movie."

I go still. *Are we? Is that all this is?* Just a movie, just nostalgia, just a moment between two people who've known each other forever?

Or is something else happening?

My stomach tightens. *Fuck.*

She shifts again, this time with intent. Not an accident. Not just leaning in for comfort. *This is something else.*

I feel her eyes on me, studying me, weighing something.

Then, "Fidel," she says, voice low, "how come you've never asked me out?"

I freeze. I can't answer. My mind is a blank.

Not because I don't have reasons. Because I have too many.

Because I work for her father. Because I work for her. Because Raul would have Elias cut me open, bleed me like a pig, chop me into tiny pieces, and bury me in some remote desert if I touched her.

Because she's not just off limits. She's sacred. Untouchable.

And worst of all? Because she could do better than me. A lot better. I know it. We both know it.

"Maria, I..." The words catch. They're too big, too dangerous. "I can't... you know. I..."

I shut my mouth. Swallow hard. My throat tightens. My brain is still buffering, trying to come up with something smart. Something safe. But nothing comes.

Her face is so close now, her breath barely grazing my jawline. Not a kiss, but so close I feel it everywhere.

I grip the cushion under my fingers. I should push her away. I should stop this now.

I don't.

Maria waits a second. Then two. Just long enough for me to realize how badly I want to turn my head. Close the distance. Feel her lips on mine.

She smiles. Soft. Certain.

"It's okay," she murmurs.

I see it from the corner of my eye. She smirks. Then pulls away. Slowly. Deliberately.

Like she just tested a theory and got the exact answer she wanted.

She settles back against my shoulder like nothing happened, watching the movie again.

My hands are clenched. My body is on fire. I cut my eyes towards her and catch her smile. Subtle. Barely there, like she knows I can see it. Like she just won.

And fuck me—she did.

38

MAVFEST DAY 9

Timestamp: 1:24 a.m.

**Recovered Voice Note from Maria Sandoval's Phone.
Flagged and archived by Fidel Cedillo as part of digital security protocol. Not intended for upload or publication. Private access only.**

[Audio begins]

Okay... Book Three... maybe this works...

[soft exhale]

Lady Juliana is back on the Marquess of Ravenshire's ship.

She's furious—because of course she is. Because he lied. Again. Because he thinks protecting her means controlling her.

She storms into his private quarters, throws open the entry hatch, ready to tell him off...

And then she sees him.

He's at the edge of the room, half-shadowed in blue light.
Stripped down. Raw. One hand braced on the wall, the other
wrapped around his...

Member? Appendage? Shit.

Let's just go with his cock for now.

[sharp inhale, slight laugh]

Yeah. That.

She should leave. She should run. But she doesn't.

She whispers his name. Not the title. Not "your grace." Just...

[5 second silence]

Fidel.

[2 second silence]

Oh shit!

[fumbling sounds, mic cuts]

39

MARIA

After orchestrating a totally healthy breakfast—berries, protein smoothies, not a pastry in sight—I settle at the dining table, across from Fidel, who is buried in whatever deep-web hellscape he's mining for cartel information.

I'm *supposed* to be working on *A Marquess from the Stars,* but my focus keeps drifting.

"Hey," I say, stretching. "Let's talk logistics."

Fidel doesn't look up. "No."

Is he uncomfortable about watching the movie with me last night? Nothing happened. Even though I practically threw myself at him. He sat there, staring straight ahead like a statue. Such a coward.

So, I continue. "Say you're an alien prince. Your species is planning an invasion of Earth, and you're sent ahead to gather intel. But then you fall in love with a human and decide Earth is worth saving. How do you do it?"

His fingers still on the keyboard. He lifts his head just enough to give me a flat, unreadable look.

"You want me to strategize an alien invasion?"

"An invasion and a possible rebellion," I correct. "Remember, you might want to save Earth."

A slow blink. "Maria." He looks at me like I've lost my mind.

I grin and continue.

"Louis Blackmere—the Marquess of Ravenshire—is an alien prince whose people are scouting Earth for colonization, but his love for Lady Juliana De Winter makes him betray his own kind. He has to outwit both humans and aliens to stop the invasion and save the planet."

Fidel runs a hand down his face, muttering something in Spanish. *Me rindo?* He gives up? Good.

Then he says, "What is it with your alien nobles betraying their entire species for one girl with great tits?" He picks up something that's sitting next to his laptop, leans back in his chair, and stares at the ceiling.

He's definitely read my books. I knew it.

"I just need to know if it's feasible," I continue. "Because if Earth's defenses are too weak for the alien weapons..."

And then—I notice it. What he picked up. Something small and silver. Something that has been sitting on the table all week long but I hadn't really looked at.

A silver flip-top lighter, balanced between his fingers, his thumb flipping the lid open and closed with quiet, rhythmic clicks. He isn't lighting it. Just running through the motion absentmindedly, over and over, like he's done it tens of thousands of times before.

It takes me a second to register exactly what I'm looking at. My breath catches.

It's *my* lighter.

The one I gave him for his high school graduation, when I was fifteen, thinking I was so grown-up, so mature, for picking out a cool, manly, totally adult gift for him. The one I had engraved.

FC Don't Burn Anything Down Without Me 🖤 *MS*

I'd completely forgotten about it.

"You still have that?" I blurt out, before I can stop myself.

Fidel glances at me and then at the lighter in his hand as he continues to flip the lid. Open, closed, click, click.

"Yeah."

I stare at him. "You use it?"

He shrugs, like it's not a big deal. Like this isn't something he carries everywhere. Like it hasn't been sitting next to his laptop this whole time. Like he hasn't kept it for years.

He's had it all this time. How many times has he flipped that lid open and closed without thinking? In the back of a car, waiting for a job? Late at night, staring at the ceiling? Has he ever thought about me when he did it?

The idea sends something hot through my chest.

I try to smirk, to cover whatever it is I'm feeling. "Wow, fifteen-year-old me really picked the perfect gift."

"You picked a lighter for a high school kid who didn't smoke."

"Because I was *very* sophisticated." I grin. "The engraving? Chef's kiss." I bring the tips of my fingers to my lips and kiss.

At that, his lips twitch.

He kept it. Through college. Through years of working for the Sandovals. He kept it. And then he brought it here.

It isn't just some random object. It means something special to him. Doesn't it?

Maybe I mean something special to him.

That thought is too much, too big. I push it away.

Fidel, completely unaware of my mental crisis, stares back up at the ceiling. "So, the alien invasion?"

I swallow the knot in my throat and try to brush off everything I was thinking about the damn lighter. It doesn't mean anything. But I can't let it go.

I tap my chin dramatically as I consider every possible implication of the lighter. "So, you carry the lighter *everywhere* because deep down, you've always—"

"Maria." His voice has that low warning tone, the one that usually makes people shut up.

"Loved it." I grin wider.

He sighs, still staring at the ceiling. "Jesus Christ. It's a lighter." There it is. The break.

"That wasn't a no."

"It wasn't a yes, either."

"Sounds like a yes to me."

He goes back to his laptop, placing the lighter on the table. I go back to my manuscript although my mind is definitely not on *A Marquess from the Stars*.

It's on Fidel. And on the lighter he never let go.

An hour later, we're still working. "Fidel?'

"No, Maria."

I grin. "Great, Fidel. Always so helpful. I was just going to tell you that I gave Zara my terms for a possible deal with UltraVision so she's reached out to them and is working on that."

That got his attention. His brows lift, just slightly.

"Zara's working on it?"

I nod. "At my request. I told her to make an initial offer. She's keeping Carlos out of it."

Fidel doesn't respond, but something flickers in his expression—that brief moment of approval before he catches himself.

I lean forward, lowering my voice. "Are you proud of me for being assertive, Fidel?"

His jaw flexes. "No."

"Yes, you are."

I go back to my laptop, trying to work out the logistics of the alien invasion when my phone buzzes.

> Natalie: UltraVis moving screening tonight
>
> Paramount Theater - you must attend!!!
>
> movie - The Last Apology
>
> made in Texas, Kara acquisition
>
> UltraVis team will all be there
>
> You BE THERE!

I stare at the screen for a second. Then, without looking up, I say, "I need to go to a movie screening tonight."

Silence.

Then a dry, unimpressed response. "Not on the schedule."

"It's an UltraVision movie," I say, arms crossed. "Natalie says I need to go. I can be with you the whole time. And Elias. And Daniel's guys. We'll be safe. We'll make sure."

Fidel's expression is pure stone. "No."

"Please, Fidel. Please?"

He pinches the bridge of his nose and shakes his head. "Goddamn it Maria. This is serious."

I try again, using the sweet tone I know will cause him to break. "Pretty please, Fidel. I'll be a good girl."

I blink my eyes at him.

He lets out a growl. "Aarrggh!"

I knew it would work.

"No after-party," he snarls. "No 'Natalie says we need to meet execs at this rave.' Movie only."

"Yes sir. Whatever you say, sir."

"You'll stay at my side."

"Yes sir."

He narrows his eyes. "And if I say no to this whole thing?"

I smile at him. "Then I'll figure out a way to go anyway. I'm your boss, remember?"

His jaw locks. "Your father is my boss."

"Well, maybe we should call him. See what he thinks when I say I'm unhappy with my security detail." He hates that I'm pulling this card. That I would do it.

But I know I've already won.

"Jesus fucking Christ," he mutters. "Fine. But if you get into trouble—"

I look at him and see his scowl. "I promise I won't," I give him my best innocent face.

I grin as Fidel curses under his breath. I've definitely won.

But somehow, winning doesn't feel like enough anymore.

I look at him, really look at him. His tense jaw, the way his fingers drum against the table, that fucking lighter still sitting next to his laptop.

He's spent years trying to keep me at arm's length. Years pretending he doesn't want me.

But I've seen it now. Felt it.

The way he tensed when I curled into him last night. The way his pulse was hammering when I leaned in too close. The way he's kept that damn lighter nearby all these years.

He wants me. I know he does.

And I'm done waiting for him to admit it.

I push my laptop closed and stretch, slow and deliberate. Across the table, Fidel doesn't even glance up. He's focused on his screen, like if he ignores me hard enough, it'll make a difference.

It won't.

"I'm taking a break." I walk toward the stairs, my steps unhurried, intentional.

Fidel still doesn't look at me. That's fine.

But before I make it to the stairs, he says, "Just so you know, after the museum incident, I enhanced surveillance on all devices."

"Oh? Good for you."

"Including your phone."

"Great job, Fidel. Keep it up."

A pause.

"Including any voice memos you might've composed." He glances up. "Or deleted."

I stop. Turn. He meets my eyes. Smirks—just a flicker—and then goes right back to his laptop.

He heard it. The voice note. My little slip, using his name during the Marquess jerking off chapter.

I deleted it but he knows.

Good. I'm glad. I want him to know.

And while I don't know exactly what my next move is, I do know one thing.

I'm done waiting on Fidel.

40

FIDEL

THE PARAMOUNT THEATRE is a hundred-year-old shrine to cinema—ornate balconies, red velvet seats, a grand gold arch framing the screen like a stage set for royalty. It's packed. Industry power players, influencers, and locals all crowded shoulder-to-shoulder in the velvet-draped lobby, buzzing with the kind of excitement that only comes from limited tickets and too much money.

Maria stands in the center of it all like she belongs there.

Because she does.

She's radiant tonight. Cool confidence layered under barely contained nerves. Her short red dress stands out under the lobby chandeliers. She's smiling, laughing with Natalie, like she hasn't put herself under intense pressure.

But I see it. The way her eyes flick toward Kara Lasater, the UltraVision exec, across the room. Kara's talking to another producer, nodding, calm, polite.

Calculating.

I take my post next to Maria. We've done this right. The theater's been swept. Elias is inside with us. Jorge's posted near the theater entrance, Luis in the lobby. The rest of Daniel's crew is covering the edges of the crowd.

I've got the live feeds from the perimeter running through my phone. No changes. No tripwires triggered. So far, everything's clean.

If something goes wrong tonight, it won't be because we got sloppy.

Daniel checks in through the comm, "Fidel. Buddy. You look like you're about to body-check a studio head."

I grunt. "Depends on how this night goes."

Across the room, Kara spots Maria and walks towards us. Natalie sees it too—steps in to intercept but Kara doesn't slow. She's all high-end polish and business casual menace in a cream-colored suit and a black silk blouse. UltraVision money and power prefers to look understated.

Maria smiles and extends her hand. "Kara. So good to see you. We're very excited to see tonight's movie."

Kara takes her hand, but her smile is practiced. "It's a project I'm proud of. Glad you could come." She holds the handshake a beat too long. "You've certainly made an impression this week." A pause. "Most of it good."

Maria's posture doesn't shift, but I see the breath she holds.

Kara adds, offhand. "That was quite the scene at the museum yesterday. Very... dramatic."

My jaw clenches.

Maria answers smoothly. "A misunderstanding. Handled quickly."

Kara nods, her tone light but deliberate. "Still, you have a compelling story. Amazing genre, viral success, huge streaming potential. People are watching. But the attention's a double-edged sword."

Maria's smile never falters, but her eyes flash. "Only if you don't know how to use it."

Kara lifts a brow. "Well, UltraVision has definitely noticed. We're reviewing a few standout titles this week. Including your offer as relayed by Zara Caldwell. But the competition's fierce. We'll see what rises to the top." She offers a final handshake. "I'm glad you could be here tonight, Mercede. Enjoy the film."

Natalie lets out a soft, warning laugh, placing her hand on Maria's forearm. "We'll let you get back to your VIPs. We're looking forward to the screening."

Kara dips her head and disappears back into the crowd.

Maria exhales—barely—and catches my eye. A beat passes. She turns to me and slips her arm through mine. "Come sit with me?"

I nod, and let her guide me to our seats.

Inside, the lights dim. The film begins. Some polished, prestige-drama from UltraVision—shot in Texas, big-name actors, heavy on dramatic close-ups and emotional piano.

Maria leans in close. I feel the whisper of her breath against my neck.

"This could be my work. My movie," she murmurs.

I glance at her. She's not smiling.

She's serious. Hopeful. Desperate to belong to this world, on her own terms. Not because of her family name. Not because of fear.

Because she earned it.

I don't say anything. Just watch her as she turns back to the screen, her face bathed in the soft blue glow of the opening credits.

And for the next hour, I don't watch the movie. From the corner of my eye, I watch her.

41

MARIA

THE LIGHTS DIM inside the Paramount Theatre, and I settle into the plush red seat between Fidel and Natalie.

Fidel's on the aisle, his arms folded, jaw clenched, eyes fixed forward like we're here for a military briefing instead of a film screening. Natalie's scrolling her phone right up to the last second before the film starts, her legs elegantly crossed. Somewhere across the room, I know Daniel and his guys are scattered like shadows, posted at exits, corners, and balconies. Elias is out in the lobby, keeping watch. MAVFest security is nowhere near as tight as the Sandoval perimeter tonight.

But all I can feel is Fidel.

His body radiates tension, even seated beside me. Every line of him is sharp, immovable, impossible.

On screen, the UltraVision logo blooms into cinematic gold. The movie—*The Last Apology*—starts to play. It's the kind of elevated, emotionally-charged drama I'm sure Kara Lasater likes to brag about. The kind of project I could write. If I can just get the deal.

If. If. If.

That word repeats in my head. Kara's polite condescension

still echoes in my ears—"*the attention's a double-edged sword*"—and all I can think is: this movie could be *The Dark Duke*. If I land UltraVision, I could be watching *my* work up there one day.

I shift in my seat. I sigh. I try to watch the movie. But I can't.

I'm thinking about this afternoon. Talking to Fidel. Seeing the lighter. Listening to his apology. Thinking it all means something. And I decide this is the moment. This is when I stop waiting. When I take charge and finally do something completely, beautifully reckless.

I slide my hand onto Fidel's thigh.

He tenses instantly. Not a flinch—just a full-body alertness that ripples through him like electricity. He doesn't look at me. Doesn't say a word for a beat.

Then, under his breath, he whispers a single word: "Maria."

A warning. Sharp. But he doesn't move to stop me.

I press down, just slightly. The theater is dark. The lighting in this movie is dark. No one can see this.

His thigh is solid under my palm, warm even through the tailored fabric. My fingers drift higher—slow, deliberate strokes. Back and forth. Testing.

Fidel exhales through his nose. A whisper of sound. His jaw tightens.

Then I feel the shape of him through his trousers, beneath my hand. Long. Hard.

Very hard.

My heart is pounding in my ears. The room is dark, hushed, faces glowing in the reflected light from the screen. And all I can think about is the way I can feel him, the way his cock pulses under my palm. The way he still hasn't told me to stop.

I stroke him, light, slow movements, back and forth.

"Maria," he whispers again, voice thick, gritted. I can see his hand, gripping the armrest between us, his knuckles white. "Please."

I don't stop. But I slow. Just enough to let the moment stretch between us like a live wire.

He's breathing hard now, nostrils flaring, and I swear I can see a faint sheen of sweat at his temple.

I don't know how much time passes. Minutes? Hours? But I keep my hand in place, slowly stroking his thigh, the hard length of him, and Fidel doesn't stop me.

Then the screen brightens. The film fades into credits. People around us begin to clap.

Fidel doesn't move.

Natalie leans forward to whisper something to a producer down the row, while I sit very, very still, my hand still resting over the small damp spot on the fabric of his pants. Precum.

I glance at him. His head is tipped back against the seat. Eyes closed. Lips parted just slightly. Barely breathing.

I grin as I remove my hand and stand.

Eventually, he exhales hard through his nose. Mutters something in Spanish that sounds an awful lot like a prayer. Or a curse.

And finally, he gets to his feet. Quickly buttons his coat to cover himself.

I smooth down my dress, utterly composed. The theater lights rise. People begin filing out. We move with the crowd, Natalie stepping ahead of us in the aisle, still talking to the producer.

The lobby is buzzing with energy—filmgoers and industry execs sipping cocktails and trading opinions. The air smells like wine and expensive perfume. Flashbulbs pop near the front as a couple of actors pose in front of an UltraVision backdrop.

Fidel doesn't say anything about what just happened in the

theater. But his hand rests at the small of my back, firm and steady as he steers me toward the exit.

Outside, the night is warm and electric, humid, the sidewalk lit by marquee bulbs and traffic lights. A VIP valet zone has been set up just past the entrance, roped off from the crowd of festival-goers still spilling onto Congress Avenue.

Natalie stands beside me, deep in conversation with Elias. Daniel is scanning the crowd like a man hardwired for threat assessment. Fidel's hand still rests on my back, guiding me to the valet. We're waiting for Jorge and Luis to pull up with the SUVs.

And that's when I notice him.

A man slipping through the crowd. Noticeable because he's got facial tattoos and a weird, almost manic, grin on his face. He's elbowing people aside and carrying a bouquet of blood-red roses. Blood-red. Just like the bouquet at FutureFic.

He moves with unsettling calm, his steps directed and sure. Ignoring the crowd. Moving straight toward me.

"Pardon me, miss," he says, stopping a foot away, fixing on me with that unhinged smile. "Are you Maria?"

Fidel steps between us in one brutal motion. Instinctive. Lethal. No words. No hesitation. Just immediate, controlled violence coiled tight beneath the surface.

His entire body shifts—from alert to dangerous, like a weapon unsheathed.

And just like that, the air around us sharpens.

Because something's coming.

The crowd keeps buzzing. The night keeps shining. But I know.

Everything's about to break.

42

FIDEL

THE MOMENT I see the man's eyes, I know something's wrong. He's not some clueless delivery kid or low-rent gofer. He moves too smooth, stands too still. His smile is deranged. The bouquet he's pushing toward Maria is an act. A cover.

I'm immediately in motion. And when he says Maria's name, I shove her and Natalie behind me, hand already out, Elias flanking my right.

"Get them out. Now," I snap at Daniel. Jorge is pulling up in one of the SUVs. Daniel hauls the door open and pushes both women in. Maria starts to protest, but Daniel doesn't give her the chance to argue. He slams the door shut and pounds the side, signaling for Jorge to go.

Elias grabs the guy's arm. "Let's go, *compañero*." He frog-marches him down the sidewalk, through the crowd and toward a dark, narrow alley beside the theater.

The guy doesn't resist, still clutching the bouquet. But he's watching everything. Counting exits. Measuring distance.

Daniel and I flank Elias and the guy, scanning for any backup he might have or any eyes on us. There's nothing. Looks like he's working alone.

Did he really have the balls to just walk up to us? This motherfucker's got no credentials. No wristband. No badge. How the fuck did he get this close?

We drag him deep into the alley, away from the lights and the crowd. We stop between a few dumpsters. No one can see us here. No one can hear.

The air smells like piss and rot. Elias and Daniel hold his arms, pinning him against a brick wall. A dim security light several feet down flickers, giving off just enough light to see the guy.

He looks to be mid-thirties. Buzzed head. Greasy mustache. Facial tattoos curling down to his neck. Prison ink. Two teardrops under his left eye. Bad teeth. Beat up leather jacket barely hiding a shoulder holster. Not just scum. Hardened scum.

"So you're here to deliver something?" I ask, voice low, even. I need him talking before I tear his jaw off.

"Just a gift," he says with a smile that oozes contempt. He still has the bouquet in one hand, holding it like he's at a fucking wedding. "For Maria. From an admirer."

I snatch it out of his hand. Blood-red roses. Tied to the stems is a slim black gift box.

My stomach drops.

I take the bouquet, tear off the gift box and open it. The necklace inside gleams like a snake. Heavy platinum links. Large emeralds. Oval cuts. Halos of diamonds. A match for the earrings delivered to Maria at FutureFic.

A set.

The message is louder now. Whoever the stalker is, he's dressing her in jewelry. He thinks she already belongs to him.

I toss the necklace and the bouquet down into the trash strewn in the alley.

Elias tightens his grip. "Start talking."

The man doesn't flinch. "I just deliver what I'm paid to."

"Paid by who?" I growl.

"Don't know. Doesn't work that way." He shrugs like we just asked about the weather. "Client with deep pockets. Said it was for Maria. Said I needed to make sure she got it and she'd know what it meant."

"You working for Los Cuervos?" I snarl.

That finally gets a reaction. He barks a laugh. Ugly and sharp. "Los Cuervos? Los Gringos? I got no fucking idea, man. I work for whoever pays me the most. I don't ask questions."

Elias and I exchange a glance. This guy's not Los Cuervos. Not cartel. He's local scum. Brought in for one job. And I don't think he knows who the fuck we are.

"You're lying," I say, stepping in close. "You know exactly who sent you."

"Buddy, I don't get paid enough to lie," he sneers. "So if you're just asking questions I don't have answers for, I suggest you—"

I punch him in the gut—hard.

He grunts and folds over. Elias and Daniel pull him back up. I punch him in the face. Then punch again. And again. Until blood spatters across him. Across me.

Elias leans in. "You really should answer him, *buddy*. You don't want what's coming next."

The guy coughs, spitting blood. Then grins. "I've had worse. And the guy who sent me? Pretty sure he's just getting started."

I stop caring. All I can see is the frightened look on Maria's face when she saw the roses.

Jab. Jab. Uppercut. Just like Marco taught me.

It feels good to lash out. It feels amazing.

His head snaps back. Hits the brick wall. Nose breaks with a crunch. Blood pours down over his mouth and that greasy mustache. Elias and Daniel release him. He drops like a sack of bricks into the trash at our feet.

I keep going. Kick him in the stomach. Then the ribs. Then the crotch. I want him broken.

He wheezes, gasping for air. No more wisecracks now.

I raise my boot again, about to cave in his jaw, when Elias grabs my arm. "Fidel. Enough."

I don't move. Not right away. My fists throb. My pulse is through the fucking roof.

"This guy's a nobody," Elias says. "He's a hired hand. Think. You don't want to kill him. You want him to go back, deliver a message."

I step back, panting, chest heaving. Elias is right.

The guy groans.

I crouch down, grab his shirt, haul him up to his knees. His eyes are already swelling shut, his head lolling to one side. Blood covers his face, and is soaking his shirt and his dirty leather jacket, pooling on the dirty pavement under him.

"You tell your boss—whoever the fuck he is—he doesn't get to touch her." My voice is low, deathly calm. "Not ever." I lean in, close enough for him to see the blood covering my hands, my face. His blood.

"And I'm coming for him. Make sure he knows."

I drop him. He hits the pavement and doesn't move.

Elias exhales. "Let's go."

"Yeah, let's get out of here," Daniel agrees.

I glance at the necklace still lying in the trash, glittering in the streetlight.

Another gift. Another breach. Another threat wrapped in emeralds and diamonds.

I think of Maria. She's probably furious right now. She's probably scared.

I let someone get too close. Again. Maybe she thinks I can't keep her safe. Maybe she's right. I run a hand over my face. Blood. Sweat. Guilt.

I'm not just screwing this up. Someone's getting closer. I'm losing control. I'm losing her.

And if I can't protect her—then what the fuck am I even doing?

43

———

FIDEL

I STEP out of the shower still vibrating with adrenaline. My knuckles are split and raw. My ribs ache from the effort of beating the shit out of that guy. I couldn't stop. Wouldn't stop. And even now, after a twenty-minute blast of cold water, I'm still not sure stopping was the right thing to do.

I wrap the towel around my waist, gripping the edge of the bathroom counter with both hands, staring down into the sink.

I failed again. Someone got close to Maria. Again. Right under my nose. And beating the guy half to death didn't fix a goddamn thing.

I shut the bathroom light off and step into the dark. My bedroom's quiet except for the soft hum of my laptop on the desk, still running background scrapes on Sloane Cross's activity.

I sit back on my bed, towel still around my waist, head resting on the headboard, trying to just breathe.

I'm failing. I'm completely failing.

Then I hear it. Three soft knocks. Not rushed. Not urgent. But deliberate.

I look at my bedside clock. 2:37 a.m.

The door opens. Maria.

"Fidel?"

She steps into my room, wrapped in a silk robe, open and sliding off one shoulder. Silk shorts. A tiny camisole. No teasing smirk. No bratty grin. Her expression is soft. Concerned.

I pull the bed sheet over me, trying to hide everything.

"It's late. What do you need, Maria?"

She lets the door click shut behind her and crosses the room. She sits on the edge of my bed. Close. Too close.

"I wanted to check on you. Make sure you're okay."

I look away. Don't look at her soft hair falling over one shoulder. Don't look at her bare legs, curling under her.

She reaches out. Her fingers trace my wrist, my scraped knuckles. "You're hurt."

"He looks worse."

"I'm sure he does." She takes in a small breath. "You protected me. You always do." Her voice is soft, steady. She climbs up further onto the bed, shifting onto her knees to face me, her silk shorts riding up her thighs and her robe opening just enough for me to see the top of the curve of her breasts.

I feel a knot in my throat. It's hard to speak. "I have to keep you safe."

"You do keep me safe."

"Not this time." I can feel the heat from her body washing over me and my cock is already getting hard.

She moves closer, her knees against me. She reaches her hand out to my thigh. "You will. I believe in you."

My breath shudders out. I try to focus on my hands in my lap, clasping them together tightly to keep them from moving toward her. Try to focus on controlling my breathing. Try to focus on anything but Maria's breasts, moving with each breath she takes and each word she speaks. On the outline of her pebbled nipples, visible through the thin silk of her pajama top.

She lifts her hand, rests it against my chest. Her palm splayed, warm, grounding. "Let me take care of you tonight, Fidel."

"Maria—"

"Just let me," she whispers.

And then she kisses my jaw, soft and warm, her hand sliding lower.

I don't stop her.

Maria reaches for the sheet. Slow. Deliberate.

The second her fingers brush the edge of the sheet, I know what's happening. I know I should stop her. We aren't talking about her book anymore. About what happened tonight.

This is wrong. This is definitely wrong and I should stop her.

But I don't. I can't.

She slowly pulls back the sheet, inch by inch, her gaze flicking down. She can see exactly what she's doing to me.

My cock is already stiff, tenting the white cotton towel still wrapped around me. The heat of her body is so close now, coming off her in waves. Her orange blossom scent wraps around me like a noose.

She reaches out, her fingertips ghost along my length, tracing me through the towel.

Fuck.

I grit my teeth, muscles locking, every nerve in my body bracing against the stupid, reckless, undeniable need slamming through me.

Her palm flattens against me. And begins moving up and down the thick towel covering my cock which is now painfully hard.

I suck in a sharp breath. *I should stop this. Now. I can't let this happen.*

But my control is slipping like sand through clenched fists. Going. Going. Gone.

Maria shifts closer, her knees pressing into my thigh, her hair falling over one shoulder as she looks down at her hand, as if fascinated by the way my cock hardens even more beneath her touch.

Slowly, she drags her fingers to the edge of the towel, pulling back just enough to touch the head of my cock. Enough to send a white-hot pulse of heat straight to my spine.

I clench my jaw. "Maria."

"Shh," she whispers. She doesn't stop. Doesn't hesitate.

And I don't stop her. I watch her hand instead.

With a small, satisfied hum, she pulls the towel completely away, my cock now uncovered, thick and aching.

She gasps softly, and *fucking hell,* that sound—it sends something dangerous through me.

I watch her watching me, her lips parting as she gently wraps her fingers around my shaft. This might be the first time she's ever touched someone like this.

That thought wrecks me.

The thought that she's never done this before. That I might be the first. Probably am the first. That I'm the one. That she's discovering me, exploring me, learning the way I feel beneath her hand.

A bead of precum slicks over the swollen tip of my cock, and she swipes her thumb over it, rubbing it across the head, curious, mesmerized. A shudder passes through me.

"I'm going to take care of you. Make you feel good," Maria whispers, her eyes never leaving my cock.

I'm going to lose my mind. All control is gone. I will do whatever Maria wants. Give her whatever she wants.

She begins slowly moving her hand up and down my shaft. Her grip loose. And each time she comes up to the tip, she swipes her thumb over it, soft and devastating.

My head drops back and I let out a ragged exhale. It feels fucking amazing.

She tightens her grip a bit, speeds up her strokes, always rubbing her thumb across the head when she reaches it. I look down at her hand and then into her eyes.

She's watching me, paying attention to every reaction I have, learning exactly what I like. It feels so good it's almost painful. "Does this feel right?"

I give in to her.

I drag in a ragged breath. "Spit in your hand," I whisper.

She pauses her soft strokes, looking at me, questioning what I'm saying.

I barely have the restraint to choke out, "Spit, Maria. In your hand."

She obeys, taking her hand from my cock and raising it to her mouth.

A single line of spit drips from her mouth into her palm. *Fuck me.*

I groan, deep and raw, my head dropping back for half a second before I force myself to look at her again.

She wraps that slick palm around me and begins stroking me again.

Jesus.

The wet glide of her grip is so good I nearly come right then.

She keeps going, watching me carefully, listening, adjusting her rhythm, her pressure, learning how to unravel me.

"Like this?" she murmurs softly, almost breathless.

I growl, my hips jerking up, desperate for more.

I cover her hand with mine, guiding her, showing her how tight, how fast.

Her hand is so small under mine, so soft, so eager, her strokes perfect, relentless, pushing me toward the edge, shoving me over it.

I suck in a sharp breath, pleasure building, coiling tight, my spine stiffening, my abs tightening.

Her eyes are now locked on mine. Our hands pumping up and down my rock hard cock. I can feel the orgasm building. My balls tightening. It's going to be too much. Too much for her first time. But I can't get control of it. I can't stop.

"Maria—" My voice is wrecked, strangled. "If you don't stop, I'm going to—"

She grips me harder, stroking faster.

I slam my head back against the pillow.

My orgasm rips through me, brutal and unstoppable, my vision blurring as my entire body seizes, back arching, hot ropes of cum striping across my chest, my hand, her hand. Every muscle spasming. Over and over.

"Maria," I gasp out. I can't breathe. The pulses won't stop. It's the most intense thing I've ever felt.

Then. Finally. It's slowing as the aftershocks move through me.

It takes me a second to recover—longer than it should—and I realize she's still watching.

Looking at all that cum covering her hand. Covering me.

Maria reaches out toward my chest, tentatively. She touches me with her finger tips. She presses her hand to me, slowly spreading my cum over my chest, circling my nipples. Like she's marking me.

Her eyes don't leave mine as she brings her hand to her mouth and slowly licks her palm and each of her fingers clean.

Holy fuck.

My body, still trembling from release, jerks in response. It's obscene. And perfect. And I want more.

A silent moment stretches between us, charged and heavy, nothing but our breathing in the dim light.

Then, without a word, Maria slips back from me, moves off

the bed. She stands and smooths her hands down her robe. She turns, padding toward the door.

She pauses, one hand on the door handle, and looks back over her shoulder.

She smiles at me. A small, secret smile. Just for me.

Then she's gone. The door clicks shut.

I stare down at my chest, heart still pounding, body still reeling, everything I thought I knew completely fucking gone.

There's a message here spread across my chest. She left it for me.

Maria is in control now.

Of me. Of everything.

Fuck. Me.

44

MARIA

I WAKE UP WARM, loose-limbed, and thrumming with satisfaction.

I stretch beneath my sheets, my body still humming from the night before. For the first time in a long time, I don't feel restless. No edge of frustration, no creeping sense of dissatisfaction. Just an ache in all the right places, a heat that hasn't fully faded.

I don't think about the weird guy with the red roses. I don't think about Kara Lasater and a deal with UltraVision.

I just think about Fidel.

I smile against my pillow, eyes still closed, replaying every second of what happened.

Fidel's body beneath my hands. His muscles coiled so tight with restraint. How he had snapped when I finally pushed him over the edge. The shudder that had ripped through him when he came, his fingers gripping my hand. And his voice—hoarse, almost strangled as he groaned my name.

I did that to him. Me.

I'd never felt so... powerful.

Until last night, sex had been distant, theoretical. The kind of thing that worked in stories, but never seemed to land in reality.

I'd kissed a boy in high school, at a post-game party, let him touch me while his breath reeked of cheap beer and mint gum. His hands had been too eager, too clumsy, groping like he was searching for something instead of savoring. I had tried to feel what I was supposed to—heat, excitement, anything—but it never came. Just discomfort, impatience, the vague sense that I was letting him down because I wasn't responding the way girls in movies did.

I had faked a shiver when his fingers slid beneath my shirt. Let out a small gasp because I thought I should. But inside, I had felt nothing.

So then I did what I always did when reality didn't measure up to expectation. I researched.

I read erotic romances, analyzed every scene, dissected what made certain moments feel electric. I learned which words tightened the chest, which descriptions made a person ache. I watched a lot of porn, noted the mechanics, cataloged the rhythms and sounds that seemed to matter. And when I started writing my own books—especially *The Dark Duke*—I poured all of that into my stories.

And the nice thing about alien sex?

You didn't need real experience for it to work.

No one was going to fact-check you on what it felt like to have a double-tongued alien prince lap between your thighs or a tentacled warlord pinch your nipples in ways no human ever could.

I was building my career writing sex that people devoured. I was writing scenes that made strangers sweat, that made readers moan into their pillows and press shaking fingers between their legs.

And yet, when it came to me? My own body? My own pleasure? Even when I had touched myself, it had been just a release. A quick way to take the edge off, like stretching out a tight muscle or cooling down after a run.

None of it had ever felt real.

Until last night. Until Fidel.

When I finally crawled into bed, my mind had been spinning, my skin tingling, my body restless in a way I couldn't ignore. I tried to sleep. Tried to let that feeling fade.

But it wouldn't.

I had closed my eyes, my breathing shallow, the sheets soft against my bare skin. And I let myself remember exactly what had happened.

Fidel, leaning back against his pillows, exposed and powerless to stop me. His broad chest rising and falling, his pupils blown, his mouth slightly open, trying and failing to catch his breath. His cock heavy in my hand, hard steel covered in soft velvet, his body shuddering as I had stroked him.

I did that to him. Me.

That thought alone sends a fresh pulse of heat between my thighs.

I slide a hand down my stomach, my fingers slipping beneath the waistband of my silk shorts, my breath catching at how wet I am.

I exhale slowly, sinking into the feeling.

One finger first, tracing a slow, teasing circle. Then two, spreading the slick warmth, a soft whimper escaping before I can stop it. I press deeper, my other hand gripping the sheets as I rock my hips up, into my own touch, chasing the friction.

It isn't enough.

I let my mind go back to him—his hitching breaths, the sharp lines of his torso—golden skin stretched over hard muscle, a faint trail of dark hair leading down to his stiff cock. He had looked unfairly perfect—untouchable, unreadable.

My fingers circle my clit, moving faster. I think of Fidel's voice, slow and heavy, telling me to spit in my hand. Of the way he had put his hand over mine, guiding me, showing me exactly how he wanted me to stroke him. Up and down. Soft and slow at first. Then harder. Faster.

I imagine those hands on me, his mouth at my throat, his breath hot against my ear as he growls my name.

My back arches as pleasure gathers low in my belly, spiraling, winding, coiling.

I think of that hot cum, pumping from his cock, covering his chest, my hand, and how it had tasted when I put my fingers in my mouth and sucked the cum off. How absolutely feral his eyes had gone watching me.

I come hard, trembling, gasping his name into the pillow.

And when it's over, when I lay there wrecked, breathless, still pulsing with aftershocks, one thing is clear.

This isn't something I can ignore. This isn't a line we crossed. The line is gone, erased.

Something between us has changed.

I know it. And Fidel will know it too.

I practically float out of bed, grinning as I shower, throw on an oversized T-shirt and shorts, and slip downstairs. Fidel is probably already awake, probably waiting for me, probably just as affected as I am.

I find Elias in the kitchen, standing in a long-sleeved t-shirt at the counter, scrolling through his phone as he eats scrambled eggs straight from the pan.

"Where's Fidel?" I ask, grabbing a mug and filling it with coffee.

Elias doesn't even look up. "Didn't hear him come down."

My stomach flips.

That's fine. He's probably still asleep. Or avoiding Elias.

I take my coffee to the dining room and open my laptop, the anticipation still warm in my chest. I'll give him time.

He'll come down. He'll find me.

Because he wants me. I had felt it.

And then—

Hours pass.

By noon, the afterglow has dimmed.

By one, it's cracked.

By two, it's shattered.

I'm not an idiot. I know how Fidel operates, know how easily he shuts down, how he retreats into himself the second things get too real.

But this? This is different.

This isn't just avoidance. This is hiding.

My fingers hover over my keyboard, motionless, my pulse pounding with a new kind of heat.

Did I do something wrong? Did I push too far? The thought makes my stomach churn. But no—I didn't.

He wanted it.

He had been shaking.

He had *let* me touch him.

And now he's running.

I clench my jaw, slamming my laptop shut.

Fine.

Fucking fine.

I'm sick of this back and forth. If Fidel wants to be a pathetic little bitch about this, that's his problem. But I'm not going to sit around and keep waiting for him to figure out what he wants.

I go back to my laptop, trying to work out the logistics of an alien invasion when my phone buzzes.

An unhinged text from Lily. A concert tonight. She sends me the details. UltraVision has a VIP area.

And just like that, I decide. I'm going. I'm going to make a fucking deal with UltraVision happen if it kills me.

And if Fidel doesn't like that, fuck him.

I'm going to this concert. I'm the boss. He's my bodyguard. So he's taking me. No questions asked. Same car. Same venue. Same breathing space. All night.

And if he wants to pretend nothing happened? Fine. But I'm going to make sure he regrets it.

I text everyone. Lily first. *"Yes, girlie! You know I'll be there!"*

Then Fidel. Elias. Daniel. Natalie. Let them know the plan.

And then I turn off my phone.

I shove back from the table and head upstairs, my mind already shifting from hurt to strategy. I want him to suffer. Want him to see every inch of what he couldn't bring himself to face.

I throw open my closet and flip through my things. I need something for this concert that's skin tight. Something sexy. No, not sexy. Slutty. Skanky. Lewd.

Something that will make Fidel clench his jaw and grip his thighs just to keep himself from reaching for me. I want his dick to be rock hard all night long.

My fingers close around a tiny slip of fabric, a top cut to show almost everything. Black. Silk. Absolutely filthy.

I smile.

Let's see you ignore me now, Fidel Cedillo.

45

———

MAVFEST DAY 10

Text Message Thread - Lily Renshaw and Mercede Sanchez

Lily: MERCEDESSSSSSSSSSSS

Tonight. You MUST be at Neon Soundstage omg

It's going to be ICONIC. The vibes unreal.

Celebs, producers, influencers, UltraVis. Plus people I hate.

I need you.

Sending deets

Mercede: Yes, girlie! You know I'll be there!!!

———

Official App Notification, Push Alert – All Badge Holders

TONIGHT ONLY

🎤 **NEON SOUNDSTAGE** – Presented by **HelixVape x Widow-maker Records x Eclipse Cinema Collective**

East River Fields, Downtown Austin

Gates open at 8:00 PM | Show starts at 9:30 PM

🎶 **LINEUP INCLUDES**
- **The Crystal Fangs** – post-synth grunge icons
- **Nova Raye** – chart-topping alt-pop siren
- **DJ NoSaint** – live remix set with visuals by GlitchCoven
- **Special unannounced guest set** rumored after midnight

⚡ LED wristbands synced to the beat

🎥 Interactive media walls + real-time crowd cam projection

🍸 Platinum Badge Holders: VIP terrace bar + private viewing zone

⚫ **NO RE-ENTRY**

🚗 Rideshare drop-off/pick-up at 7th & Chicon ONLY

👮 Enhanced security screening in effect

This is MAVFest's final all-badge blowout - Come loud - Come lit - Come legendary

———

Text Message - Group Chat: Maria Sandoval, Fidel Cedillo, Elias Vasquez, Natalie Morris

Maria: We're going to Neon Soundstage concert tonight. Entire team. Fidel - please make necessary security arrangements.

We leave at 8 pm.

———

Text Message Thread – Lily Renshaw and Mercede Sanchez

Lily: MERCEDESSSSSSS WHERE R U

u better be coming

i have sequins on my SEQUINS

Mercede: I'm coming. Calm down.

Lily: calm is for losers

i'm by the UltraV VIP ropes

look for the disco ball in human form

Mercede: Let me guess. Gold?

Lily: duh

it's a moment

also Sloane's here—running socials, probs hunting for viral angles

Lily: BE HOT BUT STRATEGIC

Mercede: I'm always both.

Lily: hurry. they're doing crowd cam chaos in 10 min

Mercede: On my way

———

Email sent to inbox for https://mercedesanchez.com

User: WingsofBloodandGlory

You were radiant at the movie screening, Maria.

But tonight, you'll truly bloom. I hope you wear the jewelry -
one day that's all you'll wear.
And look for the roses. When the petals fall, everything changes.
I'm getting so close.

46

FIDEL

Maria comes down the stairs, and I forget how to function. My breath stalls. My pulse spikes, sharp and sudden. I can feel my face and chest heating.

I had expected trouble tonight. But not this kind of trouble.

She's wearing all black. A tiny leather skirt that's way too short. Cowboy boots that make her legs impossibly long. A silk top that's cropped, sleeveless, backless, and exposes almost everything. Her hair is down and she's let it go wild, untamed.

She looks like sex and chaos. She's doing this on purpose.

I force my hands to stay at my sides. Gripping them into fists would be too obvious. Speaking would be worse. I can't let what's happening to me show.

Elias lets out a low whistle from the front door. "Damn, Maria. Cowgirl skank. I like it."

Maria flashes him a grin. "Thank you, Elias. And also fuck off. This isn't for you."

She reaches for her jacket, but then stops.

"It's so warm outside. And with the crowd. I don't think I'll need a jacket. What do you think, Fidel?"

I still haven't said a word.

Elias flicks his gaze to me. Then to Maria. Notices. Stays silent.

I clench my jaw, forcing my expression into something neutral. I won't say anything about this outfit. "This is a bad idea, Maria."

Maria tilts her head, studying me. Eyes sharp. Gaze hard. And I know. I'm fucked.

"I want this. So we're going. Just do your job," she says. Then she brushes past me toward the door.

I grit my teeth and keep quiet. She thinks she's won. And maybe she has. But this isn't just about her outfit. Not about her ego. It's about control.

She wants this concert? Fine. But we go on my terms. With my perimeter. My eyes on every exit.

If someone makes a move tonight, I'll be waiting.

I spent the day holed up in my room, pretending to work. I told myself I was focused on figuring out who's tracking Maria and why. I thought I was making progress. But I barely absorbed a single line of text. The numbers blurred, the data refused to stick, and no matter how many times I refreshed the screen, my mind kept circling back to one thing.

Maria.

Maria, in the dark. Maria, in my bed. Maria, touching me, stroking me, dragging me to the edge and shoving me off the cliff like she knew exactly what she was doing.

Maria, licking my cum off her fingers like she was claiming me. Like she was telling me, without a single word: *You're mine now.*

I want her. I fucking *need* her. And that's the problem.

I didn't stay locked in my room all day because I was afraid she regretted what happened. I stayed locked in my room because I was afraid she didn't.

Because if Maria looks at me with even a fraction of the

certainty she had last night—if she so much as smiles at me like she knows what she did to me...

I won't be able to stop myself.

And I have to stop myself.

I can't be the man who lets Maria Sandoval strip him of control, who forgets his job, forgets his purpose, forgets every fucking reason he's spent years keeping her at arm's length.

So I hid. Like a coward. Like a pathetic fucking idiot who thought distance would be enough to fix this.

And now?

Now she's wearing this next-to-nothing outfit, and I realize exactly how stupid I am.

Because Maria isn't backing down. She isn't pretending last night didn't happen.

She's doubling down. And I'm in so much fucking trouble.

On the way to the venue, the car is too small, too confined, and Maria is too damn close.

Elias drives. Daniel and his team follow in another vehicle. Maria and I sit in the back, her knee barely an inch from mine.

She smells like orange blossoms and warm spice—something that seeps into my skin, into my lungs, until all I want to do is bury my face in her hair. Instead, I keep my gaze locked on the window, ignoring all of her soft, golden skin exposed by her damn top, ignoring the way she keeps shifting, full of restless energy.

I can't let myself want this.

"This is going to be amazing," she says. "Live music, industry people everywhere. UltraVision is setting up a whole VIP area near the stage, so I should be able to talk to Kara again. *This* is exactly what I need."

I can feel her excitement buzzing in the space between us. Excitement. Freedom. Her happiness should make me happy.

Instead, it makes me fucking furious.

"Are we sure this is a good idea?" Elias says, glancing at me in the mirror. His tone is casual, but I know what he's really asking.

Have we covered all of our bases? Is Maria truly going to be safe?

"If we pull her now, she loses everything," I say quietly. "The deal. The momentum. The visibility."

And if someone's planning to show up tonight? Good. I want him to. Let's find out how close he really is.

Maria responds. "This is a great idea. And it's what I want."

I feel her looking at me. I keep my eyes forward. If I look at her now, I'll lose whatever grip I have left.

She sighs dramatically. "Jesus, Fidel. Relax."

"You say that like I won't throw you over my shoulder and take you home if necessary."

Elias snorts. Maria, unimpressed, crosses her arms.

"Please," she scoffs. "Like you'd actually take some initiative and do anything." She turns towards me, staring at me with narrowed eyes. "I'm the only one with enough balls to take action." She turns back to her window.

Yeah. She's pissed. And she wants me to know it.

We arrive. And it's hell.

The outdoor venue is packed, a pulsing sea of bodies pressed together, music vibrating. Stale beer, sweat, and vape smoke thickens the air. The bass pounds through my chest—not in a way that feels alive, but in a way that sets my teeth on edge.

Massive screens flank the stage, flashing abstract visuals and media company logos synced to the heavy bass. Colored lights cut through the haze of vape smoke, LED wristbands blinking in sync with the rhythm.

A lighting rig spans the stage and dance floor—metal trusses and suspended FX equipment mounted above the crowd. Colored lights strobe across bodies pressed tight, dancing up against each other. The VIP section near the stage glows faintly gold, roped off and guarded, with film execs and influencers already clustering near the front.

It's loud. Unpredictable. Too many bodies. Too many exits. Too much unpredictability. I fucking hate this.

But Maria is completely in her element.

She scans the space, eyes bright, absorbing everything like she belongs here. I keep one hand near my comm, tracking our security.

"Elias, you got a visual on the VIP section?"

"Yeah, just past the bar. Daniel's guys are covering the entrance."

"Copy that."

Maria should be moving toward the VIP area. She's not. She's dancing. Hands up, hips rolling, lost in the rhythm. Her silk top clings to every curve. She knows I'm watching.

She moves like she doesn't have a last name that could get her killed. Like she's not a target.

I should grab her. Pull her away. Take her home.

Instead, I stand there, jaw clenched, watching.

She looks over to me, gives me a wink, *a fucking wink*, and then she takes it further. Moves toward some random guy. Tall. Shirtless. Tatted up. Douchey enough to flirt with anything that moves. She starts dancing with him. Laughing. Close. Too close.

This guy is a nobody. A stranger. I don't give a fuck about him. He's just a prop. Just another way for Maria to push me.

And it works. Jealousy hits me like a goddamn freight train.

She tilts her head, sends me a smirk over her shoulder. She knows exactly what she's doing.

My vision narrows. I step forward, ready to end this.

But then. Maria moves first. She pulls back, leaving the guy mid-spin. Brushes past him like he doesn't exist. Heads straight to me. Slow. Deliberate.

Her chest brushes mine as she leans in, breath warm against

my ear. "We're not going to have another museum scene, are we Fidel?" she murmurs. A warning.

My whole body is vibrating with tension. Fury. Hunger.

She leans back, eyes sharp, victorious. Then she turns and walks away.

I stand there, breathing through my nose. Grinding my teeth so hard it aches.

This girl is fucking ruining me.

Maria is finally moving toward the VIP area near the stage and I follow. I stay close. I don't trust this crowd. I don't trust anything.

I scan for known entry points, nearest exits, and blind spots. I check Daniel's location in the comm. Elias is ten feet behind us. Jorge is on standby near the bar.

If anyone makes a move, we're ready to grab her and get out of here.

Then, before we get more than a few feet, Lily materializes out of nowhere. Glittering in a gold sequin jumpsuit with full chaos energy.

"FINALLY!" she shrieks, throwing her arms around Maria. Her eyes glitter like she's a few tequila shots deep. "*Omg* Mercede! You look *amazing!*"

She turns to me. "And *hello*, handsome," she purrs, dragging her fingers down the sleeve of my jacket. "You're looking very bodyguard chic tonight."

I don't react. But I see Maria go tense beside me.

Lily, oblivious, keeps talking. "We never go out together, Fidel. We should fix that."

"No," I say flatly.

She gasps. "Oh my God, do you just hate fun?"

Maria snorts. "He does."

Before Lily can throw herself at me any further, a voice cuts through the noise.

"Mercede! There you are!"

Wes Solano is making his way through the crowd, Sloane Cross beside him, both of them with too wide smiles. Wes is grinning like he owns the fucking place. Sloane has her tablet in hand, already scanning the crowd like she's mapping threats. Or feeding them. My pulse ticks higher.

Great. Just what this powder keg needs.

A spark.

47

———

MARIA

"Mercede! There you are!"

Wes's voice is too loud, too eager. I barely turn before his arms are spreading out for a hug, like we're old friends, like we haven't spoken all week, like he hasn't been dodging every serious conversation since Tuesday.

He pulls me into a clumsy half-hug that smells like scotch and cheap cologne. "God, you look incredible tonight," he says, too close to my ear. "This crowd is bananas, right?"

Behind him, Sloane Cross appears, her smile tight and professional. She's wearing a sheer black dress that looks couture, and she's holding a phone already aimed my way like she's mentally planning the perfect social caption. She doesn't even glance at Lily.

"Mercede," she says, eyes sharp as glass. "We really need some socials of you in the UltraVision VIP area. You being seen here—*tonight*—could help close this deal. It's about momentum."

Funny how the woman supposedly running Lily's PR is laser-focused on me. Not on Lily, who's still glittering beside me in gold sequins, drunk enough not to notice she's being sidelined. Not that she minds. She's too busy twirling to the beat and waving at some producer across the cordoned-off rail.

Wes shifts awkwardly. "The lighting here's not that great, right?" he says, looking around like he's scanning for exits. His eyes don't quite meet mine. Something is off with him. He's sweating through his designer T-shirt and acting like a guy who brought a date he can't afford.

My smile stays in place, but my brain starts spinning. Why is Wes acting so weird? He's nervous. Too loud, too animated. Is he just drunk? And Sloane, who's normally detached, is watching me too closely.

Lily pipes up beside me, suddenly interested in taking pics. "Yesss! Mercede, we need pics! We need better light! Sparkles! We're going to look hot!" She grabs my hand like she's going to drag me somewhere, but Sloane smoothly intercepts, looping her arm through mine instead, pulling me away from Lily.

I glance around the VIP area.

Elias is posted next to me, pretending to be casual while his eyes scan everything. Daniel's guys are further out, one near the stage, another by the bar. Everyone's in position. I know the coverage. I know the protocols.

And Fidel? He hasn't moved. He's only three feet away, scowl in place, and I can almost feel the heat rolling off of him. But he won't make a scene. Not after the museum.

I lean in to Elias, drop my voice. "You'll let them know I'm going with Wes and Sloane for photos? We won't go far."

Elias hesitates. He's weighing the optics, calculating the risks. Then nods once. "We've got you."

I glance past him toward Fidel. Arms crossed, jaw clenched, eyes locked on me like he's willing me not to move.

Sloane takes a step closer, phone raised. "Let's get a few with Wes. Maybe one over there with the logo wall? I want UltraVision to see you front and center."

I laugh lightly, letting my fingers graze Wes's shoulder as I step forward. We're surrounded by security. Cameras. Fans. VIPs. Wes isn't stupid enough to try anything here. "You really think this'll help?"

Sloane's gaze sharpens. "We're this close, Mercede. One push. Show people you belong in this circle, and they'll stop asking questions. Start assuming the deal's already done."

Which raises the question—*why the hell does she want this UltraVision deal to go through so badly?*

She works for Wes and Lily. Not me. And definitely not UltraVision.

Unless she's playing her own game. Leave Wes? Move to UltraVision? Maybe.

"Sure," I say, smiling. "I'm all about helping push things over the edge."

Wes grins like he just got the biggest green light of his life. "Come on, we need to get you in some shots for the MAVFest page. I know Kara's keeping a close eye on media this weekend. I want everyone to see us here."

I pause. That wording.

Everyone to see us here.

Everyone. To see us. Here.

My smile doesn't falter, but my stomach tightens. Something about Wes feels too eager, like he's rehearsed the lines he's feeding me. And Sloane, normally composed to the point of boredom, keeps watching me like I'm a chess piece she's ready to move.

"It's just a photo op," Sloane says smoothly. "For visibility. Maybe we can catch the crowd cam."

I glance at Fidel.

He hasn't moved. But I can feel the tension radiating off of him. Head tilted. Hands clenched in fists. He's not okay with this. And he's trying not to show it.

But he won't stop me either. Not after his screw-up at the museum. Not with all these people watching.

So I nod, turning to follow Wes and Sloane as they lead me into the crowd.

Lily moves to Fidel, throws an arm around his neck like she's claiming him for herself. "Relax, bodyguard. She's with friends."

He doesn't answer. Doesn't move. But I can still feel his eyes on me—his glare burning through the haze and the lights and the noise.

I keep walking.

Into the music. Into the chaos.

Into whatever the hell this is.

48

FIDEL

WES AND SLOANE have flanked Maria, coaxing her into a "quick PR photo op" for UltraVision.

I narrow my eyes. Wes's voice is smooth, but there's too much urgency in his tone. Too much riding on this moment.

And Sloane, usually detached, half-bored by everything, is focused on Maria too closely, waiting for her response.

Maria hesitates. She knows. Wes doesn't just want UltraVision to see her. He wants them to see her with him.

Sloane finally speaks. "It's just a photo op," she says, coolly. "For visibility."

Maria glances at me. She knows I hate this. She also knows I can't stop her. Not without making a scene. Not without embarrassing her again.

Before I can object, Wes is already turning, Sloane on his heels, leading Maria into the crowd. Lily presses into my chest like she's trying to anchor me in place.

My muscles lock. Every instinct I've ever trained screams: Move! Pull her out!

But I don't. I stay still.

Not here. Not now. Not again.

I press my comm. "Elias, do you have her?"

"I've got her," he confirms. Calm, focused.

She's getting further away from me.

"Get on her. Now," I command.

"Copy that."

I exhale through my nose, jaw tight.

Then, I see someone bump into Maria. An older woman with glitter on her face, hair pulled into space buns. She presses something into Maria's hand.

A blood-red rose.

The woman says something to her, smiling.

Maria blinks. I see her mouth the word, "What?"

But the woman is already gone, vanishing into the crowd.

My pulse kicks harder. I shift my position, trying to keep eyes on Maria. And that's when I notice it—

Blood-red roses.

A guy with a blood-red bloom tucked behind his ear. A woman weaving a rose into her hair. A couple near the stage holding a small bouquet. The crowd is blooming. One red rose at a time.

My gut twists.

This isn't cosplay. It's not fan merch. This is a signal. A fucking synchronized display.

I see Maria, holding the rose in her hand, staring at it like she doesn't even know what it is.

Then—

Rose petals begin to fall from above.

A soft, steady rain of blood-red petals drifting down from the trusses overhead. People smile. Laugh. Lift their faces and twirl, grabbing at the petals like it's some kind of magical finale.

They don't see what I see. Every instinct in me goes razor-sharp.

I scan the stage.

And that's when I notice it.

A backpack. Wedged near the base of the stage scaffolding. It wasn't there earlier. I would have noticed it. It's sitting wrong—deliberate. Nestled too neatly against the speaker stack. No branding. No tags. I tap my comm again. "Daniel, we've got a suspicious—"

That's when the world explodes.

A sharp, concussive crack splits the air, the kind that folds your senses in half. The ground shudders under my boots. A flash of white—then black. The shockwave slams into me, knocking the breath from my lungs.

My ears are ringing. People are screaming. Thick black smoke billows out from under the stage.

A low, bone-rattling rumble follows—the stack of speakers next to me groaning, twisting in the frame. They're about to fall.

I don't think. I move.

I grab Lily by the waist and hurl her behind me. We hit the ground hard—my body shielding hers just as the speakers collapse with a deafening crash, splintering across the pavement where we'd just been standing.

Smoke. Dust. Light rigs flickering overhead. A few petals still floating down.

The crowd erupts in chaos—people shoving, bodies pressing together in panic, trying to get away. I can't hear anything but the high whine in my skull.

Blood is dripping down my face.

I don't care.

Maria. *Where is she?*

I leap up, scan the dance floor, searching the crowd where she'd been. My vision is still swimming, but I catch movement—Maria, across the floor, standing, miraculously untouched, still holding the fucking rose. Her hair loose, her expression frozen. Her eyes find mine.

Wes and Sloane bracket her, one on each side. Guiding her, moving her away. They're veering toward the edge of the venue. Not the exit. Not the VIP area. Somewhere else.

My panic explodes into fury. I start forward, lunging toward her.

But something shifts in her posture. A beat of confusion. She glances around—searching. For me? For Elias?

Wes leans in to her, saying something low, urgent. Places a hand on her elbow. Tries to keep her moving.

Maria plants her feet. Doesn't budge.

When Wes tugs again, she yanks her arms away from both of them. She shoves Wes. Hard.

He stumbles back, startled.

Sloane reaches for her wrist—gentle, persuasive—but Maria jerks away.

No hesitation. No confusion now.

She sees Elias and she's already heading for him and the security team cutting through the panicked crowd to reach her.

Good girl. Good fucking girl.

I push forward, forcing my way through the screaming chaos. Bodies slam into me. Someone falls. A voice yells behind me. I don't stop.

I can't stop. I can't lose her.

Elias's voice crackles in my comm. "I have her. I'm getting her out."

But Maria is still moving. Looking past Elias now. Scanning the crowd.

Coming to me.

She reaches me, reaches out, her fingers curling around my wrist. Her grip is solid. Anchored. She's shaking, but solid.

"You're bleeding," she says, eyes locking on my cheek. Her voice is too calm.

That's when I feel it. The sting on my face. The heat. Some kind of cut. I hadn't noticed. Not until her voice made it real.

"I'm fine." I reach up, but she's already touching me, her fingers brushing the cut.

She cups my face, thumb brushing the cut. I flinch. Not from pain. But from the way she's looking at me. Like she sees everything I'm thinking. Like she knows.

And then, from behind me, I hear it—

"Is someone filming this?"

Lily. Brushing dust out of her hair, clutching her rhinestone purse like it's the last goddamn lifejacket on the Titanic.

I close my eyes for half a second. Exhale.

"We need to go," I say.

Maria nods. This time, there's no argument. No delay. We leave.

49

MARIA

Fidel needs stitches.

The doctor, one of Carlos's private medics, met up at Carlos's house. He works quickly, threading the needle through Fidel's skin with practiced precision. The kitchen we're in smells like antiseptic, sharp and sterile, but beneath it, I can still smell him. That familiar heat. Clean. Faintly smoky. Him.

He doesn't make a sound. Not when the needle pierces his skin. Not when the doctor tugs too hard. Not even when fresh blood beads along the cut before being wiped away.

But I see the tightness in his jaw. His pulse ticking at his temple. The tension in his hands, curled into fists on his thighs.

Fidel is in pain. And he'd rather die than admit it.

Across the room, Carlos stands like a storm about to break.

"This is exactly what I was talking about," he says, his voice low, simmering. "You want independence? Fine. But if you think this isn't serious, Maria—"

"I never said it wasn't serious."

Carlos ignores me, his attention fixed on Fidel. "She needs *more* security."

Fidel doesn't react. Doesn't even look at him.

Carlos exhales sharply. "We'll talk tomorrow."

The moment he's gone, the silence feels heavier.

Fidel still hasn't moved. His shoulders are rigid, every muscle coiled, not just from pain, but from something deeper.

His eyes flick to mine.

"Do you get it now?"

His voice is low, rough, furious.

The doctor pauses, startled by the sudden movement in Fidel's face. Fidel clenches his jaw tighter, staying still.

A shiver runs through me.

"Fidel—"

"No, Maria." He turns fully toward me, his eyes burning. "They weren't taking you for a fucking photo."

My stomach flips.

"Please. Hold still," the doctor mutters. But Fidel doesn't stop.

"They planted that bomb to cause chaos," he says. "To take attention away from what they were actually doing." His voice drops, something lethal cutting through it. "Trying to take you."

"You don't know that. You don't know that bomb was about me." But the thought settles in my chest like ice. Maybe it was.

I hadn't thought about someone taking me. Hurting me. I had been too caught up in my own world, too wrapped up in making Fidel suffer for ignoring me to consider what might happen.

I swallow.

The doctor ties off the last stitch, clearing his throat like he's glad to be done with both the injury and the tension in the room. He steps away from us, leaving the room without another word.

"The roses, Maria," Fidel says quietly. "They were everywhere. You saw them. They were falling from the goddamn ceiling." He exhales slowly. "Someone wants you, Maria. And they won't stop until they get you," he says.

I meet his gaze. Something flickers in his expression, but he doesn't say anything more.

I exhale and stand, taking his hand. "Come on. Let's get you home."

Elias drives us back to our house and helps me get Fidel inside.

Fidel is running on fumes, held together by willpower and painkillers. His face is pale, dark circles under his eyes, his movements stiff with exhaustion.

The doctor told him to rest. He had nodded like he was listening. But I knew damn well he wouldn't. He's already looking toward the dining room.

I steer him toward the stairs. "No. You're going to bed."

Elias says nothing. He just watches, something tense and unreadable in his eyes, before heading toward the kitchen.

I guide Fidel into his bedroom, pressing him down onto the bed. He doesn't fight me. That alone tells me how bad it is. The house is quiet as I grab a fresh cloth from the bathroom, running it under warm water before kneeling in front of him.

When I press the damp cloth to his cheek, he exhales, slow and uneven.

"This is going to scar," I murmur.

His mouth twitches. "It won't be the first."

I smile slightly. "No, but if I do this right, you won't even have a bad one. You could be my first success story."

His brow furrows slightly.

"You don't remember?" I tilt my head. "That summer I decided I wanted to be a doctor?"

Realization flickers in his eyes. A slow exhale.

"Oh," he mutters. But I see the corners of his lips quirk. "*That* summer."

That summer when I had wrapped his head in bandages, put both of his hands in splints, made him walk around on crutches for days even though nothing was actually wrong with him.

That summer when I was the doctor and he was my only patient. And he did everything I asked. Just like he always did.

"All those fake injuries I fixed," I tease. "My skills should be excellent by now."

His mouth twitches like he wants to smile. But he doesn't.

I press the cloth along his jaw, my fingers skimming the rough stubble there. His whole body goes still.

Something shifts.

The air thickens, charged.

I should pull back. But I don't.

Slowly, gently, I climb onto the bed, straddling his lap.

Fidel's breath catches.

My hands slide up his chest, carefully, feeling the solid muscle beneath his shirt, the steady thud of his heart.

His fists curl into the sheets.

"You don't have to always protect me, Fidel," I whisper, leaning in, my lips almost brushing his. "Let me take care of you."

He's trembling.

His hands move to my waist, his fingers digging into me.

Then—he snaps.

His mouth crashes into mine, rough, desperate, shattering whatever restraint he has left.

I gasp as he pulls me flush against him, his hands gripping my hips, holding me, like he's lost every ounce of control.

I roll my hips, grinding against him, and he groans—low and wrecked—his fingers bruising against my waist.

I can feel him, rock hard between my legs. He wants this. He wants me.

I reach for the hem of his shirt, sliding my hands beneath, feeling the heat of his skin—

Then, just as suddenly as it started, it's over.

Fidel rips back from me, his chest heaving, his hands shaking as he pushes me away, pushes me off of him.

His jaw is tight, his eyes wild, tormented.

I get off the bed and stand, breathless, staring down at him, hands clenched at my sides, my whole body burning.

"This isn't happening, Maria," he rasps.

I blink. "What?"

Fidel runs a hand over his face, his fingers lingering near his stitches. His whole body is wrecked, but not just from pain.

"You don't understand," he says, voice low, rough, gutted.

"Then explain it to me," I snap.

He exhales sharply, his eyes closing. When he speaks, his voice is low.

"You're better than this, Maria. Better than me. You know that."

The words hit like a slap. I stare at him, heat rising to my throat.

"What the *fuck* are you talking about?"

He finally looks at me. And I see it.

The self-doubt. The insecurity. The feelings of inferiority. The weight of something so much deeper than this moment. His voice is hoarse when he speaks.

"I am not the right man for you."

Silence. I swallow, my pulse pounding in my ears. This isn't about me.

This is about him.

Fidel Cedillo—the man I've known my whole life, the man who has been protecting me for as long as I can remember—believes he isn't worthy of me.

"Fidel, you're wrong. You don't—"

He cuts me off. "I know what I'm saying, Maria. We can't be together."

I clench my jaw, furious now. "I cannot believe this! You are absolutely wrong!" I snarl at him.

"We don't belong together, Maria." He looks away from me, staring at the ceiling, refusing to make eye contact. "You know it."

I'm looming over him now, seething. "I know no such thing!"

But he's too tired, too resigned to it. He draws in a deep breath. "You should go, Maria," he murmurs, his voice rough. "You've had a long night."

I stare at him. He closes his eyes. He looks tired, weak. Weaker than I've ever seen him.

I want to scream at him. Grab him and shake him. And for the first time, I want to make him see what's right in front of him. Make him see me. I'm right here.

Instead, I swallow the heat rising in my throat, exhaling slowly as I stand. He's right. It's been a long night. He's exhausted. We can't do this tonight.

I drop the cloth onto his bedside table, keeping my voice even.

"Fine. You get some sleep."

He nods, still unable to look at me.

I step back, heading for the door. Pause.

Glance over my shoulder, just once.

Fidel sits perfectly still. He hasn't moved. His eyes are still closed, his expression unreadable. He thinks pushing me away will keep me safe. He thinks he's doing the right thing.

But I know. He's wrong.

And this isn't over.

50

———

FIDEL

I HAVEN'T SLEPT.

Not that I ever really sleep much, but last night was worse. My brain wouldn't shut off—flickering between the explosion, Maria's face, the kiss that shouldn't have happened, her hips grinding into me. I'd been half out of my mind when she touched me, her hands soft on my face, her breath close enough to taste. I should have pulled away sooner. But I didn't.

Because I want her.

I want her in a way that burns. Raw, locked deep in my ribs. I want her mouth. I want her pinned beneath me, gasping, her body small and perfect against mine. I want her fingers in my hair, her nails clawing my back, her moans in my ear.

I have to force myself to breathe.

I shift in my chair, jaw tight, refusing to acknowledge how fucking hard I am just from thinking about her. Pathetic. She isn't even in the house and I'm falling apart.

I force myself back into the only thing I'm good at. Finding answers. My laptop screen burns into my vision. Los Cuervos. I've spent the last six hours deep in their infrastructure. No one in that organization has the amount of data I've accumulated. Bank transfers, encrypted messages, front businesses, safe houses across Texas and Northern Mexico.

And still—nothing explains who's pulling the strings. Or why they're so fixated on Maria.

But one thing has become very clear. The Sandovals are an empire. Los Cuervos are butchers.

The Sandovals deal in power, influence. Well thought out plans. Logical moves. Los Cuervos thrives on chaos.

Raul has left the drug trade behind. These days, he focuses on weapons trafficking and low-visibility income streams that don't draw the attention of law enforcement. Los Cuervos has gone the other way, getting deeper into pioneering synthetic opioids and fentanyl, controlling hidden ghost labs throughout Texas and Mexico.

Raul builds connections quietly. Los Cuervos blackmails, bribes, and murders their way into power.

Raul would never be involved in human trafficking. Los Cuervos sees people as products. Women, children, laborers. Disposable commodities.

Los Cuervos are the antithesis of the Sandovals. They don't build, they consume. They destroy.

Los Cuervos rose to power quickly, gaining territory and traction in only the past two years. Starting in Monterrey, but rapidly expanding throughout northeast Mexico. And while I can't come up with their leader's identity, I know he's brutal, bloodthirsty.

But why the fuck does he want Maria so bad?

The front door opens.

Carlos's voice carries through the house. "Where's Maria?"

I don't look up. "She went to meet with Zara and Natalie. She has Elias with her and some of your guys."

Carlos makes a sound like he doesn't love that answer, but he lets it slide. He moves into the dining room, his presence big, weighted. I can feel him assessing me.

"You look like shit," he said.

"Thanks."

"You're going to have a nice scar on your face."

I grunt in acknowledgment. I know my face is swollen and bruised. Part of the job.

Carlos pulls out a chair, sitting across from me, elbows on the table. "How bad was last night?"

I don't need to ask what he means.

"Bad enough," I say. "Could've been worse."

Carlos exhales slowly. Then—"I met with Solano this morning."

That gets my attention. I finally look up.

Carlos taps his fingers on the table, his mouth tight. "I tried one last time to buy him out. A stupid amount of money, just to make it easy." His jaw flexes. "And he turned me down again."

I frown. "Doesn't make sense. Zara's numbers say he's still drowning. You'd think he'd want more investors, more money."

Carlos nods. "Exactly."

He leans back in his chair, his usual casual arrogance gone. Carlos is sharp, ruthless when he needs to be, but never reckless. If he's here, it means he thinks something's off.

"What did he say?" I ask.

Carlos's mouth twitches like he doesn't even believe it himself. "He said he has a backer. A big one. More money than I could throw at him. But that's not the part that matters."

Something in my gut goes cold.

Carlos's voice goes lower, words slower, heavier. "They don't care about turning a profit."

I stare at him. "What?"

"His backer. He told me they don't give a shit about his

studio making money," Carlos says. "They just want the *access* Solano can provide."

I go still.

Carlos's dark eyes meet mine. "That's what he said. His exact words were, 'It's not about business. It's about *access*.'"

He pauses for just a second before he continues, "What the fuck kind of access can Wes Solano provide? And why does he care so much about *The Dark Duke*. About Maria."

The words sit between us like a loaded gun.

Carlos exhales, shaking his head. "I don't know who's backing him yet, but I'm getting that studio one way or another." His fingers drum against the table. "You and Frank need to figure out why the fuck he's so into the fucking Dark Duke."

I don't move.

This mystery backer isn't interested in Solano Studios for the money.

They aren't using Solano as a front for laundering.

They aren't here to take over his business.

They want access. Access to Maria.

They just want Maria.

Carlos stands up, but I'm locked in place, my mind spinning through every possible reason why.

He gives me a hard look. "Tell her to be careful." A pause. "And stop looking like you want to murder someone every time she's around."

I ignore that. He leaves.

If they only want Maria, maybe there's a direct connection between her and Los Cuervos, something more than just her being Raul Sandoval's daughter. Something personal that directly involves Maria.

I turn back to my laptop, my fingers already flying over the keyboard. If this is personal, then the connection has to be somewhere. The money trail I've been concentrating on might not show it. I need a name, a face, a moment in time that ties Maria to Los Cuervos in a way I haven't seen.

Something bigger than her book going viral.

Maybe something older. Deeper.

I spend the next few hours pulling up old cartel records, birth certificates, death certificates, marriage licenses, concentrating on Los Cuervos home base in northern Mexico, scanning for a thread I've missed.

And then—

I find it.

A dead link. An archive I almost missed. A single image buried in a newspaper file from the year 2000.

A faded, scanned copy of an old article. With a wedding photo.

It had been a big event in Acuña—the marriage of the only sister of the most powerful cartel boss in the region, Armando Delgado. He had led the Delgado family's crime empire up until his death. But at the time of the photo, he was still in power. Still expanding.

And he had apparently decided one way to do that was to arrange a marriage between his sister and the leader of another powerful crime family.

Raul Sandoval. Thirty-eight years old. Standing beside his new bride, Lucia Delgado.

Lucia was only eighteen when the wedding took place, and she was stunning. She had just become Raul's second wife. She was Armando Delgado's sister. And one day, she would be Maria's mother.

Looking at the faded photo, I could see it. See the resemblance. She could have been Maria. They looked so much alike.

Maria's mother. "Lucia Delgado," I whisper it to myself. The mother she never knew. The mother we never talked about.

Also pictured in the old photo, a twelve-year-old boy

standing stoically next to Armando Delgado. His only child. His son.

My stomach drops.

While he's a young boy in the photo, I recognize him. I've seen him before.

I feel a cold sweat break out over my body. *No. No fucking way.*

It's Tommy. Tommy Dawson.

The former manager of Luz. The one who disappeared from the nightclub after the night that Ami was drugged. The night Maria was almost drugged.

But the newspaper article shows his real name. Tomás Delgado. Only son of Armando Delgado and heir apparent to the Delgado crime family. Only nephew of Lucia Delgado Sandoval.

And only cousin of Maria Lucia Sandoval.

I hear my own voice say it out loud, rough, hoarse. "Tomás Delgado." The son of the founder of a powerful cartel that had dissolved upon its leader's death. Tomás Delgado. And now, very likely, the leader of a new and even more ruthless cartel. Los Cuervos.

My stomach twists. My mind reels, rewinding, replaying that night at Luz. Ami's drugging. The too-familiar way Tommy had watched Maria, hovered around her. Like he already knew her.

It was him. Tommy Dawson. Tomás Delgado.

And now I see it. He wasn't just circling the Sandovals. He was circling *her*. Always her.

Not because she's Raul's daughter. Not because she's part of the Sandoval family. Because she's his blood.

Maria. His cousin. His fucking cousin.

My chest tightens. The roses. The jewelry. The sick comments on her website. It was all him. Of course it was him.

He knows exactly who Maria is.

And I haven't been able to figure it out, to make the connection between Maria and Los Cuervos, because I wasn't looking at it the right way. I didn't see that this has never been about business. Never about territory. Never about the Sandoval empire.

This is about bloodlines. About ownership. About obsession.

Lucia died after Maria was born. Armando died soon after that. Now it's just Tommy and Maria. The last of the Delgado line.

And I can see his sick logic. She's his family. She's the legacy. He thinks Maria belongs to him. That she's his to take. His to claim.

I exhale slowly, pressing my palms against the table, grounding myself. I've finally got the connection I've been searching for, the one no one else has seen. Raul thinks Los Cuervos have been neutralized. Carlos thinks this is about business. They're all wrong.

If I'm right, Maria is in more danger than any of us have realized.

I reach for my phone.

To call Raul. Carlos. Marco.

They need to know. Now.

51

FIDEL

I TEXT RAUL, Carlos and Marco.

Fidel: Secure video call. Now.

Within ten minutes, we're all on the call, live.

Raul immediately takes charge. "Tell me."

No greeting. No hesitation. Just Raul Sandoval at his most lethal.

I take a breath and decide to commit. I'm going to lay out a theory, one I've pieced together from fragments, hunches, and patterns no one else seems to notice. I don't have every answer. But I know I'm close. Close enough to see where this is heading.

"Maria's in more danger than we thought," I say. "This isn't just about Los Cuervos. It's about her connection to the man I believe is leading them." A beat. "Tomás Delgado."

A long pause.

Then, Raul, his voice low and hard: "Explain."

I don't waste time. "We know Tomás Delgado. We've dealt with him in the past when he was Tommy Dawson, manager of

Luz. He disappeared a few months ago, after the drugging at Luz. After the attack on the compound."

A beat goes by as they take that in. No one speaks.

"Tomás is the only son of Armando Delgado and the nephew of Lucia Delgado Sandoval. Lucia, Maria's mother."

I pause, letting this sink in. Waiting for Raul to say something. Tell us something about his marriage to Lucia.

He doesn't. I continue.

"Based on my research and recent events, I believe that Tomás Delgado is not solely after the Sandoval assets. And his interest in Maria is not random. She's his last remaining family. And I believe he thinks she belongs with Los Cuervos. With him."

Raul still doesn't speak. I can see him take slow, measured breaths, like he's considering something he's buried deep within himself.

Then—another voice cuts in. Carlos.

"Fidel. What the fuck are you talking about?"

I exhale, expecting this reaction. "Armando Delgado was the leader of a cartel out of Ciudad Acuña, Mexico. Lucia was Armando Delgado's sister, his only sibling. The Delgado bloodline is Maria's bloodline."

Carlos curses low under his breath. "I knew Lucia was a Delgado, but—why does this matter now?"

I pull up the wedding photo for them, sharing it on the screen. The resemblance between Lucia and Maria is haunting.

"Tomás was Armando's only son. Armando died in 2005, when Tomás was seventeen years old. While Armando's business fell apart following his death, I believe that Tomás has been working to rebuild the empire, basing it out of Monterrey. The result is Los Cuervos. And I think that, along the way, Tomás came up with a plan to take Maria. I believe he wants Maria because she is his blood. And I believe he thinks that, through

Maria, he can merge Los Cuervos with the Sandoval infrastructure in the U.S., and basically create his own empire."

I'm laying out the facts. The Delgado bloodline. Tommy's obsession. The truth about Maria.

Raul doesn't react. Doesn't blink. Doesn't speak.

He still hasn't said anything about his marriage to Lucia. The circumstances of her death.

I watch his shoulders rise with an inhale, slow and measured. A beat. Then another. Like he's forcing himself to breathe.

Then, finally—he speaks. And his voice is quiet.

"Lucia shouldn't have died that night."

None of us say a word. We don't know what to say. No one ever talks about Lucia's death.

She died when I was five. Maria was only two. I don't remember it. But on the very rare occasions when my mother spoke of her, it was with warmth. Reverence. Lucia had been kind. Beautiful. Loved.

But I've never heard Raul speak of her. Not once.

His voice is quieter than I expected. Not cold. Not detached. Regretful.

He exhales slowly, like the weight of a two-decade-old ghost is pressing against him.

"She had just turned twenty-one," he says. "Barely more than a girl. But she was smart. Charming."

A pause. The longest one yet. Then, softer—almost to himself—

"And I loved her."

It's barely there. A confession no one was supposed to hear. A wound so deep it still bleeds.

"When Armando proposed that I marry her, that we tie our families together, I thought it was ridiculous. I was too old for her. I had grown up with Armando in Acuña. He was my age. I never knew Lucia. She was much younger that the two of us." He pauses, his focus distant. "But then... I met her and I knew."

He doesn't say what he knew. That he loved her?

Raul's voice doesn't change. "Armando wanted power beyond Mexico. He saw our marriage as a way to secure that. He thought if Lucia married me, he'd get a seat at my table. That I'd fold the Sandoval empire into his."

A dry, humorless sound—almost a laugh. "But I don't kneel. Not for anyone."

Carlos makes a small noise of understanding. "So when he didn't get what he wanted, he tried to take you out."

Raul doesn't confirm or deny it. He doesn't have to.

"He sent men," Raul says simply. "Of course he did. To eliminate me. To take what he thought was his."

A pause.

And then—the truth.

"Lucia wasn't supposed to be there that night. She wasn't supposed to be with me." He swallows. I can see the furrow in his brow, the tightness around his eyes. The pain is raw, even now. "But I wanted her by my side. I always wanted her with me."

Those words hit differently than everything else.

It isn't a declaration. It isn't a confession. It's a wound that has never healed.

I could picture it. The chaos, the gunfire, Lucia in the wrong place at the wrong time. Getting shot, killed. Not on purpose. Just unlucky. Just collateral damage.

And Raul, who never shows weakness, sounds like a man who has carried that night on his shoulders for twenty years.

"One second she was there," Raul says. "And the next... she wasn't."

A moment passes.

"I never spoke of her after that. Not to anyone. I buried her memory thinking it would keep Maria safe. But all I did was blind us."

Silence.

Then—Carlos swears. "Goddamn it, Papa! And I suppose Armando lost his mind when he ended up murdering his own sister."

"Yes," Raul says simply. "Because it was his order that got her killed. And instead of admitting that, he blamed me."

His voice darkens.

"And because he took what was mine, took my Lucia, I went after him and took his life."

No one speaks. But something heavier settles over all of us.

Raul exhales, like he's forcing himself to admit something.

"And now his son is coming to take Maria, the only thing I have left of Lucia." He takes in a deep breath and slowly exhales. "I thought I could protect her. That if I never spoke of it, she'd never have to carry that name. Delgado. Never have to live with that bloodline." A beat. Then his voice hardens. "The fewer people who knew, the safer she was."

He goes quiet for a moment. Then—

"You don't understand what Armando Delgado was. He wasn't just power-hungry. He was insane. Unstable. He lived in his own reality, convinced that he was owed more. That everyone who stood in his way was betraying him."

Carlos mutters a curse under his breath, but Raul isn't finished.

"When Lucia died, he became worse. Dangerous in a way that had no logic. Made no sense. He twisted everything, convinced himself I had taken something from him."

Raul's voice drops lower. "I thought I had ended it when I ended him. But now his son is the same."

His voice drops to a whisper. "I never imagined Tomás was

behind Los Cuervos. Never thought the boy had the power—or the vision—to rebuild. If I had known..."

He's looks directly into the camera now, his face twisting into something dangerous. Lethal. "I would have burned them to the ground years ago."

The story finally makes sense. And a cold weight settles in my chest.

I can see what had happened to Tommy. Years of Armando's resentment, of grief twisted into entitlement, a delusion fed to him daily. For years, that boy was raised on hate. And entitlement. He grew up believing Maria wasn't just family. She was his birthright.

Maria isn't just some cartel princess to him. She's his last remaining connection to his father. His path to total power.

I don't think he sees her as a cousin. I think he sees her as a Delgado asset that was stolen from him. A blood heir. Something he can claim. Possess.

In his twisted mind, she's already his.

"So Tommy grew up believing Raul caused Lucia's death," I finally say. "Meaning this isn't just some sick revenge play. It's worse than that."

Carlos's voice is sharp. "How much worse?"

I exhale slowly. "Tommy isn't just trying to *take* Maria." I let my words settle, let the weight of them press down before I continue. "He thinks she belongs to him. That she's owed to him."

Another beat of silence.

Carlos exhales sharply. "Jesus Christ. So the Delgado family has been moving against us for years. And all that time, this bastard has been circling Maria."

Silence again.

All I can think of is Maria. Her entire life, she's thought of herself as a Sandoval. One of the heirs to her father's empire. Raul Sandoval's only daughter.

But to Tommy Delgado?

She's a Delgado. The Delgado he's planning to take.

Marco finally speaks, breaking the silence, his voice lethal and to the point.

"What's our play?"

Raul's response is instant. "Lock Maria down. She doesn't move without protection."

"Okay. She's already staying with Elias and Fidel," Carlos says.

Raul gives a slow exhale. "I want her back in San Antonio. Her time in Austin is done."

I tense, hesitating to ask the next question but it needs to be asked. "Are you going to tell Maria? About all of this?"

Raul is quiet for a second.

Then—"Yes. I've waited too long. I'll tell her tonight."

Another second passes. I see Raul's gaze harden.

"And I want Tomás Delgado dealt with. Immediately."

He exhales slowly.

"Find him."

A pause.

"Finish him."

Silence.

Click. The call ends.

I exhale. This is now a war.

And at the heart of it all— Maria.

52

MARIA

THE MIDDAY SUN streams in through the windows of Zara's office. I can smell fresh coffee, leather chairs, and a faint hint of lemon polish.

I cross my legs, forcing my posture to look composed. Professional. In control. I will not lose it in front of Zara, Natalie, and Elias.

Even if, inside, I want to scream with joy.

UltraVision wants *The Dark Duke.*

Not just wants it—they're willing to play by my rules.

Zara leans back in her chair, her expression smooth, but there's a flicker of satisfaction in her sharp brown eyes. I can tell she lives for this. For the moment when power shifts.

"They love the book," she says. "They love the world you built, the tension, the romance. They see *The Dark Duke* as an episodic series. Possibly season one of something bigger."

"I knew it," Elias says, giving me a wink.

Season one.

I exhale slowly, trying to keep my pulse from kicking up too hard.

Not just a one-and-done adaptation.

A franchise.

Natalie reaches over, squeezing my arm. "Maria, this is every-thing you wanted."

Everything I wanted. The words settle deep in my chest. Solid and undeniable.

Power. Control. The seat at the table I've been clawing my way toward since I was nineteen. My name on the contracts. My vision on the screen.

I should feel unstoppable.

Instead, my first instinct is to want to tell him. To tell Fidel.

I push the thought away, force myself to focus.

"And my terms?" I ask, keeping my voice even. "The script, the creative control?"

"They're amenable," Zara says. "They're offering you an offi-cial producer credit. They want you in the writing room."

She glances at Elias, then adds, "And they love that you're Texas-based. Lower production costs, a slate of new tax incen-tives, and," her mouth curves slightly, "Carlos's friends in the legislature smoothing the way doesn't hurt either."

I blink. Not just a name on a contract. Actual influence. Even the mention of Carlos can't detract from my happiness.

"They're also open to the casting discussion," she adds, knowingly. "Lily doesn't have to be attached. But..." She lets the word hang there.

"But they like her," I guess.

Zara inclines her head.

I sigh, leaning back. "Of course they do."

Lily Renshaw is a PR machine. She turned last night's bombing into a press tour before the smoke had even cleared.

They're still cleaning up the venue and she's already been on a local TV spot discussing the terror *she had faced* at MAVFest.

I pull out my phone, scroll, and yep—#LilySurvives is trending.

"Lily," I mutter, "is a menace."

Elias, who's leaning back in his chair, arms crossed, smirks. "She's good, though."

Natalie snorts. "The best. You have to admit. She's keeping your name in the press."

"Oh, I'm aware." I wave my phone at them. "Her 'good friend author Mercede Sanchez' gets mentioned every time she opens her mouth."

Zara exhales, but there's amusement behind her patience. "She's making herself hard to ignore. Which brings me to the next point. Kara Lasater wants to meet you in person at the UltraVision Gala tonight. She wants to introduce you to more of the UltraVision team." She pauses, then adds, "Kara's been dropping hints about wanting to anchor more projects here in Texas. You're the perfect poster girl for that expansion. Smart, marketable, and local."

"They're making moves," Zara adds. "Their initial offer came through. Strong terms, everything we pushed for. But they want to finalize in person. Tonight."

Elias leans back, arms crossed, smirking. "You're the belle of the fucking ball, Mercede. And they're about to beg you to dance."

"The contract isn't signed," Natalie says, voice smooth as silk. "You're still the one with leverage."

I nod slowly, heat building under my skin. Let them wine and dine me. Let them flash their fancy numbers and VIP invites. I already know the ending.

If I say yes, they get the next big franchise. If I say no, they don't even get the rights to stream it.

The UltraVision Gala.

The final night of MAVFest. And the biggest, flashiest, and most exclusive event of the entire festival.

Where everyone who matters will be watching.

I exhale slowly, keeping my face composed, even as my pulse hammers.

This is it.

My terms. My vision. My career. I'm not just getting a deal. I'm getting *my* deal. A rush of adrenaline shoots through me. I can't wait to tell—

I cut the thought off before it fully forms. Too late.

Fidel.

The victory should feel sharper. It should feel electric. But instead, all I can think about is last night.

The way he pulled me into him. The way his body shook when I touched him. The way he kissed me, like he wanted to ruin me.

And then—

The way he pushed me away. Telling me I couldn't have him.

I press my lips together.

I have spent years pulling Fidel into my orbit. If I wanted to play queen of the castle, he was the servant carrying my robes. If I wanted to stage a sword fight, he was the villain I heroically defeated. If I wanted midnight snacks from the kitchen, he was my lookout.

Fidel has always been there. Always steady. Always mine.

And as I've gotten older, as I've started to realize that almost no one outside of my family can really be trusted, that every supposed friend has an agenda, that every guy who has ever flirted with me was either too afraid of my last name or too interested in it, he's been there.

The one person who has never wanted anything from me.

Except now...

Now he's different.

Now I can't boss him around. Now I can't just pull him where I want him to go. And that isn't just frustrating. It's infuriating.

Because last night, I know he wanted me.

I saw it in his eyes. I felt it in the way he needed me.

And still, he told me no.

I swallow hard. Does he really want me? Does he *not* want me?

No. No, I'm not doing this. I'm not going down this path.

I've fought too damn hard for this moment. For control. For independence.

And yet—

If Fidel hadn't pushed me away last night, if he had actually let himself have me, would I still be sitting here pretending this deal was the most important thing in the world?

Would I still be pretending it was enough?

I hate the answer that forms in the back of my mind.

Because it isn't.

I want this. I want UltraVision. I want to build my own success, my own empire.

But I want him too. And maybe that's the problem. Because this victory, this moment, this deal. It should feel like everything. But it's not the same without him.

It isn't as sharp. It isn't as bright. It isn't as good.

I take a breath.

I want UltraVision. But I want Fidel too.

Because I want *my* future. *My way.*

And if he thinks he can push me away? Fine. Let him try.

53

FIDEL

I'M AT MY LAPTOP, the screen a blur. Just waiting. Waiting for Maria. Because what else can I do?

Maria is in more danger than I've ever imagined. And I feel helpless to stop it.

The front door bursts open, and Maria's voice rings through the house—

"Fidel!"

She's glowing.

Her eyes are bright, her smile wide, her entire body practically vibrating with excitement.

She drops her bag by the door and bounces into the dining room, radiating happiness in a way I haven't seen in years.

I should smile. Should let her have this moment.

But I know what's coming.

"The deal with UltraVision is happening! I have to tell you—"

Her phone rings.

She glances at the screen. Stops.

And just like that, the light in her eyes dims.

Raul Sandoval.

I clench my jaw.

Maria exhales sharply, gripping the phone tighter before lifting it to her ear.

"Papa?"

I know Raul won't drag this out. He'll tell her quickly. Cleanly. Directly. But that doesn't make it any easier.

I stay frozen, listening to the slow unraveling of her world. Her voice is sharp at first. Then confused. Questioning. Then quieter. Unsteady. Finally, nothing.

Minutes pass. She ends the call, standing frozen for a beat.

Then—she turns and walks upstairs to her bedroom. I hear the door shut.

I exhale, gripping the back of my neck.

She needs space. She deserves space. But I still find myself standing, moving upstairs to her bedroom. I hesitate outside her door. My hand tightens around the printout of the small, old photograph in my grasp. The one I found in the newspaper archives.

The wedding photo.

Her mother's wedding. Her family. The bloodline she's never known.

I knock once. Silence.

Then—a sharp inhale, a quiet sniffle.

Fuck.

I force my voice low. Steady. "Maria."

More silence. Then, finally, "Go away."

I sigh, leaning against the door frame. "I have something for you."

Another pause. Then, "I don't want anything. Leave me alone."

I slide the photo under the door.

Seconds later, I hear a rustle of paper. Her sharp inhale.

Then, her door unlocks. She doesn't say anything when she opens it.

Her eyes are red. Her face unreadable. She stares at the photo, holding it like it's something fragile. Like it might burn her if she holds it too long.

"You knew," she finally says.

I nod. "I figured it out this morning."

Her lips part. I think she might burst into tears, scream at me, say something vicious.

But instead, her face crumples. She turns and walks to her bed, sitting on the edge. She stares at the photo, like she's waiting for it to change. Waiting for it to tell her something she doesn't already know.

"I just keep trying," she whispers, tears slipping down her face. "Trying to be something more than my name. More than my blood. But I'm not. I'm just a piece of this horrible, awful world I never asked for."

My chest tightens. Because I want to tell her she's wrong. Tell her she's everything good and perfect.

Instead, I sit down next to her, feeling the full weight of how unfair it is that Maria has to carry all of this.

My chest feels tight. I reach out, fingers brushing her hand. She doesn't pull away. Instead, she leans into me. And I let her.

Because I know how bad this is for her. And right now, she can have me. If that will make things better for her, she can have every part of me.

I pull her against me, my hand sliding around her shoulders.

She presses her face into my chest, breathing hard, like she's trying to not to shatter.

I turn to her, my lips against her hair. "You're not them, Maria. You're good. You're not them."

Her fingers curl into my shirt. "Then why does it feel like I'll never escape it?"

I exhale, tightening my hold. "You won't *escape* them, Maria. They're your family."

Her body tenses. But she doesn't pull away.

"And now I'm connected to another *all-powerful* crime family —the Delgados." Her voice is raw. Bitter. "And because of my mother, who I never really knew, and my uncle, a cartel crime lord, and my cousin, the cartel's unhinged heir, I am once again being controlled and managed and told what to do. Like I'm some pawn in a big game of chess. It never, ever ends."

I run a hand down her back. "But you're more than all of that. You're the only person I know who gets exactly what she wants. Always. And you deserve to get what you want."

Her sobs have stopped but she's still drawing shallow breaths, her face still pressed into my chest.

"Do you really think so?" she asks me as if my answer is all that matters.

"I don't think so," I tell her. "I know so." It's true. "You'll get everything you want, *princesa*."

I'm not thinking about whether it's the right thing to say or the smart thing to say or what she'll think of me saying it.

I'm saying it because it's what I believe. It's what is in my heart.

And before I can stop it—before I can think, or breathe, or remind myself of all of the reasons I shouldn't let her—

She raises her face to mine. And she kisses me.

That's when I break.

A soft, desperate sound slips from her lips as our mouths come together, and it wrecks me.

I groan, dragging her against me, gripping the back of her neck, tilting her head up, deepening the kiss. I let her feel just how bad I need her. How much I want to give her everything.

Her lips are soft, warm, eager.

I shouldn't let myself taste her, but now that I have, I can't stop.

Maria moans into my mouth, her fingers digging into my shirt, pulling me closer. And she feels so fucking good.

I want to give her everything.

I kiss her harder, rougher. My tongue slides against hers, and she moans, arching into me.

Her body is soft, molding against my chest.

I don't even realize I'm pushing her back until her spine meets the mattress, her thighs parting as I follow her down.

Heat rolls off her skin, sinking into mine.

I feel the shape of her beneath me, the press of her breasts against my chest, the curve of her hips as my hands slide down, gripping, pulling her closer.

Maria tilts her hips up—just slightly, just enough for my cock to drag against her, thick and aching through my sweatpants.

Fuck.

I tear my mouth from hers, panting against her lips.

She's breathless, flushed, eyes dark and burning.

But she isn't done.

She pulls me back, kissing me deeper, tongue sliding against mine, her hands threading through my hair, nails scraping against my scalp.

A shudder rolls down my spine.

I groan into her mouth, and she swallows it like she wants all of me.

And I want to give it to her.

I press harder against her, letting her feel exactly how bad I want this—how bad I want her.

Her legs tighten around my hips, locking me in place. Another gasp. Another moan. Rocking her hips against me.

She's driving me insane. The way she clings to me. The way she needs this. Needs me.

I want to feel more of her. To taste every inch of her. To pin her down and make her completely mine.

And then, out of nowhere, I remember.

I can't have her. I'm not the man who gets to have her.

I'm scarring her. Staining her. She deserves more than a man like me. Someone whose only value is tied to crime, to violence, to killing.

I tear myself away, even though it feels like ripping something out of my own chest.

Maria makes a sound of protest, reaching for me again.

She tries to pull me back down. I nearly let her.

But I grit my teeth, breathing hard, shoving the need back down.

"Maria," I say, my voice rough, uneven. "This can't happen."

Her breath stutters. Then she stiffens. And her face— shatters.

Her breath comes sharp and ragged as she shoves me away. She stands up, face hard, lips swollen from my kiss.

"You're afraid," she whispers.

I exhale sharply, dragging a hand through my hair. "Yeah, Maria. I am."

Her brows pull together and she frowns. She wasn't expecting that.

I shake my head, forcing myself to say what I should have said a long time ago. Forcing her to face reality. "I'm not good enough for you."

Maria blinks. Once. Twice. Like she can't process what she's hearing.

"What does that even mean?"

I get the words out before I can stop myself, the words she

needs to hear. The truth. She deserves to know what I am. And what I can never be.

"One day, you'll have someone who's good. Not a criminal like me. Someone who's rich. Powerful. Someone worthy of you. Someone Raul will approve of."

Her nostrils flare and she spits out, "Rich? Powerful? *Who Raul approves of?*" Her eyes are hard as she stares into mine. "Do you *honestly* think I give a shit about any of that? Is that who you think I am?"

My voice is low when I answer, almost a whisper. "Maria, you've never even been with another man. I know that." I swallow and my throat is tight. "That should be something special. Something for the man you'll spend the rest of your life with."

"Special? *Special?*" she snaps. "You don't want me because *I'm a virgin*? Are you fucking serious?" Her voice is rising. She's incandescent now, shaking with rage. "Fuck you, Fidel! I decide what's special! I decide who I want! Me. Not you. Not my father. *Me!*"

Her words slice through me.

Her hands ball into fists at her sides. Her voice goes quiet now, her tone scathing. "You're scared because you think Raul Sandoval would never approve of me ending up with you?"

I laugh. A low, bitter sound. "Raul Sandoval would put a bullet in my head before he'd let me touch you."

She takes a step toward me. Her chest is rising and falling fast. She's angry. Furious.

"You are so goddamn blind."

I say nothing.

She hisses her next words at me. "You don't even see what I see, do you? You don't see us."

I don't answer. She exhales sharply and I can see her entire body vibrating with anger.

"You always get what you want, Maria," I murmur. "Right or wrong. But you won't this time. Not if you think you want me."

She doesn't blink. Doesn't flinch. Her eyes burn into mine. "That's where you're wrong, Fidel," she says. Her voice is soft now. Dangerous. For the first time ever, it occurs to me that she sounds exactly like her father. She sounds like a Sandoval.

"You know me better than anyone." A slow, deliberate pause. "And you know I *always* get what I want."

She takes a step back, her smile twisting into something feral. Lethal.

"Always."

She turns and walks out of the room.

I stare after her, pulse hammering.

Maria always gets what she wants. But this time, I know—she won't.

And that will fucking destroy me.

54

MARIA

I have fucking had enough!

Enough of the lies. Enough of the control. Enough of every single man in my life thinking they know what's best for me.

I've had enough of the manipulation. The patronizing lies. The absolute fucking bullshit.

Raul kept the truth about my mother from me for *my entire life*. Carlos has made it his personal mission to manage me like I'm one of his startups. And Fidel—

Fidel. Fucking. Cedillo.

He kissed me like I was the only woman in the world. Like I was something sacred. Like he wanted to devour me and then worship what was left.

And then he *stopped*. Again.

Pulled away. Again.

Said I deserved something "special." Someone better. Someone worthy.

He looked me in the eyes and reminded me that I've never been with another man. Like my virginity was some fragile prize I was supposed to save for a nice boy from the right kind of family.

Like *he* was doing *me* a favor by rejecting me, by walking away.

I can still feel the weight of him on top of me. Still taste his mouth. Still hear the way his voice broke when he said my name.

Motherfucker.

And then there's my father.

"This is bigger than you, María."

That's what he said when I confronted him.

Not "*I'm sorry I didn't tell you.*" Not "*You deserve to know about your mother.*"

Just more of the same—power and control dressed up as protection.

And now I'm once again being managed by the Sandovals. And, *newsflash!*, turns out I'm also a Delgado pawn. A daughter of two bloody, violent empires. Used. Moved. Controlled.

But not tonight.

Because if Fidel doesn't want me—

If Raul thinks he still owns me—

Then I'll prove to both of them that no one handles Maria Lucia Sandoval.

I'm not some delicate thing. I'm not a legacy. I'm not a fucking virgin prize that gets handed over to whoever someone else decides is appropriate.

If I haven't learned anything else, I've learned what it means to be a Sandoval. To take charge. To take what I'm entitled to. To take what's mine.

Everyone in this house is preparing to go back to San Antonio.

But not me.

Not tonight.

55

FIDEL

Maria's leaving.

Raul's decision is final. She's out of MAVFest. Out of Austin. Headed back to San Antonio tonight.

I should feel relief. Should be grateful. Once she's back in San Antonio, buried under the layers of security Raul will throw around her, Los Cuervos won't be able to touch her. She'll be safe.

Safe from them. Safe from me.

So why does it feel like my ribs are caving in?

I sit at the dining room table, fingers flying over my keyboard, focus shot to hell. The code on my screen blurs, my own logic slipping as I force my way into Los Cuervos' network. I've done this a thousand times before. I can crack this system in my sleep. But ever since this afternoon—

Since her.

In my arms. On her bed. Pressed against me, her breath hot against my neck, her nails dragging over my skin. The way she kissed me. Like she's been waiting years for that moment.

I exhale sharply, gripping the back of my neck.

I have to shove the memory back. Seal it off, lock it down,

bury it under every firewall I've ever built in my head. Because if I don't, I'll lose whatever's left of my goddamn sanity.

But I can still feel her. Still hear the soft, breathless sounds she made against my mouth.

And then I see the look in her eyes before she left.

Hurt. Anger.

Determination.

She didn't walk away defeated. She walked away knowing exactly what she was going to do next.

I push back from the keyboard, forcing myself to breathe, to focus. I was right to push her away. To reject her.

I'm not good enough for her. I never will be. She deserves someone untouched by this life. Someone Raul will approve of. Someone who can give her a life away from all of this. Someone who doesn't have blood on his hands.

And yet—

I've never wanted anyone the way I want her.

Elias walks in, coffee in hand, tossing a folder onto the table and taking a seat. "UltraVision's deal for Maria," he says. "Zara sent over the details. Thought you'd want to see it."

I ignore the way my chest tightens and flip the folder open.

The terms are exactly what Maria wants. Creative control. A seat in the writer's room. A producer credit. It's everything she's worked for, fought for. The deal is a dream for any author trying to break into Hollywood. And Maria has it.

And now she's supposed to walk away from it.

Elias stretches his legs out, watching me carefully. "They wanted her at their big gala tonight. Kara Lasater is apparently dying to introduce her to the rest of the UltraVision team. Lock the deal down. The board still has to sign off, and tonight was supposed to seal it. But I guess that won't be happening."

He pauses. Takes a sip of his coffee. Waiting for a response from me that isn't coming.

Then, "So that's it? You're just gonna let her lose everything she fought for? Sit here doing your little coding thing while Raul pulls her off the board like she's a piece in his game?"

I look at him. "What the hell do you expect me to do, Elias? Kick down Raul's front door? Put a gun to his head until he lets Maria do this?"

He shrugs. "I don't know. Maybe you could not sit here looking like someone just shot your dog." He leans back in his chair, crosses his arms. "Carlos *might* be able to salvage something for her if he gets his hands on Solano Studios. But come on—we both know. It won't be the same. If Maria leaves Austin, she loses *this* deal. The UltraVision deal. The one she fought for. The one she wants. It'll be dead."

I exhale, staring down at UltraVision's proposal.

Maria has spent her entire life trying to build something outside of her last name. This proposal is it.

But Raul has made his choice. And I've made mine.

I don't look up at Elias. I can't. "My job is to keep Maria safe," I say quietly. "I'm just doing my job."

I close the folder and turn back to my screen. If Maria is going back to San Antonio tonight, then my focus is on that version of events. What Raul wants. What keeps Maria safe.

I need to finish my work. Los Cuervos isn't done with her yet. They're still watching her. Tracking her. Waiting. The second they realize she's leaving Austin, they'll shift their focus to San Antonio. But until then, they're still here. Watching Maria.

I've spent hours doing my own watching, tracking Sloane Cross. I've been mapping her movements, tracing every attempt she's made to guide Maria to where Los Cuervos wants her. She's tracking Maria, wiping logs, changing access codes, rerouting surveillance, adjusting plans.

It's clear. Los Cuervos isn't finished. Tommy Delgado isn't finished. He's planning something more. Something big.

I lock onto Sloane's digital signature. I have to admit that she's good.

But I'm better.

I embed myself deep into her network, Los Cuervos's network. Watching. Waiting for Los Cuervos to make their move.

Because they will.

And when they do? I'll be waiting.

56

MAVFEST DAY 11

Invitation to UltraVision Gala - Hand-Delivered, 12:15 p.m.

To Ms. Mercede Sanchez, in Care of Ms. Zara Caldwell, Langston, Blake and Saavedra

[Printed on 25 lb. cream cotton bond, center-aligned, black engraving in Didot serif font]

UltraVision Entertainment
requests the pleasure of your company
at a private gala
in honor of distinguished achievements
in media and storytelling
on the occasion of MAVFest

Saturday, May 24
Grand Ballroom | Hotel Zavala
Austin, Texas
Black Tie | Invitation Non-Transferable
7:00 PM - Midnight

Cocktail Service | Seated Dinner | Private Showcase
Attendance is reserved for selected guests.

57

MARIA

I STAND in front of my full-length mirror, slipping on a silver bangle to match my dress. The gown sparkles under the soft light of my bedroom—tiny silver sequins catching every movement, reflecting like stars against my skin. The fabric clings like liquid metal, molded to every curve.

It's short. Very short.

The hem barely skims my upper thighs, the plunging neckline leaving just enough to the imagination. Paired with my dangerously high nude stilettos, the look is all things bold, glamorous, unstoppable.

I smooth my hands over the fabric, inhaling deeply.

I am in control of my life. No one else.

A flicker of doubt slithers in. *But if they're right, if the danger is real, am I making a mistake?*

I exhale sharply, shaking it off. *They're wrong. They're paranoid.*

My phone buzzes.

Lily: OMG QUEEN!!! I'M OUTSIDE IN THE UBER!!!!

I smirk, firing off a quick thumbs-up before dropping the phone onto the nightstand. Time to put my plan into motion.

Step One: Lose the tracker.

I've already disabled location services, but I'm not taking any risks. Let them think I'm still in my room. Packing to leave. Being quiet. Being manageable. They won't realize I'm gone until it's too late.

I slip off my stilettos and move.

Step Two: Disable the security system.

Sneaking past security isn't hard. Not for me. I've been doing it my whole life.

Carlos installed his usual top-tier surveillance system in the house, but he made one mistake.

He underestimated me.

I know the failsafes, the emergency overrides, the blind spots. I've watched Marco and Fidel install security systems since I was a teenager.

And I paid attention.

I move to the closet, reaching behind a row of handbags to the matte-black panel hidden on the back wall. Carlos has these override panels in every one of his properties. Backup access in case someone hacks the main system.

No one has any idea that I know about them.

My fingers fly over the screen, inputting the emergency bypass code.

Raul's middle name: Eduardo.

The month Raul married my mother: 04.

The month I was born: 07.

A soft click.

Security disabled for exactly seven minutes.

I have seven minutes to get out, unseen.

Step Three: Trick the bodyguard.

I hold onto my heels, throw a robe over my dress, and make my way down to the kitchen, steps light, heart pounding.

I turn the corner and find exactly what I expected—Luis, one of Carlos's security guys, stationed at the back entrance. Young. Muscular. Probably too smart to fall for a dumb excuse but just gullible enough to fall for *me.*

Time to sell it.

I quietly place my heels on the kitchen counter, reminding myself: *I am the spoiled and entitled daughter of his boss, a rich-as-shit crime lord.*

I let out a breath, running a hand through my hair as I stride toward him, flustered and impatient. Channeling my new bestie, Lily Renshaw, I huff out, "Luis! Oh, thank God!"

He straightens immediately, eyes widening. "Miss Sandoval?"

"I *need* your help." I put just enough urgency into my voice to make him uneasy. "I know it's late, but I'm *dying.* And before you panic, no, not in an actual emergency way, but in an I will *literally* cry if I don't get what I need." I exhale dramatically, hand on my chest. "The kitchen is out of my chamomile tea. I *cannot* sleep without it. And if I tell Carlos I couldn't get any sleep on the drive back to San Antonio, well, *you know how he is.* He'll *blame you.*"

Luis blinks, startled. "Uh, I thought you were—"

His hesitation tightens my pulse. It all sounds ridiculous but I just have to sell it.

I push harder.

"So Luis, *please,* I need you to run to that organic market off West Seventh. They're the only ones who carry it. I checked." I give him the most helpless princess expression I can muster. "I hate to ask, but I don't want to ask Elias. He's busy packing the weapons. And I *really* don't want to deal with *Fidel.* You know how he is."

At Fidel's name, Luis's expression hardens.

Perfect.

He hesitates. His gaze flicks toward his phone, like he might text someone.

Shit.

I lunge slightly and place my hand over his phone before he can reach for it. I'm now in super hard sell mode. "Oh my god, Luis. It's late! *We're leaving soon! I need* my tea!"

And just like that—he caves.

"Okay, Miss Sandoval," he says. "I'll get it. I'll be quick."

"And have Jorge drive you in the SUV. It'll be faster," I beam. "I'll wait right here for you. Omg, Luis. You're the *best*."

He runs out the back door, and I listen as the SUV starts up, then pulls out of the driveway a minute later.

A flicker of guilt creeps in. *Sorry, Luis. Hopefully, you'll understand later.*

The second he's gone, I tear off the robe, grab my shoes, and bolt.

Step Four: The getaway.

The night air hits my bare skin as I run down the long driveway, heels clutched in one hand, dress glittering under the streetlights.

Down the road, a black Uber idles at the curb, Lily practically bouncing in the backseat.

I yank open the door and slide inside.

Lily shrieks. "BABE, THIS IS ICONIC!" She grabs my arm, eyes wide with excitement. "You're *actually* a bad girl? Why didn't you tell me we were doing a great escape? I would have brought champagne."

I laugh, slipping on my heels. "No need. We'll have plenty at the gala."

Lily gasps. "*I love you.* Like, extra plus massive love. I knew we were meant to be besties. You saved me, babe. I was NOT invited to this gala. Do you understand what this means?" She grips my hands dramatically. "We are walking into that hotel as *queens*."

I smirk. "Damn right we are."

The Uber pulls onto the main road, the bright lights of downtown Austin flickering ahead of us.

I exhale, rolling my shoulders, forcing myself to relax.

I've done it.

No phone. No tracking. No security. No leash. With two minutes to spare.

For the first time in weeks, I am *completely, entirely* on my own terms.

The feeling is exhilarating. It's terrifying. I love it.

I lean back against the seat, letting the streetlights dance across my skin.

Tonight, I stand on my own. I take control of my future. My work. My life.

And I'll prove to everyone—especially to *Fidel fucking Cedillo*—that I don't need anyone to keep me safe.

But a very small, nagging voice in the back of my mind whispers otherwise.

Raul doesn't make decisions lightly. Carlos doesn't overreact. Fidel would never let you out of his sight if he thought you were in danger.

I exhale sharply, forcing the thoughts away.

They're wrong this time. Overprotective. Paranoid. Controlling.

I have to believe that.

So I do. Because I have to.

This is my night. My choice. My future.

58

FIDEL

MARIA IS GONE for twenty-three minutes before we realize it.

Which means I'm already twenty-three minutes behind.

Unacceptable.

I have to be ice-cold now, all feelings locked out, cooly sorting priorities as I move. Find her location. Assess the risk. Mobilize.

Meanwhile, Elias tears into Luis.

"¿Qué carajo? You went out for fucking tea?!"

Luis flinches. "She—she said it was important!" He holds up the box of chamomile tea like it can somehow shield him from Elias's wrath. "She looked upset! She said Carlos would be mad. She said she couldn't sleep without it, and she told me not to..."

He hesitates.

Elias narrows his eyes. "Not to what?"

Luis swallows. "...Not to tell Fidel."

A pulse of something sharp, electric twists in my chest.

I ignore it. I'm already moving. Pulling security footage. Checking logs. Reconstructing her escape in real time.

"Luis. Check her room. Elias. Text Carlos," I order flatly.

Luis practically sprints upstairs, desperate to redeem

himself. *"Maria!"* he calls out, like she's going to cheerfully answer from under her bed.

Elias mutters death threats against both Luis and Jorge as he pulls out his phone, but I tune him out. I've found what I need.

I roll back the footage. 7:37 p.m.

Maria, stepping outside. Barefoot. Dress glittering under the security lights, heels clutched in her hand.

Something dangerous and possessive surges in my blood.

She was fucking barefoot. The hem of her dress skimming her thighs, skin catching the light, hair loose over her shoulders. She looked... stunning.

I clench my jaw. Focus.

She moved with purpose. No hesitation, no looking back. She sent Luis and Jorge off like goddamn idiots, bypassed the cameras, disabled security for seven minutes.

She knew exactly what she was doing.

I force down the flicker of begrudging admiration. Focus.

7:38 p.m.

Uber. Maria sliding into the backseat. I can see Lily waiting inside, probably hyperventilating with excitement.

I switch feeds. Track the Uber's route through Lily's phone. No detours. No suspicious activity. Destination: Hotel Zavala.

The UltraVision Gala. Of fucking course.

Elias comes up behind me, still fuming. "Where is she?"

I exhale slowly, clicking the monitor off.

"Where do you think?"

Elias swears. "That little—"

I ignore him. Focus. I have Maria's destination, but no way to track *her*. Her phone? Left in her room. Luis shuffles forward, handing it over, still looking like he might puke. So no GPS. No digital breadcrumbs.

Lily's phone gives me the car's location right now. But once they're inside the gala, if Maria breaks off on her own, which she will, I'll lose her.

I need something better.

I need Sloane Cross.

I'm already in her system. If Los Cuervos so much as blinks in Maria's direction—if Sloane checks security feeds, sends coordinates, accesses the hotel's cameras—I'll see it.

I roll my shoulders, turning to Elias. "We leave in three minutes. Get dressed."

The Guard Dogs don't roll into high-profile events looking like mercenaries. We infiltrate. Dominate. Command.

Elias and I move fast, swapping out sweats and t-shirts for black suits, custom-fitted concealable soft armor vests, crisp black dress shirts, and black silk ties. All black. Doesn't show blood.

I text Carlos.

Fidel: Maria UV gala at Zavala. Full team. Now.

I return downstairs, adjusting holsters for three guns beneath my jacket, as I head to the living room where we have our store of weapons. Luis and Elias are already there, grabbing gear.

Elias tightens his tie, then yanks open a case. Knives gleam in the overhead light. "Let's load up," he says.

"Luis," Elias barks. "Clips. Silencers. Flashbangs. Now."

Luis freezes for half a second. Fucking Luis. "Uh—y-yeah. I mean, got it. I mean, yes sir." He nearly trips over his own feet scrambling for the gear.

I ignore him, pulling together my own loadout. Three pistols under my jacket, one in each boot, extra clips, and several small, high-impact explosives.

Elias catches sight of them. "The fun stuff. Good."

"If this goes sideways," I say coolly, "let's be ready."

Elias huffs out a dark laugh. "This is the version of Fidel that I like."

I don't bother responding. I'm only thinking of one thing right now. Getting Maria out.

Luis is breathless, arms overloaded with gear, looking winded and wide-eyed as fuck. I toss him my padded tech bag and he struggles to get his footing. "I—I thought this was just a security gig tonight," he stammers.

Elias shoots him a look. "Jesus Christ. You work for the Sandovals, Luis. That means *you don't think*, you do whatever the fuck I tell you."

Luis nods quickly. "Right. Got it, sir. No thinking."

Elias rolls his eyes. "Just make sure you've got a gun, grab the extra clips, and go load the SUV. Tell Jorge to get ready. Make sure he's got a gun." He pauses for just a second. "And don't either of you die tonight."

I barely register them.

My phone buzzes.

Carlos: Copy. Full response Zavala ETA 10 min

Good. That's enough time. I finish adjusting my tie, checking the fit of my jacket, making sure everything conceals my weapons perfectly.

I check my screen one last time. The tracker I planted in Sloane's system is still running, her digital footprint now moving fast. I exhale sharply. *She's knows something. She's trying to get to Maria.*

Elias adjusts his holsters, securing his knives. "You thinking worst-case scenario?"

I exhale, pressing everything down—anger, worry, the sharp edge of something deeper that I can't afford to feel right now.

"I'm thinking she just walked into the open, and the second Sloane Cross clocks her, she's a target."

Elias exhales, dragging a hand through his hair. "Then let's move, *jefe*."

7:56 p.m.

We pull out of the driveway in silence, Jorge driving, engine roaring as we tear down the street, heading straight for the Hotel Zavala.

Maria hasn't just slipped away. She's made herself visible to the enemy.

I exhale slowly. And for the first time in a long time, I'm thinking about Maria and I don't feel panic. I don't feel rage.

I feel calm. Cold, clear, precise.

Like I've finally let go of the things that kept me soft. The fear. The guilt. The need to deserve her.

All I feel now is purpose.

And a rising, calculated hunger to destroy anyone who thought this was the moment to take her from me.

Let them try. God, I hope they do.

Because tonight, I'm not the hacker in the shadows. I'm not the smart one. Not the quiet one. Not the obedient one.

I'm the one they should've feared from the beginning.

I am the reckoning.

And I will burn the world to the ground before I let them touch her.

59

MARIA

THE HOTEL ZAVALA'S Crystal Ballroom isn't just a venue. It's a spectacle. A temple to wealth, power, and the people who decide what the world will watch next.

Gold-trimmed elegance drapes across the room, glinting off every surface. The chandeliers, massive and dripping with crystal, refract light across tuxedos and couture gowns, making the entire room glow. Conversations hum at a polished, controlled pitch. Deals are being closed, alliances being formed, careers being shaped.

This isn't just a party. It's a marketplace.

The UltraVision section is even more exclusive. A cordoned-off space with velvet ropes and mirrored walls, where the highest-ranking players in Hollywood move with the kind of confidence that comes from shaping billion-dollar franchises. Studio execs, award-winning directors, A-list actors—all mingling together, making power moves look effortless.

And tonight? I'm not just an observer. *I'm one of them.*

My dress catches the light with every step—a silver constellation against bare skin, unapologetically short and gleaming among a sea of floor-length gowns. I see the glances as I move, some admiring, some judgmental, and I lift my chin higher. I know exactly what I'm doing.

Beside me, Lily is buzzing with excitement. She's clutching an UltraVision swag bag to her chest like it contains the secrets to the universe.

"Oh my God, Mercede," she whispers, barely holding in a squeal. "You're not going to believe what's in here." She peeks inside, eyes going wide. "This is real luxury swag. Look! A freaking UltraVision-branded Montblanc pen! Do you know how much these cost?"

I barely glance at her. "Uh-huh."

Lily gasps louder, digging deeper into the bag. "Is this—an UltraVision monogrammed Dolce & Gabbana Casa bathrobe?" She presses it against her cheek and sighs. "I've never felt anything this soft."

Before I can respond, Kara Lasater appears. UltraVision's polished, immaculately put-together executive, exuding money, power, and effortless confidence.

"Mercede," she greets me smoothly, her smile warm but measured. "I'm so glad you could make it."

She barely spares Lily a glance, which doesn't seem to faze Lily at all. She's already distracted by the passing trays of cocktails.

She snatches up a dark red drink in a crystal coupe glass, reading the label attached to the stem. "The Duke's Blood." She takes a sip and moans. "Oh, this is dangerous. It tastes like... sexy betrayal."

Kara's lips twitch. "UltraVision loves a theme."

I arch a brow. "You have Dark Duke-themed cocktails?"

She gestures to a sleek bar setup, where customized drinks are displayed on an illuminated menu, each tied to one of the three major projects UltraVision is pushing for tonight.

Signature Cocktails
Inspired by UltraVision's Next Big Projects
The Duke's Blood – Aged bourbon, smoked cinnamon, and cherry bitters. Inspired by The Dark Duke.
The Perfect Lie – Champagne, grapefruit liqueur, and a hint of sage. Inspired by The Witness.
The Last Horizon – Mezcal, passionfruit, and chili salt. Inspired by Gravity's Edge.

The names alone tell me everything I need to know. UltraVision isn't here to impress me. They're here to close deals. And not just with me.

They've got three potential franchises lined up tonight. Which means I'm not just being courted. I'm competing. And if I don't seize this moment, someone else will.

Kara watches my reaction carefully. "This," she says smoothly, "is what UltraVision does. We don't just make entertainment. We create experiences."

She guides me deeper into the UltraVision space, past sleek digital displays looping concept trailers, toward a floor-to-ceiling glass wall lined with dramatic lighting.

And then—

I stop dead.

Because there, displayed like a statement of intent, is a huge mock-up poster for *The Dark Duke*.

It isn't finalized—just a concept—but when I see it, my breath catches.

A towering, shadowed castle. A lone, masked figure in a black military coat standing at the gates. A storm brewing overhead.

The title emblazoned in silver gothic font:

THE DARK DUKE

by Mercede Sanchez

I imagine it on billboards. On posters in Times Square. Streaming previews. Merch with the name stamped on it. A future I built from nothing.

I think I'm about to cry.

This was just an idea once. A story I worked on in stolen hours, in library corners, and through late nights, clinging to the hope that it mattered. Only a few people believed in it then. Ami, Natalie. Fidel. They helped me make it real.

And now it's here. In a room like this. On the brink of becoming something massive.

"You're on our shortlist," Kara says, watching me. "We've been developing materials to show the UV board. But I wanted you to see this. To get a sense of what UltraVision is ready to do for you."

I swallow hard, pulse hammering.

I want this. I fought for this. This deal is going to be mine.

Carlos wants to control the rights if he can take Solano Studios away from Wes. Control me.

And Fidel—

I shove him out of my head.

I'm here, in this moment, standing in front of the future I've built for myself.

"Mercede!"

I don't see her at first. I feel her. A presence slipping into my space.

Sloane Cross.

She appears at my side, sleek in a long, high-fashion emerald-colored dress, confidence dripping off her like perfume.

"Kara," she greets, polite but indifferent. Her real focus is on me.

"I was hoping to track Mercede down," she says smoothly.

"We need to go over some PR strategy before she's bombarded by press—"

"I'm here for the gala, Sloane," I interrupt, keeping my tone even.

Lily, on her way to tipsy from her second Duke's Blood cocktail, leans toward me. "She's very intense," she whispers loudly.

Sloane's smile doesn't falter. "Just making sure you're covered," she says. "Your profile is only going to get bigger after tonight."

Something about the way she says it made my skin prickle.

I narrow my eyes. "What does that mean?"

Sloane tilts her head. "You know. UltraVision." Her hand sweeps toward the Dark Duke poster. "You're a hot commodity right now."

The way she says it. Too casual, too confident. It sets off alarm bells in my head.

How does she know what's happening with UltraVision? The deal *just* came together. Only a handful of people know the details. So why is she talking like she's already been briefed? How is she looped into any of this?

Something isn't right.

The air around me has changed—just slightly, just enough to make the hairs on the back of my neck stand up.

I scan the room. It feels like things have shifted.

A man near the bar, laughing with another exec, but his eyes are me.

A woman near the entrance, turning away too fast when I glance over.

A man on a phone, speaking too quietly, gaze flicking toward me, like he's waiting for something.

Am I being paranoid?

I glance back at Sloane. She isn't just *here*. She's watching. She's maneuvering.

Why is she so focused on *me?* Isn't she supposed to be doing Lily's PR? Or is she here for something else entirely?

Around us, the gala hums with power and influence. Business deals, handshakes, the quiet exchange of money and control. But beneath the glamor and luxury, something feels off. I'm a Sandoval. I know how to read a room. And this room is wrong.

Was I stupid to come here? To ignore every warning I was given? Is Sloane something more? Is she positioning me? And if she is—

What have I just walked into?

60

MARIA

Sloane grabs Lily's arm.

Not a guiding touch. A hard grip.

"Come on," she says smoothly, her heels clicking against the polished marble floor as she pulls on Lily. "We'll do a few quick shots and be right back. The terrace is this way."

Sloane glances back at me. A knowing smile curving her lips. There's something in her eyes. Something calculated. Like she's already won. She knows I'll follow.

And I do. Not because I trust her. Not because this feels right.

But because I'm not letting her lead Lily off alone.

Lily, oblivious, giggles, stumbling to keep up. "Oh my God. The terrace? Mercede, this is such a good idea," she gushes. "Hashtag UltraVision glam! Hashtag Mercede and Lily take over! Hashtage Lady Penelope goes Hollywood! We should totally do a video!"

Sloane hums in agreement. "Yes, a video. The terrace is right through here," she says. "Perfect lighting, privacy, and a great skyline view. We'll get some incredible shots."

We move deeper into the Hotel Zavala. Away from the gala, down a side hallway. The music dims, the conversations fade.

Something's wrong. It's too quiet. The air is too still. The marble beneath my heels feels too quiet. I slow my steps. "Who's taking the photos?" I ask.

Sloane doesn't hesitate. "Someone from UltraVision's social team."

I glance back over my shoulder. A man in a suit steps into the hallway behind us. Blocking the exit. My stomach tightens.

Lily, completely unaware, keeps moving ahead. "I love a well-curated aesthetic. I mean, picture us, standing at the edge of the terrace, backlit by the city—"

Sloane reaches the door at the end of the hallway. She pushes it open. Instead of the crisp scent of night air, there's nothing. No terrace. No skyline. No sound. Only darkness. A hollow, empty space.

My pulse spikes. My instincts screaming. *Trap!*

I stop short. "Lily, wait—"

A hard shove from behind sends me stumbling forward.

Lily screams.

I catch myself, twisting just in time to see—

Men.

Six, maybe more. All in black. Balaclavas covering their faces. No features, no expressions.

The door slams shut behind us.

And Sloane?

Gone. She didn't come in the room.

They move fast, no shouting, no wasted movement. This isn't amateur hour. This is professional.

Lily's still screaming, flailing as one of them grabs her.

A gloved hand clamps around my arm. I react instantly—twisting, driving my elbow into his ribs—

A grunt. Pain. But not enough.

I kick out, heel slamming into another's shin. Another set of hands grabs me. A gun is jammed against my ribs.

"Move." Low. Flat. Professional. Not a threat. An order.

I freeze. Not in fear. In calculation.

Lily gasps, her breathing sharp and frantic.

"Mercede!" she chokes out. "Oh my God, oh my God, I *knew* this would happen—this is literally my worst nightmare—"

"Lily." Firm. Steady. "Look at me."

Her wild, terrified eyes lock onto mine.

"We're going to be fine," I say. Controlled. Even. "Don't fight. Just breathe."

She nods—too fast, too shaky—but she listens.

One of the men yanks off my heels and tosses them aside.

Not Lily's. Just mine. Because they know.

They know I'm a Sandoval. They know I'm trained. They know I might turn my stilettos into weapons.

Lily's purse and UltraVision swag bag are ripped from her grip, flung to the floor.

She gasps. "Oh my God. Do you even *know* what was in that bag?!"

No response. Lily pouts and says quietly, "It has... a Montblanc pen."

A man steps closer. Slow. Unrushed. Gloved hands run over my body. Waist. Hips. Thighs. A calculated search.

His fingers pause.

Shit.

He's found the small knife strapped to the inside of my thigh. He yanks it free and tosses it aside. I tilt my head. Calm. Controlled.

"Careful," I murmur. "It's sharp."

No response. Just cold efficiency.

Lily, on the other hand, is watching with wide, horrified eyes.

"What the hell is this?" she blurts. "Is this like… some kind of robbery thing? A kidnapping thing? A cartel thing?"

She gasps. "Oh my God, I was in an episode of *Law and Order* just like this!"

One of the men pulls out plastic zip ties. They bind my wrists in front of me, tight. Too tight. Good.

They do the same to Lily, but less precise. She isn't the target. She's collateral. They aren't amateurs. But they aren't perfect either.

They tied my wrists in front—rookie mistake. They didn't gag me. Didn't knock me out. They must need me conscious. Talking.

Why?

They move fast, pushing us toward the exit. My feet scrape across the floor, fighting for balance. Lily stumbles beside me in her heels.

"I can't—I can't walk this fast in these—"

One of the men yanks her forward harder.

I scan the hallway. No cameras. Someone already cleared this route. I clench my teeth. Fucking Sloane.

I look back at Lily. At the guy dragging her forward. At the tattoo on the back of his hand.

A black crow. Wings spread. Mid-flight. And suddenly, a cold wave rolls through me as everything clicks into place.

Los Cuervos.

Fidel was right.

This isn't just Sloane. This isn't just a setup.

This is Los Cuervos. Tommy Delgado. His trap.

They shove me through the last door. The night air hits my skin. Cool. Crisp.

A blacked-out van waits at the loading dock. A gun presses against my spine.

"Get in."

My heart is slamming against my ribs. I walked into this. I knew something was off, and I still let it happen.

Maybe if Lily wasn't involved, I wouldn't keep moving. Maybe I could figure something out.

But she's here. And I can't leave her.

I glance back. Hotel Zavala looms behind me, golden and glittering. And I think of only one person.

Because I know that, by now, Fidel realizes I'm gone.

Find me, Fidel. Find me before it's too late. Because this time, I don't know if I can save myself.

61

FIDEL

THE SECOND we step into Hotel Zavala's grand ballroom, the world shifts.

The music keeps playing, the champagne keeps flowing, but something under the surface fractures.

It's not just that we walk in, armed and ready. It's the way the air contracts. The way conversations choke off mid-sentence, silence slowly descending. The way heads snap toward us, instincts flaring before logic can catch up.

Because people with power know it when they see it.

And people without it? They get the fuck out of the way.

We move like a single organism.

Ten Sandoval men. Elias. Me. Carlos. Our team. All black. Suits, shirts, ties. Polished shoes, precision in every step.

No shouting. No weapons drawn. Just cold, silent inevitability.

Hotel security is standing down. Carlos called ahead and made sure of it.

We're here with a purpose. And no one—not the starlets, not the executives, not the politicians sipping cocktails in their tuxedos—wants to be standing between us and whatever the fuck we're here to do.

The crowd parts without a word. The music dies down. People retreat to the walls. Conversations dip into hushed whispers. The smell of fear, heavy with expensive perfume and adrenaline, starts to permeate the air.

We're the wolves at the masquerade. And the sheep know it.

Carlos is with us, but he lets me take the lead. Even he knows it. For me, this is personal.

Because no one knows how to track Maria like I do. And right now, there's only one outcome I'm willing to accept.

Bring her back.

Even if I have to burn this city to the fucking ground to do it.

First priority: Scan the room. Find Sloane Cross.

I spot her instantly.

Green dress. Laughing too hard at something some low-level producer has just said. Too relaxed. Too cocky. No fucking idea that her life just ran out of runway.

I tap my comm.

"Luis. Green dress at UltraVision VIP. Take two guys. Come in slow. Grab her, find a room nearby, and lock her down. Take everything—phone, tablet, anything she's carrying. Nothing leaves her hands."

Luis responds immediately, voice taut. "Copy that."

He and two others peel off, slipping through the ballroom like predators among cattle.

The rest of us fan out. I keep Elias close.

We're hunting.

The UltraVision VIP section is a gleaming pocket of desperate ambition. Custom cocktails, sleek promo displays, concept art projected across the walls.

At the center: The Dark Duke.

A stormy castle. A masked figure. Maria's future—glossy, stylized, monetized.

But Maria?

She's not there. She's gone.

I feel the hollowness of it like a void in my chest. A vibration just below rage.

Elias closes in on Kara Lasater, UltraVision's shining star executive. His smile is so charming it should be illegal.

"Ms. Lasater," he says smoothly, "you look devastating tonight."

She blinks, thrown off for a second, before her social instincts click back in. "Elias Vasquez," she says with a professional smile. "I didn't know you were here."

"Always where the action is," Elias says. Then, casually, "You happen to see Mercede tonight?"

Kara frowns, irritation creeping into her perfect veneer. "She was doing great. I was about to make introductions to the board. And then—" she gestures vaguely toward the empty VIP cordon — "her PR girl dragged her off. Supposedly for photos."

Her voice drips with disapproval. Not of Maria. Of whoever had the audacity to pull a prime prospect off the auction block.

"Her PR girl?" Elias prompts, voice all lazy curiosity.

"Sloane someone?" Kara says, exasperated. "Honestly, it was weird. She kept saying something about the terrace. Some perfect spot." She shakes her head. "But there's no terrace nearby. Frankly, she's not too good at her PR job."

A cold, sharp certainty slices through me. Not a photo op.

A setup. A trap.

I meet Elias's gaze, and I see the same conclusion written in his eyes.

"Sloane. Now."

We move. No running. No shouting. Just precision, dark suits slicing through the crowd like blades.

We find the private conference room Luis has taken over. The two guards stationed outside straighten when they see us coming. Instinctive, silent acknowledgment.

Luis opens the door for us without a word.

Inside? Sloane Cross. Seated at a massive oak conference table. Phone and tablet laid out neatly. Hands folded. Face calm.

But there's a twitch at the corner of her mouth. A crack in the mask?

She's fucked.

And we're about to make sure she knows just how much.

62

FIDEL

THE CONFERENCE ROOM IS COLD. Quiet. Clinical.

Sloane Cross sits at the heavy wooden conference table like she owns the place. Legs crossed, hands folded neatly on the polished surface. Not a single hair out of place. Not a single crack in her composure.

Yet.

Luis stands by the door, arms crossed. Gun in his waistband, visible, deliberate. He's finally understanding the job now.

Elias pulls up a chair next to Sloane, swinging it around and dropping into it backward, casual and predatory, arms folded across the back.

I stand on her other side, arms crossed, leaning against the table. In her space, boxing her in.

"Where is she?" Elias asks, voice smooth as silk, sharp as broken glass.

Sloane tilts her head, offering a slow, coy smile. "You'll have to be more specific."

She's trying to play us? Okay, let's play.

Elias exhales, slow and bored. "Mercede Sanchez. Lily Renshaw. Last seen with you. Now they're gone."

Sloane's eyebrows lift, amused. "Mercede?" she purrs. "You mean Maria Sandoval, right?"

I feel my fists clench at my sides. But I keep it contained.

Focus.

No mistakes.

No rage.

Only cold, clinical disassembly.

Sloane leans back in her chair. "Maria left with me willingly," she says, glancing at her manicured nails. "If she's missing... that's her problem, not mine."

Wrong answer.

I move. Fast.

Fist in her hair. Yanking her head back hard enough to make her gasp, exposing the delicate line of her throat.

I lean in, so close she can feel the heat of my breath against her ear.

"I'm going to ask you only once," I murmur, deadly quiet. "Where the *fuck* is Maria?"

Her throat bobs with a swallow. But she recovers fast.

Tries to smirk. "If you're so good at finding things, why don't you figure it out yourself?"

Challenge delivered. Her last mistake.

I release her abruptly. Letting her jerk back into the chair, clutching her pride like it might save her.

It won't.

I turn to Luis without even looking at her. "My laptop."

Luis moves instantly, crossing to the tech bag tucked against the wall.

What's happening here isn't unplanned. Not an improvisation. I came ready for this bitch.

I take the seat next to Sloane. Luis places my bag onto the table in front of me.

I unzip it calmly. Pull out my laptop. Power it up. Load the cloned interface of her system. Make sure she can see the screen.

Sloane leans forward, she sees the layout. Recognizes it. Realizes it's hers.

"Good luck, bodyguard," she scoffs, leaning back. "You don't have the clearance to break into that."

She's wrong.

I plug in a black USB stick I've kept with me, waiting for this moment.

Frank's backdoor access.

The one thing Sloane didn't realize had escaped her system, waiting for someone smarter to find it. Use it.

I sit next to her. Calm. Icy.

A few keystrokes. A few seconds pass. Access granted.

Sloane blanches.

I turn and give her a smile. All teeth. "It's Blackmatch, right?" Her face pales at the sound of the name she thought she burned. "I've got your key, Blackmatch. I don't need your permission."

In less than six seconds, her entire system cracks open for me.

Every file. Every text. Every buried GPS ping and wiped security video.

Because I'm not some hired gun in a suit.

I'm the fucking apex predator of the digital world.

And she just wandered into my kill zone.

"You're a bodyguard," she breathes, horror dawning. She looks up from the computer screen, wide eyes locking on mine. "Who are you?"

I don't answer. I don't owe her anything. I skim rapidly through her decrypted files. Encrypted texts. Offloaded hotel security footage. GPS records.

There. Storage room. Then loading dock. Black van.

Maria. Lily.

Dragged. Disappeared.

I push the laptop toward Sloane. Let her see the evidence in glowing clarity. "You're going to tell me where they took her," I say, low and lethal.

Sloane's pulse hammers at her throat.

Her eyes dart to the screen—

Then to Elias—

Then to the door—

Calculating.

Frank said she's done cartel work before. She's smart. She knows if Los Cuervos finds out she cracked, she's dead.

But she also knows if she doesn't crack right now—she won't walk out of this room alive.

Elias smiles.

A slow, lazy grin as he flicks his butterfly knife open and closed, with a casual click-click-click that echoes loudly through the silence in the room.

He leans in close. Slow. Deliberate.

He presses the tip of the blade lightly to the soft hollow of her throat.

"You know, Sloane," he says conversationally, voice low, "your carotid artery is right here."

He presses the knife just enough to dimple her skin.

"One quick puncture... you're unconscious in twenty seconds. Dead in under two minutes."

Sloane's breath stutters. She's staring at her hands as they clench into fists against the table. I watch her mouth—quivering slightly, biting down panic.

Elias traces a slow line up her neck with the tip of the blade. A single bead of sweat slides down her temple.

"Of course, the problem with that is," he says, his voice low, his mouth right at her ear, "then you're dead. And you can't tell us what we want to know."

Sloane takes in a shuddering breath. But stays silent.

"And what we want to know is exactly where Maria is," Elias whispers.

Sloane stays silent. A few seconds pass by slowly.

Elias stands, pushing his chair back. "Okay, Sloane" he says, sounding just slightly exasperated. He's good at this. "Let's do it your way. Luis, can you help me?"

Luis steps in behind Sloane. Elias tells him, "Hold her head still. If she moves, it gets sloppy."

Luis grips her skull with both hands. Sloane flinches, letting out a low moan. But Elias is already turning her head, exposing her left ear. "This will only hurt for a minute, Sloane." He pulls down on her earlobe, places the blade of his knife at the cartilage at the top of her ear, and begins a small slice.

Sloane whimpers. She's still thinking about Los Cuervos. What could happen with them. But now she's realizing—Elias might be worse.

"Nothing to say, Sloane?" Elias asks, flicking blood from his knife onto her cheek.

"I... I don't know... I don't know where they are... " she whispers, still trying to hold on. "Tommy didn't tell me."

Elias exhales. "Not the right answer." He pulls down on her earlobe again, and makes a second cut, taking a small notch out of the cartilage in her left ear. A precise, deliberate slice. Enough to hurt, enough to scar.

Sloane lets out a sharp, terrified shriek. Luis doesn't flinch. Elias smiles faintly as he finishes his work on her ear.

"Please," she gasps, voice cracking, chest heaving. "I don't know. I don't know." She gulps in a breath. She gets it now. "Just... please. Stop."

Her breathing is shallow, eyes wild and wet with tears, shoulders curled inward. Her facade crumbles.

Elias releases her ear and flicks the skin and blood from his knife onto her face. Luis exhales a low, satisfied laugh.

I think we almost have her. I step in, lean into her other ear.

"The problem with you, Sloane," I say, my voice soft and steady, "is you think a little blood is the worst thing that can happen." I unzip the outer pouch of my tech bag. Sloane watches with wide eyes as I lay out pliers, wire cutters, a compact cordless drill. Matte black. Clean. Unassuming.

"Huh," Elias mutters, eyebrows lifting.

I set the drill on the table with a soft thunk. Open the bit case. Choose the largest one. Screw it in.

"I use it for hardware extraction," I say. "Bypassing tamper-proof casings. You've probably got one, right Blackmatch?" I say.

I meet her eyes. "Today it has a different function."

Sloane starts to shake her head. Her mouth opens. I stand and grab her right hand.

"You went to work for the bad guys, Sloane." My voice is low, almost kind. "How did you think this would end?"

I brace her wrist flat against the table. She screams before the drill even touches skin. Then I pull the trigger.

Her scream rips through the room like a blade. Luis doesn't flinch. Elias watches with quiet approval.

I stop after half a second. Not enough to cripple. Probably.

"Still worried about Los Cuervos?" I ask calmly.

Her lips tremble. Tears are rolling down her face as she sobs. Her mouth opens. And this time—she talks.

63

MARIA

THE BLACK BAG over my head smells like cheap polyester and somebody else's sweat.

I sit on the metal floor of the van, knees bent, zip-tied hands resting in my lap. The vehicle rumbles beneath me, jostling slightly as we take a turn.

Forty minutes. That's my best guess at how long we've been driving. Not far enough to leave Austin, but far enough to get out of the city center. Surface streets, then freeway. I felt the shift, the way the van picked up speed. Maybe twelve minutes on the highway, then a turn. Longer stretches of road. Fewer stops. The terrain changed too. Smoother, less urban.

Not a warehouse district then. Not a hideout in some crumbling back alley. Suburbs maybe. Or some remote estate tucked away from curious eyes.

Three men total. Two in the back with us. One driving. So they didn't all get into the van. Maybe a separate car?

Beside me, Lily lets out a small huff.

"Ugh. This is going to absolutely ruin my hair," she says, voice muffled under her own bag. "*And* my dress. It's a rental, you know. Do you think UltraVision will reimburse me for this? Probably not, right?"

One of the men growls. "Shut the fuck up."

Lily pauses. Then, quietly: "... Just asking."

I almost laugh.

Not out of amusement. Just out of pure disbelief.

We're in the back of a van, kidnapped, restrained, on the way to God-knows-where, and Lily Renshaw's biggest concern? Her hair and the rental fee on her cocktail dress.

I turn my head slightly, whispering through the suffocating fabric. "Lily, breathe. We're fine."

She sighs dramatically. "I mean, except for the part where we're being *kidnapped*, sure."

Yeah. Except for that.

The van slows, then stops.

A door slides open, cool air rushing inside. We're at the "second location."

Hands yank me forward. I stumble but catch myself, adjusting my balance as I'm hauled out of the van.

A hard shove between my shoulder blades. "Move."

I move.

Lily yelps as she's dragged alongside me. "Okay, okay! I have heels on, asshole! I can't just—ow, *rude*! Also, are we *at* a place? Like, is this it?"

No answer. Just the sound of a door unlocking, heavy and deliberate.

Then—polished floors beneath my feet. Soft air conditioning. The faint scent of leather and expensive cologne.

This isn't some abandoned warehouse. This is a house. A very nice house.

The bags are ripped off our heads.

Lily gasps. "Ow!" And then, "Oh, wow."

I blink, eyes adjusting to the sudden light.

We're in a massive living room. White leather couches, glass tables, dim golden lighting, enormous windows with a sweeping view of the Austin skyline, gleaming in the distance.

Lily's eyes sweep over the decor. "This is way swankier than I was expecting. I mean, you hear *kidnapping* and you think *grimy basement.* But this is amazing!"

The nearest thug shoves her onto a couch.

"Okay, rude. You could *ask* me to sit down," she mutters, shifting her weight as gracefully as someone zip-tied in a cocktail dress can manage.

I'm forced down next to her, my own restraints digging into my wrists. They're too tight, almost cutting off circulation. But that's good. Easier to break when I have the chance.

Lily's? Looser. Because she isn't the target. And I think she's starting to realize it.

Then footsteps. Slow. Deliberate.

And, a voice. Low, slick, and far too self-satisfied. "I've been waiting a long time for this."

I don't need to look up to know who it is. But I do anyway.

Tommy Delgado steps into view, outfitted like a cartel prince playing dress-up for a photo shoot.

Black silk shirt, open to the waist. White designer slacks. Black crow tattoo sprawling over his chest—wings outstretched, talons curled. He's lean, almost gaunt, with sharp cheekbones and the over-bright eyes of a man who's spent too long chasing power and not enough time living in reality. Slicked-back hair. Too much cologne.

Smile just a little too wide. Eyes a little glassy. Maybe he's high on something. He's definitely unstable.

He paces slowly in front of us, basking in the moment. His eyes are locked on mine.

"Maria Sandoval," he says, savoring the name. Then, grinning wider, "Or should I say... Maria Delgado?"

Something cold shifts in my chest. But I keep my face blank. He wants a reaction. I won't give him one.

"I know it's a lot to take in," he says, with fake sympathy. "But you must know. You were never really a Sandoval, Maria. Not truly. You're a Delgado. Our blood runs thicker than theirs ever could."

I stare at him. Waiting.

He steps closer, crouching in front of me like he's about to share a secret.

"You remember me, don't you Maria? That night at Luz? I was the manager. I tried to help you. Remember?"

This motherfucker.

"You mean the night you drugged my friend? Tried to drug me?"

I see a gleam in his eyes. Wild. Feral.

"Maria." His voice softens, twisted with warped sincerity. "I was trying to save you. You were stolen. Taken from your real family. Taken from me. But I'm here to fix that. I'm here to fix everything."

He reaches out to me, gazing at me with a strange look of longing? Desire? He tucks a strand of hair behind my ear and I try very hard not to flinch. I'm unsuccessful. Next to me, Lily mutters, "What exactly is happening?"

Tommy ignores her, still watching me. I don't think he hears anyone but himself right now.

He straightens up, pacing again, hands clasped behind his back like a general inspecting his troops. Like a D-list actor performing dinner theater.

"My father was old-school. Narrow-minded. He believed in building power through fear. Through loyalty and bloodshed." His lip curls slightly, contemptuous. "But I'm smarter. I see the bigger picture."

Lily leans toward me, whispering, "He's monologuing."

I almost smile. Almost.

Tommy keeps going, utterly in love with the sound of his own voice.

"Everything the Sandovals built? It was supposed to be ours. Mine. But your father—" His voice curls with contempt as he paces back and forth. "He stole what belonged to the Delgado bloodline. He took our power. He took my father's sister, your mother, my Aunt Lucia. He took my father. He took you."

I feel Lily stiffen beside me. She's starting to see, little by little, just how terrifying our situation is.

Tommy continues with his delusional remarks. "Los Cuervos will not stay caged," he says, voice rising. "We were born to rise. To rule! We're expanding. Further into Mexico, into Texas. Then into the rest of the United States, into every city that thinks it can resist us." He pauses, looking toward the ceiling, seeing something that no one else sees. "Together, we will rebuild what the Delgados lost. A new empire. A blood dynasty that will outlast them all."

He looks down at me and smiles. He leans in, taking my chin in his hand, speaking as if I'm a child who just doesn't understand. "Maria, you were born into the wrong family. But it's not too late." He stops, hands going behind his back, but leaning in further. "You and me? We're going to fix things."

I pull my head back. "Fix things?"

His smirk deepens. "By doing what should've been done years ago. Merging our bloodlines."

A pause.

"You'll marry me," he says softly, his lips much too close to mine. "And together, we'll be unstoppable."

A beat of silence.

Then Lily—being Lily—interrupts with, "Wait. Sorry. Are you saying you want to marry your cousin?"

"Family is everything," he says, almost lovingly. "It's in our blood."

I tilt my head, trying to move away from him, from his lunacy. I let my voice go soft, almost curious. "And what if I say no?"

His smile sharpens. "You won't." A small pause. "But if you do..." He stands, shrugging his shoulders. "There are other ways I can handle this."

There it is. The glint beneath the charm. The violence simmering just below the surface.

This isn't a negotiation. Tommy Delgado believes he's already won. He thinks I'm already his.

My fingers twitch. The need to slap him is becoming unbearable.

He straightens, pulls on the cuffs of his silk shirt.

"Get them settled in my bedroom," he orders the guards. "We're leaving for Monterrey soon. I have calls to make."

And just like that, he turns his back on us. Because in his mind, this is already over.

And in mine? It's only just begun.

64

MARIA

"Maria?" Lily whispers, confused, her wide eyes darting between me and the guard moving toward us.

I cut my eyes at her and give a quick shake of my head.

Play dumb, Lily. For once.

"Stand up," the guard barks. "And don't do anything stupid, ladies. No one's coming for you." He grabs each of us by the arm, yanking us roughly to our feet, and marches us down a wide, silent hallway, to the bedroom Tommy has ordered us to.

My wrists ache from the zip ties, the plastic digging deeper into my skin with every step. But I can't do anything yet. I'm still calculating, trying to form a plan.

Forty minutes in the van. No phones. No trackers. No way for Fidel to know exactly where I am.

That thought hits hard. What if he can't find me?

No. No, he will. He always does.

I take a slow, steady breath. *Keep your head, Maria. Stay sharp. Find the cracks.*

The guard shoves us through a door at the end of the hall. I stumble but catch myself. Lily trips over the heels she's somehow still wearing, landing hard on her knees with a loud "Oof."

"You'll stay in here," he snarls, "and don't cause problems." He slams the door closed. A lock clicks. And then silence.

For half a second, neither of us move.

Then Lily stands, brushing imaginary dust off her cocktail dress with her zip-tied hands. "Seriously?" she mutters.

"Lily," I whisper, "are you okay?"

She tilts her head, staring at me with a confused little frown. "Mercede? Are you really named Maria? I don't get it."

"Yes," I whisper. "I'm Maria. Tommy is my cousin. And you need to keep your voice down because I'm going to get us out of here."

She holds her breath for just a second. Blinks. And then seems to accept what I'm telling her.

She nods and says, very seriously, "Okay, but I'm still calling you Mercede. Also, I know how to get out of zip ties. I learned when I was an extra in an episode of *Serial Killer Confessions, Season 2*."

I smile at her, whispering. "I know too, Lily."

"And for some reason, they haven't taken my shoes away." She looks down at the scuffed but intact stilettos she's still wearing. "I played Call Girl Number Four in a straight-to-DVD movie called *New Orleans Hookers*. Maybe you saw it?"

I shake my head, trying not to lose it.

"That's okay," she whispers. "It wasn't very good. I mean, *I* was good. But the movie, not so much. Anyway, in the movie I stabbed my pimp through the eye with the heel of my shoe. That's how I got away from him. So maybe that's an idea."

I look into her eyes and for the first time since we were tossed into that van, I smile. Maybe Lily's not dead weight after all. Maybe she's actually an asset. And suddenly, I feel like we're going to get out of this. Because I'm not doing it alone.

"Lily, you are truly awesome," I tell her, keeping my voice low.

She beams at me. "Thanks, bestie," she says, still whispering. "And that's not even the best part." She looks around dramatically, then tugs at the side seam of her dress. A small smartphone falls from a hidden pocket. It glints under the dim bedroom light.

A phone. A fucking burner phone.

I suck in a sharp breath. "Lily! You have a phone?" I whisper-yell.

"Always!" she says proudly, still speaking in a quiet voice. "Sometimes they take your phone at the door, so I always bring a backup. You never know when you need to post a TikTok at an after-party."

I'm torn between laughing and sobbing with relief.

"They didn't even check me that hard," she continues. "I guess because I wasn't like, *the target*."

No, they didn't. While the kidnappers had patted me down thoroughly, they'd barely touched her. Just ripped away her purse and swag bag and tossed her into the van like baggage.

They hadn't planned for Lily. They hadn't planned for the two of us.

I inhale slowly. I have a partner now. An unexpected one, but maybe the only person in the world right now who can help me tip the odds.

"Okay," I whisper. "Here's what we're going to do." I crouch closer, our heads nearly touching. "We break the zip ties first. Quietly. No noise. Then, we text one number and one number only."

Lily nods, suddenly very serious. "Who?"

"Fidel," I say. My voice is steady. "No one else. No 911. No friends. No UltraVision. Only Fidel."

Her brow furrows. "Okay, but like... he might ignore it because he won't know my number. So what do we text?"

I think for a second. Then grin.

"I know exactly what to text. He'll know it's us. And believe me, he'll come."

65

FIDEL

Sloane Cross is gone.

Elias dragged her out of the conference room, handing her off to Carlos's guys with a simple, "Take care of her." By fucking with the Sandovals, Sloane had earned a death sentence.

Now, it's just me, Elias, Luis, and a table full of Sloane's pathetic attempts at cybersecurity.

Whatever Los Cuervos paid her, they got scammed. I'm easily tearing through everything. She's got weak AES keys, recycled passwords, encryption slapped on with duct tape. Sloppy. Lazy.

Sloane Cross wasn't slick. Wasn't untouchable. Shit, she wasn't even that good.

And she didn't know Maria's location. But she knew the exit plan. The destination. The timeline. The transport.

After what we did to her, she finally gave up enough to help me trace it.

Elias lounges at the end of the table, flipping his butterfly knife open and closed. Click-click-click.

Luis hovers nearby, watching the screens, glancing at me, smart enough not to ask questions.

Then I find what I'm looking for. A buried text thread. Tommy's burner number. The last message sent to him:

> Sloane: M secured. En route to safe location.

Timestamp: 39 minutes ago.
My pulse slams in my chest, hard.
Another ping:

> Sloane: Confirming travel arrangements. Private jet to MTY. Flight plan filed.

I still. Private jet to Monterrey, Mexico. Not just a hostage situation. They're planning to move her. Out of the country.

I should be panicking. My hands should be shaking.

But they're not. There's no rage. No fear. No second-guessing. Just focus. Cold, exact, ruthless.

That part of me that used to lose control? Gone for now. What's left knows exactly what to do. "Okay, motherfucker," I mutter.

Elias's knife pauses mid-flip. "What?"

"They're taking her out of the country," I say flatly.

Luis swears under his breath.

Elias's eyes narrow but he stays calm. "Where is she now?"

"Still looking."

I switch to Tommy's handset metadata. Every burner he's ever used left breadcrumbs. I find a GPS ping. Just outside Austin city limits. I cross-reference it with my files on Los Cuervos holdings, looking through a list of nearby properties.

Then—

My phone buzzes. Unknown number. I open the text anyway.

> Unknown: hi boots dora hrry

I go still.

Everything else drops away. The room. The sounds. The people. Gone.

Nothing exists except the text. Dora the Explorer. Boots. It's her.

Maria.

Alive. Messaging me. Giving me clues. The words aren't perfect. Maybe there's a guard nearby. Maybe she's got to be fast. But it's her. She's alive. I text back.

> Fidel: yes dora what do you see

A reply. Immediate.

> Unknown: big win city pool tes driveway

I exhale sharply. Big windows. City view. Pool. Tesla in the driveway.

She's in a house. Somewhere high up. A Delgado-owned property in Austin.

> Unknown: going mex soon

No. Not happening.

I switch screens, confirming a Delgado house near the GPS ping. Satellite imaging. Pool. Massive windows. Modern architecture. Traffic cams. Silver Model X in the circular driveway.

There it is. The house where they have her.

Got you, you little shit.

I grab my gun, my voice cold and sharp. "I've got it."

Luis tenses. Elias flicks his knife closed. "Where is she?"

"Tommy's house."

Luis exhales sharply, checks the mag in his Glock. "Sloane give that up?"

"Her phone confirmed it," I say. She talked. Just not fast enough.

I tap my comm. "Carlos. Sending coordinates. Bring Daniel and an assault team. Ten minutes."

Carlos's response is instant. "Copy. Clean sweep."

I text Maria.

> Fidel: stay put princesa coming he's dead

The reply is a fucking heart emoji. I smile.

I adjust my jacket and turn to leave.

Tommy Delgado thinks he has Maria.

By the time I'm finished, he'll have nothing. Nothing at all.

66

MARIA

Fidel is coming.

I know it the second I send the text. He's already tracking me, already moving.

But Lily and I can't just sit here and wait. We've got to buy time. Give Fidel a chance to get here.

Tommy and his men are somewhere in this house, prepping for the next phase. Getting us out, getting us on that plane, disappearing us into Mexico.

Or maybe they'll kill Lily and just take me.

I clench my fists. Not happening.

Our first obstacle is the single guard outside the door. One man between us and freedom. And he's about to have the worst, and possibly last, night of his life.

I turn to Lily, voice low. "Okay Lily. Time for some acting."

She exhales. "Oh, thank God. Finally."

I smirk. "You're gonna convince the guard to open the door and take you to the bathroom. He's going to come in and then I'll handle it."

Lily closes her eyes and takes a deep breath, getting into character. I move into position, pressing myself against the wall next to the door. The overhead light is too bright, so I snap off the switch.

Now the only light is coming from the bedside lamp. Dim, uneven. Perfect.

I nod at Lily. She nods back. She knocks on the door, gently at first, voice high-pitched and whining. "Sir? Hello? Sir? I *really* have to pee."

Nothing. She knocks again. "Hey? You? Guy with the gun?"

No response.

Her tone shifts—syrupy, seductive. "You can watch me in the bathroom if you want." Her tone drips with soft suggestion. "To make sure I don't do anything *bad*. I'll be *extra* nice."

Silence. She looks at me and shrugs.

Then she takes a deep breath and switches tactics. She bangs on the door with both of her fists and starts screeching. "I *swear* to goddamn fucking GOD! If you don't let me out, I will *literally piss* on this extremely expensive carpet. And I will make *sure* Tommy knows it's *your* fault!"

A heavy, irritated sigh from the other side of the door. Then —footsteps. The lock clicks.

The door cracks open and I lunge, exploding forward. I'm on his back before he can react, one arm around his throat, the other gripping Lily's stiletto like a dagger.

I slam it into his neck. Hard. Again. Again.

A wet noise gurgles from his mouth. He staggers forward, trying to shake me off.

Then Lily moves in before I even tell her to. She kicks him in the balls. Hard. He drops to his knees, choking.

Lily finishes it. She has the other stiletto in her hand and drives the heel straight into his eye socket.

It slides in like it's going through butter.

I let go. The body hits the floor.

More gurgling. Some twitching. And then silence.

Lily, panting, stares at the corpse, her stiletto still jammed in his eye. I reach out, touching her arm. She didn't grow up in this world. This might be the first time she's seen someone die.

"Lily," I whisper. "Are you okay?"

She's panting, staring at the man still bleeding out at her feet. She sucks in a deep breath. Then, she looks up at me, pouting. "I loved those shoes."

I almost laugh. But there's no time. I grab his gun. "Let's go."

We don't go for the front door. Too predictable.

Instead, I look around as we slip into the hall. Massive house. Marble floors. Expensive furniture. A fortress disguised as a mansion. Our exit options are limited. I decide we'll move deeper into the house, try to go out a window at the back.

Then, a voice—another man coming down the hall.

I don't hesitate. I raise the gun. I fire once—clean headshot. He drops. Dead.

The silence shatters.

Gunfire erupts. A door slams. Voices shout. They know we're loose.

Lily grabs my arm. "Where—?"

We run. Left, right. Deeper into the house. I push open a heavy door. We've barely cleared the threshold when I realize where we are—and immediately regret it. We're in a wine room.

Massive, climate-controlled room. Rows of floor-to-ceiling racks crammed with bottles of obscenely priced wines. A narrow tasting island anchors the center: crystal stems, a silver champagne bucket, corkscrews, a foil cutter.

Lily gasps. "Holy shit. A wine cellar! This is amazing!"

I press my back against the cool stone wall, breathing hard. Problem. The door we just ran through? Thick glass. Framed by heavy wrought iron. Meant to lock things in. Not keep people out.

Which means...

If Tommy finds us before Fidel does?

We'll be trapped. I have the gun. But not many bullets.

I hear footsteps. Voices. Close. I grab Lily, pulling her behind one of the racks. My heart pounds.

And then a familiar voice. Tommy.

His tone is almost amused. "Really, Maria? Hiding?"

Lily sucks in a sharp breath. I put my finger to her lips, motioning for her to stay quiet.

Tommy's voice floats in, amused. "You think I won't find you?" A pause. And then his voice lowers. "You know," he muses, "maybe you're not that special after all. Maybe you're not worth keeping."

A slow, deliberate step.

"If you insist on acting like some pathetic, scared little girl— perhaps you're not as valuable as I thought."

I clench my jaw. He's unraveling. Good.

His voice sharpens. Hardens. "Come out, Maria. Let's stop playing games."

Another pause. Then—he snaps.

"COME OUT," he roars, "OR I'LL BURN THIS WHOLE FUCKING HOUSE DOWN WITH YOU IN IT!"

Lily's head jerks towards me. Eyes wide. Mouth forming silent words.

"What is this guy's problem?"

I exhale. Trying to stay calm, gripping the gun tighter. Tommy's losing control.

And that's a weakness I can use.

67

MARIA

SUDDENLY, Lily's phone vibrates. A barely audible buzz, but in the suffocating silence of the wine room, it might as well be a gunshot.

She looks down at it, eyes going wide, then turns the screen toward me.

A text.

Fidel: get ready we're coming

A sharp breath catches in my throat. My vision blurs for just a second.

They're coming.

I smile at Lily, squeeze her arm, my whole body flooding with relief. If we can just hold out a little longer...

Then—movement. Through the glass door, Tommy sees us. His eyes lock on mine and an ugly grin crawls out across his face.

"There you are, *mi amor*."

A chill goes down my spine. Tommy has crossed the line

from dangerous to delusional. He was teetering on the edge, but now? Now he's untethered. There's no coming back from this.

He lifts his gun, gesturing lazily toward the glass door. "Drop the gun, open the door and we can put all of this..." he waves his gun in the air, gesturing like this is all nothing, "...behind us."

I look at the gun in his hand. Look at the gun in mine. I am not handing myself over to the insane heir to a vicious cartel throne. Even if he is my blood.

Maybe I can stall, bargain with him, draw things out just a little longer.

I take a slow, measured breath. "Tommy..."

And then the lights cut out. The world stops.

Seconds pass.

BOOM! BOOM!

The sound of two huge explosions rips through the house.

Lily shrieks, slapping a hand over her mouth.

Another two seconds—

BOOM!

Even louder. Several more seconds.

BOOM! BOOM! BOOM!

More explosions.

The floor beneath us shudders violently, shockwaves rattling the racks of wine, bottles crashing to the floor, wine spraying.

Then—

CRACK!

A flashbang detonates, a piercing, metallic noise filling the air.

I squeeze Lily's hand. And grin.

"They're here!"

68

FIDEL

We roll up in a silent convoy, four blacked-out SUVs gliding up the winding drive. The house sits on a secluded hill, city lights flickering in the distance.

Expensive. Isolated. Poorly defended.

I sit in the passenger seat, scanning my laptop, blowing through Tommy's security system in under ten seconds. Amateur. No redundancies, no encrypted firewall, no automated defense response.

The live feeds flicker onto my screen—six men outside, three inside. Two of them guarding the first-floor entry points. One posted upstairs, probably watching from a window. Weak. Predictable.

Then I see him.

Tommy.

Pacing in a hallway near a massive glass door, waving a gun in the air, ranting like a deranged asshole to someone I can't see. His movements are erratic, his posture all bravado, but his body language is screaming something else.

Maria and Lily are behind that door. I know it.

My grip tightens on my gun.

I text Maria.

Fidel: get ready we're coming

Then I press my comm. My voice is flat. Controlled.

"On my cue, I'll cut the power. Then we move in. Carlos. Daniel. Your team handles the six outside. No survivors."

Carlos—"Copy that."

We're already moving, stepping out of the SUVs, loading weapons, checking gear.

"Elias, Luis. Front entrance with me. Jorge. Take the west side. Clear anyone who tries to flank."

Jorge nods. Focused. Ready.

"Blow the vehicles. All of them. Tommy gets no escape."

Carlos huffs out a laugh. "So dramatic."

I see Daniel move to the back of an SUV, pop the back door open, and reach inside. When he straightens, a rocket-propelled grenade launcher rests on his shoulder. Because of course he has a fucking RPG.

"Man, I've been waiting to use this." He sounds pleased.

I ignore him.

I tap a few commands, using my phone now. Power grid override. The house and the surrounding property plunge into darkness.

We move.

Carlos's team splits off, vanishing into the night. Suppressed shots hiss through the air as they take down the perimeter guards, one by one.

Elias, Luis, Jorge, and I move up the driveway. I pull two micro grenades from my belt, flicking the pins off with my thumb.

BOOM. BOOM.

Two explosions. The Tesla and Lamborghini parked in the

front erupt into flames—metal shearing apart, glass shattering like gunfire.

Maria will hear that. She'll know we're here.

But before I can move—

FWOOOSH.

A streak of fire slams into one of Tommy's SUVs.

And the fucking thing detonates.

The blast rips through the night, flames bursting sky-high, sending metal shards whistling through the air.

Daniel steps forward, casually unshouldering the RPG.

I blink. Elias laughs and calls out, "Jesus, Daniel."

Carlos, still moving toward the back, howls with laughter. "I fucking love you, Daniel."

I exhale. Fine. That's one less SUV to worry about.

I speak into the comms. "Hit the rest."

Daniel reloads. Another streak of fire—another detonation. Then another. Then another. Tommy's entire fleet of vehicles— gone. He won't be going to the airport tonight.

Luis shoots at the locked front door, kicks it open, and hurls a flashbang in. A blinding white explosion. A crack of white light and explosive sound.

Jorge moves in tandem, circling to the west entrance, covering our flank, his suppressed rifle barking once. A guard drops before he even knows he's dead.

We breach.

69

MARIA

THE AFTERMATH of the flashbang hangs thick in the air. I smell acrid smoke and my ears are ringing.

Outside the glass door we're trapped behind, Tommy snaps. "FUUUUCCKKK!"

Then—gunfire.

CRACK. The top half of the glass in the door shatters.

The bullet slams into the racks, exploding bottles of champagne in a burst of glass shards and foaming liquid. A cold mist sprays across my skin, sharp with the scent of alcohol.

Lily screams, ducking.

Shit.

I yank her down behind the nearest row of shelves. The wine racks won't save us. They're nothing but thin wooden beams, glass bottles, empty spaces. But they're all we have.

I press the gun into her hands. Her eyes snap to mine, wild with panic. *God, I hope this is the right move.*

Tommy's voice slices through the chaos. "You think you're fucking safe in there? You think someone's gonna get here in time to save you?"

I wipe my wet hands on my dress, brain racing. No back door. No way out. The only exit is through Tommy.

And he knows it.

His voice changes. Lower. Smoother. Pleading. "Let's not play games, Maria." Like he actually thinks he can reason with me. "You're coming with me. One way or another."

CRACK. A final gunshot blasts through the glass door— shattering it completely.

Time to move.

I grab Lily's wrist, hauling her up. "We have to go. Now." We stumble forward, broken glass crunching under our feet. I barely feel it as small shards cut into the soles of my feet.

But Tommy is faster. The second we step into the open, he yanks at what remains of the door. And then he's on me. A strong arm pulling me back, hard, dragging me so that my back is pressed against his solid chest. Cold metal presses under my jaw.

Tommy's gun.

"Drop it," he orders.

My stomach clenches.

He's not talking to me.

He's talking to Lily.

She freezes. She's got the gun raised but it's shaking in her hands. She looks at me—then Tommy—then the gun. Her hands tremble and she can barely keep the gun level. Her breath comes in sharp, uneven gasps.

Tommy sighs, exasperated. "You're not gonna shoot me, sweetheart. You don't even have the safety off."

Lily whimpers. I know the second she makes her decision. Her fingers uncurl from the gun. She lets it drop.

Tommy kicks it away, hard enough to send it skidding across the floor. He tightens his grip on me. His arm locks around my throat, securing me to his chest like a human shield. He jams his gun harder into my temple.

His lips brush my ear. His voice is soft, gentle. Almost intimate.

"Whatever happens, my love, dead or alive, you're leaving with me."

A shiver crawls down my spine. He means it.

Lily lets out a broken sob. I try to breathe, but I can't.

This isn't a standoff. This isn't a negotiation.

Tommy is completely, fully unhinged. And he has me. For the first time, there's no angle to play.

There's no way out.

70

FIDEL

INSIDE THE HOUSE, shadows ripple through the smoke in the air. Two guards in the foyer, guns half-raised, still sluggish from the flashbang. I don't let them react.

I shoot the first one clean through the throat. He crumples, soundlessly. Elias takes out the second with a shot to his chest.

Luis quickly heads upstairs to take out the man there.

Carlos's team breaches through the back, silencers hissing as they execute the last men outside.

Then—gunfire. A single shot. A pause. Then another shot. Inside the house. The sound is sharp and shattering, sending adrenaline knifing through my veins.

Maria.

I'm already moving before I register Elias at my side, both of us swift, silent, lethal. Guns drawn. The emergency lights have kicked on, bathing everything in a dim, eerie red glow.

We make our way to the back of the house, check a corner, turn. And then—there he is.

Tommy Delgado.

Gun pressed to Maria's temple. Arm locked around her throat as he holds her to his chest.

I can just see a black crow tattoo peeking above the open collar of his shirt, rising and falling with each ragged breath. His breathing is uneven, shuddering. Sweat gleams along his hairline. The look of a man who has already lost but refuses to accept it. Behind him, Lily trembles, hands curled into helpless fists.

Maria is still. She isn't screaming. She looks scared but I know her too well. She's waiting. Waiting for an opportunity she can use.

Tommy's eyes flick to me.

"You want her alive?" His voice is like ice, edged with something unstable. "Drop your fucking guns."

Elias and I don't move. Our weapons stay trained on him.

Tommy snarls, tightening his grip on Maria, yanking her even closer. A sharp inhale from her. A flicker of pain. He's pulling too tight, the barrel of his gun jammed against her head.

My grip on my gun tightens.

"She's mine!" He's screaming, completely unraveling into full-blown madness. "And she's coming with me! If you want her alive, drop your fucking guns and let us walk out of here! Or I swear to God—"

Maria flinches. A barely-there reaction, but it's enough. My stomach clenches.

I tilt my head slightly, my voice cold. "You think you're walking out of here?"

Tommy's lips curl.

"I'm a Delgado," he spits. "I rule Los Cuervos. The Sandovals are fucking finished. You're over. When I burn your empire to the fucking ground, *my name* will rise from the ashes."

Elias exhales slowly, muttering, "Jesus Christ."

Tommy doesn't hear him. His entire world has narrowed to me. "Put. The guns. Down."

Tommy doesn't know the Sandovals. He doesn't know we don't bargain with people. We bury them.

I can't help when my lips quirk into the smallest of smiles. He's already dead. He just doesn't know it yet.

I meet Elias's gaze. A silent exchange. We'll play along.

I loosen my grip on my pistol. Slowly, deliberately, I crouch, placing it on the floor. Elias follows suit. I straighten.

"All of them," Tommy says with a smile.

I pull a second gun from inside my jacket as does Elias. We place them on the floor, next to the other two.

Tommy grins. A moment of smug, delusional triumph.

Idiot.

The backup pistol at the small of my back sits heavy and waiting. Elias has knives strapped to every inch of his body. We're both wearing bulletproof vests. Tommy is wearing a thin black shirt.

Two guns each? You think that's it?

We're ready to take him out. And Maria? Maria just needs an opening.

Then—

I see it. Lily, behind Tommy, her hand slipping into her dress. A pocket.

She pulls something out... a corkscrew? A fucking corkscrew?

Before I can react, Lily moves. She slams the corkscrew into the back of Tommy's neck. She draws back and does it again. And again.

His body jerks. He screams.

His grip on Maria loosens. Just enough.

Maria moves fast. Her elbow snaps back, driving hard into his ribs. His gun jerks away from her head for half a second— enough for her to tear herself free.

She doesn't run. She spins away from him, grabs Lily, and drags them both down.

Giving me a clear fucking shot.

I pull my backup gun.

First bullet. Chest.

Second. Throat.

Third. Gut.

Tommy staggers, coughing, a wet, choking sound. He tries to raise his gun as his knees buckle, but he can't. He manages to stay upright, swaying, refusing to fall. His eyes find mine. Furious. Disbelieving.

And I smile.

Good. One round left.

I don't rush it. I want him to feel this. To know exactly who put him in the fucking ground. Blood is spilling down his torso, soaking the black ink of that crow spread across his chest—wings disappearing under a curtain of red. He sways once more.

I meet his eyes. And pull the trigger.

The shot hits right between his eyes.

Tommy stumbles. Face slack. Eyes wide.

He convulses. Then crumples. Dead before he hits the ground.

Silence.

The air is thick with gunpowder and the iron scent of blood. The emergency lights flicker, bathing everything in a hellish red glow.

It's finished. Tommy Delgado is finished.

But then—

A sharp inhale of breath. Lily, sitting on the floor next to Maria, blinking at Tommy's corpse.

She exhales.

"Corkscrew to the neck, asshole. *Pure Bloods, Season 7.*"

71

———

FIDEL

MARIA PUSHES HERSELF UP, steady, blood smeared across her cheek. Her torn dress clings to her. Her shoes are gone and her feet are cut and bloody from the glass sprayed across the floor. She's scraped and bruised, covered in bloody gore, hair a mess. And she's smiling.

That smile.

She turns to me, eyes meeting mine. They're dark, burning. Alive.

And she moves. Straight to me. No hesitation. No doubt.

Still with that fucking smile that's just for me.

Sultry. Defiant. She's never looked more beautiful, more seductive.

She stops in front of me and reaches up, wrapping her arms around my neck, pulling my forehead down to hers, her breath warm against my lips.

"I knew you'd come for me."

My hands find her, one on her waist, one on the back of her neck. I pull her flush against me.

"I'll always come for you, *princesa.*"

And then—

I kiss her.

Our mouths crash together. Hard. Desperate. A kiss that tastes like a promise.

Like a claim. My fucking claim.

She kisses me back, fierce and wild.

Footsteps. Boots crunching over broken glass. A voice. Carlos. He and Daniel come down the hallway toward us. I can hear the rest of his team in the house. Checking bodies, securing exits, ensuring that no loose ends remain.

Carlos stops a few feet from us, eyes sweeping over Maria, taking her in—torn dress, bruised wrists, blood streaked across her face and in her hair.

His jaw tightens. Like he's trying not to lose it. And then he exhales, shaking his head, something like resignation in his eyes. "I should've seen this coming."

Maria turns, still tucked against my chest. She doesn't let go of me.

Carlos watches us, his expression unreadable. Maybe he doesn't want this.

Then, he looks at me. No anger. No disbelief. Just a long, measured stare.

"Do you love her?"

I don't blink. "Always."

Carlos exhales sharply, dragging a hand down his face. He mutters something under his breath and turns away.

"Good," he says, finally. "Take care of her."

That's it. The only approval I'll get from him.

Carlos doesn't waste any more time. He nods at Daniel and Elias. "Clean the house out. And then torch it. Erase everything."

Daniel hefts the rocket launcher, giving it a pat and grinning. "Oh, hell yeah. I'll be outside with my baby. Ready and waiting."

Elias is already barking orders. "Luis. Take care of Lily. Jorge. With me."

Luis goes to Lily, pulling her to her feet. "Thanks so much," she says. She looks up at him, asking in a suddenly sweet voice, "So, you're Luis?"

Elias and Jorge turn to move through the house—grabbing phones, laptops, weapons. Anything that might be worth keeping, might give us intel. Because this house is about to be burned to the ground.

Carlos pulls out his phone. Making the calls that will ensure this whole fucking mess goes up in smoke. He finishes, snaps the burner in half, drops it, pockets the SIM. Everything will be handled. Everything will disappear.

Maria looks up at me, her fingers still curled into my shirt. Her lips ghost over mine, her voice a whisper as she grabs my face and pulls me down to her.

"You're mine, Fidel Mateo Cedillo. Mine."

"Yes." I swear it.

"Now, take me home."

I pick her up and carry her out.

72

—————

FIDEL

MARIA LEADS me up the stairs like she already knows how this night will end.

She pulled the glass from her feet in the car as I drove us back to the safe house. It's quiet as we enter. We're the only two here.

She's barefoot, scraped-up, blood still smeared on her face and in her hair. She's the most beautiful thing I've ever seen. She moves with purpose. Slow, deliberate, leaving no room for hesitation. No second-guessing. She's already decided.

And I follow. Because I always do. I always will.

We drove away, leaving the rest of the world behind. The blood, the bodies, the fire. Maria claimed me, led me away from the destruction, away from everything. She's finally stripped me of every excuse, every reason I've ever had to resist her.

She doesn't look back at me until we reach her bedroom. Then—just for a second—she stops at the door. Her dark eyes lock onto mine, and I brace for the aftershock, for the weight of everything that's happened tonight to hit her all at once.

But there's no fear. No hesitation.

Only want.

She turns and walks inside. I follow.

The bathroom light flickers on. She steps to the shower, turns the knobs, and the steam begins to curl into the air.

I'm still standing there when she peels her dress off.

It slides down her body, pooling at her feet, and she doesn't stop. She removes her bra, lets it fall, pushes her panties down her hips and steps out.

I can't move.

I've imagined her like this before, fucking countless times, in the privacy of my own mind. But none of those moments—none of those fantasies—were ever *this*. Never Maria standing in front of me, bare and perfect, looking at me like she's about to ruin me.

Because she is.

She already has.

She tilts her head, noticing my lack of movement, and smiles.

She steps to me as I reach for her, hands skimming up her bare sides, over the smooth, soft heat of her body. But she doesn't let me take control. Not yet.

Her palm lands on my chest. Firm, commanding. Her fingers work each button and buckle open, sliding my jacket and holsters from my shoulders. Takes off my armored vest and shirt. Works my belt loose and shoves my trousers down. Pulls off my boots. Peels my boxers away. Stripping me until I'm bare, just like her.

Her hands run down my chest, nails scraping lightly, teasing. My muscles flex under her touch, heat rolling through me.

"You're tense," she murmurs, pressing her palms against me, smoothing over my skin, like she's memorizing me. Her hands skim lower.

I barely swallow the groan before she catches my wrist, leading me into the shower.

Hot water streams over my chest as Maria stands behind me. She reaches for the soap, lathering it between her hands and then smooths it over my skin.

I stand there, letting her do it. Letting her take her time.

Her fingers work over my shoulders, then lower, into my back, my hips, pressing into the knots of tension that have been there for so long. I exhale, head tilting back.

This shouldn't be happening. She deserves better than—

"Stop thinking," she whispers.

She reaches for the shampoo, putting some in her hand and then reaching up to massage it into my hair. Her nails scratch against my scalp, making my breath hitch.

No one has ever touched me like this. Not in a way that makes me feel like I belong to them.

Maria does it like she already owns me.

Because she does.

When she finally rinses the suds from my hair, her hands slide down my back. She wraps her arms around me, pressing into my back, and I can feel her hard little nipples brushing against my skin. I turn to face her and lock eyes with her. Her pupils are blown wide, black swallowing the brown.

She looks down at my cock—hard and heavy between us, aching for her.

I swallow hard. "Maria—"

"Shhh." She takes the soap again, runs her hands down my abs, lower, slow, too fucking slow. "I'm taking care of you."

Fuck. Me.

I let her touch me. Tease me. Let her be in control.

And when I can't take it any longer—

I take over. Now, I'm in control.

I grab the soap from her hands, and turn her to face the spray of the shower. From behind, I press against her, glide my soapy hands over her and watch as my hands slide down her bare skin. She leans her head back and I run my hands over her shoulders, down her sides, over the curves of her ass. I pull her close, gliding my hands up over her stomach, her perfect breasts, pinching and rolling her hard nipples between my fingers. My cock nestles between the cheeks of her ass.

I can feel her heartbeat pounding and her breathing is ragged.

I clean her the way she cleaned me, slow and reverent, smoothing my fingers over every inch of her body.

She sighs, body relaxing under my touch. Leaning back into me.

She's mine. Mine.

I turn her to me and back her up against the shower wall, her chest now pressed to mine.

She gasps, but she doesn't stop me. Doesn't hesitate. Just smiles.

Fuck. That smile.

She puts her arms around me and drags her nails down my back.

I kiss her. Hard. Desperate. My tongue sliding against hers, my hands gripping her ass, pulling her flush against my cock.

"You like this?" I murmur, nipping at her bottom lip, dragging my fingers up over her nipples, pinching, rolling them until she gasps.

"Yes," she whispers. Then she arches her back, pressing harder into me.

I growl, sucking a line down her throat, across her collarbone, lower. Lower. Down between her beautiful tits, pausing to suck on one nipple, then the other.

I drop lower, licking her from hip bone to hip bone.

Finally, I'm on my knees, at her feet, my hands on her hips, staring up at her.

Maria's fingers fist in my hair, yanking me closer as I kiss her thighs, teasing, breathing against her, nudging her legs apart, kissing the pretty curls there.

Her nails scrape against my scalp, pulling me closer, pulling me into her wet, hot cunt.

"Fidel," she murmurs, voice low and dark.

Fucking hell.

I spread her open, lifting one leg over my shoulder, and lick her up and down, tasting her. Teasing her. Slipping my tongue through her wet folds.

Then—finally—devouring her.

Her moan rips through the steam-filled air as I lave my tongue up and down. I flick it over her clit and she pulls me in harder. I'm sucking, licking. Biting. She gasps, thighs trembling.

I pin her against the tile with my forearm across her stomach so I can get deeper. So I can ruin her the way she's ruining me.

"Oh fuck, yes." She gasps. Her hips are rolling into me, fucking my face.

I bring a finger to her entrance, circling there, teasing, while I keep sucking her clit.

"Yes, please, please."

I slowly inch that finger into her and hear a gasp. Even though my face is buried in her pussy, I can look up and see her, head thrown back against the shower wall. She is immaculate. Perfect

I fuck her slowly with my finger and keep sucking and licking, swirling my tongue around her clit. I can feel her wetness dripping down my hand. I add another finger. Pumping my fingers in and out of her hot cunt as she rides my face, licking, sucking and biting her sensitive clit.

"Fidel, I'm—"

I pump harder, faster. Suck harder. I want her to explode on me.

And then she comes, with a violent, sudden spasm, gripping

my head with her hands and thrusting her hips into my face over and over. She cries out, convulsing. "Oh, fuck! Fidel!" She's shaking, gasping, moaning my name like a prayer.

Her orgasm goes on and on. Her cunt in my face, thigh caging my head, drowning me in her heat. Her body spasms as I hold her up.

When she finally releases me, I sit back on my heels, look up at her and put my fingers into my mouth, sucking every bit of her off of me.

She looks exhausted. But she gives me her little smile. My cock is so hard I could come just looking at that smile.

I turn off the shower and guide her out. I dry her skin, her hair, I kiss her neck. "You good?" I murmur in her ear. She nods and I wrap her in a towel. I dry myself. Then I carry her to the bed and lay her down.

I toss the towels to the floor and lay down on my side next to her, heart pounding, mind racing, my hard cock pushing against her thigh. Her damp hair is spread across the pillow and her eyes are half-lidded, focused on mine.

She's breathtaking.

I want to take my time. Worship her. Make her feel everything I can't say.

This is her first time. I know it and I need to be careful. I need to—

She grabs my face and pulls me down.

Her lips brush against mine, soft but insistent, and when she speaks, her voice is raw, unforgiving.

"I don't want slow. I don't want safe. I want you to fuck me, Fidel. Hard. As hard as you can."

I shatter.

Maria doesn't want gentle.

She wants *me.* All of me.

I move over her, my weight on my forearms. I slam my

mouth over hers as I reach down and line up my cock at her dripping entrance. I slowly push inside. Slowly. Carefully. Her slick heat clenches around me, taking me deep, stretching around my cock.

She gasps—I know there's a sting of pain for her first time. I want to be so careful with her. But she drags my hips closer, her fingers digging into my back.

I groan, barely able to hold on.

She wraps her legs around my waist and rolls her hips up, pulling me in deeper, taking even more. I bottom out inside her tight, hot cunt.

"More," she demands, her voice breathless, wrecked. "Give me what I want."

I snap.

I thrust into her hard, deep, burying myself in her completely.

Giving her what I've never given anyone else.

Because Maria is mine.

Because I'm hers.

And I'm going to give her what she wants.

"I want you to come for me, Maria. Come while my cock is buried in you," I command.

"Yes, Fidel." Her voice is uneven, like she can't catch her breath. "Yes, yes."

She pulls me in further with her legs wrapped around me, and as I pump into her, she bucks her hips up, fucking me just as hard as I'm fucking her.

"Are you mine?" I ask. I need to hear it.

Her eyes are locked on mine, fierce, craving.

"Yes. I'm yours. I'm yours."

Supporting myself on one forearm, I reach with my other to pinch her hard nipple and then to pull her hair back, exposing her throat, driving into her hard.

I'm thrusting into her, stretching her open, sucking and biting her neck, hearing her moan in pleasure as she takes my cock.

"Fidel, I'm—" Her voice breaks on a scream as her cunt clenches. I feel her orgasm. She arches her back, repeating my name. The walls of her hot cunt are squeezing around my cock, over and over.

I can feel my balls tighten, feel my own orgasm building. "Yes, Maria, my *princesa.*"

And it hits me. My orgasm is hard. Harder than anything I've ever felt.

It's blinding. "Fuck, Maria, fuck! Fuck!"

It seems to go on and on. I empty hard, pulse after pulse, buried deep inside her. So much of it. All for her. Only for her.

My thrusts are slow now, stuttering. When I can finally open my eyes, as I rest my forehead on Maria's, I feel spasms still convulsing through my body.

I come down slowly, and finally pull out, rolling to the side of her, my arm resting across her.

Maria sighs, and turns toward me. Throws her leg and arm over me. She gently traces a scar along my ribs, then leans up, brushing a soft kiss to my throat.

Her voice is a whisper, but I feel it everywhere.

"Mine."

And for the first time, I feel it bone-deep. She's claimed me. I'm hers. And Maria Sandoval is mine.

The scent of her skin, the weight of her hand on my chest. The quiet in my head. I've never belonged to anyone more.

73

MARIA

Two Weeks After the Kidnapping

L os C uervos is finished.

The fire is out. The ashes are still warm. And the future? That belongs to me.

Fidel and I are in Austin for now, staying in the same house, tucked away on the city's edge. Quiet, secure, far from the noise.

No security. No guards. No interruptions.

Just me and Fidel.

Publicly, there are still a lot of questions about the kidnapping. The media latched onto the UltraVision Gala attack like vultures—hungry for scandal, sniffing for blood. But UltraVision was smart.

Kara Lasater may not have said the words *Sandoval* or *cartel*, but I'm pretty sure she's figured out exactly who I am. And she hasn't asked questions.

When the press started speculating about the attempted kidnapping of a rising author and a beloved actress at one of the most exclusive events of the year, UltraVision did the smartest thing they could.

They let Lily handle it.

And she absolutely delivered.

Within hours, her statement was everywhere: Lily Renshaw, still shaken but perfectly styled, explaining it all away with wide eyes and a practiced tremble in her voice. "An obsessed group of my fans. Nothing to do with the studio or my bestie Mercede, the brilliant author of *The Dark Duke*, who was kidnapped with me. We're just so grateful our private security stepped in before anything really bad happened. Thank you so much for your thoughts and prayers."

She turned it into a promo moment.

She didn't need to mention *unhinged admirers, cult-like following,* or *dangerous fanbase*. The media did that for her. Lily just gave them the angle—a tabloid-friendly tale of obsession and survival—and let them run with it. By the next morning, the hashtags *#LilySurvives* and *#DarkDukeBesties* were trending.

As for Luis and Jorge?

I'll admit I still feel a little bad about tricking them that night with the whole chamomile tea thing. Which was incredibly stupid. But it worked out.

Luis hasn't left Lily's side since. He's technically still on Carlos's Austin team. But in practice, he's Lily's personal bodyguard now. Which means he goes where she goes—Austin, LA, New York. Lily doesn't like to sit still.

And if her Instagram stories are to be believed, and I think they are, he's also her boyfriend. Or the latest arc in Lily Renshaw's romantic content universe.

Every time I see him in the background of one of her posts, wearing his signature *"how did I end up here?"* face, I have to laugh.

I tried to warn him. Told him that Lily is a full-time job with no off switch. He stayed anyway. And honestly? I think he likes it.

Jorge's thriving, too. Solid in Daniel's Austin team—sharp, efficient, focused. And after my little trick that night, I doubt anyone will ever catch him off-guard again.

As for my cousin Tommy Delgado, the deranged leader of the Los Cuervos cartel, the psycho who thought that marrying me would hand him the Sandoval empire. He's gone. Erased. Like he never existed.

His mansion burned to the ground within hours of his death, with his body in it. Carlos made sure of it. Made sure the fire crews arrived just late enough for the place to be unsalvageable.

No weapons. No bodies. No sign that the Sandovals were ever there. Just ashes.

That hilltop estate—once Delgado territory—is his now. Carlos claimed it in the fallout, and this time, it's not just business. He and Chris Harding are finally moving in together. Officially. They're building a house, a mansion really, and they're deep in architectural plans. I've seen the renderings. Clean lines, glass and steel, the kind of view that refuses to end.

Chris calls it their "forever home."

Carlos calls it a much-needed upgrade.

And my deal with UltraVision? I got even more than I asked for. After Lily worked her magic with the press, UltraVision was begging me to sign. The publicity, the trending hashtags, the image of a rising author caught up in the drama of a celebrity kidnapping—it was too much for them to resist.

They gave me everything I asked for and more. Creative control. Casting input. A seat in the writers' room. Producer credit. Final script approval.

My vision. Untouched.

We officially named the series *The Celestial Empire*. *Season One: The Dark Duke* starts filming in six months. *Season Two: The Stellar Sovereign* is already in development.

And who's playing Lady Penelope Hargrove?

Lily Renshaw, of course.

She was born to play the scandal-prone noblewoman torn between duty and her obsession with the Duke. She's already declared this her "alien Regency era" and posted seven videos about how she manifested the role. One of them features a Pinterest vision board, a candle shaped like a suction-cupped tentacle, and Luis staring dead into the camera like he's begging for rescue.

She's a nightmare. But she's my nightmare. And together? We're about to make something unforgettable.

Somehow, I've built the future I wanted out of the wreckage meant to bury me.

And now, at night—every night—I crawl into bed with Fidel, who fucks me until I forget how to breathe, then holds me like I'm the only thing keeping him alive.

He touches me like I'm his light, his anchor, his salvation.

Because I am. And he's mine.

I scroll through Lily's latest story while Fidel cooks breakfast for me. He's shirtless and I can see his first and only tattoo, still healing over his heart—*Princesa Maria* in a flowery script surrounded by pink roses. Pink. Not blood-red.

I show him my phone and he chuckles when Luis's dead-eyed glare pops onto the screen, a tentacle candle in his hand, held aloft, while Lily's voice prattles on in the background. Fidel comes up behind me, loops his arms around my waist, and presses a kiss to my neck as I sip my coffee. Domestic bliss.

I wanted control. I wanted a life of my own. And I got them.

But now? What I want most is him. And as my father, Raul Sandoval, is about to find out, I always get what I want.

Including Fidel Cedillo.

74

——————

FIDEL

Two Weeks After the Kidnapping

Los Cuervos is dead.

Their U.S. holdings—shell companies, laundering networks, real estate—devoured by the Sandovals. Everything they built, I've taken apart line by line, until there's nothing left but ghost traces.

Their operations in Mexico? Passed to La Firma, a quiet, ruthless cartel based in Matamoros, with deep roots and older blood than most people realize. Raul opened the door. I handled the rest.

A handoff like this usually bleeds for weeks. We bled Los Cuervos dry in four days. I scrubbed digital trails, wiped owner-ship records. Shell companies fell like dominoes. Routing numbers, rerouted. Ownership records wiped. Money that once propped up the Delgados is now either sitting in Sandoval-controlled accounts or was transferred to La Firma, strength-ening the alliance.

Raul's been laying the groundwork for this relationship for years. Now, it's locked in.

We gave La Firma what was left of Los Cuervos in Mexico—safe houses, territory, personnel. They took the bones, we kept the blood. Everyone walks away richer. No mess. No mistakes. No survivors.

Surgical. Strategic. Efficient.

The Delgado name is erased. Tommy Delgado's insane ambition? Dead in the fucking dirt.

Carlos saw to it that Tommy's house burned down first, then paid off two nosy Feds sniffing for a RICO bust. Now the hilltop estate is his, one more Delgado asset flipped to the Sandovals.

The rest of the Delgado U.S. holdings? What little there was has been absorbed, repurposed, or liquidated.

We left no trace.

And Solano Studios? Doesn't exist anymore.

Carlos removed Wes Solano from the picture. No headlines, no arrests, no questions. He's just gone. I don't know if Carlos paid him off and sent him out of the country or truly got rid of him. Not my problem to worry about.

Same with Solano Studios. It's gone. Lone Star Studios rose in its place, quietly on track to become a Texas film powerhouse. Carlos built a front team led by Frank—tech-savvy, diverse, professionally clean. Then hired the kind of people the film industry loves to praise. Creative. Innovative. Visionary. The kind who'd never be suspected of working for the most powerful crime family in Texas.

So Lone Star is laundering money and power in broad daylight, and no one even realizes it.

And Maria? She's a star now.

UltraVision bent over backwards to finalize her deal. All it took was one terrifying night, a few trending hashtags, and Lily Renshaw going full tabloid-icon on every major outlet.

Maria has everything she wanted. Everything. She's happy. I've never seen her this alive.

And she's safe at my side.

We haven't left Austin. Not yet. The official reason is recovery. Security coordination. Cleanup. But that's only part of it.

The truth? I'm not ready to leave this place where she's unequivocally mine.

We're staying in the Austin safe house. Elias left for Houston last week to handle the remaining Delgado properties there, but Maria and I are still here.

Alone.

At night, when the house is quiet, she crawls into bed with me—warm, bare, soft against my skin—and I pull her close and hold her like she's the only thing anchoring me to this fucking earth.

Because she is.

She lets me worship her. Lets me fall apart in her hands. She moans my name like it means something. Like I mean something.

She touches me like I'm her shield. Her protector. Her weapon.

And I touch her like she's mine.

I watch her sleep, when she's wrapped around me like she's trying to fuse us together, and think about a future with her.

Can I be enough for her? Can I keep her safe? Not just from cartels and enemies, but from all the ways she can get hurt?

Will Raul truly accept me? He must know what's happening. Carlos would have told him. Will he allow me to be hers? Or is he waiting—watching—thinking I'll fail?

I've lived my whole life in the Sandoval shadow, earning their trust piece by piece. But I know that claiming Maria wasn't what they wanted from me. This relationship isn't some footnote in a security report. It's everything.

I think about rings. Gold bands. Diamonds. I think about

what it would mean to ask her to be my wife. About what it would mean to claim her as mine. Legally, publicly, eternally.

She already owns me.

But I want everyone to know it. I want her to know it. To see it. To wear it.

I've never been good at this kind of thing. Never let myself want something like this. Like her.

But I want it now.

Because for the first time in my life, my future doesn't belong to the Sandovals.

It belongs to Maria. Only Maria.

And wherever she goes?

That's where I'll be.

75

MARIA

Three Weeks After the Kidnapping

WE'VE COME BACK to San Antonio. Just long enough to walk away again.

We'll leave the Sandoval compound behind for now. Leave the home we both grew up in. Not in some desperate escape. Not in secret.

We're walking away on my terms.

For the first time in my life, I'm making a decision that Raul Sandoval can't control. And he knows it.

I step into my father's office without knocking.

He's behind his desk, jacket off, tie loose, sleeves rolled up. His eyes are sharp as he looks up. A crystal glass of tequila sits half-full beside a thick stack of paperwork—deals being finalized, acquisitions settling into place.

"*Mi cielo,*" he greets me warmly. "I'm so proud of you. You handled yourself like a true Sandoval."

I smile but it doesn't quite reach my eyes. This next part will be hard but I'm determined.

"I want to speak with you, Papa. I want to let you know

how things are going to be now." He arches an eyebrow, clearly wondering what I'll say next. "How my life is going to change."

I move forward, heels clicking against the hardwood. Deliberate. Steady. I sit in the leather chair across from him, assuming his favorite posture, elbows on the chair arms, fingertips templed beneath my chin, staring at him intently.

Classic Raul Sandoval move.

He leans back, adopting the same posture, watching me the way a general might study an incoming attack.

"Go on," he says.

I know he knows what's coming. Know that Carlos has briefed him. Told him about me and Fidel. But I lay it out, clear and firm. As if it's already been decided.

"I signed with UltraVision. *The Dark Duke* is moving forward, and I'll be participating in the production." I let the words settle before adding. "In Houston for now."

He leans forward, raises his glass and takes a sip of his tequila. Then gestures for me to continue.

"I'm moving there. To work on the script. To assist with production. To continue publicity for *The Stellar Sovereign*. To complete my third book."

He nods, not necessarily in agreement, just in understanding that these are my terms.

"And Fidel is coming with me."

His fingers tap against the glass. A slow, measured beat.

He places his glass on his desk, once again mirroring my pose, fingers templed under his chin, elbows on his desk. "And you think I'll allow this?"

I inhale slowly. He is my father and I love him, but I am in control of my life now. "It's not about what you'll allow anymore, Papa."

A muscle ticks in his jaw. He hates this. Hates the idea of me out of his reach. Hates that he isn't the one controlling the decision.

But I know he isn't going to stop me. And he knows it too.

"Houston is not our's the way this city is," he says carefully. "We don't own it in the same way. Your brother, Raul Jr., is doing well, but—"

"RJ is doing fine," I cut in. "And I'll be fine, too. You don't have to worry."

That earns a dry laugh. Raul Sandoval worries about everything.

"*Mija*," he sighs. "I only ever wanted to protect you."

His voice is softer now. Lower.

"You think everything I've done, I've done to control you, but that wasn't it." He runs a hand down his face, looking—not upset. Just... weary. "I didn't want you caught up in this life. I didn't want you to end up like her."

Her. I know who he means.

"Like your mother." His throat bobs as he swallows and, for the first time in my life, I see real pain in his eyes.

"Lucia was the love of my life and..."

He doesn't finish. He doesn't have to. We've never spoken of her. My mother. Lucia Delgado Sandoval.

He loved her. And she died because of it.

I was too young to remember her death, but I've felt her absence every day since.

"It's my fault she died, Maria." His voice is steady, but I can hear the guilt woven into his words. "The bullet that killed her was meant for me."

I know that now. She died in an assassination attempt gone wrong and he's never forgiven himself.

My throat tightens. I feel tears welling up, but I won't cry. That's not the Sandoval way.

"I'm not her," I say softly.

His eyes flick up, assessing me.

"No," he agrees. "You're not her."

He exhales, reaching for his drink again, but his grip is looser this time. He tilts his head to one side as he watches me, a small smile on his face.

"You look so much like her. Beautiful. But you're not her, are you? You've grown up, *mija.*"

I arch a brow. "You only just noticed?"

His mouth twitches—the closest thing Raul Sandoval ever gave to a grin.

"You trust Fidel?" he asks after a beat.

"Completely."

Raul studies me for a long moment, weighing something. Then, he nods once. "Yes, I trust him too."

That's it. That's how I know. I've won.

I stand, smoothing my hands down my silk dress. "Good. I'll be leaving in two days. I wanted you to hear it from me first."

"And your brothers?"

"Carlos already knows. He's busy swallowing up Solano Studios. I think he's extremely satisfied with the outcome."

Raul huffs. We both know Carlos is already turning Solano Studios into a money laundering machine.

"And Raul Jr.?"

"I've spoken with him. He has a property we can use, a high-rise apartment. I think he's happy we're coming."

Raul nods his head in agreement. He knows there's no stopping this.

I turn to leave, but just before I reach the door, I pause.

"Oh," I say, glancing back. "One more thing. No. Two more things."

Raul arches a brow.

"I haven't told Fidel yet, but within the year, we'll be getting married."

His brows lift slightly.

"I'll want a huge wedding. Here in San Antonio." I smile sweetly. "It's going to cost you a lot of money, Papa. So get ready for that."

For the first time in maybe my entire life, Raul actually laughs, loudly and with surprise.

"Cabrón," he finally mutters, shaking his head. "You are just like your mother." He pauses. "She would be proud of you, *mija.*" He smiles at me. "And the second thing?"

I swallow hard. This shouldn't be hard but it feels like the end of something.

"I want you to know I love you, Papa. I always will."

He nods his head. *"Yo también te quiero. Eres mi orgullo, mi vida. Siempre lo has sido."*

His words mean the world to me. *I love you too my life. You are my pride. You always have been.*

I nod, holding back tears. And then, without another word, I walk out.

76

FIDEL

Three Weeks After the Kidnapping

THE LATE-NIGHT AIR is thick with heat, the last remnants of a Texas summer clinging to the sky.

I lean against the wrought-iron railing of the terrace, looking out over the Sandoval estate. Below, security moves in controlled, methodical shifts, patrolling the grounds with the precision Marco has drilled into them.

I helped build this system. Fortified these walls. And now, I'm leaving.

Not forever. Not completely.

But for the first time in my life, I won't be answering to Raul Sandoval first.

Maria comes first now.

Behind me, I hear the terrace door open. Footsteps—heavy, deliberate. My brother, Marco.

He doesn't say anything at first. Just walks up and stands beside me. For a long moment, neither of us speak.

Finally, Marco exhales. "So. You're really leaving." It isn't a question.

I nod. "Maria wants Houston. So we go to Houston."

Marco grins. "Since when do you let Maria tell you what to do?"

I huff a quiet laugh. "Since always," I admit.

Marco's chuckle is low, unsurprised. He nods, like my words make all the sense in the world.

He leans on the railing, studying me. Measuring me.

"You know what this means." His voice is quieter now. "You're not just her guard, *hermano*. You're hers."

I don't look at him. Just exhale, watching the lights of the city. "I always have been."

That's the truth. Marco has always known it. Since we were kids. Since Maria would boss me around, and I'd let her.

Since I'd come back from college and seen Maria—really fucking seen her.

Since I'd spent years keeping my distance, convincing myself I wasn't good enough. That I had no right to want her.

Now? None of that matters. Because Maria chose me.

Marco sighs, shaking his head. "You know, I used to think you'd fight it forever."

I let out a quiet laugh. "I tried."

"Yeah." His smile is knowing. "Didn't work out so well, did it?"

"Not even close."

He turns toward me. "You've been part of the Sandovals since we were kids, Fidel. Even more than me. You and I both know Raul sees you as one of his own."

I nod. Because I know that's true.

"But it will be different now."

His gaze is steady. Assessing.

"You're not just part of this family anymore. You're building your own." He pauses, letting it sink in.

The words hit me hard. Because Marco is right.

"You remember what I used to be like," Marco says after a beat.

I glance at him. "Yeah. You were a cold-hearted bastard."

He smirks. "Exactly. And proud of it."

Then his voice drops, lower, quieter. "And then I met Ami."

He gazes out over the property for a long moment, into the darkness. Then he speaks again.

"I spent my whole life thinking love made you weak. Made me weak. That really loving a woman would be a liability."

He shakes his head. "But I was wrong."

I stay quiet. Because this? This is rare. My brother doesn't talk about his feelings. Not like this.

"She doesn't make me weak, Fidel. She makes me better. Stronger."

He turns to face me, eyes sharp.

"You think you're just protecting Maria?" He shakes his head. "But she's going to change you."

I swallow hard. Because I already know that. She already has.

"You're going to fight it at first," Marco continues. "You're going to want to keep control. You're going to want to be the one leading her."

His smirk returns.

"And then, one day, you'll wake up and realize—she's the one who's been leading you all along."

She's already claimed me. Already decided I'm hers. And I've never wanted to belong to anyone more.

"I trust you with her," Marco says suddenly.

No hesitation. No doubt. And fuck, that means more than I can ever say. Because Marco doesn't trust easily. Because Marco has spent most of his life protecting Maria, too.

"But," he adds, pointing at me, "don't let her run you over completely."

I huff a laugh. "You think I could stop her?"

"No," Marco admits. "But try."

I shake my head. "I don't need to stop her. I just need to make sure she gets everything she wants."

That earns me a crooked grin.

"You're a Sandoval alright," Marco muses. "We all give Maria everything she wants."

He claps me on the shoulder, a solid, final gesture.

Nothing else needs to be said.

I let out a slow breath, looking out over the compound one last time. Tomorrow, Maria and I leave for Houston. A new city. A new future.

But the Sandovals aren't my past. They're my foundation.

And Maria? She's my future.

I push off the railing, turning to head inside.

Marco lingers behind, still watching, still assessing.

"One more thing," I say, pausing at the door.

He turns to me, lifting a brow.

"Maria doesn't know it yet," I murmur. "But we're getting married soon. Very soon."

Marco's smile is slow, knowing. "Yeah?"

"Yeah."

"You tell Raul yet?"

"Not yet. I will. Soon."

That makes him laugh. A deep, satisfied, older-brother laugh.

"Good. He always needs something to worry about."

77

THREE MONTHS AFTER THE KIDNAPPING

Text Message Thread - Lily Renshaw and Mercede Sanchez

Lily: MERCEDE!!!!! Wheels down in H-town, bestie!

Luis says hi (and "for the love of God please send help" whatever that means)

Maria: Tell him new city, same full-time job 😅

You two at the hotel yet?

Lily: Pulling up now. I brought you a tentacle candle

Maria: You know the rule: if it glows in the dark, it stays in your suitcase.

Lily: Rude. Anyway—casting brainstorm tomorrow

I've got three contenders for the duke

Hunter still my fav

But all big boys packing where it counts ••

Just so you know - I'm talking about their penises

Maria: Stop. You're killing me. I know you mean penises

Coffee at 9? No tentacle props allowed

Lily: Make it 10. Luis insists on "area sweeps."

Maria: Fine. 10.

And Lily—thank you for doing this.

Lily: Babe, I live for drama and screen time. See you in the morning

———

Source: Reddit
Reddit Thread: r/TheDarkDuke
Thread posted 5 hours ago | 2.0k upvotes | 14 downvotes
Posted by u/dukeskisses4life

Thread Title: **Fancast round-up - who's your dream Duke and Lady P?**

u/dukeskisses4life (MOD)
Heard UltraVision is screen-testing *Ridge Donovan* for the Duke 🙄 Thoughts?

u/dukeanddestroy
NO. I need someone who can smirk like sin *and* cry on cue. Ridge only does Blue-Steel-In-High-Def. Give me Hunter!!!!

u/mercedehasmyheart

Hot take: IRL author Mercede Sanchez should cameo as the librarian in Ep 3. GIVE THE QUEEN HER CROWN.

u/tennisfixated

Lily Renshaw confirmed for Lady Penelope and I'm 128% here for it.

u/tentaclelover

Hear me out-Brad Pitt as our Duke and Savannah Guthrie as lady P-just think about it - the tentacle sex would be UNREAL!!!!

u/dukeskisses4life (MOD)

u/tentaclelover - Don't make me ban you again. Also Brad Pitt way too old.

78

MARIA

Three Months After the Kidnapping

HOUSTON HAS STARTED to feel like home.

Not RJ's city. Not Raul's empire.

Mine.

I step onto the balcony, stretching in the warm night air, watching the sun dip lower behind the high-rises. From here, I can see one of the newly acquired Sandoval properties—a sleek, glass-covered tower that used to belong to Los Cuervos.

Three months ago, it was theirs.

Now, it's ours.

Fidel is the one who secured it. He's spent the last three months fortifying every inch of the new assets across Texas. Setting up surveillance. Tightening defenses. Making sure nothing and no one will ever touch me again.

But that isn't the best part of life in Houston.

The best part is that Fidel and I wake up together almost every morning. He fucks me senseless, showers with me, makes me breakfast. All before I start work.

And he has never once tried to stop me from being exactly who I am.

The Dark Duke is officially in pre-production. Which means I'm working my butt off. I'm writing the scripts. The novel has been adapted, but I'm making sure every word still feels like mine.

I'm co-producing. And UltraVision wants my input on casting, locations, and branding.

And I'm building my own fucking empire. UltraVision has already optioned *The Stellar Sovereign.* If *The Dark Duke* hits big, my second book will be adapted next.

This is my dream. It's happening.

Lily Renshaw flew in last night to help with casting. Lady Penelope Hargrove herself.

She's still a beautiful, chaotic gremlin, and I love every bit of her.

And Luis? Lily has acquired him. And she's not letting go.

I grin as I hear their voices inside the apartment.

"Babe, I told you, I don't need a jacket." Lily's voice rings out.

"It's cold. If we're going out for dinner, you need a jacket," Luis grumbles.

"It's seventy degrees! I'm fine! And that jacket clashes with my heels!"

"Put it on anyway."

I turn, stepping back into the living room, just in time to see Luis draping a leather jacket over Lily's shoulders.

Lily rolls her eyes. But she doesn't take it off.

I grin. "You two are disgusting."

Lily flips her blonde hair. "I prefer the term 'deeply in love and painfully hot.'"

Luis just shakes his head. "She's exhausting."

"Oh, I know."

But I love her for it.

Lily flops onto my couch, kicking her stilettos up onto the coffee table. After stabbing a man in the eye with the heel of her shoe, she refuses to wear anything else.

"So," she says casually. "When are you and Fidel getting married? Because I have a feeling it's soon, and I need at least four months to plan the bachelorette party. I'm thinking Telluride. No! Charleston! No! Vegas!"

I snort. "I'm sure it'll be soon."

Luis shoots me a look. Lily shoots me a look. Even I'm not convinced by what I just said.

I'm trying to be patient, to let Fidel take charge on this. I'm not going to push him. I want him to come to me. I want him to ask me to become his wife. *But honestly, what is the hold-up?*

Then the front door opens.

Fidel steps inside, kicking the door shut with one boot.

His dark eyes land on me. Steady. Unreadable.

"Out," he says simply.

Lily blinks. "Excuse me?"

"Out," Fidel repeats, his voice deadpan.

Luis doesn't ask questions. He just grabs Lily's hand and drags her to the door.

"Hey!" she squawks.

Luis wrenches the door open, shoving Lily out.

"You can't just—hey! Okay! Text me later, bestie!" she yells as she disappears into the hallway and the door closes.

Silence.

Fidel locks the door. Turns to me. His dark eyes are calm. Certain.

"I was in San Antonio. Talking to Raul." His voice is quiet.

I swallow. "Yes, of course. About security—"

"No, Maria. Not about fucking security."

He pulls a box from his pocket. Flips it open.

Inside sits a ring with a massive emerald-cut diamond.

I stumble back a step. Is he doing it? He's doing it. Fidel is actually doing it.

"Jesus, Fidel. What the hell is that?"

"This was your mother's." He steps closer. "When I asked Raul for your hand, he gave it to me. He wanted you to have it."

"You asked my father for my hand?" I'm stunned. Tears are starting to fill my eyes.

"Yes, of course I did."

My father had never let my mother go. Now, he's given Fidel her ring. Given me her ring. He's giving us his blessing.

I stare at the ring. The one my mother had worn. A piece of her, now mine.

Fidel gets down on one knee. My chest tightens. I thought I was ready for this but suddenly I'm overwhelmed.

"Maria, you're my *princesa.*" His voice is low, steady.

Through the tears now rolling down my cheeks, I stare at the ring. At him.

My heart is racing. This is more than I ever expected.

Fidel has always belonged to me. But this? This is him taking charge of our lives. Him choosing me. Him choosing to belong to me forever.

"I love you, Maria. Hopelessly." He stares up at me, his voice quiet. "I've always loved you. Always. And now I can't live without you. I can't breathe unless you're with me. I'm lost without you. I... I don't know how to handle it. All I know is I can't lose you. I want to be with you, always."

He pauses and I see him swallow. "Marry me, Maria."

Tears blur my vision.

"Please. Marry me. Please."

My lips part. I step forward.

And then—I grab his collar, yank him up, and kiss him. Hard. Deep. Wrecking both of us.

I pull back, breathless.

"Yes, Fidel." I smile against his lips. "Yes, I'll marry you."

His face relaxes and he smiles. He takes the ring out, tossing the box aside, sliding the ring onto my finger. His fingers curl around my jaw. Pull me in.

"You're mine, *princesa.*" His voice is a whisper, a promise. "You've always been mine. And you'll always be mine."

I swallow hard. "I've always been yours, Fidel. And I always will be. And you're mine."

His lips quirk into a smile.

"Good."

He kisses me again, hard, and lifts me, cradling my ass as I wrap my legs around his waist, and walks us toward our bedroom.

I press into his cock—

He's hard. Very hard.

His forehead presses against mine. I feel his pulse hammering under my fingers.

His voice is a whisper against my lips.

"You'll be my wife soon, *princesa.* And then—"

His grip tightens on my ass.

"I'm going to spend forever ruining you."

"Good," I whisper into his lips.

He kicks the bedroom door open, carries me to our bed, and spends the next several hours fucking me into bliss.

And as Fidel makes good on his promise to ruin me, I know.

I've finally, finally gotten everything I ever wanted.

79

———

ELIAS

THE CLUB IS A FUCKING DISASTER.

I sit back in the deep booth, tequila glass resting against my fingertips, and watch as a crew struggles to install the latest addition to the decor.

Fantasma. The Ghost.

That's what this club will be called once I finish stripping away every last trace of Delgado filth. Right now, it still looks like something out of a cheap '80s cocaine dream—neon grids, fluorescent palm trees, sticky black leather booths too soaked in alcohol and sweat to be salvageable.

Los Cuervos let it rot. But now the Sandovals own it. And I'm turning it into something better.

A high-end, high-security nightclub. One of a kind.

For once, Chuck of all people, king of the dad jokes, has actually come up with a good idea. He called in from San Antonio to see if I needed help. I don't. But he had an interesting idea for the dancers.

"Show the dancers, but don't *show* them," he'd said.

So, behind the bar and at various points throughout the club, huge shadow screens are being installed that will show the silhouettes of dancers behind them, making them appear to be dancing completely nude without actually exposing them. This isn't a strip club after all. But we'll present our mainly male clientele with a fantasy wrapped in an illusion.

Just at the entrance, I see two workers carefully hoist an expensive sculpted art piece into place. A woman's seemingly nude figure, larger than life, her body completely draped in flowing, clinging fabric that looks like it's been dipped in molten gold.

It gleams under the dim lighting, a ghost caught between flesh and a dream.

I roll my tequila glass between my fingers, watching. There's something poetic about it.

Then—

I hear the hurried click of high heels entering the club.

Click. Click. Click.

I don't turn my head, don't react. Just watch from the corner of my eye as Natalie Morris strides through the club, scanning the room like she's searching for a target.

Tall. Long legs. Nice tits, full curves.

I'd be lying if I said I haven't spent some time thinking about that body, what I'd like to do to it.

But I've kept it professional with her. For the Sandovals. For Maria.

And because it isn't her body that intrigues me as much as her brain.

I've watched her work. Calculating, cutting, shrewd. She brought in Zara Caldwell, the entertainment lawyer, before Maria even knew she needed her. She spotted every flaw in the UltraVision deal before Zara had uncapped her pen.

And she knows exactly who the Sandovals are. And has no problem with it.

She's smart. Dangerous, in the right way. That's what makes her so fucking attractive.

Her face goes into a scowl the second she spots me. Then she stalks toward me.

I exhale slowly, smirking to myself.

This is going to be fun.

She slides into the booth across from me, her movements controlled, like she's the one who owns the space.

"Just who I was looking for," she says. Her voice is smooth, but her shoulders are stiff. She places her phone on the table and folds her hands as if to keep them still.

I swirl the tequila in my glass. Look up. Don't blink.

"Natalie Morris." I say it like I'm indulging her, like her name is a game piece I might play with.

She bristles but keeps going. "Yes, it's me. Elias—"

I cut her off. "Drink?"

"What? No, I don't want a drink."

I shrug, take another sip of tequila. No rush.

She inhales sharply, visibly restraining herself. "Elias, I need some help, and I think you are exactly the help I need."

I grin, stretching out lazily in the booth. "I hear that a lot."

She rolls her eyes, but there's something else behind it. A flicker of hesitation. Not like the razor-sharp woman I've seen in Maria's meetings.

Then she shoves her phone at me.

A text. I pick up the phone, scanning the message.

Nika Petrovna Morozova 9 PM tonight

An address I don't recognize.

Then—a string of text in Cyrillic. I can't read it, but I have a damn good guess that it's something bad.

Not Natalie Morris then.

"Nika Petrovna Morozova," I murmur, testing the name, tasting it.

Her jaw clenches. "Yes."

"Russian?"

A slow, measured blink. "Obviously."

I glance back at the text. Screenshot it. Text it to myself so I can send it to Katya back in Raul's kitchen in San Antonio and get a translation.

"So, someone wants you to be at this address at nine o'clock tonight. What does the Russian part say?"

She hesitates. A fraction of a second. But I catch it.

Then—her voice, flat and resigned.

"The blood oath must be honored."

That's probably what it says. Maybe. Katya can confirm.

I set the phone down, finally looking at her.

Natalie Morris—also known as Nika Petrovna Morozova—is good at hiding emotions. But right now, there's something hollow behind her eyes.

I exhale, slow. Take another sip of tequila.

"So. A blood oath." I pause, stare at the ceiling for just a moment, because I actually know what that means. "Russian mafia, then. Bratva?"

She nods. One sharp movement.

I tap my fingers against the side of my glass. If the Bratva is making moves into Houston, into Texas—

That means they're making moves into Sandoval territory. That means I need to be on top of it. And Nika Petrovna Morozova just became my way in.

I cock my head, watching her, letting the moment stretch.

Then—"Sure, Nika Petrovna Morozova. I can help."

Relief flickers over her face for exactly half a second.

Then annoyance. She hates needing me.

I smirk. Lift my glass.

"Drink?"

This time, she nods.

I gesture to the bartender and call out. "Mandy, two vodka shots. And the bottle. The good stuff."

When I turn back, Natalie's watching me carefully. Calculating. Like she's trying to read me.

Like she hasn't yet decided if she made the right choice.

I let my smile widen.

Mandy brings us our shots and the bottle, setting them in front of us.

I lift mine. *"Za nas!" To us!* I throw my shot back.

Natalie cocks one eyebrow at me, probably curious about that little bit of Russian. Then, the scowl returns to her face as she quickly tosses back her own shot.

She's a complication. A problem. Maybe even a liability.

But fuck if she isn't interesting.

GLOSSARY

Below is a quick reference of non-English words and slang used in *Watch Dog*. Non-English words in the text and in this glossary are written in simplified phonetic form rather than their original script (Cyrillic, for example) for ease of reading and pronunciation by readers. All translations are by the author who is solely responsible for any errors.

Spanish

- Borracho beans - a flavorful Tex-Mex dish featuring seasoned pinto beans cooked in beer, the word "borracho" means drunk or drunken
- Cabrón - fuck or shit as an exclamation, fucker as a noun
- Carajillo - a cocktail made with coffee or espresso mixed with a liqueur, often brandy, rum, tequila, or mezcal
- Chile con queso - a Tex-Mex appetizer consisting of melted cheese, chile peppers, and tomatoes
- Compañero - comrade, buddy

- Enchiladas verde - enchiladas made with corn tortillas, usually filled with chicken or cheese, and covered in a green sauce made with tomatillos
- Fantasma - a ghost or phantom, can also mean a haunting presence
- Hermano - brother
- Jefe - boss
- La Firma - The Firm
- Los Cuervos - The Crows
- Luz - light
- Me rindo - I give up
- Mi cielo - my darling, my sweetheart
- Mi preciosa - my precious
- Mija - daughter, dear
- Oaxaca cheese - a semi-soft, white, string cheese from Oaxaca, Mexico
- ¿Qué carajo? - What the fuck?
- Yo también te quiero. Eres mi orgullo, mi vida. Siempre lo has sido. - I love you too my life. You are my pride. You always have been.

Russian

- Za nas - To us

ACKNOWLEDGMENTS

I have many people to thank because I promise you - it is impossible to write a book alone. When friends shared a word of encouragement or readers gave me a "thumbs up" rating, it definitely kept me going.

To my husband, thank you for letting me write absolutely unhinged things at all hours, for never asking what I mean by "spicy dark crime romance," for acting as my bartender at my book drop happy hour (and not asking if the Luz Lemonade is drugged) (or even if that's a legitimate concern), and for being my biggest cheerleader. I couldn't do all of this without you.

To all of my family, thank you for your support. Your constant questions and genuine curiosity about just what I'm talking about is what keeps a smile on my face.

To all of my many friends, especially my Literally Speaking ladies, my BAT Book Club, my Electra friends, and my tennis buddies, thank you, thank you, thank you! Just wow! The outpouring of interest and enthusiasm is beyond anything I ever expected. Thank you!

And finally—to all of my readers. The ones who love morally gray men, heroines with bite, and endings that feel earned and deserved. You're my people. Thank you for stepping into the dark shadows with me. I hope *Watch Dog* wrecked you in all the right ways.

With love, smut, and an every-growing body count,

Katt Andrews

ABOUT THE AUTHOR

Katt Andrews writes dark, spicy romance with dangerous men, smart women, explosive tension you can feel across the page, and just a bit of snark. A proud Texan and lifelong writer, she lives in Houston with her family and an opinionated dachshund named Daisy. When she's not writing, she's probably playing tennis—or plotting her next morally gray hero. You can find her at: https://kattandrews.com

A NOTE FROM THE AUTHOR

Thank you so much for reading Watch Dog!

I hope you loved crashing through MAVFest with Maria and Fidel as much as I loved writing it. Their journey was messy, chaotic, a little dangerous—and totally worth it. And come on... Fidel's proposal? Swoon doesn't even begin to cover it!

Of course, you already know we're not done with our favorite bodyguards. Elias kept things strictly professional in *Watch Dog*. But how long is that going to last now that he's helping Natalie, or should I say Nika, a secret Bratva princess? *Sly Dog* is next, and it's going to be explosive. Because let's be real—playing with a butterfly knife in every other scene is definitely not a sign of emotional stability.

If you want to be the first to know when *Sly Dog* is out—or you want sneak peeks, bonus content, and behind-the-scenes chaos from the entire Guard Dogs world, sign up for my updates by going to https://kattandrews.com/newsletter or scanning the QR code:

Yes, there's a mailing list but I promise to never, ever spam you (because I hate it too). Come for the bodyguards. Stay for the dark romance (and just the right amount of torture).

And one last thing—if this story wrecked you in the best possible way, I'd love for you to spread the word. Shout it out on Goodreads, BookBub, and Amazon. Share it on BookTok. Text it in your group chat. Discuss it in your book club. And most of all? Leave a review. That's the good karma that keeps dark romance alive.

Thank you again for reading. And for loving these dangerous bodyguards and the women who burn with them (and for them).

Katt Andrews

www.ingramcontent.com/pod-product-compliance
Lightning Source LLC
Chambersburg PA
CBHW071736110726
47908CB00006B/1608